ROSE SOMMERVILLE;

OR,

A HUSBAND'S MYSTERY AND A WIFE'S DEVOTION.

A ROMANCE.

BY ELLEN T.

[AUTHORESS OF "THE HEIRESS OF SACKVILLE," "RAVENSDALE," ETC., ETC.]

For a woman's heart is possest
With love, and love alone:
The grave is her only rest
When that sweet hope is gone!
Old Ballad.

LONDON:

PUBLISHED BY E. LLOYD, 12, SALISBURY-SQUARE, FLEET-STREET.

PREFACE.

"The old, old fashion!" As far back as the light of history or the glimmer o ftraditionary legends can throw any reflections, human nature, in its passions both for good and evil, has been much the same. Young hearts have loved and beat for each other, and formed schemes and anticipations for future happiness, as well when the earth was in its infancy, as they do now. Youths and maidens have loved as truly, without the least taint upon their passions, in those times when Rome held sway; and the course of their true love, as is too often the case at the present day, even then has not run smoothly : "it is the old, old fashion," and so it will be until the last day.

In every phase of human life, changeable and various as they may be, "the old, old fashion" peeps forth—there is nothing, there can be nothing new in it; and the world—that is, that portion of it whose nature can sympathise with the kindly and better feelings of the heart—still loves that fashion as it did in days of yore.

"Rose Sommerville," the heroine of our Romance, is one of those creations of the fancy, formed upon the model which has been used by the Almighty hand ever since the day when Adam first saw Eve. The Authoress lays no claim to originality in the formation of the character; Rose is a simple and single-hearted girl, rich in all the charms, both of mind and person, which make a heart of so much value. She is but one of many, whose presence has shed a bright lustre over the dreary paths of life, and whose sunny smile, and absorbing, devoted love, have smothered a wrinkled brow, and driven the cloud of care from before a darkened mind.

Loving the "old, old fashion" as she does, the Authoress of "Rose Sommerville," in the history of her heroine, and in detailing the many trials by which the young girl's love was tested, has endeavoured to enlist the sympathy of her readers in favour of one whose character they can understand, and whose virtues they can appreciate. No false halo of a romantic nature has been thrown around her—she has been given to the world as such a character should be given, in the unadorned dress of virtue, innocence, and love; and if she has found favour with the reader, the Authoress's ambition is satisfied.

The Authoress gives her thanks to those who, week after week, have followed her through her eventful tale, and shaking them by the hand for the present, bids them farewell! though not without the hope of meeting them again, and that, too, at an early day.

London, 1847.

ROSE SOMMERVILLE.

ROSE SOMMERVILLE, sweet, fairy, bright-eyed Rose Sommerville—I think I see her still tripping across the lawn with the light buoyant step of early youth—earth surely never held a fairer creature than Rose; the sweet smile that played around her dimpled mouth possessed all the soft beauty of infancy, her light auburn tresses waved luxuriantly around her fair and sunny brow, and for figure never did I see a more sweet and graceful form.

Rose was Nature's child; of humble birth, she knew nothing of the gaieties of the world; her father was a farmer, an upright honest man, respected by his neighbours and loved by his family, his circumstances were flourishing, and his children had all received a plain but good education. Rose was the youngest of four; idolized by the whole circle, she had been petted from infancy, and yet her disposition was so soft—so gentle and loving—that she had not been spoilt by indulgence; at sixteen, half child, half woman, like the flower whose name she bore, just bursting into bloom, what a fair and lovely creature was Rose! her clear and ringing laugh struck on the ear like distant music, as, bounding on before her more serious companions in search of wild flowers, she laughed at their sober, steady pace.

Poor Rose! she had never known sorrow, or even discontent; her wishes and hopes were all

No. 1:

confined to her own family, and they were too happy to be able to make her so. The three eldest of the family were sons, and they almost idolized their little sister Rose, whom they still regarded as a child.

The farm Mr. Sommerville occupied was situate in a particularly salubrious village, and it was his custom to receive as inmates during the summer months, persons desirous of a change of air, and Rose had just attained her sixteenth year, when a gentleman whose health had become impaired through over-study, came to reside with them. He was a tall, dark, melancholy-looking man, of at least six-and-thirty, and his brow was lined and indeed somewhat wrinkled with deep thought; he seldom smiled, but when he did, it lightened up his whole face with so pleasing an expression that you hardly recognised it as the same countenance; when in repose it was habitually very pale, and his raven hair, which hung rather loosely about his face, afforded such a chilling contrast, as almost to awe the beholder; indeed, he had, altogether, an air of sternness and reserve that made him rather an object of dislike to the open-hearted farmer and his family, with the exception of Rose, who from the first seemed taken with him: whether it was that his eye never encountered her fairy form without the sternness of his brow relaxing and giving place to the smile of pleasure, or whether it was the interest youth and health ever feel for the sorrowing brow and pallid cheek, we cannot tell, most probably the latter. In his absence Rose would carefully arrange his room, dust his books, of which he had a large stock, and not unfrequently take a peep inside them. One day Rose had found the book she opened so interesting, that forgetful of all else, she had sunk upon a chair absorbed in its contents. The stranger, unexpectedly returning, surprised her thus: Rose, covered with blushes and confusion, endeavoured to stammer out an apology: the stranger approaching, with an air of almost parental kindness, placed his hand upon her head, and while his deep thoughtful eyes rested upon her face, said, 'My dear girl, make no apology, I am but too proud to know that the book has interested you; this you will comprehend, when I tell you that it is written by myself.'

'You, sir,' replied Rose, reassured by his air of kindness. 'You wrote this? oh! then indeed, you must be proud.'

'That it has interested you, I am,' he returned, still gazing on her speaking countenance.

'Then you will allow me to finish reading it, sir; it has, indeed, pleased me, but it will much more, now that I know by whom it is written. I had no idea, sir, that you were an ——'

'Author,' rejoined Mr. Moreland, (such was the stranger's name,) 'but you will oblige me, Rose, by accepting of the book, it will serve sometimes, to remind you of me.'

'It will, indeed, sir,' said Rose, 'and I am infinitely obliged to you, more so than I can tell,' and she left the room with her treasure.

Oh! how Rose pored over that book, it was scarcely ever out of her hands. She read and re-read it, till she knew it all by heart, and yet perused it again: in all her walks, it was her constant companion. It was a volume of poetry, and of poetry Rose knew little or nothing, yet she felt and appreciated the glowing, beautiful language of the book, even on the first perusal, and for the author, Albert Moreland, she felt a sublime admiration which deepened, alas! only too soon, into a warm, passionate love. Gentle, innocent, childlike, she yielded her heart almost without knowing it, and to whom? A man more than double her years, naturally gloomy and austere, in every respect unworthy to win and wear so bright a gem. Her parents and brothers could not, at first, conceive it possible that Rose, little more than a child in years and experience, really loved a man so entirely opposite to herself in thoughts and pursuits, and regarded the admiration so strongly, yet blushingly confessed, as appertaining entirely to the author, and having little or nothing to do with the man; but they were soon undeceived. She loved, all things told it—she crimsoned beneath his earnest gaze—she gathered the fairest flowers to deck his room, was uneasy and anxious in his absence, happy but in his presence, gay if he but smiled upon her, sad if he passed her unheeded by: these are, indeed, true signs of love—of a love ' such as life only once may know :' and Albert Moreland, the successful, flattered, and caressed author, and man of wealth and independence, who had but to make proposals to the high-born ladies of fashion, and was certain of being well received, did he, could he return the pure affection of the little village maid, who had nothing but her own sweet beauty and guileless heart to recommend to his notice? This was not so easily discovered; that he liked, that he admired her, could not be doubted; but his feelings for her seemed more of a parent than a lover. He would sometimes accompany her in her walks, and, when he did so, they were long ones; for their absence would extend over hours, but whether or not he spoke of love, could only be guessed, if he did, Rose never mentioned it. Thus months rolled on, when, one morning, Mr. Moreland, solicited a private interview with Mr. Sommerville, which was instantly granted. The conference was long, and, oh! how poor Rose trembled when her father desired her presence; she could hardly support herself into the room.

' I have sent for you, my child,' said Mr. Sommerville, with tearful eyes, as he drew his daughter closer to him, ' on a matter of most serious import. Mr. Moreland has just made a proposal to me for your hand, and much as I dread being separated from you, my dear child, I wish to hear from your own lips if the proposal is pleasing to you ; in short, my Rose, do you love him well enough to become his wife? It is a solemn and holy connexion to enter into, and oh ! my child, do not rush lightly into it.'

He ceased, and there was a silence of some moments, during which time Mr. Moreland sat erect in his chair, gazing calmly and vacantly around him, with nothing of the anxious, hopeful look, a lover might be supposed to wear on such an occasion. Rose glided tearfully and timidly to his side, and placed her hand in his. He started as from a dream, but recollecting himself, he pressed it in his own, and, bowing his head, imprinted a kiss upon her brow, then turning to Mr. Sommerville, he said:—

' May I hope that you will immediately arrange all preliminaries, and appoint an early day for our marriage, as my health being now fully re-established, I am anxious to be again in town ?'

Mr. Sommerville's heart was full at the thought of parting with his child, and he could only bow in reply. The month that intervened previous to the bridal was indeed a sad and gloomy one. Mrs. Sommerville, with all a mother's fears and forebodings, when she is about parting with a darling child, wept almost incessantly ; in vain her partner strove to comfort her, he was himself nearly as much overcome.

' If I were only sure she would be happy,' said Mrs. Sommerville, ' I would cheerfully resign her ; but he is so unsuited to her in every respect, so utterly different to the man I would have chosen.'

Yet, Rose herself seemed to look upon the future with rapture. Her brothers, even, almost thought it unkind that she should be so willing to leave them for a stranger, of whom she knew but little. But Rose loved with all woman's fond devotion, and sacrificed all other feelings to that. Albert Moreland had no relative but an only sister, to whom he was tenderly attached, his junior by six years. She was already married to a man of affluence, with whom she lived on the most affectionate terms. Her brother had written to acquaint her of his approaching marriage, when she signified her intention of being present at the imposing ceremony. Her arrival was anxiously looked for by Mr. Sommerville and his family, no excepting Rose, who earnestly hoped to find favour in the sister of the man she loved so dearly. Sweet Rose ! thy soft winning bashfulness—thy gentle, touching earnestness of manner, upon thy first introduction to Marian Trevors 'found its way to her heart, and she threw her arms around thee, and bade Mrs. Sommerville have no fear for the future, for she would watch over thee with an elder sister's guardian love, and the tears that had been gathering in thine eyes rolled slowly till they bedewed thy fair face.

The morning sun shone bright and beautiful upon the bridal of Rose Sommerville and Albert Moreland. The church was crowded with villagers to witness the ceremony, and never did Rose, smiling through her tears, look more beautiful than at the moment she pledged her troth to Albert. Her soft, liquid blue eyes were raised beaming with pride and tenderness to the man she had chosen. But, oh ! it was strange to mark the contrast between the two. His years and mien betrayed no sympathy with hers, and his vacant eye seemed wandering around as if in search of some object ; his face was paler even than usual, and his whole appearance care-worn and abstracted. And when all was over, and they left the church, and every one crowded round Rose to pour blessings on her head, and hope she might be happy, she smiled and thanked them, and never doubted but her lot would be bright and blessed.

The parting with her relatives was, it is true, accompanied with bitter tears, and a promise of a quick return to spend some weeks under the parental roof, and Mrs. Sommerville was reassured by the kindness of Marian Trevors, who promised to watch carefully over Rose's health and happiness.

Arrived in town, installed as mistress of an elegant home, surrounded with luxuries she had never before dreamed of, introduced by her husband to a numerous circle of friends, all of whom were delighted with the beauty of the bride and the sweet simplicity of her manners, need it be said Rose was happy? After the first visits of ceremony were over, Albert, naturally studious, seemed rather averse to society ; but, in company of her sister-in-law, Rose visited every place of amusement. With the theatres she was, indeed, delighted, especially operas. Of them she thought it impossible she could ever weary, and wondered how any one who had ever seen London could be content with a country life. Her letters home to her parents were to them a constant source of pleasure ; to know by Rose's own assurance that she was 'happy (to use her own words) beyond description,' relieved their minds of the fears they had naturally entertained at parting with their beloved child.

As the wife of Albert Moreland, the admired author of several beautiful poems and other works of fiction, Rose was everywhere received with pleasure ; indeed, her company was not unfrequently sought for among the highest classes of society, and it was with rapture she felt that the husband she dearly loved was so universally admired; and when she heard him spoken of as possessing wonderful talents and rare ability, even beyond his brightest compeers, her breast heaved with joy; at the same time, she would almost doubt herself worthy of being his wife, and, after reading his sweet poetical effusions, of which she never tired, would blush at her own simplicity—would even term it ignorance. Thus roll on the first months of her wedded life, when, with anguish, she frequently remarked her husband wore a troubled brow, and began to tremble lest his love decay.

'Oh! that I were more worthy of sharing his every thought,' she exclaimed to his sister who had called upon her one morning.

'You have too humble an opinion of yourself, dear Rose. Albert has chosen you for his wife in preference to all others, and consequently must deem you worthy.'

'Oh! but,' returned Rose, 'I have lately fancied he has been reserved, I was going to say cold, in his manner to me.'

'It surely can be only fancy,' replied Marian, rather anxiously.

'I hope so, indeed,' said Rose; 'and yet,' and she paused—

'And yet what?' replied Marian. 'I entreat you, tell me all.'

'His rest has of late been much disturbed, and he is constantly talking in his sleep, though, in so indistinct a tone, that I have not been able to catch anything he said till last night, when he breathed the name of Florence, accompanied with such a bitter groan, that it went to my very heart; and this morning he is dejected in the extreme, and, when I inquired after his health, answered me almost unkindly. Oh! Marian, dear Marian,' she continued, bursting into a flood of tears, 'I fear that he loves another; perhaps he has met with one whose talents may render her more worthy his regard than the poor untutored village girl.'

'Be comforted, dear Rose,' replied her friend, kindly straining her to her bosom, 'It was probably the name of some new heroine you heard him utter, and over whose fictitious woes he heaved the groan that has had the effect of making you so sad.''

'It cannot be,' said Rose, '*that* surely would not make him look so miserable this morning. He has been for upwards of an hour pacing the floor of his study, with such a troubled look that could proceed from no fancied woe of another, it must be from some grief of his own; and when I connect the name I heard him utter with his altered manner towards myself, I cannot but think he regards another more favourably.'

A shade of deep care crossed Marian's open brow, which she endeavoured to conceal by treating Rose's fears as foolish and absurd.

'You are wrong, dear Rose, I am confident, and must not indulge in such idle fancies. Ladies who marry men so devoted to romancing as Albert is, must not be jealous of their, husband's heroines, that indeed would never do,' she continued, assuming an air of gaiety, 'and here comes Edward to confirm you in my opinion. Would you believe it possible?' she said, turning to her husband, as he entered. 'here is our little sister, Rose, half mad with jealousy, because she fears Albert adores the fancied beauty of his heroines more than the real bewitching sweetness that sits upon her own fair countenance.'

'I cannot for a moment suspect him of such bad taste,' replied Edward Trevors, turning a look of admiration upon the blushing face of Rose, 'but were it possible he could be guilty of such a thing, Rose might well be angry with him; there are but few men, I think, who would not prefer Rose before all other living beauties. How weak and silly then must be the one who could give the preference to the ideal creations of his own brain!'

'That will do, Edward,' said Marian, affecting to be vexed, 'it is my turn to be jealous now, and not without cause either, only I love Rose so dearly that I must even be contented to stand second in your admiration; but all this talk has made me forget the real object of my visit, which was to take you out, dear Rose, for a drive round the parks, the morning is so beautiful that I know you will not refuse to accompany us. Come, come, I shall positively take no denial, I insist upon your getting ready immediately.'

Rose had lately, for the first time in in her life, carried about with her an aching heart; she had begun to suspect, and oh! what bitterness it cost her, that she was unworthy to be the wife of one who possessed such talents as the husband she adored.

'How many,' poor Rose would frequently say to herself, 'if not so clever as Albert, have at least sufficient ability to converse with him on topics I dare not mention an opinion upon; and then of her beauty, the theme of admiration and envy of all others, she held so humble an opinion herself that she thought but little of it, and would have indeed have willingly exchanged it for one tittle of the talents possessed by Albert; and then the conviction would force itself upon her, 'He is not happy, and why?' Oh! how often Rose considered the question, and yet found no satisfactory answer, till he breathed in his sleep the never-to-be-forgotten name of Florence. Oh! that, thought Rose, was a sufficient explanation of everything. He loved another, it must be so ; and yet when she had confided all to Marian Trevors, and found that she treated it so lightly, Rose thought she must be wrong, and with a lighter heart equipped herself for the drive. As she passed her husband's study on her way down stairs to the drawing room, where Marian and Edward Trevors were awaiting her arrival, she paused a few moments and then knocked timidly at the door. Albert's voice bade her enter, she did so, and acquainted him with her intention of going out.

'I am very glad to hear it, my love ; you have been too much confined lately, and, doubtless, the air will be serviceable to you. You must not allow a town life to banish the roses from your cheek, which you know I admire so much. Farewell, my love, I wish you a pleasant drive. You must excuse me to our friends ; tell them that I am busily engaged in my study, and cannot at present be disturbed.'

This was spoken in a kind and cheerful manner, and had the effect of lighting up Rose's face with one of her sweetest smiles, and she joined her friends in the drawing-room with such a beaming countenance, that Marian gaily rallied her upon it.

'She has seen Albert in her absence I am convinced, she has obtained an interview on some excuse or other, perhaps even, intruded on the privacy of his study, and found him engaged in reading some dusty old volume of abstruse literature, when she feared to find him describing some glowing beauty with darker hair and eyes than her own, which, of course, he could not do without arousing her jealousy.'

'Well, Edward, you must excuse me, but I really cannot give you such convincing proof of my affection as our little sister Rose does Albert. I cannot, for the life of me, be jealous. I tried once, and found it made me so miserable that I was only too thankful to cast from me such a troublesome companion, I hope, for ever ; but time stays for no man, and I see by my watch that it is flying fast, so let us begone without another word.'

The day was beautiful, the air was soft and balmy, and everything looked gay and brilliant, the park was crowded with carriages, and ladies fair, bedecked in silks and satins, smiled upon smartly-dressed cavaliers, mounted on high-mettled steeds, who, in return, bowed and kissed their hands, sometimes stopping to exchange a few words, or make appointments for the evening. All were gay and richly dressed, and all seemed happy. Rose, a creature of impulse, was delighted.

'How pleasant,' she exclaimed, ' to see so many happy faces ! there cannot be a single aching heart in all this crowd.'

'' You judge too hastily,' said Marian, ' there is often deep anguish concealed under a smiling countenance.'

'Impossible,' returned Rose : ' how could any one smile so gaily if their heart was sad?'

'It is, nevertheless, very frequently done ; but you, dear Rose, have never been taught to conceal your feelings, and consequently, cannot imagine it possible ; but persons educated in the world never carry such an expressive face as yours. Those, indeed, often smile the most, and appear the gayest, that have the greatest cause to be unhappy.'

'And others,' said Edward, ' put on their bonnets and smiles together, to be worn as out-door ornaments, which they invariably lay aside on their return.'

'Now, you are harsh upon our sex, Edward,' replied Marian, ' which reminds me that I must call upon my milliner to see if the hat I ordered is finished, for if it is not ready for me this evening, my smiles will certainly be turned to frowns, so give John orders to turn into Bond-street. You, my dear Rose, know so little of dress, that I will not take you in with me, therefore, remain with my liege lord till I return.'

Edward Trevors was a fine, perhaps, even some might term him a handsome man, but there was a boldness in his looks and manners which ever caused Rose to shrink abashed from his gaze, and avoid, if possible, being left alone with him. Yet her friend, Marian, ever spoke of him in the highest terms, and with the tenderest regard, as being a kind and affectionate husband, and a good and generous master. Rose even felt vexed with herself that she could not conquer a dislike she had conceived for him on their first interview, and now, as he fixed his dark eyes upon her, with an expression that brought the rich blood to her cheek, although he spoke on some light topic of the day, she wished herself anywhere but by his side. After a while, Marian appeared, and informing them she should be detained some time, advised them to take a short drive, and call for her on their return. To this Edward yielded ready assent, and though Rose would have prefered alighting, and waiting with her friend, she could not at that moment think of an excuse for doing so. As soon as the carriage was in motion, Rose rallied herself, and endeavoured to enter into conversation with her companion, who after some confusion, as if he was about saying something which might not be well received, began with,—

'Will you oblige me, Rose, by informing me what conversation you had with Marian, before my arrival this morning?'

The colour receded from Rose's cheek at this abrupt question. What had passed between herself and her friend. she intended to be strictly confidential, not even to her parents or her brothers would she have breathed a word of distrust concerning her husband, how much less then to Edward Trevors!

'I ask not, Rose,' he continued, 'from motives of idle curiosity, but I may be able to throw some light upon the subject. I cannot suppose you are weak enough to be jealous of the beauties Albert describes in his poems, none half so fair as yourself, were they real instead of imaginary beings.'

'It is scarcely worth mentioning,' replied Rose. 'Albert, I have reason to believe, is commencing a new work, and his thoughts have been so engaged with the distress of the heroine, that he breathed her name in his sleep, and it being rather a singular one, I told it to Marian when she laughingly insisted upon it that I was jealous.'

'And what may be the name; I suppose it is not a secret?'

'Oh! dear no, it is Florence.'

Edward started from the careless attitude he had assumed, with an air of surprise too evident to be feigned, and said—

'Florence! is it possible that Albert is writing a romance, with such a name for the heroine? then, indeed, I think it will greatly resemble truth.'

Oh! what a tumult of agonising sensations filled the heart of Rose at these words; she was correct then in her surmises, Albert loved another; this was the foremost thought that, quick as lightning, shot through her brain, bewildering her even with the intensity of anguish it caused. Yet she spoke not, her face was deadly pale, and she trembled violently, still not even a sigh escaped. Edward kindly took her cold hand in his, and begged her to forgive him for having thus thoughtlessly alarmed her.

'I entreat you, dear Rose, to be composed, and will only now say that I have alarmed you needlessly. You have indeed no cause for grief; there was a lady who bore the name of Florence, who loved, and was most passionately beloved by Albert, but it is many years ago, and that unfortunate lady is long since numbered with the dead.'

These words, together with his kind, earnest manner, at length reassured poor Rose, yet she earnestly longed to know the history of Florence, and entreated him to tell her all he knew concerning it. Florence—was she beautiful? anything like the brilliant dark beauties she read of in Albert's poems?

'I never saw her, dear Rose; yet I have heard she was very handsome, and doubtless she was dark, being an Italian; but we will say no more about it; her history is a very painful one, known only to few.'

'But Marian—does she know it?'

'Certainly; although like me she never saw her, yet she is well acquainted with her unhappy fate.'

'And why should not I be made acquainted with the truth? it would relieve me of many fears. I beg of you, Mr. Trevors, if it is not a secret, to tell me all you know.'

'It is a secret, dear Rose, and one I should be sorry you heard from me; but rouse yourself, my dear girl, I see here is Marian already looking out for our return—I fear we have kept her waiting for us.'

At this moment the carriage stopped, the door opened, and Marian was again seated by the side of her friend.

'Upon my word, I am infinitely obliged to you for keeping me so long! I have had sufficient time to select dresses enough to stock my wardrobe for the season, if I do not weary of them before the close:' then turning to Rose, upon whose brow some marks of agitation were still visible, she said,—'I am afraid you have extended your ride too long, we will order the carriage home immediately. I see Rose looks pale and tired, and will want time to refresh herself, or she will not be able to accompany us to the opera in the evening.'

'Oh dear no!' said Rose; 'I would rather, indeed, be at home this evening.'

'Nonsense, child! I shall not allow you to do anything of the sort; so do not think of it! Mind, if you are not dressed by the time I call, you will incur my severe displeasure.'

On reaching home, Rose experienced a languor of spirits she had seldom known. It was the day on which she invariably wrote to her parents, and she considered it a duty to be punctual, and never allowed them to be disappointed in their expectation of a letter; it was a duty, indeed, she had ever performed with pleasure—but now, seated at her desk, with pen in hand, she scarcely knew what to write; the thoughts and feelings uppermost in her mind she must conceal from those dear relatives, or it would render them unhappy: not that she entertained any weak, foolish jealousy on account of one she was assured no longer existed, but she had a strange, undefinable curiosity to learn the secret of Albert's love—a secret which Edward had told her was a painful one, and enclosed the fate of Florence. Was it possible that Albert could have acted otherwise than honourably towards the being he had loved? No, no; that could not be! Whatever the secret contained, of one thing she was convinced beyond the shadow of doubt—Albert was the injured, not the injurer. So intently was she wrapped in these thoughts, endeavouring to find some clue to the secret she almost dreaded, yet wanted to fathom, that the door to which her back was turned opened, and her husband entered without her being aware of it till she felt a touch upon her shoulder, when, starting with surprise, she beheld Albert leaning over her, pale as ashes, and the muscles of his face working convulsively, while his raised finger, which shook like a leaf when exposed to the breeze, pointed to the paper which lay before her: her eye instantly fell on the spot indicated, when, what was her surprise to find that, lost in thought, she had unconsciously traced the name of Florence. Young and inexperienced in deception, yet Rose instantly resolved how to act.

' What is there, dear Albert, in that name to alarm you thus?''

" How came it there ?—did you write it ?"

' Yes, yes, though I was not aware of having done so till you pointed out to me.'

' What reason had you then for writing it.'

' None whatever, dear Albert ; you were restless last night, and I heard you mention the name in your sleep, and concluded it belonged to one of your heroines. I was just now going to write home, and not having much news to tell them, was thinking what to say, and, connecting you with all my thoughts, have, without knowing it, traced that name.'

Albert gazed upon her fair, ingenuous face, heaved a deep sigh, and seemed relieved.

' You have indeed, my dear Rose, been in a fit of abstraction, for the dinner bell has rung without arousing you.'

Rose blushed, accepted his arm, and accompanied him to the dining-room.

' Have you any engagement for the evening, my love?' said Albert, as, dinner over, Rose was about leaving the dining-room.

' Marian made me promise to accompany her to the Opera; indeed, she wont take a denial, or I would not have given my promise.'

' And why should you not wish to go, Rose? I thought you were fond of operas.'

' So I am, but—'

' But what ? I hope you have nothing to make you unhappy.' This was accompained with a sigh.

' Oh! no, dear Albert, I have everything to render me happy.'

' Then go, my love, and I hope you will be amused.'

At the appointed time Edward and Marian called for Rose, who, scarcely bestowing a thought upon her appearance, followed them to the carriage. They were accompanied by a friend of Edward's—an agreeable looking young man of about five-and-twenty, with prepossessing manners and elegant exterior, whom he introduced to Rose as Mr. Melville. As his first glance fell upon her lovely face, he seemed struck with her soft feminine beauty, and the sweet graceful outline of her fair form. On reaching the opera, the gentlemen alighted from the carriage, and Mr. Melville was about to offer his arm to Rose, but was prevented by Edward, who, drawing Rose's arm through his own, bade his friend to take care of Marian.

' Really, gentlemen, I have a great mind to be offended with you for thus so rudely giving the preference to Rose,' said Marian, as she took Melville's arm, and entered the house. Edward contrived to linger a few moments in the lobby, and said, pressing the small white hand that rested on his arm, ' I hope, dear Rose, you have entirely recovered from the fright I caused you this morning.'

' Oh! yes, perfectly,' replied Rose ; ' and yet I wish you had not told me there was a secret concerning Albert, unless you were at liberty to impart it. I am certain at least, that I should hear nothing prejudicial to him: he may be injured and oppressed, but he has never been the oppressor.'

' How kind of you, dear Rose, to think thus of him ! it shows how generous is your disposition.'

' It would be wicked and ungenerous to think otherwise, knowing Albert's noble mind so well as I do.'

' He may mean kindly towards you, Rose, and yet I think, did I possess so great a treasure, I should guard it more carefully.'

Rose made no reply, and they entered the box, where Marian and Melville had preceded them. Rose felt herself compelled to occupy a seat by the side of Edward, and never before had an opera appeared to her so long: the music and singing were indeed beautiful, and the company brilliant in the extreme ; it comprised nearly all the smiling faces and gallant cavaliers they had seen in the park in the morning, and though their voices cried 'encore,' and bouquets of flowers were showered upon the favourite performers, how very few seemed really interested in what was going on ! Finely dressed gentlemen peeped through their opera-glasses, not at the scenery, but at some fine beauty in the opposite boxes, and dashing ladies laughed and flirted with some favoured exquisite, who in return prided himself upon the curl of his moustache, and the

set of his cravat: Edward appeared resolved neither to listen himself nor allow Rose to do s
for, from their first entrance, he kept up an incessant whispering conversation, which sh
answered chiefly in monosyllables; her own thoughts were filled with Florence, and the secre
she was now determined the morrow should unravel. Yes, she had made up her mind t
seek an explanation of Marian, without compromising Edward in the matter. Thus circumstanced
Rose felt thankful when the curtain dropped, and they were once more seated in the carriage o
their return. On taking leave of her friend, Rose said, ' I wish Marian, you would oblige me b
calling early to-morrow, and do not order the carriage, as I wish to spend a quiet morning alor
with you !'

' Certainly, dear Rose, I promise to be with you at an early hour.'

' Am I to consider myself excluded,' said Edward, ' or may I add a third to your number

' If it comes to that,' said Melville, gazing admiringly upon Rose, ' I shall be wanting to mak
a fourth.'

' Oh, I cannot receive gentlemen to-morrow,' said Rose, ' mind, dear Marian, you com
alone !'

' I promise,' replied Marian, ' and till then, dear Rose, farewell.'

' What a splendid creature,' said Melville, as the carriage was again in motion. ' I wonde
not, Mrs. Trevors, that your brother should have fallen in love with such an angel, indeed
would have been wonderful if he had not.'

' She is certainly very beautiful,' said Marian with a sigh, ' but that is her least charm, fo
she is good, generous, and amiable, in a degree seldom found comprised in one person.'

' She looks it all,' replied Melville, rapturously; ' would that I could find her equal, I woul
gladly become a Benedict immediately !'

' Come, come,' said Edward, moving uneasily in his seat, ' her heart, as the old song say
is another's, and never can be thine.'

' I know it,' returned Melville, ' would that it were otherwise; for, notwithstanding sh
scarcely gave me a single glance the whole evening, I acknowledge myself desperately in love.'

' Pshaw !' said Edward, ' Love cannot be felt so suddenly, and for one who is the exclusiv
property of another it would be madness.'

' Such madness as I glory in,' resumed Melville, and pointing to the moon, which was shinin
resplendently in the heavens, ' beauty like yonder orb shines alike for all.'

' And on all, I suppose you would say,' said Edward, evidently annoyed.

' Even so,' replied his friend, ' and such being the case, there will be no harm in ende
vouring to catch a few of the smiles she so lavishly bestowed upon you this evening.'

' I warn you,' said Edward, hastily, ' against doing anything of the sort ; the husband, wh
seldom goes out, confides her to my protection, and I shall most certainly resent an
endeavour to attract her notice.'

' Why, Edward,' said Marian, anxious to put an end to the discussion, which promised t
grow warm ; ' you speak as though Rose was your wife, instead of my brother's, and you, M
Melville, I am certain would never offer her any affront.'

' If no one respects her less than I do, Marian, she will never have occasion to complain c
insult.'

' I hope not,' rejoined Edward ; ' did any person ever offer her even the slightest affron
they would soon bitterly repent it.'

Determined to turn the conversation, Marian began speaking of the opera. Melville out c
politeness joined her, and they were soon engaged in discussing the merits of the performers
but Edward continued silent the remainder of the ride.

Arrived at their respective homes, the gentlemen coldly bade each other good-night, and, onc
more alone, Marian turned rather anxiously to her husband, as the words, ' impertinent fellow
dropped from his lips.

' I think, Edward,' she ventured to say, ' you are really unjust to Melville, he is surely a
liberty to admire Rose ; and when he offered insult, it would have been time enough to resen
it. I am sorry you should have affronted so old, and, I fully believe, sincere friend.'

' Affront him! was it not enough to cause any one to affront him, to hear him talk in the
manner he did of Rose ? Insufferable puppy ! I wonder at his impudence ; however, I shall take
care to warn Rose against him.'

' Rose is my brother's wife,' said Marian, in a tone that implied he needed to be reminded of it

' I know it, Marian, and as such I love her dearly, and will ever be the first to protect he
—her very innocence makes her stand in need of greater care.'

Marian made no reply : she loved Rose herself with the affection of a sister, and was too
generous to nourish even an unkind thought towards her, yet she thought her husband migh
have spoken less warmly. Rose was, indeed, her brother's wife, and she knew he loved he
devotedly, and Rose likewise so loved him, and that, she deemed, would be a sufficient safeguar

from every snare; but then, Rose was beautiful: to be seen was to be admired, and she could not wonder Edward should be so ready to espouse the cause of one so young and fair, and, perhaps, Melville had meant more than he said in declaring his passion for Rose, at least, men read deeper into men's motives than a woman could do; and, in short, she was vexed with herself for having for a moment felt vexed with him, for Edward, she was certain, meant kindly towards Rose, and thus she dismissed the subject from her thoughts.

The following morning Rose anxiously awaited the arrival of her sister-in-law—she should hear the secret of Albert's early life, that sometimes, even at this distance of time, cast a shadow on his brow. Yes, she was convinced that Marian would tell her all she knew concerning Florence, and her untimely fate; and yet Rose almost dreaded to hear the painful tale; her colour came and went, and her heart beat, and when Marian entered, her voice became so tremulous, she could scarcely greet her.

'Well, Rose,' said Marian, ' you see I have done your bidding, for here I am, and alone: but are you not well this morning? or what have you done with your usually glowing cheeks? I declare you look quite ill.'

'No, dear Marian, there is nothing ails me, but I have a favour to ask, and I dread your refusal.'

'Then dread it no longer, I promise to grant it you.'

'Listen, then, Marian: after I returned home from our drive yesterday I sat down to write to my dear mother, but my thoughts were so filled with the conversation we held together in the early part of the morning, that I could not find words to begin, and had unconsciously traced the name of Florence on the sheet of paper before me, when Albert suddenly entered, and his agitation at seeing the name was so great, as to convince me there was some secret cause for it, which I think, dear Marian, you also must know of. Will you unravel this mystery to me?'

'My dearest Rose,' replied Marian, 'it is a very painful story, even I do not know the exact truth, but as it may relieve your anxiety, I will tell you all I know, though, had you not discovered there was a secret connected with the name, I would gladly have concealed it from you.

'You must know, then, dear Rose,' she commenced, ' that myself and Albert were the only children of our mother, who died leaving me almost an infant. Some few years after our father formed an intimacy with a young person in rather humble circumstances, who died in giving birth to a boy, of whom he acknowledged himself the father, and caused to be removed to his own home, provided suitable attendants, and in short, as he grew older, treated in every respect as ourselves. Charles (such was his name) was indeed a fair, a beauteous youth, he possessed almost feminine gentleness of manners, which won upon the hearts of all who knew him, not excepting Albert and myself; we considered him as a dear younger brother, and were ever ready to yield to his wishes; this unity of feeling was, of course, a constant source of pleasure to our dear father, who was never happy but when he saw his children so. When Charles was old enough, he joined Albert at college, and the affection that existed between the brothers excited universal admiration. Albert was then, Rose, very different to what you see him now; he had an open careless manner, that rendered him a general favourite; he had also an inexhaustible fund of humour, which caused his company to be eagerly sought for by the gayest of his companions, his brow was unclouded by "e'en the lightest touch of care," and indeed the Albert of the present day would never be recognised by those who knew him then.

'Albert had left college, and was waiting at home with myself and our father, till Charles should have nearly completed his studies, when they were to pursue their travels together. Our father had already selected as tutor a person he deemed in every respect suitable to take charge of them, when he was unexpectedly seized with a fit of illness, which terminated fatally in a few days. Immediately on his illness assuming an unfavourable appearance, an express was sent for Charles, but on his arrival our father was in a dying state, speech had already left him, still he was perfectly sensible, and, taking the hand of Charles, he placed it in that of Albert, accompanied with a look which bade him, more that words alone could have done, to love and protect him. Albert well understood this mute appeal, and replied by clasping his brother to his heart. I shall never forget the smile that passed across our dying father's face, illumining every feature, as he thus saw his last request was felt and understood. He feebly raised his arms to Heaven, as if invoking blessings on our united heads, and then, ere the smile had faded from his countenance, without a groan or a sigh expired. He had died intestate, and Albert, as the eldest son, could have laid claim to the entire estates, to the utter exclusion of Charles, whose illegitimacy was beyond the shadow of a doubt; but, so far from taking advantage of this circumstance, Albert, immediately after our father's funeral, caused one-half of the estates to be made over to Charles, by a deed of gift, which put it even beyond his own power to revoke.'

'Dear, noble Albert!' exclaimed Rose, her eyes suffused with tears. ' I was certain he could never act otherwise than generously.'

'Indeed he did not,' resumed Marian; ' nay, so determined was he to possess no more than
No. 2.

one-half of our deceased father's property, that even the ready money, plate, and furniture, were scrupulously divided between them. I had forgotten to mention that I was already amply provided for, under my mother's will. Having thus settled these preliminaries, he placed me under the care of my dear Edward's mother, who resided a few miles from town, and prepared, accompained by Charles and the tuter our father had chosen, to prosecute his travels. Having no other relation in the world, I naturally looked forward to the departure of my brothers with a sorrowing heart. Indeed, from the first, I had an unaccountable gloomy foreboding that I should see Charles no more. He was then but eighteen, tall for his years, and possessed such symmetrical proportions of limb and figure as almost to give him the appearance of effeminacy, which his light hair, hanging in loose curls around an unusually fair forehead, rather increased. The day before their departure they spent with myself and Mrs. Trevors. The evening was so fine, that it tempted us to walk out, and, as I leant upon Charles's arm, and gazed with an elder sister's love upon his fair young brow, I felt it was for the last time; as the thought crept through my heart, I clung tighter to him.

'"Oh, Charles!"' I exclaimed, '"it is not even now too late; let Albert travel alone, and you, dear Charles, remain at least for another year behind with me."'

'Charles was naturally gay and light-hearted, and never had I seen him in better spirits than on that evening; consequently, he laughed at my fears, and Albert gently chid me for encouraging such foolish fancies.

'"Charles is dear to me as my own life, Marian, and it will be at once my duty and my pleasure to protect him from every snare."'

'"And bring him safe back,"' I added rather anxiously.

'"And bring him safe back,"' rejoined Albert.

'"Why, Marian,"' said Charles, laughing, '"you seem determined to consider me still as a child, although, I believe, I am a good three inches taller than yourself, and turned of eighteen to boot; and I think, with all due deference to your sisterly fears, that I am able to look a little after my own welfare; self-preservation, you know, is the first law of nature, and if I have not learnt that yet, I know not when I shall."'

'We sat together till a late hour of night, conversing on the past, the present, and, what to me seemed fraught with sadness, the future. How often did I warn them to be wary on their voyage against every accident, and extort from them a promise of writing at their earliest opportunity! At length we parted for the night, but met again at early dawn. I accompanied them to the sea-shore, saw them embark, waited till the ship sailed, and strained my eyes in gazing after them so long as I could see the outline of Charles's form, who stood upon the deck waving a white pocket-handkerchief; and when the vessel, increasing the distance between us, became but a speck upon the ocean, I still stood upon the sands gazing upon it till even the speck was lost, when I sunk fainting into the arms of Mrs Trevors. Oh! how anxiously I watched the breeze, and trembled as I fancied it freshened into a gale. My thoughts were scarcely absent from them a moment, till I received a letter which relieved me of my fears. They had safely arrived at their destination—the voyage had been a very pleasant and unusually speedy one—they were in Italy, delighted with all they saw—the gayest of the gay, visiting every place that was deemed worthy of notice. Time passed on, and I again heard from them. They still remained in Italy, of which country they spoke in raptures. After this came a long pause. I would not at first be uneasy, as a letter coming such a distance might have miscarried on the road, or a thousand little incidents might have occurred to prevent them writing, but when double the interval had elapsed that usually intervened between their letters, and I still heard nothing, I began to be seriously alarmed, and wrote, begging an immediate answer to my letter. Alas! the distance was so great that I should still have to wait many dreary days before it was possible for me to receive a reply. Still I comforted myself with the hope that I should hear sooner or later, as a letter might pass mine on its passage. Still time wore on, and I heard not. I had hoped, till hope itself began to sicken at the delay, and I knew not what to think. To know the worst, be it what it might, I deemed would be preferable to the dreadful calamities my brain was conjuring up; when one day a letter was placed in my hands—it bore a foriegn post-mark, and the writing was that of neither Charles nor Albert. I tore it open—comprehended almost at a glance the sad tidings it conveyed, and fell senseless on the floor. I was carried to bed, where I lay for many weary weeks in a state of utter unconsciousness. The dreadful anxiety I had so long endured, and now the certainty that a dreadful tragedy had been enacted, and the principal actors in the awful scene my two brothers, bound to me by the dearest and tenderest ties, had such an effect upon my frame as to cause a brain-fever, which nearly deprived me of life. After tossing to and fro in high delirium for many days and nights, I at length once more awoke to consciousness. My first feeling was a sense of heavy sorrow pressing on my heart, and I cast about in my mind for the cause, but I have never to this day had more than a vague recollection of what had occurred. As I grew stronger I remenbered having received a letter, which, indeed, was the cause of my illness; and not having even a knowledge from whom it came, and but a very obscure recollection of its contents, I inquired for it, wishing to satisfy myself on these points, when I was told it had been destroyed, and none of my attendants would allow me to speak on the subject; at least they would never answer my questions, or if by chance they did, it was only to involve me in further mystery. After a lapse of years, Albert returned alone, and I was strictly cautioned to make no inquiries of him concerning Charles, or even mention his name. He was sadly altered; like me he had been stricken with disease, and brought low, but his recovery, unlike mine, had been marked by a settled melancholy. He took to writing, and it is remarkable that affliction has brought out and fully developed a genius he had never before shown any signs of possessing.'

'It is indeed remarkable,' replied Rose: 'but Charles, have you never heard anything concerning him?'

'Nothing, although I have reason to believe he is still living; at any rate, his share of the estates is regularly forwarded abroad.'

'That, indeed, I should think was a proof of his being still alive; but you have told me nothing of Florence.'

'Of her indeed I heard but little. It appears, from what I can remember of the letter, that a beautiful Italian lady, who bore that name, was introduced to my brothers, after their arrival in Italy, and had secretly encouraged the attentions of both. Charles loved her with the strongest affection, and had the greatest confidence in her purity. Indeed, he had mentioned to his tutor his intention of marrying her, and bringing her back with him to England. Albert also loved her, with less devotedness, and was, unknown to his brother, carrying on a guilty correspondence with the object of his love.'

'Is it possible?' exclaimed Rose, horror-struck at the recital.

'As far as my memory serves me, I am correct; but I must do Albert the justice of stating he knew not of his brother's love. Florence, artful and designing, had stipulated with each that her regard for them was to be kept entirely secret.'

'Still I am sorry,' replied Rose, ingenuously, 'that Albert should have led her astray.'

'It was wrong, doubtless, but men will sometimes take advantage of a woman's love; and in her case it was more pardonable, for she must have been badly inclined, or she would never have encouraged the attention of two brothers at the same time.'

'Surely not,' replied Rose; 'and yet the tale has make me sad. Pray go on.'

'Well, then, Charles had made every preparation for a private marriage with Florence, and one evening, eager to make her acquainted with the pleasing intelligence, he abruptly entered her dressing-room, and surprised her in the arms of Albert. Enraged to madness at this convincing proof of her duplicity and baseness, he snatched a poniard which unfortunately lay near, and before Albert could arrest the blow, plunged it into the heart of the wretched girl.'

'How very, very dreadful!' said Rose, veiling her face in horror. 'I wonder no longer at Albert's pallid countenance when he saw the name of Florence—I shall never even think of it again without a shudder; and poor Charles—how wretched he must be to have thus caused the death of one he loved!'

'Yes, yes,' said Marian, sobbing convulsively; 'but oh! Rose, had you known him, you would scarcely believe it possible: so kind, so gentle: he never before hurt even a worm—he was, indeed, almost too forgiving—never resenting an injury or insult. Dear Rose, the conversation has opened wounds that time had but partially healed, and my heart is wrung with anguish for the fate of that unhappy youth; did I know where to find him, I would travel to the most distant part of the globe, and offer him a sister's solace and affection. Doubtless, he bitterly repents the rash act, and when we consider the provocation he received, we may, at this distance of time, pity, and forgive him.'

'We may, indeed,' returned Rose; 'and Albert, too, what heart-rending anguish he must have endured, to think that though him the unhappy object of his own and brother's love met with such a dreadful and untimely end.'

'Yes, Rose; and it should warn us against giving way to feelings of jealousy, since we know not where they may lead us.'

'But, oh!' replied Rose, 'if Charles had really loved her he could never have done her an injury, let her conduct have been ever so bad.'

'You, doubtless, think so, dear Rose; but, oh! it must be very awful to find one, upon whose love and purity we have prided ourselves, so utterly base and unworthy as Florence. I can well conceive a man, maddened and blinded with passion, committing the fearful deed, especially when the weapon was at hand.'

'Oh! talk not thus, dear Marian,' replied Rose shuddering, 'you absolutely alarm me. The bare thought of one human being taking the life of another is too awful to dwell upon.'

'It is, Rose; therefore let us change the subject—nothing but your own earnest desire would have induced me to impart the dreadful secret to your bosom, but do not, I entreat you, let it lower Albert in your estimation.'

Rose was silent; had she spoken, she was too ingenuous to have concealed from her friend the deep anguish of her heart the knowledge of Albert's early life had cost her. She had been educated in such strictly virtuous principles, that, though she had nourished an affection for Albert before he had spoken to her one word of love, yet she would have been ready to die with shame had she for one moment suspected he had discovered it; and though she dearly loved him, she was so truly modest and unobtrusive, that it required all the powers he was master of to woo and win her; consequently, she could not conceive that any woman could be lightly won, and gained over to his pursose; for none ever loved dearer than herself: therefore, unlike most of her sex, she would not have heaped the whole shame and obloquy upon the head of the seduced, and entirely exculpated the seducer. Rose thought only of the baseness of the man who could take advantage of a woman's love, 'For she must have loved him,' said poor Rose 'or she never would have fallen into sin.' Alas! that love which was designed to be the sweetest solace and comfort of our lives, should, through our own evil, unrestrained passions, plunge us more frequently into the depths of misery and vice! It has indeed often caused bitter animosities between the dearest friends, separated the wife from her husband, the mother from her child; indeed, out of the many tragical events recorded in history, how very many may be traced to have originated with love; and yet it is an utter profanation of the word to apply it to the restless feeling of desire, which is satiated with the object almost as soon as obtained. No, true love binds but never loosens affinity; it throws around all our actions beauty and grace, refines and purifies our feelings bears us triumphantly through all our temptations, and crowns us at last with joy and happiness.

A man who coolly seeks to seduce a woman from her high estate, though he swear in the most impassioned language that he loves her, has not towards her in his heart even a shadow of true affection.

If women would but think of this, how much less misery there would be in the world!

'Well, Rose,' said Marian, 'we have had a very long conversation this morning on a painful subject, and I fear it has affected your spirits. I shall now bid you adieu till the evening, when I will call to take you with us to Mrs. Melville's. She entertains a large party this evening in honour of her only daughter, Lucy, coming of age, and she particularly desired me to bring you. Lucy is a very interesting girl, and I am sure you will be pleased with her. *Apropos*, you saw her brother last night at the opera, and I can assure you you made a complete conquest of him.'

Rose smiled faintly.

'Indeed, Marian, I have not much spirits for company; but as you wish it—'

'You will go of course. There is nothing, my dear girl, like gaiety for dispelling *ennui*. Mind you put on your most becoming dress, and wear with it your sweetest smiles. I have spoken of you to Lucy as a beauty, and, for the honour of my opinion, should be sorry if she did not think you one.'

Henry Melville, whom we have already cursorily introduced to the reader was the only son of a widowed mother, her husband having died and left her with two children, a girl and boy only a few years after their marriage. She was then young and handsome, and had several opportunities of settling in life anew, but she declined them all, and devoted herself to the education of her orphan children, who fortunately proved both dutiful and amiable. Henry, the eldest, had become acquainted with Edward Trevors at college, and they conceived a sincere and lasting affection for each other, which was 'ne'er roughened by those cataracts and breaks, which humour interposed too often makes.' The bosom of the one had ever been the repository of the other's secrets, and Edward was also a great favourite with Mrs Melville, and it was a constant source of satisfaction to her that her son should have chosen for his most intimate friend and companion so steady and deserving a young man, for Edward was never addicted to the follies, and even vices, which very many fashionable young men pursue as amusements; and Lucy too had regarded her brother's friend with warm feelings, which, perhaps, had they been carefully analysed, might have been found to border upon love; but Marian Moreland, who greatly resembled Albert in his brightest days, had shot with her brilliant dark eyes such bewitching glances as had found their way to Edward's heart, and to Melville's ear he first breathed the secret of his love; and when his friend had seen and ardently approved of his choice, then, and not till then, Edward solicited from her brother the fair hand of Marian.

They were married, and Melville, who officiated as father, was the first to salute the bride, and gave the bridegroom joy on the occasion; and Melville was particularly fortunate, for, go where he would, he was sure to be liked, if not admired, and Marian most certainly cordially extended the hand of friendship, not only to him, but his mother and sister also, consequently she could not but feel grieved that a coldness should have arisen between him and Edward, who had never before, during the whole of their acquaintance (which should now be numbered by years,) ever had a word of disagreement, and when she returned home from her visit Rose, she reminded him of their engagement for the evening, and expressed a hope that he would meet Melville with his usual cordiality.

'I am quite convinced, dear Edward, that Melville is by this time sorry for having expressed himself so warmly, and will be anxious to forget all that passed between you ; and I should be indeed sorry if Mrs. Melville (who since the death of your mother has all but filled her place towards us both) should observe any coolness between you ; and poor Lucy, too, just as she is celebrating her one-and-twentieth birthday, it would cast a shadow over all her joy, for she is so tenderly attached both to you and her brother, that to know an unkind feeling existed between you would have the effect of rendering her very sad.'

'Rest assured, Marian, that I shall not renew the discussion, especially as Rose is to accompany us ; at the same time, knowing Melville's feelings towards her, I shall regard him with a jealous eye. Think what an opinion your brother would have of me if, through any want of caution on my part, Melville should succeed in seducing her affection from him.'

'Oh ! I cannot conceive Melville capable of such premeditated baseness.'

'A man passionately in love, as he declares himself to be, is capable of anything that tends to gain the object of his wishes.'

'Really, Edward, I am confident you think too seriously of the matter ; that Melville admires Rose exceedingly, I do not doubt, for she is so beautiful that I think few men could gaze upon her without admiration ; but that he really loves her in the way you imagine, I cannot believe.'

'You have his own words in proof of it, Marian.'

'Yes ; but how often do men express themselves in a similar manner, without, for an instant, seriously meaning what they say ? it is but natural that men should endeavour to attract the notice of a handsome woman, which they may surely do without entertaining any bad design ; and I must think, Edward, you were too severe upon Melville last night. I never deemed you unjust before, and Rose is, you know, so devotedly attached to Albert, that it would be next to impossible for any one to estrange her affections from him.'

While this conversation was taking place between Edward and Marian Trevors, Mrs. Melville and Lucy were making active preparations for the evening. Lucy in a light undress, with a beating heart, trod the floor of the ball-room, anxious to see that all was arranged to her satisfaction. She was, as Marian had described her, a very pretty, interesting looking girl, not that she could be for one moment compared to the brilliant beauty of Rose, yet her features were regular and good, and her pale cheek and slender form never failed of awakening an interest in the beholder. As she stood in the centre of the room gazing around with proud satisfaction, apparently in deep thought, her brother entered, and walking gently up behind her, placed his hand on her shoulder : she turned instantly, and with a look of tender affection exclaimed—

'Well, dear Henry, what do you think of the arrangements ; for I suppose, like me, you have come to see that all is perfect ?'

'I have come dear Lucy, to give you a brother's greeting on this important day.' And, drawing from his pocket a row of costly pearls, he clasped them round her neck, and, affectionately kissing her cheek, said,—

'My dear girl, may you never be less happy than at this moment !'

'Thank you, dear brother,' she returned. 'If your kind wish is granted, my lot will indeed be a bright one. But I dare not hope to pass through life so easily.'

'Why not ? If any one ever deserved it, I am sure it is you.'

'You regard me, dear Henry, with a brother's fond partiality, but even putting that aside, those who most deserve happiness in this world rarely attain it.'

'Dear Lucy,' he returned, 'you must not speak or look sad on a day which should be the brightest and most joyous of your life, except one.'

'You allude to marriage,' said Lucy, a slight colour mounting to her usually pale cheek.

'Most certainly,' replied her brother. 'I hope one day to perform that office for you that I have already done for Marian Trevors.' The colour faded from her cheek, and a slight agitation shook her frame, but she answered calmly,—

'That is the only subject on which I cannot allow you to speak to me ; you have frequently heard me express a determination never to repeat the marriage vows. There is so little faith in man, that I am resolved never to trust my happiness to another's keeping.'

'Are you not rather bitter against our sex, Lucy ?'

'I may have reason to believe so,' she returned.

The colour mounted to the very temples of Melville, suffusing his face with one rich glow, as he replied,

'Lucy, tell me this instant, has any one dared to—'

'Stop, dear Henry, there is no occasion for your anger, I may have loved and been deceived but it is no uncommon case,'

'Did I but know,' he returned, as he grasped her hand convulsively, 'who the villain was that had deceived you, my own dear gentle sister, I think naught but his death would appease my anger,'

'My dear brother,' she returned, clasping her white arms round his neck, 'I needed not this to convince me how dearly you loved me, yet I am sorry to see you give way to such ungovernable anger; for had any one ever injured me, which, indeed, they have not'—and the bloom again crept over her pale cheek—'I should not dare to impart it to my brother.'

'You are yourself, dear Lucy, so mild and forgiving, that you can scarcely make any allowance for my fiery temper.'

'Say not so, Harry; none, believe me, ever admired your noble spirit more than I; and should not a sister make allowance for a brother's anger, especially when it is roused in her defence?'

'Well, dear Lucy, time is speeding on, and I fear this conversation has already kept you from your toilet, so I will detain you no longer.'

When the brother and sister again met, it was in the broad blaze of light that illuminated the ball-room, where all was gaiety and confusion; the company were arriving fast, which was announced to the entire neighbourhood by thundering knocks at the door. Lucy remarked that Henry seemed agitated and confused. Every time the door opened, his anxious gaze was bent upon it, and as often turned away in disappointment, till at length Edward Trevors entered, supporting on either arm Marian and Rose. He flew to welcome them, and introduce Lucy, whom he led by the hand to Rose, who received her most kindly—indeed, there was something in Lucy's gentle unobtrusive demeanour that struck a chord in the heart of Rose, which instantly vibrated at the touch—she was conscious of an unity of feeling existing between them, and kindly pressed the hand Lucy presented to her. The four stood chattering together in friendly converse, neither Edward nor Melville appearing to remember the coldness that had arisen between them the preceding evening, till Melville solicited the hand of Rose for the quadrilles that were forming. She answered, politely, she was engaged to Edward for the first three sets, when a deep shade of disappointment passed over his countenance, which Rose observing, she added, 'that if not too fatigued, she would be happy to oblige him afterwards Milville thanked her with a smile of pleasure.

Rose's heart had been very heavy in the morning, after hearing Marian's account of the early life of Albert. Dearly as she loved him, she could not refrain from shedding a tear, when alone, as the thought forced itself on her mind, that his life had been less free from stain and blemish than she had fondly painted it. She had, indeed, in her almost fond adoration of him, deemed his honour bright and untarnished as her own—then what painful emotions it cost her to find there was a spot upon it which could never be wiped out! Some, would, doubtless, have regarded it as a very venial offence. Not so Rose. If a man wilfully brought a woman to vice whom he professed to love, and won her affection for the sole purpose of taking advantage of that affection to gain her to his wishes, she rightly judged it was a crime of no light magnitude, and one for which he must give an account on that day when the secrets of all hearts are laid open; and though in this world he goes free and unscathed while the flower he has blighted sinks 'neath the withering touch of vice, unpitied, to the tomb, yet God looks with a more tender eye upon a woman's frailty, and, unless he bitterly repents, will most assuredly visit her sins upon the head of the seducer.

Such thoughts as these, we have said, made Rose's heart sad and heavy; yet now, in the midst of bright smiles and happy faces, she for awhile forgot her care. Dancing was, as the papers invariably say, kept up with great spirit till a late, or rather early hour. Rose had danced with Melville, and afterwards seated between him and his sister, held a long and agreeable conversation with them; in them she found feelings and thoughts akin to her own; their spirits, like hers, were free and unshakled from Fashion's chains, which held in bondage most all by whom Rose had been surrounded since her marriage, and with a lighter heart than she had brought with her she obeyed Marian's summons to depart. She could not but remark during their ride home, that Edward seemed to lack his usual spirits, and was surprised, when, on assisting her to alight, he took the opportunity of saying, unheeded by Marian—

'Will you oblige me, Rose, by granting me a private interview to-morrow?' and seeing she hesitated, he added, 'there is something I particularly wish to impart to you, and which I cannot so well trust to another, or Marian should be my deputy, and I think you need not fear trusting yourself with me in your own house.'

'Oh dear, no,' returned Rose, rather hastily, 'will four o'clock suit you?'

'Your time is mine.'

'Then let it be four;' and freeing her hand from his ardent grasp, with heightened colour she entered the house.

Poor Rose seemed doomed to have her curiosity awakened. No sooner had she been made acquainted with the secret she was most anxious to learn, than another mystery sprang up before her. What could Edward have to say that he could not impart to Marian? was a question she asked herself over and over again; sometimes she felt vexed with herself for having appointed a meeting with him, and then, again, she wished the morrow had arrived, and all was explained. Well, there was nothing for it but to wait as patiently as possible. Lucy and Henry Melville were her earliest visitors in the morning; they called to inquire how she felt after the fatigue of the preceding evening, and were gladly admitted; their conversation was exactly of the description that pleased Rose—it reminded her strongly of her own quiet family circle, ere she had mixed with the gay world, and it refreshed and invigorated her spirits. She could talk to them without experiencing the languor she so often felt while conversing with Edward and Marian Trevors, unless on some particular topic, and this thought reminded her of the visit she expected from Edward, and for which, when she had taken leave of her new friends, she found by her watch the hour drew nigh. She had been pleased—much pleased, with the company of Henry and Lucy, and Albert, too, had left his study for a short time, and joined her in the drawing-room, and his manner towards her had been particularly marked with kindness, and this had illuminated Rose's charming face with the smile of pleasure that so well became it. When Mr. Trevors was announced, although striving hard to maintain her usual firmness and self possession, yet Rose was conscious of trembling and looking confused when Edward entered, and when, on receiving her hand, he warmly pressed it in his own, the colour on her cheek deepened, and she almost repented having granted an interview; yet, making an effort to regain her composure, she said,—

'I believe, Mr. Trevors, you have something important to impart to me.'

'Rest assured, dear Rose, I have, and yet it is an unpleasant subject to speak on; would that I did not feel it a bounden duty to tell you all I know.'

'If it is for my benefit to hear what you have to tell, I entreat you, Mr. Trevors, to speak at once.'

'I will, my dear Rose; I feel for you as a brother, and as such, be it my care to guard you from every ill; and though it is necessary for me to denounce one who has hitherto been my dearest friend, yet your welfare requires it, and therefore I shall not hesitate an instant to do so. Rose, it was to warn you against the temptations of Melville that brought me here this morning.'

'To warn me against Melville!' replied Rose. 'I know not, Mr. Trevors, what you can see in my conduct to think I require such advice.'

'Nothing, dear Rose: your conduct has ever been above reproach; but Melville passionately loves you, and has not hesitated to declare it, almost publicly.'

'You are wrong, Mr. Trevors, I am convinced,' said Rose with dignity; 'he may regard me as a friend; indeed I have every reason to believe he does; he was here with his sister Lucy this morning, and——'

'He was here with his sister this morning!' repeated Edward. 'He has then, kept his word, and been beforehand with me. I told him that I should warn you against his base attempts.'

'Base attempts! I am quite at a loss to understand you, Mr. Trevors,' replied Rose.

'I have nothing but your good at heart,' rejoined Edward; 'this, I think, you will do me the justice to believe, when I tell you that I have ever regarded Melville as a sincere friend to me and mine, and have on more than one occasion experienced his friendship, and was ever willing, in return, to assist him to my utmost whenever he required it; but now we have quarrelled, and can never again be to each other what we have once been, and all because I could not bear to hear him use your name in the manner he did at the club yesterday You are silent, and perhaps scarcely believe what I say; it is, nevertheless, true. I can have no reason for wishing to deceive you; but even if you still persist in disbelieving me, you shall know all, and then I shall have discharged my duty, and whatever may happen, my conscience will be free from reproach.'

'Well,' said Rose, with a mournful expression of countenance, 'pray proceed; let me hear all I have to fear from Mr. Melville.'

'On the evening he accompanied us to the opera he conceived a violent attachment for you, and declared it to Marian and myself. I reminded him of your being married, but he treated it with contempt; still, having known him so long and well, and never before having had a doubt of his honour, I did not suppose for an instant he entertained any wrong feeling towards you. Judge then, of my surprise, on meeting him at the club yesterday, to hear him laying a wager with a young man present that he would gain you to his wishes in less than six months. I could not quietly stand by, and hear you treated with insult, and yet, not wishing to quarrel, I gently remonstrated with him on his conduct, and finding it of no avail, I warned him, if he still persisted in the wager, I would acquaint you with all that had passed, when he insultingly declared that he would be beforehand with me, and so far win your regard that you would pay no attention to my statement.'

' Is it possible ?' replied Rose ; ' if so, how much—how very much I have been deceived in him !'

' Not more so than myself, Rose. I thought him the very reverse of what he has proved himself to be ; indeed, had I not been present, and heard all that passed, I should, like you, have deemed it almost impossible.'

' I am truly unfortunate, replied Rose, ingenuously, ' for I must confess that I thought better of him than I did of you ; can you, Mr. Trevors, forgive my injustice, when I tell you that I had conceived, I know not why, an unkind feeling towards you, as you have in this affair (the truth of which I cannot doubt) proved yourself my sincere friend ?'

' Forgive you, Rose, most certainly, though I grieve you should have thought ill of me, but you will now, I hope, know me better.'

' I shall indeed, Mr. Trevors ; but oh! tell me how I am to guard against Henry Melville. I have promised Lucy to spend to-morrow evening with her, and Henry will, most probably, be of the party ; had I not better think of an excuse for not being present ?'

' No, go, dear Rose, by all means ; you are now on your guard against him, therefore it is impossible he can injure you.'

' Yes ; but what you have told me has caused me to feel a horror of his very presence, and if I show it, he may guess you have told me of his conduct, and that may be the means of causing fresh quarrels between you.'

' It will doubtless, Rose, be as you say, but do not let that make you unhappy. I have only done what any other man of honour would, in acquainting you with what took place, and care not for the result, No,' he continued, half aside, ' should Melville send me a challenge he will find me ready and willing to accept it.'

Rose turned deadly pale. No, no, Mr. Trevors, oh! do not, I entreat of you, make me wretched enough to be the means of causing bloodshed, perhaps, even death ;' and at the thought she shuddered, and the blood forsook even her very lips. ' Oh! I would submit to insult and degradation a thousand times rather than another should be injured through me ; the very thought is productive of such bitter anguish as I should be sorry for my worst enemy to feel.'

— ' Compose yourself, dear Rose, it shall not be—I will, for your sake, cautiously avoid giving Melville offence, and he need know nothing of this conversation ; you can keep him at a distance without mentioning what I have told you.'

' Oh! yes, Mr. Trevors, I can and will, and pray accept of my best thanks for your kindness. Had it not been for you, regarding Melville with the feelings I did, into what a vortex of misery I might have been plunged ! how wrongfully, indeed, I may well say how wickedly, I have judged you ! but knowing how ignorant I am of the world, you will, I am convinced, pardon me.'

' Yes, Rose, for I well know that it was an error of the judgment only, not of the heart.'

' Thank you, Mr. Trevors, for doing me that justice, and for the future I shall know and appreciate you better.'

' One word more, dear Rose, before we dismiss the subject from our thoughts. You will not, of course, mention anything I have told you to Albert. If the bare idea of Melville or myself falling in a duel caused you such anguish, what would you feel, were Albert the victim ? and I am certain, did he know of Melville's conduct, he would instantly call him out. He is of an exceedingly jealous disposition, and, when roused, of a very vindictive spirit : of this you must be well aware, for Marian told me she had acquainted you with the unhappy fate of Florence, who unfortunately fell a victim to Albert's jealous passion.'

' To Albert's ? You mistake ; he certainly led her astray, and so far was the innocent cause of her death, but it was Charles who, having surprised them together, in a fit of passion struck the dreadful blow that deprived the unhappy girl of life ; but Albert, Marian assured me, did his best to arrest the weapon ere it descended, but unfortunately it was too well aimed and his efforts to prevent the deed were useless.'

' Did Marian tell you it was Charles who struck that fatal blow ?'

' Most certainly ; and if there was a doubt upon the subject, his remaining abroad, while Albert has returned to his native country, I should think was a convincing proof of it.'

' It is not so, Rose ; I am sorry to undeceive you, but I have good proof that it was Albert's hand that committed the awful deed.'

' You wring my heart with anguish : but it cannot be, or why should Charles remain abroad ?'

' That is a secret I cannot myself fathom ; that he willingly remains in a foreign land is, doubtless, perfectly correct, but why, being innocent, he consents to do so, while the guilty party returns and spends his days in peace and happiness with his relatives and friends, I cannot for a moment pretend to account for, unless I ascribe it to his generosity. You know that after their father's death, Albert provided for Charles in a most handsome manner.'

Yes, yes,' repeated Rose, with beaming eyes, as she reflected there was at least one trait in Albert's character—one portion of his life she could lways look upon with pleased satisfaction, that she could speak of as generous and noble, though no more, perhaps, than was strictly just. Yet how many would have acted otherwise, and if they had made a trifling allowance to the illegitimate son, have deemed they were performing a generous action! But Albert had done just what Rose felt assured she should have done herself—divided the inheritance between them. It is true that, shared, it afforded an ample provision for both, yet few would have been content with half when they could rightly have claimed the whole: but if all knew how sweet is the performance of a good action, what a constant source of comfort to fall back upon in our saddest and dreariest hour, is the thought that we have ever acted uprightly, even when surrounded by the fiercest temptations, and when we might have taken advantage of another, without one voice being raised against us except the still small voice of conscience, which will make itself heard, and though our outward actions may bear the strictest scrutiny of the world, and yet be pronounced faultless, if conscience whispers we deserve not the praise bestowed upon us, and tells of sins unknown perhaps to all but our own hearts, we have no longer any resource for our moments of sorrow and despondency, which chequer even the happiest life—ah! better, a thousand times better, had we suffered unmerited calumny, and have our best and purest actions misinterpreted by those who know not the difficulties and trials that beset us, if our own conscience (which is indeed a faithful monitor and never leads us into error) tells us we have ever kept integrity for our guide and honour for our goal, renouncing our dearest hopes if indulging them would cause us to deviate, even in the slightest, from the path it is our duty to pursue. There is no retracting; if once we fall into sin we must do it with our eyes open. It is weak and foolish to urge, 'I did not know;' all do, or at least may know, if they choose to listen to the voice God has placed in our bosoms, for the sole purpose of reminding us, and preventing, if possible, by its wise counsels, our feet from slipping—one false step is often, alas, fatal! It is frequently difficult to resist evil, but oh! how much more difficult it is to return; this should indeed make us cautious, especially when walking, as we are sometimes obliged to do, in slippery places, and it is a sad thought that though we may repent with anguish and with tears, we can never undo the sins we have foolishly and wickedly committed, often, very often for the mere want of a little firmness and resolution to resist temptations that will constantly spring up around our path.

But, to return from our digression: we were saying that Rose felt thankful that there was a portion of her husband's life she could reflect upon with pleasure, but oh! what bitterness to know that there were other parts she could not for a moment dwell upon without the deepest horror; still she could not think he was the principal actor in the dreadful tragedy that had deprived a fellow-creature of life, one to whom, by all she could learn, he had paid his first and earliest vows of love; in that Edward must be mistaken, and Marian's account of the awful affair not only the most probable but surely the most correct one. Still Edward persisted he was right, and after Rose had urged him to acquaint her with proof, he assured her that he was perfectly convinced he was correct in his statement, and at length acknowledged he still held possession of the letter which Marian imagined destroyed.

' You remember, dear Rose,' he said, ' that at the time Marian received the letter conveying to her the sad tidings which plunged her into such severe distress, she was residing with my mother, who was seated with me in a room exactly beneath the one occupied by Marian, and we were conversing together on some topic of no great interest when we were aroused by a shriek and the falling of a heavy body on the floor: we instantly repaired to Marian's room; we found her senseless, with the letter, which had only arrived a few minutes previously, grasped tightly in her hand; on removing her to bed it was with difficulty I withdrew the letter from her hand, and in doing which it was torn and somewhat defaced, yet enough remained entire to inform me of the dreadful calamity which had taken place in Italy. When Marian, some weeks after, recovered sufficiently to make inquiries concerning the letter, we deemed it best to tell her it had been destroyed, for we dreaded the effects of a second perusal, but I carefully hoarded it, thinking it might some day be turned to account; and as it may satisfy you that Albert, and not Charles, was the assassin, I will bring it for your perusal, only be careful not to allow Marian to suspect it is still in existence.'

Poor Rose's heart seemed ready to break; the more she heard of Albert the deeper he seeme plunged in vice. To think, for an instant even, that the husband she adored had ever with fell intent seized the murderous knife and driven it into the bosom of the helpless victim of his jealous love—the thought was madness; her reason reeled till it seemed ready to desert its throne; a flood of tears at length afforded her a little relief, and being anxious to sati sfy,

No. 3.

herself of the truth of Edward's statement, she begged he would bring her the letter, if possible, that very day.

'I am indeed wretched,' she said, as Edward strove to comfort her, 'and never can be happy again unless I find that by some most fortunate mistake you have been led into error. Oh, God Almighty! ordain that such may be the case!'

Never did Rose, mourning in all the soft beauty of youth and health, look so fair and heavenly as now: pale and wan, she raised her sweet blue eyes, overflowing with tears, to Edward's face, as if beseeching him to acknowledge that he was wrong, that he had deceived her, or at least that there was a hope that such might prove to be the case. He shook his head.

'It would be useless, dear Rose, for me to tell you aught but the truth, although had I known it would have affected you thus I would gladly have continued you in error; for I cannot bear to see you shed such bitter tears for a deed that was committed so many years ago, that doubtless it is almost forgotten by one who has most reason to deplore it.'

'Never, never! Mr. Trevors,' said Rose in bitter agony; 'such a deed cannot be forgotten. Oh! no; if indeed it is as you say, Albert remembers, fearfully remembers it yet. Yet what do I say?' she continued, gazing wildly around. 'Oh! if it were possible for him to live for thousands of years nothing surely could ever efface that awful scene from his mind! It must remain vividly there till his dying day, and oh! if not repented of, what a dreadful death-bed it will be.'

'My dear Rose,' said Edward, with an air of surprise, 'you think too seriously of it. It was certainly a sad affair, but then the provocation was great; indeed, altogether, I can not regard it in the light you do.'

Rose sobbed convulsively. Taking her unresisting hand in his, Edward kindly begged of her to subdue her emotion. 'What would Albert think if she me him at dinner with such palpable demonstrations of grief in her countenance? She would be under the necessity of telling him that she knew his secret—a secret he was desirous of keeping from the knowledge of all, but of course more especially from her, his young and tenderly loved wife; and then to know that the knowledge of it cost her such intense anguish, he would conclude that he was no longer regarded with the fond affection she had hitherto given him, but would deem he was despised, if not hated, on account of the past.' With such words as these, intermingled with kind and endearing epithets, Edward at last succeeded in reducing Rose to something like composure; her tears ceased to flow, and the paleness of her lovely countenance gave place to a flush of feverish excitement, which somewhat resembled the bloom that usually sat upon it. Delighted with these signs of returning fortitude, Edward, still retaining her hand in his, particularly cautioned her to avoid, by every means in her power, allowing Albert to discover that she knew aught of his early life, likewise to say nothing to Marian of what he had told her, either as regarded Melville, or ———. At this moment the room door opened, and Marian appeared on the threshold, surprise plainly depicted on her countenance.

'You here, Edward! I am indeed surprised to find you thus engaged. I have been for some time closeted with Albert, who I am grieved to find suffering from a fit of *ennui*, and have been doing my best to cheer and amuse him, while his truant wife, regardless of the sorrow of her lord, is herself seeking solace and amusement in the society of a younger and gayer knight.'

Rose, trembling and covered with blushes, essayed to rise from her seat, but was prevented by Marian.

'No, no, child! Albert will not wish to avail himself of such protracted politeness: remain where you are, he is now busily engaged with his lawyer, and will not thank you if you interrupt him.'

'Indeed,' replied Rose, 'I knew not he was ill.'

'Not ill, child; low spirits, I assure you, nothingmore.'

'That is often,' said Rose mournfully, 'worse, far worse than bodily illness, and I would gladly have been with him, only when he retires to his study, I always know that he wishes to be alone.'

'Very likely, but it is not at all times proper to indulge him. You study him so much, Rose, that I thought you would have known when the evil spirit was on him, and which requires charming away with winning smiles and tender words; it was fortunate I called here this morning, or he might have met you with a darker spot upon his brow than you will now observe there.'

'He was with me in this room not long before Edward called, and was then in excellent spirits.'

'Indeed,' replied Marian, 'you surprise me! for I have ever observed that *ennui* creeps upon him very gradually, when to-day it must have been sudden, for I have been with him some considerable time, and when I arrived here I was immediately struck with his extremely dejected appearance, which induced me to remain with him, instead of, as was my first intention, seeking for you. There must surely be some cause for it more than usual. Have any letters arrived from abroad to your knowledge, Rose ?'

'None.'

'Because he has a correspondent in Italy, for I have frequently known him to receive letters, and which ever have the effect of causing him excessive dejection.'

'A letter may have come without my knowing it,' replied Rose.

'Doubtless. Indeed, I think that must have been the case, for I cannot account for the sudden alteration in his appearance in any other way; but I came to inform you, Rose, that I have seen Mrs. Melville this morning, who has engaged to dine with me to-morrow, accompanied by Henry and Lucy, on the consideration that you were to be present.'

'I had promised to spend to-morrow evening at Mrs. Melville's.'

'Yes, I know; but they have consented to waive that pleasure till the day after. So mind, Rose, I shall expect you. I have been persuading Albert to make one of our number, but it seems useless, although he is perfectly willing that you should come. And now, Edward, if your conference with Rose is at an end, perhaps you will have the politeness to attend me home ?'

From the moment of Marian's entrance Edward, hastily dropping the hand of Rose, remained perfectly silent, seeming to fear that his wife had overheard part of their conversation, and dreading she would require an explanation, and he now, with alacrity, obeyed her summons to depart. That he had fondly loved Marian, ere their marriage, was beyond a doubt, but it was a love that had no foundation on which to build domestic happiness. She was a dark, handsome woman, of no small ability; indeed, she possessed a great share of her brother's talent; but, being naturally of an indolent disposition, she had never made use of it, beyond occasionally composing a few verses, which were allowed, by competent judges, to be far above mediocrity. Edward, as we have said, loved her, but never for an instant considered, as a man should do, whether her tastes and pursuits were in consonance with his own. She possessed, as she well knew, a vein of satire, which frequently, during the days of courtship, was directed against himself, and which, though he bore it patiently, galled him more than he would have cared to acknowledge. Indeed, satire is a talent that, however much admired by some, need not be coveted by any; for the possessor is always more or less disliked: it was this that ever kept Rose, in a manner, in fear of Marian; she could speak to her of Albert, for was he not her brother, one, too, whom she loved and admired ? but of her own thoughts and feelings she never breathed a word to Marian—she dreaded her raillery, and, although she was certain ever meaning most kindly, Marian had, unfortunately, so much accustomed herself to speak satirically, even of serious things, that she had very few real friends. Edward, previous to their marriage, had borne from her much in this way, but he little expected its continuance afterwards, and Marian, seeing it was hurtful to his feelings, certainly did less frequently direct it towards him; but then it must have vent somewhere, and, in the absence of other objects, Edward was made to feel its edge, and, now, his visit to Rose, without her knowledge, afforded ample opportunity for her indulging in her favourite talent, and, consequently, Edward almost dreaded the ride home, and would gladly have availed himself of an excuse for not accompanying her, had it been possible. How great, then, was his surprise to find her silent and apparently thoughtful, replying to his observations on the weather, or any other subject he could think of, chiefly in monosyllables, and paying so little attention to his remarks, that she sometimes gave him anything but an appropriate answer; for this he was quite at a loss to account, he had never seen her thus before, and it completely puzzled him. Had she, as he had first feared, overheard any part of his conversation with Rose, he felt certain she would never have allowed it to pass so quietly. So, blessing his lucky stars that he had escaped her raillery for once at least, he determined to make himself as agreeable as possible the remainder of the day, consequently, at dinner he was unusually attentive, but Marian still preserved an abstracted and thoughtful demeanour; yet she sometimes fixed her dark eyes on his face with an expression of sorrow, and then, again, with a look so deep and searching, that he stopped abruptly in his converse, and, with a confused manner, endeavoured to avoid her gaze.

In the mean time poor Rose, left alone, had leisure to think upon what had passed. How wrong and rashly she had judged of Edward and his friend Melville was her first thought, and thankful she felt that Edward had communicated to her the real character of Melville. Warned of his baseness, she need fear nothing for the future: on that score, she had only to treat him with the cold contempt his conduct so well merited, and all his attempts to injure her would fall harmless to the ground, and Edward she generously resolved to confide in as a sincere friend, and Lucy; too, in whom she had found a sister spirit, she could still lavish on her the affectionate regard of a sister; for, though her brother was so utterly unworthy, she was certain Lucy knew it not, or even if she did, it would be wicked to make her answerable for it; and then her thoughts turned to Albert, and all she had heard of his early life, and she could scarcely believe it possible that such opposite traits should be found in one character; yet she could, at least, do him the justice of feeling that he had ever been kind and indulgent in the extreme: indeed, she was so young and innocent, so almost child-like in her want of knowledge of character, and experience in the world, whereas he was so well versed in the windings of the heart, could so easily detect deception, was older both in knowledge and appearance than his years, and, when he conversed with her, seemed, so to speak, to unbend and suit his language and ideas to the simplicity of hers—that any one, not knowing the relative character they bore to each other, would unhesitatingly have taken them for father and daughter; and when he addressed her it was always with the affectionate tone of a parent, and which, in a measure, repelled and forced back to her own heart the fond warm feelings she would otherwise have lavished upon him. He never appeared to forget that he was her senior by years, or that his thoughts and feelings soared far above her own. From their first acquaintance she had mingled reverence with the love she felt for him; had deemed herself unworthy of sharing, as she was desirous to do, his every thought; and now, alas! with bitter agony she learnt that not only had he been guilty of follies and vices, to which all are exposed—that would have been sad enough, but, oh! a thousand times worse, his character was blackened with positive crime. Weighed down with such bitter thoughts, it was with a very heavy heart she obeyed the summons of the dinner-bell and descended to the dining-room: it was empty; but a note was handed to her by the servant—she opened it, and read these words:

'My dearest Rose,—I am grieved I shall not be able to meet you at dinner this day. I am engaged on business of a very painful nature, which will detain me the rest of the evening; make yourself as comfortable as possible, and if you have any engagement do not hesitate to fulfil it, without applying to me.   'Your affectionate husband,
                                                                'ALBERT MORELAND.'

Seated alone at the dinner-table in solitary state, surrounded by every luxury that could tempt the most fastidious appetite, while obsequious servants hastened to fulfil her slightest wish—oh! how thankfully would Rose have parted with all to be again the happy light-hearted village maid, who had never known what sorrow meant. In vain she essayed to eat—the dishes were sent almost untasted away, and she could scarcely check the starting tear till she had gained the privacy of her own room, when, throwing herself on the downy pillows of the couch, which luxuriantly invited to repose, she wept long and bitterly, not for her own but others' sins, till at length, like a fair and beauteous child, she sobbed herself to sleep. She had slept for hours, and darkness, like a curtain, had gathered round her couch, yet none had dared to disturb her slumbers, till Albert's study door turned on its hinges, and, stern and erect, he issued forth, bearing a small lamp in his hand. Ascending the stairs, he was about to enter the bed-room, when Rose's maid opened the door of her dressing-room and looked out.

'How is it, Milford, you are up and in your mistress's room at this hour?'

Mrs. Moreland had fallen asleep on her couch, and she was waiting to assist her in undressing, in proof of which she threw the door open to its fullest extent, and Albert's eye fell upon the sweet form of Rose: her head rested on one soft white arm, the other lay listless by her side, while her beautiful auburn tresses drooped to the ground; her eyes gave evident signs of having shed tears, and as Albert stooped down to look upon her face, she heaved one deep sigh and awoke: making an effort to arise, she became conscious of her husband's presence.

'Is that you, dear Albert? Oh! how glad I am you have come!'

'Tell me, Rose,' he replied, with an air of sternness he had never shown to her before, 'what you have to render you unhappy?'

'Unhappy, dear Albert! Oh, I can never be unhappy when you are with me,' said Rose, endeavouring to avoid telling a direct falsehood.

'You have been weeping, Rose: it is useless to deny it; and I desire to know what cause you have for shedding tears.'

'You did not dine with me to-day, and I felt dull and low-spirited—perhaps without sufficient reason,' stammered out poor Rose, covered with blushes.

'The one you have given is, indeed, a silly and childish one; and I could scarcely have thought it possible you would have wept because you were obliged for once to dine alone. Are you sure there is nothing else? If you are desirous of visiting your relatives, from whom you have been long absent, fear not to tell me so, and I will make arrangements for your departure.'

'You will go with me, dear Albert?' replied Rose, evasively.

'It will be inconvenient for me to leave town just now but that need make no difference to you.'

' I would rather, indeed, dear Albert, remain where I am, unless you accompanied me.'

' Well, Rose, you can do as you please. I suggested it only out of a desire to make you happy; either way, it is all the same to me. But you had better now let Milford assist you to retire for the night, and to-morrow we can talk further on this subject, only do not allow me to see you unhappy, if I am not to know the cause.'

Rose thought he was almost unkind in treating her with such indifference. In consulting her pleasure he had put himself completely out of the question: whether she left him to visit her parents, or whether she preferred remaining with him, he had assured her was a matter of indifference; she could not so think of him. No: though he were proved guilty of every crime, she would still have loved and clung to him—he would not have been the less her husband, whom she had vowed at the altar, in the presence of God, to love and honour; and strictly indeed she had performed her vow; yes, she, all innocence and purity, still loved him and clung to him, as her heart's best treasure.

When they met at breakfast the following morning, Albert seemed to have forgotten the conversation of the evening before, and addressed Rose with all his wonted kindness, although at times plunged apparently in a deep reverie; before leaving the breakfast-room, he alluded to her engagement at Marian's for the evening, hoped she would find company dissipate all feelings of *ennui*, and then added he was sorry he could not accompany her himself, but his thoughts were too busily engaged to admit of his doing so.

' You well knew, dear Rose, previous to our marriage, that I was wedded to books and solitude, and, therefore, will not think me unkind for permitting you to go out alone.'

' Oh, no, dear Albert, I never think unkindly of you.'

' I am glad to hear it, my love,' and he left the room.

' Oh,' thought poor Rose, ' that I, too, might be allowed to remain in solitude; but I am obliged to pay and receive visits, let my heart be ever so sad; and, oh! worse than all, I must conceal my real feelings under an assumed gaiety, and which has only the effect of rendering me in secret more wretched.'

Marian, brilliantly dressed, her dark eyes flashing with pride, and all smiles and beauty, received her company with graceful dignity. Rose was the last to arrive, and was gently chid by Marian for her want of punctuality.

' Allow me to introduce you, my dear Rose,' she said, leading her by the hand to a tall handsome man, of about five-and-twenty—' to Sir Charles Mortimer, who is especially desirous of making your acquaintance;' and then, turning round, ' here is another claimant for the honour of an introduction, Mr. William Fairford.' Rose and the strangers exchanged polite greetings. ' The rest of my company are known to you, Rose, and therefore my office is done,' said Marian, glancing round the room. Rose's eyes followed hers, and with evident pleasure she addressed Mrs. Melville and Lucy. Edward, too, was warmly received, but on Henry presenting his hand she drew back with more pride than she had ever assumed before, and curtsying coldly turned away. Henry could scarcely believe the evidence of his senses, and the colour mounted to the cheek of Lucy on seeing her brother treated with such rudeness; yet Henry could not feel offended—there surely must be some mistake, or Rose had unintentionally avoided him; this he resolved to ascertain before the evening was over.

The servant now announced ' Dinner waits,' and the company prepared to descend to the dining-room. Edward had advanced, in accordance with a look from Marian, to offer his hand to Mrs. Melville. Thinking this a favourable opportunity, Henry proffered his to Rose, but pretending not to see it, she stepped before Mrs. Melville and took Edward's: it was received with a smile of pleasure, and Melville even thought triumph, as he glanced for one moment towards him, but that was neither the time nor place to notice it. Sir Charles Mortimer politely presented his hand to Mrs. Melville, and Mr. Fairford did the same to her daughter, thus leaving Marian Trevors to Henry Melville. Whether or not Marian had observed the coldness with which Rose had treated Melville, and the marked preference shown to Edward, it was impossible to guess from her manner; at any rate, she showed no outward signs of having done so, although, generally speaking, nothing escaped her searching glance.

After dinner, when the ladies rose to leave the room, Edward opened the door and Rose being the last to pass out, she lingered an instant to exchange a glance full of meaning with Edward which was not lost upon Melville; the door closed, and Edward again having resumed his place at the table, the wine began to circulate more freely, and conversation, which had been restrained in the presence of the ladies to the polite attentions of the dinner-table, now found vent on all the commonplace topics of the day, as if each was eager to make himself amends for his previous restraint—all but Melville, who remained silent, intently watching Edward's countenance, who appeared exerting himself to keep up the spirits of his guests, without feeling much interest in what was going on, till Sir Charles Mortimer suddenly exclaimed—

' By-the-by, Melville, the young and beautiful Mrs. Moreland seems to have imbibed some terrible antipathy to you. I always gave you credit for being a favourite with the ladies, but it appears you have lost caste. I little thought, when Mrs. Trevors introduced her to me, that it was possible she could assume the air of *hauteur* with which she returned your address; there must be a reason for it, so tell us, my boy, what you have done to offend her.'

'If you require an explanation of Mrs Moreland's coolness to me, you must seek it of Mr. Trevors, and I have no doubt he will be happy to satisfy your curiosity,' said Melville, turning a look of reproach on Edward.

'I!' replied Edward, hastily; 'seek an explanation of me! I know not whether you mean to offer me an insult.'

'Nothing is farther from my thoughts,' returned Melville. 'I merely meant what I sa and what I still think, that, if you choose, you could give a very satisfactory explanation of Rose's behaviour to me. I called on her with my sister Lucy yesterday morning, and we parted on the most friendly terms, and to-day she scarce deigns me so much as a look, unless it is one of offended dignity.'

'Well,' replied Edward with an air of pique, 'am I to be made accountable for a woman's whims?'

'Rose is not whimsical—she is too much a child of Nature to be addicted to such fashionable follies. No, I am convinced the alteration in her conduct is attributable solely to you. I wish not to prolong this discussion, painful to me on every account; yet, let me tell you, Edward, that my eyes are now opened to your real character, therefore henceforth be cautious and guarded in your actions, for, should you attempt to take advantage of the confiding innocence of Rose, know there is, at least, one arm will ever be ready to avenge her wrongs.' Melville spoke with considerable excitement, and his brow was flushed with anger.

'This is language,' replied Edward, 'I cannot bear; although the speaker is an old and long-esteemed friend, it would be worse than cowardice to submit to it.'

'I have not spoken,' returned Melville, 'without due consideration, and I am willing to meet you as a man of honour should.'

Sir Charles Mortimer and Mr. Fairford here put an end to the discussion, and, not without some little difficulty, succeeded in amicably settling the dispute. And if friends (so called) would more frequently interfere with kindness and consideration for the wounded feelings of others, instead, as is too often the case, of being so ready to take up the dispute, and to encourage the adverse parties in their ill-will towards each other, till there remains no course but the awful one of standing face to face, breaking down all barriers of tenderness and pity which have at one time dwelt in the bosoms of all, and deliberately seeking each other's life as a sacrifice to their wounded honour, whit, instead of all this, a little—sometimes indeed a very little—gentle interference on the part of their mutual friends, the dispute would have ended in a renewal of intimacy and good feeling. While this was passing in the dining-room, the ladies were each amusing themselves, according to their own fancy. Mrs. Melville turned over some beautiful prints, regarding them with the air of a connoisseur. Rose had endeavoured to enter into conversation with Marian, but was checked with a very cold reply; she then turned to Lucy, who was of too amiable a disposition not to receive her kindly, and yet she felt there was a want of that warm animation that had hitherto marked their conference. Thus thrown back upon herself, Rose sat buried in deep and painful thought, often wishing she had never left her peaceful, innocent home to mix in a world with which she was so unfitted to contend. But when she thought of Albert, oh! she loved him so dearly that to be his she would endeavour cheerfully to bear with all. Oh! how she longed that they could fly together to some sequestered spot, where he would allow her to soothe his sorrow, attend to his every want, and know herself his sweetest solace and support under the bitter grief that so frequently weighed him down. What to her were riches? how little she cared for the splendour by which she was surrounded—how gladly she would have cast it all from her, if with it she could have laid down the sorrows and anxieties with which she was encompassed! Aroused from these thoughts by the entrance of the gentlemen, Rose endeavoured to look less sad. Sir Charles Mortimer seated himself by her side and strove to win her into conversation; Melville appeared resolved to mould his manner after her own, and strictly avoided even looking at her. This was some relief, for she felt convinced he must have become acquainted with her knowledge of his base designs, and consequently determined to withdraw his attentions from her altogether: thus she would be spared all further mortification from him, and thankful indeed she felt when the party broke up. On taking leave of Mrs. Melville, that lady expressed a hope of having the pleasure of Rose's company to-morrow. Alas! poor Rose had no choice; she could only bow and politely accept the invitation. From Marian, for the first time since she had known her, she parted with but a very cold greeting, and yet Rose knew not why. Never had she felt more friendly than now; but Marian was very distant to her, and Rose unconsciously followed her example. Edward led her to the carriage, and as they passed through the hall she said,—

'May I ask, Mr. Trevors, have you forgotten the letter we were speaking of?'

'No,' he returned; 'and if you are still desirous of perusing it, I will bring it with me to Mrs. Melville's to-morrow.'

'I shall, indeed, be exceedingly obliged if you will do so.'

'Then you may depend on me, Rose; but you will not feel offended with me for advising you not to treat Melville with such marked discourtesy as you did this evening; it caused him immediately to suspect that I had communicated to you what passed at the club; and had I not patiently borne from him such contumely as few men would have done, it would have caused what you so much dread. Believe me, dear Rose, it was for your sake alone I put up with his insults.'

'Oh! thank you, Mr. Trevors,' she replied, earnestly; 'I am, indeed, grateful to you, but my path is, alas! so beset with thorns that I know not where to tread.'

'Have courage, dear Rose, and in time, depend they will all be cleared away.'

'I dare not hope it, Mr. Trevors; every step I take seems to plunge me deeper in mystery and sorrow. Sometimes, you know not how wretched I feel, as the thought crosses my mind that Albert may get estranged from me.'

A smile of peculiar meaning passed over the face of Edward, but the darkness prevented Rose from observing it, and he answered, pressing her hand in his own,—

'If ever that should happen, remember, Rose, you have still a friend in Edward—one who will cling closer to you in misfortune and trouble than in your brightest and happiest days. Will you, Rose,' he continued, 'promise to apply to me for advice and comfort when all others forsake and turn against you?'

'Oh! Mr. Trevors, if that time should ever come—which God forbid!—I should need but little advice or assistance; all I could desire would be to lie quietly down and die.'

'Do not talk so, dear Rose, you wring my heart with anguish; one so young and lovely should not be so ready to talk of death.'

'It is our common lot,' replied Rose; 'and I have ever had a presentiment, which I now feel stronger than ever, that my life would be but a short one. Yet I will not, Mr. Trevors, make you uncomfortable with my sad forebodings: let us never speak on this subject again.'

'Be it as you wish, Rose; I cannot myself think but you will yet live many years in happiness and peace, perhaps even smile at these mournful presages. I must now say farewell till to-morrow, when we shall meet again, and I hope to see you in better spirits.'

'Farewell,' repeated Rose: 'do not, Mr. Trevors forget the letter.'

'Never fear, Rose, but I will do your bidding.'

The following morning, Mrs. Melville, Henry, and Lucy, met at breakfast. With them it was always a pleasant, sociable meal; they were, strictly speaking, a happy family: Lucy and Henry were most devotedly attached to each other; neither would have hesitated an instant to sacrifice their best wishes, if it could have conduced to the other's happiness; and as to Mrs. Melville, their widowed mother, they considered it their bounden duty to consult her welfare and comfort before all else on earth, and she, we have already said, was devoted to her children. With these feelings and views it would have been impossible for them to be otherwise than happy; though each may have had some little secret cause of anxiety, that they could not perhaps impart to the other's bosom, yet in each other's love and tenderness they were ever blessed.

Lucy was the first to observe on her brother's countenance an air of deeper thoughtfulness than usual, but she made no remark, out of consideration for their mother's feelings, till Mrs. Melville herself inquired of Henry if he were unwell?'

'Never in better health, dear mother, than at the present moment,' he replied.

'Has anything occurred, then, to make you anxious, for I am certain you are less cheerful this morning?'

Lucy said nothing, but fixed her eyes upon her brother's face, apparently waiting with great interest for his answer to her mother's question.

'Well, then,' said Henry, 'you know I never have any secrets from such near and dear friends; and must therefore confess that I had a few angry words with Edward Trevors yesterday, concerning Rose Moreland.'

'My dear Henry,' replied Mrs. Melville, 'I could not of course do otherwise than observe the cold, I was going to say rude, manner that Mrs. Moreland assumed towards you last evening, and was very much surprised and puzzled to account for it, feeling certain you had in no way given her cause to behave so.'

'Indeed, my dear mother, you only do me justice in saying so.'

'I am convinced of it, Henry, and also that it was that very coolness which caused words between you and Edward.'

'You are right, mother; I feel sure in my own mind I have to thank him for Rose

Moreland's altered demeanour to me. Lucy, my dear, you well know how friendly we parted the aay before?'

'Yes, yes, Henry, but what motive can Edward have in wishing her to think ill of you?'

'That he does wish it I am well aware, and that he has succeeded in imposing on her credulity there cannot be a doubt, and, irritated by the remarks of Sir Charles Mortimer, I taxed him with it.'

'And what said he?' returned Lucy, eagerly.

'He merely evaded my charge, which has the more convinced me that my surmises are correct.'

'But the motive?' said Lucy.

'Must be a bad one,' replied her brother.

'Oh! I hope and trust not,' returned Lucy, with deep emphasis.

'My dear sister, do not let it make you uneasy; I have warned him to act with caution, and bade him beware that, did he injure her, I would avenge the wrong.'

'Oh! no, my brother, my dear and only brother, not you!' and Lucy clung to him with all a woman's tenderness.

'Why, Lucy, any one would think that I was on the eve of some fearful peril, you cling so tightly to me; and see, you are alarming our mother; your foolish fears have absolutely chased all the colour from her face: depend upon it, my girl, Edward will be careful how he behaves to Rose, especially as he is well aware that I suspect him.'

'Yes, he will, I am sure he will; and, dear mother, forgive me for thus arousing your fears without any reason; there is none, I assure you—there cannot be. Henry will never forget how necessary his life is to both of us, so far as to risk it on any little quarrel, will you, dear brother?'

'On any little quarrel, most certainly not, dear Lucy.'

These words reassured Mrs. Melville, as they were intended to do; but Lucy felt that, did Edward wrong Rose, Henry would assuredly call him to account for it, in the only way men think they can redress an injury; and Lucy had been so accustomed to consider duelling as the most right and proper mode for men of honour to settle their disputes, that though she shuddered at the thought of her brother being engaged as principal in one, yet she admired his spirit in thus rising in defence of the weak, and owned to herself that had she been a man, her conduct would have resembled his; for with all her mild, feminine gentleness, Lucy possessed herself a fiery spirit, which, though it took much to rouse, yet, when once done, it transformed her into a different being; her eye would appear to flash fire, and her slight form, attaining its utmost height, would fill the beholder with a feeling of awe that was not easily forgotten.

Edward and Marian Trevors were among the early arrivals at Mrs. Melville's in the evening. It was a mixed assembly; and dancing commenced previous to Rose's entrance in the room. Edward had begun to fear she would not come, and, though standing aloof from the dancers, endeavoured in vain to conceal his uneasiness, till at last, when he had entirely abandoned the hope of seeing her, 'Mrs. Moreland' was announced. Edward wished, yet did not like, to be the first to greet her; and consequently Mrs. Melville received her first address. Apologising for the lateness of her arrival, she stated, in excuse, that she thought Mrs. Trevors would have called for her. Here Edward stepped forward, and hoped she would acquit them of all negligence. He had, indeed, proposed calling, but Marian had concluded, as nothing was said on the subject, that Rose would not expect them.

Rose returned that it was of very slight importance, and begged he would say no more about it; indeed, had she consulted her own feelings, she would not have been present that evening; as it was, he must excuse her for not fulfilling the promise she had made to dance with him, as she was really too unwell to bear the fatigue.

Edward, perceiving he was closely watched by Melville, deemed it best to join in the dance, therefore, seeking a partner, Rose was left seated alone by the side of Mrs. Melville. They entered into discourse with each other, and Rose was charmed with the kind and matronly manner in which she inquired after the cause of her ill-health, and Mrs. Melville found no difficulty in drawing from her the secret that she was likely to become a mother—a secret that had not before been breathed to any.

'But it is wrong, my love,' said Mrs. Melville kindly, 'not to acquaint your husband. When he discovers it, he will deem it positively unkind of you not having imparted it to him, and I would, therefore, seriously advise you to do so without delay.'

'I will endeavour to follow your advice,' said Rose, 'and yet—'

'Surely, my love,' interrupted Mrs. Melville, 'there can be no difficulty with your husband; he has a right to know it, and better he should do so from your lips than another's.'

Rose made no answer. She could not tell Mrs. Melville that, though loving Albert most dearly, there was ever a restraint existing between them that prevented her communicating freely with him on any subject, then surely more especially on this. Yet now she resolved, cost her what it might, she would tell Albert the following morning, and he would no longer be desirous of her mixing so much in gaieties and amusements that were not amusing to her. Having made up her mind to this, she felt a little relieved of the care that pressed so heavily on her bosom. It might be the means, she fondly deemed, of winning Albert from the sadness of the past, and causing him to forget his sorrows—of binding him more firmly to her and; then, spite of the fearful crime he was accused of having committed, she would still love and cherish him, as all the world

to her. Edward suddenly aroused her attention by placing in her hands the letter he had promise to bring with him. She turned very pale, but hastily concealed it, as she thought, unseen by any one present, but, alas! there was an eye that observed the action, and also the hurried and confused manner by which it was accompanied.

'Will you allow me, dear Rose, to call on you to-morrow, when you can return that letter to my keeping?' said Edward, as he took leave of Rose.

'Yes, certainly,' she replied. 'It ever will afford me pleasure to see you, who have, indeed, proved my best friend.'

'I am, indeed, pleased to hear you speak thus, dear Rose, and hope you will ever think as well of me as now.'

No. 4.

'I should be ungrateful indeed if I did not, for it was your kind warning that has kept me aloof from danger.'

Rose was naturally very timid, and required kindness and encouragement, and had, previous to her marriage, been so accustomed to be considered and indulged by her fond parents, that it was a very sad change to her to be suddenly placed in a situation of life wherein she was thrown almost entirely upon her own resources, and though surrounded by every luxury, she sighed after the sweet, fond endearments that had hitherto made up her every-day life, and life is nought without them. Oh! it is the mutual and constant exchange of affection that makes the family circle in which we move so dear and sacred to our hearts. We care not how humble the abode; happiness may dwell, nay, often does, in the cottage of the labouring man, while it as frequently forsakes the splendid mansion of the rich; and the passer-by, who gazes upon the numberless windows illuminated, perchance, for some gay festival, need not covet the lot of those who dwell therein. No! happiness consists not in outward show. Alas! how many

'Aching hearts in rich brocade are drest,
And jewels glitter on an anxious breast!'

For happiness, depend, we must look into the privacy of the domestic circle; and when there is an habitual cheerfulness, a tender regard for each other's feelings, a willingness in one to resign their wishes, without a murmur, for the sole sake of pleasing another, and that other to accept the resignation with gratitude and tender words of love—then we may conclude, without hesitation, that happiness dwells there, no matter in what grade of society the inmates may be placed.

Albert meant to be, and judged he was, acting kindly towards Rose; but, with all his knowledge, he knew little of a woman's heart, and her fond devotion to one she loves. His lot he deemed a dull and gloomy one; his thoughts and feelings were all tinged by a sombre hue, and unfit, he thought, to be shared by such a young and light-hearted girl as Rose. Oh, no! he shrank from her participating in his sadness—she, still little more than a child, and one, too, that had never known care. Oh! it must not be—no, although he could never more mix in the gay world himself, yet, under the protection of Edward and Marian Trevors, Rose could visit those scenes usually so delighted in by the young and fair; and when, night after night, he sat alone buried in deep and often melancholy thought, he deemed that Rose was the gayest of the gay, the happiest of the happy, till the evening he unfortunately discovered she had been weeping. Rose to weep! she that used to be the very type of mirth! what cause could she possibly have for tears? so brilliant, so admired; and oh! he felt more, a thousand times more than all, so innocent, so utterly free from crime. Why, why should she weep? and then his own morbid fancy fixed the cause on himself. True, the cause did lay there, but not in the manner he put it.

'I am, indeed, a wretch,' he exclaimed, 'and poison the happiness of all that come within my reach. Was it not enough for me to know that my own was blasted for ever, but must I seek to link the fate of another with my own dark destiny? Had I not already proof enough that all I loved was doomed to wither beneath my blighting touch? Was I mad, or what devil tempted me to rush thus blindly on, involving the happiness, oh, God! perhaps even the death of that fair creature? for thus it has been before. But, oh! cease such thoughts, my brain is on fire, and nowhere can I seek for peace; and yet what have I done? only fulfilled what was allotted for me. Yes; fate, fate, thou hast done it all.'

Thus did Albert wickedly ascribe to the ordination of a wise and merciful God the crimes he had himself wilfully committed; and oh! how often do those who have the most cause for repenting, bitterly repenting of their sins, boldly stand forth and shield themselves behind that most fatal of all doctrines, fate! How frequently are our ears pained with hearing, when we are kindly striving to convince them of their error: 'You cannot understand it, the doctrine is only known to few. You may one day see as I do, and then you will feel convinced that I could not have acted otherwise. It was ordained for me to act as I have, and it would have been utterly useless for me to have striven against my destiny.' What can we urge to such reasoning as this? Nothing; and then the boast, 'it is such a comfortable doctrine!' well may our tears flow, but those for whom they are shed regard us as weak and foolish. The saddest thought connected with this doctrine is, that it cuts off the believers in it from all hope of repentance; of course, they cannot repent of sins they hold it as part of their creed that God ordained them to commit; and, consequently, if they persist in their error, must die with all their sins upon their head. The thought is too painful to dwell upon, and we return to our narrative.

Poor Rose, trembling and covered with blushes, had managed, not without much confusion and embarrassment, to acquaint Albert with the important intelligence that she was likely to become a mother. But oh! how differently was the news received to what she had fondly pictured it! instead of pledging his love for her anew, and vowing to love and cherish the unborn babe, as the sweet offspring of their mutual affection, which would ever be dear to him, if only for her sake, a dark shade of sorrow passed over his face, and he seemed far more troubled than pleased at the intelligence: of this she judged from his countenance, for he spoke not a word. Rose's heart was full; she had so depended on seeing him pleased, if not delighted, with what she had told him, that this want of sympathy with her situation so overcame her, that she burst into an involuntary fit of tears.

Albert gazed upon her with astonishment. 'You are unhappy, Rose, and seek in vain to hide your sorrow from me; any longer concealment is now useless. I must, I will know all.'

'I really cannot tell you, dear Albert, but I have not felt well lately, and it has affected my spirits in the way you see; pray forgive me, and I will endeavour to be more cheerful for the future.

'Alas! Rose,' replied her husband, 'I see, I feel you will never be happy with me.'

'Not happy with you, dear Albert? Oh, say not so; indeed, indeed you are wrong.'

'I have acted cruelly in transplanting you from your own happy home to the cold, bleak hearth, which chills all who sit beside it.'

'I know not what you mean, dear Albert.'

'No, no, dear Rose, it is not fit you should; and yet you already exhale the poisonous vapour which destroys all that ever love me. Oh, it was ever thus: not the brightest virtues, the purest devotion that ever dwelt in human breast, could save those who were wretched enough to cast a thought upon me; and, oh! Rose, if I see you droop and fade, what will become of me? But no, I must save you at any cost; had you not better for a while return to your parents in the country? the fresh air of your native hills may perhaps again win you back to health and spirits. What say you, Rose? it is long since you have seen them; suppose you set off at once?'

Rose could only stammer out, 'And you, dear Albert—'

'Will remain here; you can acquaint your mother with your situation, and she will sympathise with and comfort you.'

Rose could offer no objection, and so anxious Albert seemed to send her from him, that, contrary to his usual wont, he was active in giving the servants orders, and, indeed, superintending the preparations for her departure himself. Rose was too sad to take any interest in what was going on in Albert's presence. She strove hard to assume a cheerfulness she could not feel, and when at night she laid her head on the pillow, with the consciousness that the morrow would wake her to parting with the one best loved on earth—and oh! when the thought crossed her mind that it was possible they might never again meet—she had, as she told Edward Trevors, often entertained a feeling that her pilgrimage would be but a short one; and oh! if it should close before they again met: but the thought was such anguish that she was only too thankful to use every endeavour to banish it from her mind.

Early in the morning Rose was up and dressed; Albert followed her example. They had both passed a sleepless night, and, seated together at the breakfast-table, calmly spoke of their approaching separation.

'You must remember me kindly to your parents, Rose, and tell them it is my earnest desire for you to remain in the country for some weeks, and I hope you will enjoy yourself.'

'If, dear Albert,' returned Rose, and her voice trembled, 'I find my health fully re-established, you will have no objection, I trust, to my returning sooner.'

'I consider only your happiness, Rose, and if you would consult it likewise, it would tend greatly to my peace of mind. Will you promise me to do this?'

Rose thought if she had consulted her own happiness she should not have left him, even to visit her dearest friends, but she only replied—

'Oh, yes! dear Albert, I promise to do as you wish.'

'Well then, my love, you have a long ride before you, and I think the sooner you commence your journey the better.'

With a sad and aching heart Rose completed the few preparations that yet remained unfinished, and, attiring herself in her travelling dress, descended to the drawing-room. Albert kissed her pale cheek, and, bidding her be careful of her health, led her to the carriage.

'You had better, my love, allow Milford to ride inside with you, it will be company for you on the road.'

Rose quietly acquiesced, and, fixing a look full of anguish on Albert, faltered out a mournful farewell. It was returned with a lingering pressure of the hand, accompanied with a wish for her happiness; and the parting was over, and poor Rose conscious of being whirled away from the great metropolis. She was, indeed, not sorry to leave it, for how much anxiety she had endured, how many sad and weary days, and lately too long and sleepless nights. Oh! if her husband so loved and treasured, had been but by her side, with what renewed hope and spirits would she have commenced her journey—with what rapture have flew from the gay scenes and fashionable assemblies she no longer felt any interest in! but to leave him behind, to know that every mile bore her further and further from him, was fraught with such bitter sorrows, that she could only droop her head and weep in the very fulness of grief; he thought so much of happiness; oh, did he but know how she loved him, how much dearer to her heart was care and anxiety with him, than every blessing and peace if he shared it not!

'If,' she involuntarily exclaimed, 'if he did but know this, he would never have sent me away from him, but I will shortly return; I will, at least, feign cheerfulness, if I feel it not.'

Thus soliloquised Rose, as all the sadness of parting pressed upon her heart.

Who has not felt it? a cold, heavy chill, that wraps everything with which we are surrounded in the deepest gloom. There is nothing on earth so mournful as parting from one we love and that one oftentimes endeared to us by a thousand little thoughts and feelings, known perhaps to none but our own bosoms, and which, if told again, would appear to others light and trivial, but they have connected the loved object to ourselves, have linked them to our hearts with ties, that have so turned and interwoven themselves, that to tear them out seems like rending our very lives; there is something in the very sound of the, word 'parting,' that strikes on the ear as the knell of expiring happiness, that tells our brightest days are o'er—that what is past can never be again: there is such pure ecstatic bliss when souls and hearts meet and blend together, that were there no such thing as parting, this world would approach so closely to Eden, that we should forget it was not our rest, and feel grieved when the summons came to call us away.

While Rose is speeding away to her native village, we will linger a little longer in the busy city, and then follow her to her childhood's home. About the time Rose took her departure from town, Marian Trevor made an unusually early call at the house of Mrs. Melville, and required a private conference with Lucy, which was instantly granted.

'My dear Lucy.' began Marian, 'I know I can confide in you as a sincere friend, and am consequently about to impart to your ear a great secret, and I which have not yet dared to mention, even to Edward.

'You rather alarm me,' replied Lucy, 'for to judge from your appearance, the secret is a painful one.'

'Not altogether.' rejoined Marian, 'but you shall hear. You are well acquainted, dear Lucy, with the painful affair, which occurred many years ago, in Italy; and which, though I often appear to have totally forgotten it, can never be erased from my memory; you have heard me, Lucy, frequently express the affection I entertained for Charles, and though so long a time has passed since I last heard from him, I have never given up the hope that we should meet again; and now, dear Lucy,' she added, trembling with eagerness, 'I have at last discovered where he is to be found, and my earnest desire is to set out for the continent immediately, that I may once more see and embrace my brother, dear to me, no matter what crimes he may be accused of committing, Lucy. I know you dearly love Henry, you can then feel for my impatience.'

'But are you certain you have obtained his correct address? because, if so, would not a letter——'

'Oh no, dear Lucy,' interrupted Marian, 'my eagerness to see him is so great that I wish to go to him at once.'

'But would it be advisable to act upon such an impulse? consider how great your disappointment would be, if, on your arrival, you discovered that the person you take to be him should prove a totally different personage.'

'I think there is no fear of that, Lucy; but I forget, I have not told you how I became acquainted with the fact that he is still residing in Italy, and also the exact spot.'

'Well,' replied Lucy, 'tell me, and then I shall be a better judge.'

'Sir Charles Mortimer has just returned from his travels, and conversing with me about the country and climate of Italy, accidentally asked if I had a cousin, or other relative, residing abroad. I replied in the negative, and naturally inquired what reason he had for supposing so; he informed me that there was a young Englishman resident in Italy who bore the name of Charles Moreland; you may judge of my astonishment, dear Lucy; the surprise was such that I was very near fainting, and it required all my presence of mind to prevent Sir Charles Mortimer discovering that I was deeply interested in the individual he had named.'

'But it is possible,' replied Lucy, 'that it might not be your brother; the name is not so uncommon but that it is probable it might belong to another. Did he see him, and could you from his description form any resemblance between that individual and your brother?'

'Unfortunately, he never saw him, and yet I know not why; but I feel convinced that it is no other than my dear Charles, whom I have so long endeavoured to track out, but till now without success.'

'My dear Marian, to make a voyage to the continent on such slight grounds for supposing you will meet with your brother, would be worse than folly, and end, in all probability, in severe disappointment. If, which is natural, you are desirous of inquiring into the fate of the absent Charles, why not apply to Albert, who, doubtless, knows well where to find him?'

'My dear Lucy, had you seen the state of mind I threw Albert into once, by only hinting as to whether Charles would ever return to England, you would not propose to me to adopt such a painful course.'

'Well, then, Marian, be persuaded by me: obtain his address from Sir Charles Mortimer, and write to the person you apprehend to be your long-lost brother; that will, of course, bring an answer, and solve all your doubts.'

'When I came to you, Lucy, this morning, I felt assured, in my own mind, that I had at length found my brother, but now, your cool reasoning has involved me in doubt, and I remember, too, what in my excitement had escaped me, that Sir Charles Mortimer said the young man he alluded to lived in a lone chateau, with his mother and aunt, who kept a numerous retinue of servants, and bore the character of being very rich.'

'All of which makes it very improbable that it is your brother,' replied Lucy.

'It does; and I feel sadly disappointed, yet can blame no one; it is attributable to my own foolish imagination alone, which, directly I heard the name, made me instantly believe what I was desirous to prove true; yet though my hopes are but faint, I think it will be advisable to write and ascertain the truth.'

'I certainly think so,' returned Lucy.

'Then without mentioning it to another creature I will do so at once, and wait as patiently as possible for an answer.'

'You cannot, I am convinced, do better under the circumstances. Had Sir Charles Mortimer seen the individual he spoke of to you, and ascertained that it really was Charles, I would have been the last to have chided your impatience, but as it is——'

'The best thing I can do will be to return home and write without delay, so I will say, farewell at once. Mind, Lucy, I shall depend on your secrecy.'

After Albert had bidden Rose adieu, he returned to his study, and having closed and bolted the door seated himself at his desk, on which already lay a sheet of writing paper, and commenced writing. The task occupied him but a short space of time, and having folded it in the form of a letter he sealed it, and directed it to Italy: this done, he sat a long time, heedless of all around, apparently engaged in communion with his own thoughts; that they were painful ones was evident, from the troubled workings of his brow, and the look of deep care that sat upon his features. After gazing on vacancy for some time, his eye gradually moved round the room till it fell upon the letter he had written; he immediately unlocked the door, and then rang the bell: the servant entered and waited his orders. He pointed to the letter, and without a word more the man, as though thoroughly accustomed to his master's eccentricities, and therefore manifesting no surprise, took up the letter and withdrew. Albert, heaving a deep sigh, said, half aloud, 'I am glad it is gone! I feel easier now it is out of my sight.' His thoughts then appeared to recur to Rose, and he exclaimed fervently, 'God bless her! and grant that she may yet again recover her health and cheerfulness! Oh, how willingly would I deny myself the gratification of ever beholding her again if that could be the means of restoring her to her wonted spirits; had I not discovered that she loved me, never, never would I have made her my wife. My wife! Oh, how did I dare, before the presence of an offended God, take those vows, knowing as I did—— But stop, I cannot pursue these thoughts. Oh, that my death had saved the life of one so justly dear—all that was noble and worthy to be loved! but oh, how useless; my destiny is fixed, and I have nought to do but fulfil it. All that I have done was allotted for me the moment I breathed the breath of life; it is useless to struggle against fate.' Thus screening himself behind his favourite doctrine, Albert endeavoured in vain to pick up some crumbs of comfort; and it is a strange fact, that those who most believe in what they term fate, and boast of it as 'such a happy doctrine,' we have rarely found bear the ills of life so bravely, and bend so meekly to the blast, as others who repudiate it as absurd and wicked, and who would blush to be thought for a moment to entertain such a ridiculous notion.

In the course of the morning, Edward Trevors called, and inquired for Mrs. Moreland, and was almost thunderstruck, on learning that she had gone to pay a visit to her friends in the country, alone and unattended, save by her own maid. He turned from the door, sadly vexed, and grieved he had been prevented calling as he had promised Rose to do, the morning after they parted at Mrs. Melville's, for Marian had enlisted his services to attend her in a drive, which was protracted till the hour was too late for him to visit Rose; and now, when he had got a long morning entirely at his own command, and had built upon spending it with her, had thought of all the news with which to regale her, and enable him to stay as long as possible, to find the bird flown was vexatious indeed; but there was no help for it; and yet it must have been a very sudden determination on her part, or she was more artful than he had given her credit for, never having said a word to him on the subject.

After she had travelled some miles, Rose dried her tears, and endeavoured to compose her ings, to meet the dear relatives she was now fast approaching. How surprised they would be at her coming so unexpectedly, yet not the less pleased. Oh, no! how delighted they would be to have her again under their roof; and now, too, she as began to recognise objects on the road—familiar things, such as a tree, a house, or a field—her feelings almost overcame her, as she thought with what different ideas they were last beheld: she was no longer the happy village maid, but was transformed into the elegantly dressed lady, and with the change had come tears and sorrows she had little dreamed of; and, oh! now she has caught a glimpse of the farm, where, in happier days, she has roamed free and merry as a bird; and now the stile, whereon she has stopped to rest when weary, appears in full sight, and a gush of fond emotions thrill her heart at the remembrance of other years. Oh, it is sweet to return to old familiar places! How dear and sacred is every spot that is consecrated by past happiness; everything wears a friendly aspect and appears to bid us welcome back. Oh, sweet and hallowed feelings take possession of the heart, on viewing places and scenes we have delighted in, in our best and fairest days; the sweetness of the return almost reconciles us to the pain of parting, if we could, after our absence, bring back with us the fresh warm thoughts and pure feelings we took away. But, alas! that is seldom, we had almost said never, the case; when we mix with the world, one bright dream vanishes after another, till at length all are gone, and we are but the wreck of our former selves. It is the being able to nourish such fair hopes for the future, without entertaining the least fear that we shall be doomed to see them dashed away at the moment we think them within our grasp, that makes youth, such a sweet and happy season, all smiles and beauty.

Arrived at her paternal home, oh! what kind warm greetings were showered upon Rose: her mother wept over her, and mingled sobs with affectionate inquiries; her father and brothers almost carried her into the house, and seated her on the chair which had been her own, and never since her departure been profaned to other's use—no, there it stood just as she had last seen it—she would have thought it had never been removed since; and there, on either side, were the old quaint arm-chairs that belonged to her father and mother; and, in the middle of the room, the dear old-fashioned carved oak table, round which in mirthful hours they had gathered to partake of the nut-brown ale or home-made wine, while they listened to the song or laughingly re-echoed the joke; and presently the tea-table was brought in, and, with her father on one side, and her mother on the other, and her three brothers opposite, Rose once more partook of that pleasant and refreshing repast, and questions were poured close and thick upon her concerning Albert and Marian, and wherefore she came upon them thus suddenly and alone; and her father and brothers remarked that she did not look well. Her mother said nothing till tea was over, when, taking her daughter into a private apartment, she soon learnt from Rose what she deemed a satisfactory reason for her altered appearance; for that she was altered she had not failed to note at the first moment of her arrival, for there is no eye so tender and watchful as a mother's, so difficult to deceive with an outward appearance of tranquillity, for she looks far beneath the smiling surface, down, down into the innermost recesses of the heart; and when Mrs. Sommerville inquired of Rose if she were happy and blessed in her husband's love, the sunny smile that for a moment lighted up her countenance told that he was still all in all to her.

'And why, my dear Rose, did he not himself come with you? The apartments he occupied when last here, he must have known, would be entirely at his service.'

'Yes, dear mother, but he could not leave town just now without inconvenience.'

'Then, dear Rose, pleased as we are with your company, we would gladly have waited for it a little longer, and had his at the same time.'

Rose stooped down, under the pretence of picking up something from the floor, in order to hide her blushing cheeks, and Mrs. Sommerville, seeing it pained her, said no more.

'You had better retire, my love, early this evening, for you must need rest after your journey, and to-morrow we shall be able to converse more freely.'

Rose gladly acquiesced, and the little room she had occupied from childhood was prepared for her reception.

After the fatigue of the day, and previous sleepless night, Rose slept long and well, and awoke refreshed. She had dreamed of Albert, and, on first opening her eyes, turned over, expecting to see him by her side; but, instead of the large and elegantly furnished room, with its separate dressing-rooms to correspond, she lay upon a small couch, with curtains and sheets of snowy whiteness; the sun streamed in at the little casement window, and down upon the tiny dressing-table, where all was arranged with such exact neatness, that it looked the work of some fairy hand. Oh! how often had Rose awoke in that very chamber to joy and happiness; but now she began to cast about in her mind for the care she was conscious of being an inmate of her bosom, but which, on first awakening, she had missed; and then came remembrance, with all its busy train of thought, to weigh her spirit down.

Throughout the entire day, there is no time so sweet and pleasant as the first awaking in the morning. We have been refreshed and invigorated with sleep, and we cast off many of the cares and anxieties which we carry with us to our couch, and which are the result of the strife and worry of busy day; and then, too, all things like ourselves look fresh and pleasant, especially in summer. Oh! then it is delightful to wander out among the fields and trees, to see how sweetly the plants that were ready to droop and fade at eve now hold up their heads, as it were in thankfulness for the refreshing dews, and the sunshine of another morn. All things appear springing into renewed life: the lark rising, soars on grateful pinion high up towards the deep blue sky, while he pours forth his song of praise and gratitude for the blessing of another day. The insect world, too, are all alive, eager to take advantage of the early morn, while, with shame be it said, man rests the longest on his pillow, and is the very last to give God praise for his wondrous works. Rose had been accustomed from childhood to very early rising, but the gaieties of town, which keppt her from her repose at night, had made sad innovations on her morning hours. She now hastily rose, and summoning her maid, was soon ready for the breakfast-table; but only Mrs. Sommerville was present, Rose's father and brothers had long partaken of the repast, and gone forth to the labours of the day.

'Why, my dear mother, did you not awaken me? I had fully depended upon the pleasure of breakfasting with my father, and feel quite vexed with myself for having slept so long.'

'I am glad, my dear child, to see you so refreshed this morning, and forbore to disturb your slumbers, thinking rest needful for you; and, let me warn you, Rose, to be careful to guard against fatigue; in your present situation, it might be the means of your losing the hope you now so fondly nourish, and which would of course greatly disappoint your husband.'

Rose thought her mother spoke in a tone of inquiry, and therefore answered,—

'I scarcely know, dear mother, whether Albert would be disappointed. Indeed, I thought he seemed sad when I told him of my expectation.'

'Doubtless, my love, that arose from uneasiness as to the result regarding yourself; but he is rich, and will, I feel assured, be delighted at having a family. What would your father and I have been without you, my dear Rose, and your brothers? Children, depend, if they bring some anxiety, which, if people are in but middling circumstances, they, of course, will, yet for all that they are a great solace and comfort to their parents' hearts; their little winning ways and fond endearments often charm away sorrow, and certainly bind a man more closely to his domestic hearth.'

'Do you indeed think so, mother?' replied Rose, eagerly.

'More than think so, I am confident of it, having proved it in many instances, and have always found that where there have been children, a man's heart and affections have been more concentrated in home; he seeks far less for amusement away from his family; in them centre all his dearest hopes and wishes, and consequently his heart dwells with them.'

'Dear mother, I am glad to hear you speak thus; it has made me feel thankful that I am likely to have a child; and, oh! if it should, as you say, charm away sorrow, I shall indeed be blessed.'

'You, dear Rose, I trust have no sorrow that requires to be charmed away,' replied Mrs. Sommerville anxiously.

'No, dearest mother, but—'

'You would say, Rose, that your husband has.

'I have fancied that he is sometimes melancholy, but then, you know, he writes and studies so much that it may affect his spirits.'

'Very probable, Rose; and then, supposing that to be the case, a child will call his attention from his books, and be the means of making you both more happy.'

'Oh! may God grant it,' returned Rose, fervently, and her heart felt lighter than it had done for a long while.

Breakfast over, her mother proposed a short walk, which Rose gladly acceded to, and they visited what used to be Rose's favourite spots.

'How fresh and beautiful everything seems, dear mother! and oh! how much preferable this sweet walk, to a ride in the dusty parks of London.'

'I thought, Rose,' said her mother, smiling, 'from your early letters, that you much preferred a town life.'

'So I did at first,' replied Rose, 'but then it was when all was new to me; but I assure you I have been quite wearied of balls and parties, and would never visit one again if I could help it.'

'And operas too,' said her mother, 'of which you sent us so brilliant an account?'

'Not quite of them, dear mother, but then I would visit them only in winter, and not then very frequently.'

'You see, my love,' said her mother, kindly, 'that a woman is formed for domestic life. A constant round of pleasure has the certain effect of enervating her character, and unfitting her for the performance of those social duties in which a woman shines preeminent; and believe me, never does she look so lovely in the eyes of her husband, as when quietly pursuing the avocations of every-day life, and which she is especially called upon to fulfil.   Home should ever be a woman's delight, however exalted her situation in life may be, and it should be ever her highest ambition and earnest endeavour, to make her home pleasant and cheerful to her husband, for I am well convinced roving husbands are more frequently than many suppose attributable to the want of management in their wives, and a happy, well-conducted home; how rarely we find men, who have pleasant, agreeable wives, and a cheerful, well-ordered home, ever ready to receive them, where they know that after a short absence they will be greeted with kind smiles and tender words—I say how very rarely we find such men truants from their own fireside! on the contrary, they are ever eager to return, if they occasionally seek amusement elsewhere, they but come again with warmer zest; you will not think, my love, I mean to reprove you, far from it, but we are none of us the worse for a little advice.'

'No, indeed, my dear mother, and I am much obliged to you for this; I think it may be the means of making myself and Albert happier than we have hitherto been.'

'I would not, Rose, say a word in my letters to you, that might sound unkind; but when I heard of such continued gaiety, I trembled for my child.   I knew that in those scenes you would never find true happiness; indeed, the taste for such amusements as you have lately been mixing in, frequently becomes a habit, and is indulged in for the want of other and more exalted pursuits more often than for any satisfaction, or even pleasure, that they afford.   You, Rose, have been educated in a far different manner to most of those you have, since your marrige, associated with, and consequently have sooner wearied of those gay, but idle frivolities. You were not happy, Rose, though surrounded by every comfort, and even luxury.'

'No, indeed, dear mother.'

'No, my child, you sighed for what can only be obtained by a right and proper performance of duties which are incumbent on our sex, and which, well performed, ever bring with them a sweet and sure reward.   Your task is, perhaps, more difficult than many, for your husband is of a melancholy disposition, and fond of retirement, even to the exclusion of his wife—is it not so, my love?'

'Yes, exactly,' replied Rose.

'Well then, my love, you should endeavour to win him from his solitude, not by reproach or upbraidings—those are weapons a woman should never use, especially to her husband; but by gentle words, a kind consideration for his feelings, and a smiling face, strive to throw around all your actions an air of habitual cheerfulness; never, without you are prepared to give him a good reason for it, look sad in his presence; should he desire it, mix occasionally in the gay world, but let him see that your heart and affections dwell in your own home, that you need no society but his to make you happy, and that his love and kindness are everything to you.'

'Thank you, dear mother, I will endeavour to profit by your advice; but do not think it was altogether my own wish that induced me to spend so much of my time from home; at first I certainly did find pleasure in those amusements, but lately I have been completely tired of them; but Albert was ever so desirous for me to go, indeed would not allow me to refuse the invitations I received, or I would much rather have done so.'

'He thought, no doubt, that you would be dull by yourself, and therefore wished you to seek amusement in the society of others; but you should, Rose, have kindly explained to him your real feelings, and he would have been pleased to think that your home was to you the dearest place on earth.'

Here, Rose felt, was the difficulty: she had never been able to tell Albert her thoughts and feelings; it was a subject on which neither ever conversed to the other, and it was this want of sweet communion, and which, in her own family circle, she had so delighted in, that had thrown over Rose's married life such an air of cold, melancholy reserve, which had made Rose, hitherto so light-hearted, sad and mournful; but though she did not like to breathe this even to her mother's ears, yet Rose resolved for the future to do her best to cast it off.   Why need she mind imparting every thought of her innocent bosom to that of Albert?   Was he not her husband, with whom surely there should be no restraint; he might have, and the thought was a bitter one, (indeed she had good reason to believe he had,) secrets that he could not impart to her;   but then she deemed they were secrets of the past, which had nothing to do with the present or the future, to which she now looked forward with pleasure, hoping that it would prove sweeter—happier, than she had once dared to expect. Her mother's advice was thankfully received and treasured in her memory, and ardently did she long to return to Albert, and, moulding her conduct after that advice, perhaps be rewarded by the joy of winning him back to peace and happiness.   Oh! if it should be hers to chase away the dark cloud from his brow, to heal his wounded spirit, and see him smile upon her efforts

and bless her for them—oh! what a fund of happiness would be found in this; and if she
failed in her attempts she would at least possess the proud consciousness of having done
her best—of having, at all events, fulfilled her duty, regardless of all things else; and this
thought alone was fraught with joy. Oh! yes, she was convinced that she had not yet
strove to win Albert from the too close confinement of his study. She had merely bent to
his will, and when sorrow sat upon his countenance had never inquired the cause, or sought by
cheerful converse, to banish it from him; she had only mourned it in secret, without ever
breathing a word of sympathy, or showing, by her outward demeanour, that she even
observed it. It is true that she had acted from diffidence and motives of delicacy;

but now she felt to rise above her natural timidity: although humble, in point of birth
and talents, when compared to him, yet she was his wife, and as such it must be her duty to
console him under affliction, to share in his sorrows, be they what they may, and to bring
every thought and hope to bear on his happiness; this she had ever desired to do as a sweet
pleasure, but never till now had she regarded it as a positive duty. How little, thought Rose,
do we, poor weak-sighted creatures as we are, knew what is most for our own good! She had
felt grieved and wretched at leaving Albert—would have avoided doing so at any cost, had
not he so much wished, and indeed desired, her to visit her friends; and now she had, in

almost the first conversation with her mother, received advice which she would have
deemed cheaply purchased by a much greater sacrifice of present feelings.

'Well, dear Rose,' said her mother, after they had prolonged their walk to some distance
from home, 'I think it is time we thought about returning. I am afraid I have already
fatigued you ; I had forgotten that you have not been so used to walking lately as when we
were last together.'

'I am not at all tired,' returned Rose, 'and have enjoyed this walk with you, dear mother,
exceedingly. I must confess that I have not been either in good health or spirits these last
few weeks ; and, indeed, that was the reason Albert was so desirous of m coming to you;
but I feel better now than I have done for some time.'

'I am thankful, indeed, to hear it, Rose ; and this reminds me that you have not written to
your husband, who, of course, must be very anxious to hear of your safe arrival. We will
therefore hasten home, and then you had better write immediately ; it would be not only
unkind, but positively wrong, to keep him in suspense.'

Rose made no reply, but quickened her step in obedience to her mother, recollecting
with sorrow that Albert had never asked her to acquaint him with her well-being—had manifested no desire for her to send him a single line ; and this being the first time, since they
had become known to each other, of their ever having been separated for more than a few
hours, they had consequently never before had occasion to correspond by writing ; and Rose
felt a difficulty in being the first to commence doing so. Yet she hesitated not an instant in
compliance with what she now deemed her duty. She resolved, immediately on their return
from their walk, to write a few lines to him ; also to kindly request an answer, that she might
feel assured of his health, and, what was so dear to her, his happiness. Arrived home, she therefore hurried to her room, and, opening her desk, sought for writing materials, when the first
thing that me ther eye was the letter Edward had given her, and which, on her return home
from Mrs. Melville's, she had placed there for security, without having made herself acquainted
with its contents, and the bustle consequent on her leaving home so suddenly had caused her
totally to forget, till now that she accidently discovered it in her writing desk ; and oh !
what sad thoughts and feelings did the very sight of it bring back to her memory—thoughts
that she was using every endeavour to forget. She had acted throughout wrong and unkind
towards Albert, in using every means in her power to fathom a secret it was his evident
desire to keep from her knowledge. What right had she to seek from others an account of
his early life? others too, who, prejudiced against him, seemed anxious to make her believe
the worst and darkest shade of his character to be the most true to nature and himself. Yes,
even Marian, she felt, would gladly, if possible, exculpate Charles at the expense of Albert—
Albert, who had been to him so kind and affectionate a brother ; who, all allowed, was ever
ready and willing to sacrifice his hopes and wishes for him. Was it then possible that he
would leave that brother in a foreign land, alone, and unaided by even one kind friend, while he
himself returned to England, to spend his days among those who loved him, and were bound
to him by the dearest ties? Oh, no, he never would voluntarily have returned to his boy-
hood's home, and left one who had shared equally in the affection of a beloved father, who,
dying, had bequeathed him to his love and protection, an exile from all that renders life sweet.
No, whatever sins, or even crimes, he might have committed, she was assured Albert would
not, without some stronger motive than any she was acquainted with, have thus left his
brother behind, while he himself came back to take possession of what, through his gener,osity,
had become their joint estate ; how much less then, if he, in a fit of jealous passion and
committed the deed which had kept Charles an alien from his home, would he have consented
to take advantage of his brother's loss, and allow him to be stigmatised as the guilty party,
while he bore the open front and unspotted brow of the innocent ! Never ; nothing on earth
but his own avowal would ever induce her for a moment to entertain so base an
opinion of her husband ; and yet, Edward had more than hinted that such was the case ;
but she now felt how very wrong she had acted in talking to Edward of Albert's life and
conduct—in listening one moment to the crimes he was accused of committing. If Albert
chose to have a secret from her, she had no right to seek a knowledge of it from any but himself. And what benefit would the knowledge of it (even if she could arrive at the exact
truth, which seemed almost hopeless) prove to her? none whatever ; on the contrary, all
she had been enabled to learn had only the effect of plunging her into deep sorrow and anxiety.
She would have blushed to have owned to her mother, whom she so dearly loved, and in whom
she was wont to confide every thought, how very meanly she had striven to arrive at a
secret Albert had wished to keep from her. Now she coolly thought it all over, she was
surprised she could so far have forgotten the respect due to herself, as to converse with Edward
concerning her husband, and even listen to his remarks on his conduct.

While these thoughts passed through her mind, resulting in a great measure from the conversation she had just had with her mother, and from whose advice she determined to mould her future conduct, Rose held the letter in her hand; it was put into a sealed envelope, and addressed, on the outside, to herself; she turned it over and over, laid it down, again took it up, and was half unconsciously breaking the seal, when recollecting herself she stayed her hand and determined to put the almost irresistible temptation she felt to open it beyond her power, she hastily took a sheet of paper, and seizing her pen with a trembling hand traced the following lines:—

'DEAR SIR,—You will be surprised at receiving the letter I was so importunate to obtain from you, back, unopened, but I have repented of the error I had thoughtlessly fallen into of desiring to learn anything further concerning the secret of my husband's early life, feeling assured in my own mind that some sad mistake alone had induced you to think him guilty of crimes I never will believe he has committed. I think it best to return you the letter at once, as the only effect of reading it would be to make me more sad and unhappy than I was at your recital. With best wishes,   'Believe me, dear sir, yours respectfully,

'ROSE MORELAND.'

Having written this, she folded it and placed it in an envelope together with the letter she had once been so anxious to peruse, and addressing it to Edward Trevors, left her room in search of a servant, that she might send it to the post-office at once, and thus put it entirely out of her own power to alter her determination.

'Well, my love,' said her mother, who met her on the stairs, 'I see you have written to Albert,' as she glanced at the letter Rose held in her hand.

'Not yet, replied Rose, who was so unaccustomed to deception, that she betrayed herself, 'I intend writing directly, but this is not for him.'

'Not for Albert!' said her mother, with a look of surprise; 'who then is it, Rose, that you would write to before him?'

Rose, covered with blushes, knew not what to say; fortunately her mother looking at the letter caught the word Trevors. 'Oh, I see,' added Mrs. Sommerville, smiling, 'it is for your friend Marian; why did you not say so, child? but dinner is now waiting for us, so give that to John, and let your other correspondents wait an hour or so longer.'

Rose eagerly did as she was desired, and, with a feeling of great relief, followed her mother to the dining-parlour. They were now joined by her father and brothers, who cordially greeting her, expressed themselves pleased to see her in so much better spirits than the night before.

'Why, my dear Rose,' exclaimed her father, as he fondly kissed her, 'the fresh air has already brought back some of the bloom to your cheek, that I was so grieved to miss last night; depend, there is nothing like a country life for preserving health and beauty.'

'I think, indeed,' replied Rose, as she returned her father's fond caress, 'that a country life is most conducive to happiness; and happiness, you know, is a great beautifier of the countenance.'

'It is indeed, my girl; but I hope from that I may not infer you have been unhappy.'

Rose hesitated a moment, and then replied,—

'I must confess, dear father, that I have not been so happy hitherto as I hope to be for the future: but then it has been almost entirely my own fault, and I have this morning received such excellent advice from my dear mother, and which I intend strictly to follow, that I think in the end I shall obtain what I most desire—my husband's happiness, and my own will then indeed be perfect.'

'I am glad to hear you speak thus, dear Rose, and I am certain you cannot do better than copy in every respect your mother; be only as good-tempered, cheerful, and affectionate as her, and your husband will deem himself blessed in his choice. And now, Rose, we have a piece of news for you. Your brother Henry is about to follow your example, and marry.'

'Indeed!' said Rose, 'now you do surprise me;' and looking kindly at her brother, 'Who is it, Henry, that you think of making your wife?'

'Guess,' replied her father, laughing.

'Oh! it is impossible,' said Rose, earnestly; 'do not keep me in suspense; you know not how anxious I feel.'

'Well, then,' replied her brother, 'it is Agnes Forster.'

'What! my old playfellow? Oh! how happy I feel, Henry, that you have made such a choice, in every respect your equal, both by birth, fortune, and talents, and within a few years of the same age,' and a tear gathered in her eye, as she added emphatically, 'Oh! you must indeed be happy.'

None present appeared to notice the earnest manner in which Rose spoke, but all secretly drew their conclusions. They felt that Rose had discovered she would have been far happier had she married a man in her own station of life. Indeed, unequal marriages are seldom productive of much happiness to either party.   Parents are often proud and pleased to see their daughters married to men of fortune and talent, superior to themselves, and will not unfrequently spend a sum of money beyond their actual means, in order to render them more attractive, more likely to find favour in the eyes of persons who move in a higher class of society; will carry them about, regardless of expense (for which they must either run the risk of being styled actually mean in all their little household affairs, or, what is still worse, get really into debt) from place to place—assemblies, balls, operas, anywhere, if their daughter's beauty is likely to attract a man of wealth, and if, in the end, they gain what they have so coveted, and at length obtained at so great a cost, the probability is, a hundred to one that the marriage turns out, to the daughte, a little more than splendid misery. It is the unity of feelings, thoughts, and pursuits, and equality of birth and station, coupled with a fond, enduring affection, that makes a happy marriage; and this can seldom be found when girls have been early taught to value a man according to the length of his rent-roll or the largeness of his estate, and, ere they give their heart, particularly to ascertain that it is free and unencumbered.   This was not the case with Mr. and Mrs. Somerville.   They had from the first grieved that Rose should unfortunately have placed her affections on a man whom they rightly judged unsuited to her in every respect : still, knowing that Rose ardently loved him, and most certainly for himself alone, they had, when he sought her of them, reluctantly given their consent, because they felt they could not withhold it without making Rose unhappy.   Her first letters to them after her marriage were, as we have before said, all they could wish ; but latterly they found a difference in them; and though Rose strove hard to conceal it, and to write with her accustomed cheerfulness, yet they discovered she was less happy, but tenderly forbore to notice it, till, having her once more under their roof, her mother kindly took the earliest opportunity of affectionately pointing out to Rose the course of conduct she thought would be most likely to render her happy, and which, as we have seen, was well and thankfully received, as advice from a parent, who can have nothing but the good of her child at heart, ever should be.

'We have been thinking, Rose,' said her father, after a short pause, 'that it would afford you pleasure to be present at your brother's nuptials.'

' Indeed, indeed it would,' replied Rose.

' Then,' rejoined Mr. Somerville, ' we have made up our minds, if Agnes and her father consent, to have them celebrated before you return to town, as, when we once lose you, we know not when we shall procure your company again.'

'It is very kind of you, dear father, to consider me so; and if Agnes loves Henry, which I cannot doubt, I think there will be very little difficulty in persuading her to accede to our wishes.'

'Will you, dear Rose,' said her brother, ' walk down with me to Mr. Forster's farm this evening, and add your persuasion to mine ?'

'Most willingly, Henry, though I think,' said Rose, smiling, 'she will pay more attention to you than me.'

'I do not know,' replied her brother; 'she is still very fond of you, and often makes inquiries respecting your welfare, and will, I am convinced, be perfectly willing to put herself to a little inconvenience, in order to have your company on her marriage-day. Like yourself, Rose, you know she has no sister to give her support on such an important occasion.'

'I do know it, dear Henry, and also that, unlike me, she has no tender mother to encourage her with affectionate advice, or a brother to love and protect her, if she needs it.'

'Well, well, my girl,' said Mr. Somerville, 'she has a doting father, which is surely something, and ere long will have a husband, which is better than all, or, at least, should be.'

'You are quite right, dear father,' replied Rose; 'but,' turning to her brother, 'I am very anxious to see Agnes again, especially as she is soon to be my sister, and therefore, Henry, I shall feel much pleasure in going with you this evening.'

'Thank you, dear Rose, then we will consider it settled.'

As soon as dinner was over Rose withdrew to write a few lines to Albert, and, strange to say, she sat in front of her desk, with a sheet of paper spread before her, and pen in hand, about to address a husband to whom she was devotedly attached, and yet knew not how to begin. What should she say, was a question she asked herself, till she was ashamed of having done so, and after a great deal of anxiety as to whether he would be pleased to hear from her, he never having requested her to write, she at last determined to begin at once, and wrote as follows:—

'MY DEAR HUSBAND,—I arrived here after a very pleasant journey, last evening, and found all my dear friends in good health, and, I need not add, overjoyed at my arrival; as you particularly desired me to study my own happiness, you will be pleased to hear that I am already in better health and spirits than when I left you. My dear brother Henry is about shortly to be united in marriage to an old friend and playfellow of mine, and is very desirous for me to be present at the ceremony, so, if perfectly agreeable, I think of remaining here till that is over, when I will immediately return to you. My parents and brothers all desire to be kindly remembered. With affectionate love, believe me, dear Albert, ever yours,

'ROSE MORELAND.

'P.S.—I had forgotten to say that, if you can spare time to write me a line, it will afford me the greatest pleasure.'

After writing this she was not altogether satisfied with it, but thinking of nothing better to say, resolved to let it go, therefore sealed and directed it, after which she joined her mother in the parlour, and spent some hours in sweet and unrestrained converse : this was what Rose had so yearned after amid the festivities of London, and it is indeed delightful to have one friend to whom we can impart all the little vexations that will beset us in our road through this world, which, though but trifles, yet, pent-up in our own bosoms, grew to real trials and sorrows: and, oh! when we feel an emotion of pleasure, perhaps even as we pass along the street, on hearing some old ditty, which calls back to memory some sunny spot where we have strayed in the days gone by, or, may be, the well-known face of some loved object lost to us for years, but which the slightest thing will bring back fresh and bright as when we last saw it—oh! is it not then sweet to have a friend to whom we can turn, and tell the fond emotion that fills our breast at the remembrance—one who can readily understand our feelings, and cordially respond to them ? and surely it is our duty to comfort and support one another, and never can there be a duty more pleasant in the performance. How very few can enjoy solitary pleasures ! half the charm of the richest music is lost if there is none to whom we can say—'Is it not sweet ?' There is no recreation, no enjoyment, that is not doubled, trebled, if others share it with us, or rendered all but valueless if obliged to be enjoyed alone ; and, oh! in sorrow and grief, all know how sweet is the voice of consolation—how precious the tear that mingles with our own : oh! how it heals the broken heart, and binds up the wounded spirit, and as we all stand in need of consolation at one time or another, we should never refuse to offer it whenever occasion requires.

After tea Rose equipped herself to walk with her brother to Mr. Forster's farm; their road lay through fields the entire way, and all looked so fresh and beautiful, that Rose was delighted, and expressed herself to her brother, in warm terms, in praise of a country life.

'Having been accustomed to such lovely scenery from infancy, Rose, I almost wonder you can live for months so far removed from the country.'

'Nothing, dear Henry, but the affection I feel for Albert could render it endurable, You are in love with Agnes, Henry ?'

'I do indeed truly and earnestly love her.'

'Then, if it were necessary for her good to reside far from these sweet scenes, you would not hesitate to leave them.'

'No, not for an instant ; but I am thankful and proud to say that she is like me, devoted to this spot, and has no thought or wish beyond it.'

Rose sighed. 'It is indeed a blessing,' she said, 'when a similarity of feelings and pursuits meet in persons who are about to be united for life. I, you know, Henry, married so young, and was by nature so thoughtless, that I never considered whether Albert was calculated to make me happy. I loved him with the strongest affection, and do still, and that makes any place dear to me where he is.'

'Undoubtedly, dear Rose, I understand well the feeling that induces a sacrifice of everything for one we love, especially when that one is worthy of it all; and, I am sure, you must feel very proud of Albert's talent ! what beautiful poems he has written ! and a man who can write so well of love, must himself be capable of showing the most ardent affection.'

'Yes, Henry,' said Rose, 'and yet that talent deprives me of much, very much of his company, as the greater part of his time is spent in his study; though none, I am sure, can admire his talent more than I do, yet it raises him, in a measure, above me. I feel myself scarcely worthy of being his wife.'

'You should, Rose, for a wife must ever be her husband's equal.'

'Yes, yes, I know all that, but I cannot converse with him on subjects that he most delights in; and though ever most kind to me, I sometimes fear that I am but a very poor companion for him.'

'That is your modesty, Rose,' replied her brother, smiling: 'I have no doubt, if I were to ask him, he would tell me very different. But here we are at Mr. Forster's, and see, there is Agnes coming out to meet us; she has recognised you already, and is anxious to greet you again.'

'Perhaps, dear Henry,' replied Rose, 'it is you she has recognised and is coming forth to welcome.'

At this moment they met, and, affectionately embracing each other, Agnes kindly took Rose's other arm and led her into the house. Here, as at Mr. Sommerville's, all was simplicity and neatness, everything was arranged with an air of comfort that did Agnes credit as being the mistress of the house; and Rose, who had so lately been accustomed to move through suites of splendidly-furnished rooms, and to be waited on by numerous servants in rich liveries, who flew to do her bidding, felt thankful to be relieved of so much state, and, seated on one of the old-fashioned wooden chairs of the farm-house, while a good-tempered, happy-looking country maid brought in the plain but substantial refreshments that belong exclusively to the farm-house, drew in her own mind a comparison between the rich and the poor: she had tried both states, and, therefore, deemed herself a competent judge, and, after taking into consideration the disadvantages and ills that belong to each, she most decidedly considered the poor man's comforts to be the sweetest, his happiness the best; and who that has seen the cheerful, health-beaming face of the farmer—has watched him after the labour of the day, seated under the shade of some venerable oak, with his pipe and jug of home-brewed ale—has listened to his converse as he talked to some village crony, and heard the hearty laugh that told of a bosom void of care—and then turned and took a peep into the halls of the great, and saw the rich man surrounded by his lacqueys, sickening amid his pomp and state, chained to fashions and form, that afford him no real happiness, bound to observances that weary him far more than toil, and pay him back nought in comfort—who, that has seen and marked all this, would hesitate an instant in giving the preference to the poor man's lot?   When we say poor, we must be understood as speaking comparatively, not, of course, of those who lack the means of procuring the necessaries of life, or are obliged to live in crowded houses, situated too often in unhealthy neighbourhoods, with an insufficiency of wholesome food, perhaps even excluded, in great measure, from the sweet light of day; and there are beings, fellow-creatures with ourselves, even in England, with sorrow be it said, that are thus circumstanced, and these, indeed, are far removed from happiness; but we refer to the contented, healthful farmer, who, by his own industry, earns a moderate competence, and, if his days are spent in toil, his nights are spent in peace.

'My dear Agnes,' said Rose, after the first mutual exchange of greetings was over, 'I am afraid you will not be so pleased to see me when I announce myself as a suppliant for a favour which only you can grant.'

'Anything that is in my power,' said Agnes, blushing.

'I would not require it of you if it were not,' returned Rose, 'as that would not be fair either to you or myself, But do not alarm yourself, Agnes. I dare say you will find no difficulty in granting my request.'

'Name it, then,' replied Agnes, blushing still deeper as she encountered her lover's ardent gaze.

'I think I must refer you to Henry, for he is still more deeply interested than I am,' said Rose.

Thus appealed to, Henry took the hand of Agnes in his own, and affectionately addressed her thus:

'Dearest Agnes, I have long been informed of the tender regard you feel for me—a regard which it has ever been my pride to possess, and my ambition to deserve; and all I want to perfect my happiness is this dear hand. Say, Agnes, can you withold it, when you knew how dearly I love you—how earnestly I will strive to make you happy?'

'Dear Henry,' said Agnes, averting her blushing face, 'I feel all you say, nay more.'

'Then you will consent, dearest, to appoint an early day for our marriage? Rose's stay in the country will be but short, and I am anxious to have it solemnized while she is with us.'

'There is one thing,' said Agnes, earnestly, 'that I must insist on; in all else I am willing to do as you wish.'

'Name it, dear Agnes, and, be it what it will, it shall be granted without a moment's hesitation.'

'It is,' replied Agnes, 'that I may never be separated from my father.'

'Then if I can agree with him to admit me into his family as one of its members, I may have the transport of knowing that you will shortly give me the title of husband, and, in so doing, make me the happiest of men?'

'Yes, dear Henry, and, in becoming your wife, it will be my constant study to promote your comfort, and confirm your satisfaction in the choice you have made.'

'I know it, I know it,' cried Henry, rapturously kissing her lips.'

'Come, Rose,' said the blushing girl, freeing herself from her lover's embrace, 'I wish to have a little conversation with you in the privacy of my own room, the more especially as Henry will not be left alone, for I hear my father's footsteps in the passage.'

Rose willingly obeyed her summons, and followed her from the room.

Agnes Forster was a pretty country girl; health was plainly pictured on her glowing cheeks, and happiness and content seemed to have made their dwelling-place on her smiling countenance.   She was an only child, and had never known a mother's love or care, her parent having died in giving her birth. No wonder, then, she was doted on by her fond father, who never again entered into the marriage state; his every hope and thought seemed centered upon his Agnes, who, as she grew to womanhood, strongly resembled her he had lost, and fully returned his love and affection; they were, indeed, all-in-all to each, till Henry Somerville, whom she had known from infancy, won her first and early love, but never was it confessed until she had sought the advice and consent of her father, who, upon hearing of Henry's preference for Agnes, cordially shook him by the hand, and vowed he was the very man he would have chosen above all others as a protector for his child, when it should please the Lord to remove him from this world; and when Rose and Agnes had retired, and Mr. Forster, entering, greeted Henry with his usual hearty welcome, he found no difficulty in requesting of him to grant him what he so much desired—the hand of his daughter.

'Agnes has promised, if you consent,' said Henry, 'to fix the day, not I hope long distant when I may have the unutterable felicity of calling her mine.'

'I tell ye, boy,' replied the honest-hearted farmer, 'that I consider it no light gift ye ask of me. Agnes is my best, I may say my only treasure, and it will cost me something to part with her, still, I cannot expect her to remain single all her young days; and then, too, I might die, and it would be hard to leave her alone in the world; and I think, boy, as I have told ye before, that she loves you, and cannot doubt that you love her; and I know you to be a good lad and kind to your parents, and the old saying, I trust, will be verified, that "a good son makes a good husband;" and so you and Agnes had better settle it between you; ye may tell her that I give you my full consent, and here, lad, is my hand upon it:' and Mr. Forster wrung Henry's hand in his own, while a tear trickled down on his sunburnt cheek. Henry Somerville felt overcome by the kind and generous manner in which Mr. Forster yielded his child to his care and keeping, and for a moment found a difficulty in giving utterance to what he wished to say, but, getting the better of his emotion, he thus spoke:—

'Think not, Mr. Forster, that in wishing to become the husband of your Agnes, I desire to remove her from the shelter of your roof; but if such, indeed, had been my wish, Agnes would never have consented to leave you. She this evening expressed her determination never to become mine unless I could persuade you to receive me as one of your family.'

'Did she, indeed, my boy? Well, it was kind, but no more than I ought to have expected from such a girl as Agnes; she never forgets her poor old father, or his comfort and happiness, and consequently will not fail to be good and dutiful to a young and handsome fellow like you, and, lad, I believe you to be worthy of each other.'

'Then you will find me a corner by your fireside?'

'Ay, boy, and gladly; you know how pleased I always am with your company and Agnes.'

'God bless her!' said Henry, fervently.

'Amen,' replied the farmer, 'and you, too, my boy; and, I think, I must also add myself, for I hope to live long enough to dance your children on my knee, and play with them, as it seems but the other day I did with Agnes—but here she comes to look for you, Henry, and Rose, too. What, my little Rose, then you have not forgotten your old friends since you have exchanged a simple country life for one of gaiety and pleasure?'

'No, no, Mr. Forster,' replied Rose eagerly; 'and never, never can you know how constantly you have all been in my thoughts, or you would never suspect me of such a thing.'

'Forgive me, Rose,' returned the kind-hearted farmer, 'I should have known you better; and yet there is something in London, I know not what, but it is generally the ruin of all who visit it. How very seldom we find those who have been a-pleasuring to London, seeing its fine sights and gaudy attractions, that return to the sweet, innocent enjoyments of the country with their hearts pure and uncontaminated by the vices of that great city!'

'I think, my dear sir,' said Henry, respectfully, 'that you are rather prejudiced against London.'

'Well, boy, perhaps I am. It is certainly true that I have never seen it; and, what is more, I have never had a desire to do so, and indeed, Henry, I have seen so many good lads completely spoilt by only going there for a few weeks, that, were you to declare your intention of paying it a visit, I should tremble for the result, and should feel myself bound to withhold the hand of Agnes till your return.'

'Make yourself quite easy on that score,' returned Henry, 'for I assure you that I have neither the thought nor wish to leave this neighbourhood, especially now,' and he threw a look of love on Agnes; 'and here is our dear little Rose,' he continued, 'after mixing in the most brilliant assemblies, flattered, admired, I am certain, by all, and yet she has returned to her native home with a heart as pure and free from sin as she took with her, and would be content, putting her husband out of the question, to remain with us for ever, without the slightest desire to renew her acquaintance with that, as you consider, most dangerous place; surely this, sir, should cure you of all prejudice.'

'No, no, boy, there may be, indeed' there are, exceptions to the general rule, but yet the rule remains the same ; and girls do not run so much danger of being spoilt as boys do, especially when, as in Rose's case, they are guarded and protected by a fond husband, and one, too, who knows the world, and the danger to which the innocent are exposed.'

'I see, sir, you are determined! not to] allow me | any credit for having kept you all in remembrance, and being so willing to return ; oh, that I could spend my life among you, never more to say farewell in this world !' said Rose ; and the sentence was begun with a smile, and very nearly ended with a tear.

'Dear Rose,' said [Agnes, 'you must forgive my father; he meant not, I assure you, any unkindness, [but he has lived for so many years in the country, and has seen so little of the world, that he has become prejudiced against London, which is, I dare say, no worse than any other place.'

'No, sure,' rejoined the farmer, 'you will not, dear Rose, take to heart anything I have foolishly given utterance to, and which was never meant to wound your feelings ; so look up, girl, and give me an assurance that you will think no more about it',

'My dear friend,' said Rose, as she offered her cheek to the farmer's salute, 'I never for a moment felt hurt at your remarks, which I think approach very closely to the truth ; but sad thoughts will sometimes force themselves upon us when we least desire them. But Henry, dear,' she added, evidently anxious to turn the subject, 'is it not time for us to take our leave?'

'I believe you are right, dear Rose and we must pronounce that saddest of all words, farewell !'

'But only for a very short time,' returned Rose. 'Agnes has promised me to be with us early to-morrow, when we can arrange for the wedding ; for I doubt not you have obtained Mr.|Forster's consent.'

'He has, Rose, replied the farmer, 'and I care not how soon it is all over, and we' are settled for life ; there will be no occasion for a single tear, my Agnes, for Henry has generously resolved to come and live with us, so there will be no parting. I must insist on having no crying, all shall be joy and mirth ; and I am determined to have a dance at the wedding if my little Rose there, in token that she has not forgotten our rural sports, will promise me her hand for a partner.'

'That I will,' said Rose, placing her soft white palm in the large and rough hand of the farmer.

'Bravo! my girl, that puts me in mind of my own village maid of days gone by,' and he brushed| away a tear ; for, notwithstanding his unpolished exterior and what some might term rude, uncouth manners, Mr. Forster possessed as warm and tender a heart as ever beat in the breast of man, or, indeed, of woman either. No supplicant for charity was ever turned from his gate unrelieved; the jug of ale was ever ready to be extended to the thirsty traveller ; no matter what his degree, be he rich or poor, it was all the same to the honest, hospitable old farmer.

During their walk home, Henry and Rose spoke but little ;¨her thoughts had fled to Albert, and found there a resting-place too dear and sweet to be easily abandoned, and yet they were tinged with melancholy, as all her thoughts of him ever were ; but the hope that he would be pleased at hearing from her, perhaps answer her letter—she had never received one from him—and oh! what sweet pleasure it would be to peruse words of love addressed to herself by the being she so fondly, ardently loved, and hers, indeed, was a love worth having, and should have been proudly cherished—but, alas! it was unfortunately placed on one who did not understand her, who looked upon her as a child, and treated her as such, who never encouraged her to pour out the warm feelings of her young heart, but kept them back till they were almost frozen up in her heart. Oh! one that could love on in spite of all this, cherishing every kind look or word, mourning in secret that she was not more worthy of the one she had chosen—one that could do all this must love with sincerity and truth, must cast aside all selfish feeling which too often mingles with the passion, and love utterly regardless of self and all things else. Thus it was with Rose, and, her heart full of Albert, she walked by her brother's side in silence : he, too, spoke but little—happiness has never many words at its command, and if ever man was blessed, Henry deemed himself so at that moment ; he was shortly about to be united to one whom he had long earnestly sought, and whom he loved with no light boyish fancy, but a deep, concentrated, manly passion, a love which he felt elevated his character, purified his mind, and kept him free from sin, to which young men are only too much addicted. And if love reach not this standard, if any unworthy feelings connect themselves with the object professed to be loved, then it is a love which should be shunned as valueless, and never for a moment encouraged, as it is at best but a spurious imitation of the real coin. Women unfortunately are easily flattered into the belief that men love them, and men, knowing this, often take advantage of it, frequently for the base motive of laughing at their credulity; it is a painful thought that man, who is intended by nature and by God to be woman's support and protection, should thus wickedly trifle with her best and holiest feelings, and turn the purest hopes of her heart into ridicule for his light and mirthful hours. But the knowledge that this is only too often done should induce a woman to guard well her heart; it is a fortress which requires all her caution, or it will be besieged and taken before she is herself aware of it: there are persons constantly on the watch, ready to take advantage of a moment's oversight on her part, therefore she must block up every avenue, er love will creep in and take possession of the whole. Henry loved Agnes not only for her rosy cheeks and dimpled mouth, and the transparent whiteness of her skin,

all of which a fit of illness might have destroyed and carried away, never to return; no, he had known her from a child, and having watched her closely, when she thought it not, he had marked the clean and comfortable house of the farmer, the ready smile that ever welcomed him, the cheerful converse that made his winter evenings pass so quick and happily—had noted her as daughter and as mistress—had seen with pleasure the tender regard she evinced for her father, and the mingled love and respect with which the servants looked up to her, young as she was— had seen her bustling about the farm to see that all were engaged in their proper avocations, and not unfrequently sharing in the toil—never idle, nor anxious to forego her accustomed duties,

No. 6.

never low-spirited, for she was gay, healthful, active, and happy as a bird. Often had Henry lingered near the farm, to catch her merry laugh, or fragment of some old song, which she hummed as she pursued her task, and then would say to himself,—'That is the girl for me.'

And now he was fast approaching the consummation he so ardently desired; he knew that his love, for it was reared upon a sound foundation, would be able to bear the storms and buffets of life—that all sorrow and sickness could do, would be to bind them, if possible, more firmly to each other; for now this last proof of Agnes's kind and good disposition, the refusing to leave her father, had fully confirmed him in his appreciation of the excellence of her character; he should call her wife, a dear and holy name to bear; but Agnes was well calculated to fill that position, and he knew his honour could be safely confided to her keeping; for never was a girl more free from even that flirtation which is considered allowable between the sexes, and especially before marriage; she had been sought by many of the young farmers of the neighbourhood, and had, without the slightest approach to *finesse*, given them at once a kind but firm denial, and, not as many would have done, kept them in suspense till they had nourished a hope that she would accept their proposal, which she never intended to do: thus, those she refused, though feeling confident she would never be theirs, entertained a high respect for the openness of her character, and even spoke of her with praise; and if women would but be more true to themselves, men would certainly be more true to them, and we should hear of much less deceit and broken vows: frequently women have to blame themselves for either their too easy faith in man, or for the want of stability in their own character; a woman should love a man for something more than the flattery and praise he bestows upon her, and not be ready to yield her affections to him, merely because he vows love to her; and yet how often this is the case, especially with very young females! they set at nought the wise counsel of parent or friend, who may see clearer than themselves, that the person who seeks their love is either unworthy or unsuited to them, and rush blindly on, till they find, when it is too late, the advice they foolishly refused was meant in kindness, and if received by them as it ought to have been would have saved them from sorrow, perhaps even destruction.

Each busied in their own thoughts, and planning for the future, which both hoped to find brighter than the past, the brother and sister arrived once more at their childhood's home: the sight of it recalled their truant thoughts back to their parents and brothers, to whom they quickly communicated the pleasing intelligence that Agnes and her father had consented to their wishes, and that, ere, another month was passed, she would become the bride of Henry.

'I am indeed pleased to hear it, my children,' said Mr. Sommerville, 'and will gladly receive Agnes as a daughter; she is a good girl, and well deserves the happiness I hope she will live many years to enjoy; but life at best is but a chequered lot, and therefore I hope God will give her fortitude to endure whatever may be in store for her.'

'I trust, my dear father,' replied Rose, 'that she may never have any serious trials to bear; she is not going to leave her paternal roof, and consequently will but increase her happiness, without diminishing her own or her father's comforts.'

'Yes, father,' said Henry, 'what Rose says is perfectly correct, and I must think that Agnes need fear nothing for the future.'

'I hope not, my son; but still a married life brings with it cares and anxieties, as well as comfort and joy; the present time must be the freest from sorrow she will ever know; what think you, dame?' he added, turning to his wife.

'It depends in a great measure on circumstances, and I think with Rose, that not having to leave home, which is a thing a woman dreads above all other ills, for she passes so entirely into another's keeping as to commence her life as it were entirely afresh; and although, as it is, she will have many little cares she is now a stranger to—yet I think we may deem Agnes fortunate, both in the man she has selected for a husband, and in his so readily yielding to her desire to remain with her father; it is not every one,' and Mrs. Sommerville smiled kindly on her son, 'who, possessing the means of providing a comfortable home for himself and wife, would be content to reside in the house of his father-in-law; but the motive is good, and will be doubtless appreciated by Agnes.'

'I am sure it will—I may say it is,' said Rose, 'for I had a long talk with Agnes alone this evening, and she will be here, dear mother, to-morrow, and then you will be able to converse with her yourself.'

'I shall be pleased to do so, Rose, and though I must soon lose you again, I hope to find another daughter in her, who will not be removed far from me.'

'Yes, dearest mother,' replied Henry, 'Agnes, I have every reason to believe, regards you already in that character, and we shall often walk down of an evening to spend an hour or two with you, and then my dear father and yourself, and I must also include James and William, will occasionally, I am sure, come to Farmer Forster's of a Sunday—and then how happy we shall be together.'

'I am grieved, dear Henry,' said Rose, that I shall not be able to witness and partake of the happiness that I feel confident will be yours, but my thoughts will often stray back again to home, and I shall almost fancy that I see your smiling faces, and hear your dear voices breathing tones replete with joy; but how is it dear James,' she added, turning to her elder brother, 'that you have allowed me and Henry, the two youngest of the family, thus to get the start of you in marriage?'

'I know not,' he replied, laughing, 'unless it is that I have not yet seen the woman I could love well enough to induce me to commit matrimony.'

'And you, William,' returned Rose, 'do you not intend to be married, or is it, that like James, you have not seen the person you could love?'

'I scarcely think, dear Rose, that I shall ever be otherwise than I am now, a merry, light-hearted bachelor, free as air to admire all or any, and yet my heart still be safe in my own keeping.'

'Have a care,' replied Henry, smiling good naturedly: 'those who boast as being out of danger frequently fall the earliest victims.'

'Thank you, brother for your wise caution, but I must say, that I think I need it not. I fear my heart is rather callous to the attractions of the fair sex. I certainly love to see a pretty woman, and so I do a pretty picture, or pretty scenery, or in fact, anything else that may be so styled; still I can admire it without wishing to make picture, scenery, or woman my own.'

'You argue wrongly' said Henry, 'in comparing the animate to the inanimate, the ideal to the real; and you will some day be convinced of your error, and no very distant one—take my word for it. I have ever remarked that those who, like you, disclaim matrimony, are ever the first to enter into its bonds.'

'You do not mean to say, I hope,' returned his brother, laughing, 'that I shall enter into the marriage state before you, my boy; because if that is it, I had better try and cut you out with Agnes at once, for I do not hesitate to assure you that I admire and like her more than any woman I have yet seen, with the exception of my little sister Rose.'

'No, no, James,' replied Henry, jestingly; 'Agnes' heart is mine every bit, and I defy you to get more than a sisterly smile from her, do your utmost; and I also fully hope to become a Benedict before I see you one, which I shall do, I am certain, please God, if I only live a few years more.'

'Well, Henry, as you have settled it that I am to be married, the next thing you had better do is to seek for a wife for me, and marry us off at once to save further trouble.'

'There will be no occasion for that,' returned his brother, 'we shall see you shortly selecting one for yourself.'

'Well, my children,' said Mr. Sommorville, 'I think it is time we separated for the night; we are early risers in the country, you know my Rose, and you have walked further to-day than you did during a month in town, I'll be bound. Is it not so, my girl?'

'I think I must plead guilty to having led a very idle life, dear father,' replied Rose smiling, 'and must also confess that I feel rather weary, and shall not be sorry to retire.'

'Come then, my girl, give me one kiss and be off to bed at once; those who rise with the lark should go to bed with the lark, though I believe, Rose, you did not rise with the lark this morning, eh, my girl?'

'No, indeed, dear father, I was many hours behind him; but I hope to-morrow to meet you at breakfast, and, for fear I should oversleep myself, will take your advice and say good night at once.'

The parting kisses were soon given, and Rose once more took possession of her little bed; for a while she lay busied in thoughts which gradually took the shape of dreams, presenting to her imagination her brothers, parents, Agnes, and her father, with Albert and Edward Trevors, blended into one confused heap, and it is wonderful how often even the minutest occurrences of the day follow us in our sleep, presenting them in as vivid colours as they appeared in our waking moments. The mind, that wonderful part of man, and of which we know so little, never sleeps, is never for a moment at rest; always awake, busily engaged, either on the past, the present, or the future. When the body, wearied and worn out with anxiety or toil, lies, totally helpless and unconscious, taking that rest which is absolutely necessary for the continuance of our lives as the air we breathe, the mind, never weary, is roaming, perchance, o'er countless realms of space, peopling them with persons and things that we have never seen or heard of in our wakeful hours, and yet we bear them so strongly in our memory that when we arise from sleep we can describe the minutest circumstance connected with our dreams, and which some-times (and this is still more wonderful, though beyond a doubt) prove but the image of what afterwards actually occurs.

We will leave Rose in her slumbers, peaceful and innocent (the two ever go together), while we return to town; and first we introduce the reader into the house of Marian Trevors. It is the second morning after Rose's departure, and seated in her drawing-room she is conversing with Lucy Melville, who is paying her a morning visit, or in fashionable language we should say 'call:' they were talking of the hopes Marian still nourished of finding her brother.

'How long the time does seem!' said Marian, moving listlessly in her chair; 'would that I possessed the power to push it on a few weeks,—how glad I should be to do so!'

'It is wrong to talk thus,' replied Lucy, 'you may one day be thankful for the time you are now so anxious to get rid of.'

'Well my pretty philosopher,' said Marian, with something between a laugh and a yawn, 'you may be right and you may be wrong, it is quite impossible to say; but I would be perfectly willing to run the risk of doing so if I could make old Time mend his pace for a few weeks just now, mind you, only till I have heard from my continental correspondent, and have thus become relieved from my present suspence, which keeps my mind equally poised between hope and fear.'

'I am glad to hear that it is equal, for I have fancied there was a preponderance on the side of hope, which I cannot but think is doomed to be fallacious.'

'You are a perfect Job's comforter, Lucy, I must confess.'

'I see not that you stand in need of comfort, Marian, or I would be the first to offer consolation.'

'The truth is, Lucy, that you cannot enter into my feelings; were it your brother instead of mine, you would feel very differently.'

'You are really unjust to me,' replied Lucy mildly. 'I can well understand the desire you must naturally feel to behold a brother once more who has been separated from you for so long a period; but then Marian, you must remember that it was his own sins alone that prevented a return to his friends.'

'I know not what the truth may be,' returned Marian; 'you have frequently heard me say that I have but a very indistinct remembrance of the letter which conveyed me the tidings of that awful affair, and Charles was so completely the reverse of what you would expect a person to be who could commit such a dreadful act.'

'There can be no doubt Marian,' said Lucy, 'but there is as yet an unfathomable secret connected with the fate of the absent Charles, and which will one day be brought to light; but I cannot believe that the young man you have written to in Italy will prove to be him.

'Why not?' replied Marian, with an air of irritation; 'it is strange that a young man bearing the same name should be residing on the same spot where the tragical affair took place.'

'My dear Marian,' interrupted her friend, 'that makes it more unlikely it is him. Charles in all probability, is far, very far away from Italy, which country I should think would have become hateful to him, as being the scene of his crime.'

'Well, well, we must each think as we please till a letter arrives and proves one of us to be right.'

'And the other consequently wrong,' said Lucy laughing; 'but, Marian, I can assure you I shall be quite content, nay, happy, to own my judgment incorrect, and pleased to pronounce yours for the future infallible, should this Charles Moreland you have honoured with your correspondence own himself your brother.'

'Well, you are more generous than me, replied Marian; 'for I candidly confess that, even if he will not own me as his sister, I shall still regard him as none other than my brother. Stop, Lucy,' she continued, seeing her friend was about to interrupt her; 'consider, he may have a thousand reasons for not wishing to be known to his friends in England; sometimes, when I reflect on the generosity Charles ever evinced towards myself and Albert, I cannot help thinking that his prolonged stay abroad is out of consideration for Albert's feelings, who may have some motive for not wishing him to return.'

'Oh! do not,' said Lucy, anxiously, 'let your love for one brother lead you into doing an injustice to another, and one who has ever studied your welfare and happiness, I have often heard you say, in preference to his own.'

'It is perfectly true, Lucy, and yet—'

'And yet,' continued her friend, 'there is a secret he cares not to impart to you and doubtless for your good; probably he is well aware that the knowledge of it would have the effect of rendering you wretched. I wish I could extract from you one promise.'

'A promise! what for?'

'For your happiness. It is, that if, as I fully believe, the person you take for your brother turns out not to be him, you will at once cast from your mind all thought and anxiety respecting him, and then, perhaps, some day, when you least expect it, you may see or hear from him, Will you, dear Marian, give me this promise?'

'It is impossible, Lucy; I will never give up the hope of again meeting with my brother, or slacken my exertions to obtain a knowledge of his address; and let me once be certain where he is to be found, and no power on earth shall prevent my flying to him. Albert, I feel assured, will never allow him to revisit this country if he can in any way help it, and that is certainly wrong; years have passed since the unhappy occurrence in Italy, and it is time it should be forgotten, at least to his prejudice, and the knowledge that it was in a great measure attributable to Albert's conduct towards the unfortunate girl who lost her life, should induce him to pardon and forgive his brother——but no, his name never passes his lips, and yet he is constantly melancholy in the extreme; particularly since his marriage has this gloom increased upon him, and now Rose is away from him he is certainly less miserable.'

'It is very strange,' said Lucy, thoughtfully.

'It is, and it is not,' replied Marian. 'I am afraid, Lucy, we have been sadly deceived in her; I thought her all that was innocent and free from guile.'

'And so she is, I am convinced; dear, dear, Marian, do not be unjust, or wrong the absent. Poor Rose, I feel certain, is as good as she is beautiful. I cannot say more.'

Marian shook her head.

'None, Lucy, had a better opinion of her than I; but depend, she is unworthy of our regard. I have watched her closely, and have every reason to believe that she is base, designing and deceitful.'

'Oh, do not, do not say so,' replied Lucy. 'I will not, cannot believe it. Appearances are not to be trusted; they often lead us into error therefore, I beseech you, Marian, suspend your judgment while there is even the shadow of a doubt upon your mind. Rose is so unused to etiquette and forms, that she might innocently appear designing, and be blamed, perhaps, for another's sin.'

Lucy spoke with considerable warmth, and it gave a flush to her cheek, not usually seen there.

Marian fixed her black piercing eyes on Lucy, who cast down her milder orbs before the gaze of her friend, who thus spoke:——

'I know not what you mean, Lucy, by another's sin. I spoke only of Rose, without, I think, coupling her name with any one.'

'Yes, you did,' said Lucy, striving to escape Marian's searching glance; 'but you stigmatised her as being artful and designing, and I do not believe Rose capable of being either; and then, you know, Marian, you are so eager to take advantage of a woman, and——and——in short, I suppose you allude to her preference for Mr. Trevors.'

'Then you have also remarked it,' replied Marian, 'and wish me to understand that it is entirely Edward's fault that she so forces her company upon him. You must excuse me, but I differ from you in opinion on that, as on other subjects.'

'I cannot say what I would, Marian. Edward is your husband.'

'Edward is indeed my husband,' interrupted Marian with an air of dignity, 'but that need not prevent you declaring aught you may know to his disadvantage. We have been married several years, yet never have I heard a word breathed against his honour; in both I have ever deemed him irreproachable.'

'I meant not to wound your feelings,' replied Lucy, 'but we should be careful not to be too harsh upon our own sex.'

'If our sex forget what is due to themselves, they cannot be surprised if others should forget it also.'

'But what has Rose done?'

'Shown a marked preference for Edward, which any woman of delicacy would have avoided doing before a room full of company, whatever her feelings might be. I was shocked to observe the utter want of refinement she displayed in thus proclaiming her regard for one who had never treated her otherwise than as a sister.'

'And, oh, Marian! was it not a sister's regard she manifested towards him? Surely, surely, it was nothing more; indeed it appears to me that she was more anxious to avoid Henry than to show a preference for Edward.'

'And why should she be anxious to avoid Henry? your brother, Lucy is not generally disliked.'

'He is not; neither did Rose at one time, regard him with the abhorrence she now appears to entertain—on the contrary she seemed much pleased with his company and conversation, and indeed declared to me that he strongly reminded her of a brother of her own, who bore the same name, and myself and Henry were greatly astonished, and at a loss to account for the sudden alteration in her behaviour, which I can assure you, pained him much.'

'It is all of a piece with the rest of her conduct: it is only too evident to me that she has taken a fancy to Edward, and being conscious of her own charms, sought to please him by an open display of her preference; but she was wrong—men are not gained by such conduct, they are indeed more likely to be disgusted by it.'

'I am confident,' returned Lucy, ' that you are labouring under some sad mistake, and hope soon to see you convinced of your error.'

'Do not, I entreat of you, Lucy, suppose for a moment that I am enacting the part of the "Jealous Wife;" I know both myself and Edward too well to give way to any foolish jealousy, and all Rose's efforts will, I am certain, only recoil on her own head;' and Marian drew herself up with pride.

'Marian! you will one day be sorry for having spoken with such bitterness. Rose is innocent and guileless as a child.'

At this moment the servant entered with a waiter, on which lay a letter, and handed it to Marian; she took it up carelessly, and, before opening it, glanced at the direction; she started and turned pale, but, recovering her self-possession, she held it between her thumb and finger before the eyes of Lucy, who could scarcely believe the evidence of her senses—it was in the hand-writing of Rose, and addressed to Edward. Marian, after a moment's silence, threw it back on the waiter, and with a bitter smile said—

'Well, Lucy, what do you say to your paragon now? Think you she is still faultless; or is this (pointing to the letter) some trick of the imagination? You had better examine it more closely, and satisfy yourself beyond a doubt that it really is her hand-writing. You as well as myself are acquainted with her hand, and I believe, too, that wax bears the impression of the seal Albert had purposely engraved for her—a rosebud, which he said pourtrayed at once her name and beauty. But do not be afraid to touch the letter; that at least cannot harm you. I beg you will examine it: I am so weak-sighted, so hasty in forming a judgment, that I may very probably be labouring under an error, and will thank you to set me right.'

Saying which, she threw herself back on her chair, and, with a sarcastic smile, affected patiently to await Lucy's reply. Poor Lucy was so taken by surprise, that she knew not what to urge in defence of the absent, and, with all her desire to think Rose innocent, she knew not how to separate the truth from falsehood. Here was a letter she was convinced came from Rose, for, in obedience to Marian, she had taken it up and carefully examined it; here was her own hand-writing—her seal—and the post-mark, to convince her it actually came from Rose, and plainly addressed to Mr. Edward Trevors. And what could Rose have to communicate to him? She had only left town two days, and consequently must have found time on the very day after her arrival—a day which any one would have naturally supposed would have been devoted to the friends she had just come amongst after a long absence; and yet on this day Rose must have stolen some moments to write to Edward. Thus puzzled to account for Rose's apparently strange conduct, Lucy sat bending over the letter, anxious to urge something in defence of Rose, and yet scarcely knowing what to say, when she was roused by Marian, who said—

'Well, Lucy, have you not yet satisfied yourself of the correctness of my statement? or are you lost in astonishment at the duplicity of woman?'

Lucy only replied,—

'You will open this, Marian;' and she placed the letter before her.

'Not I,' said Marian, tossing it disdainfully away; believe me I have no curiosity to see the contents; besides I never open letters addressed to another; it is a rule I have ever most scrupulously observed, and I am not going to beeak it now.'

'Then you will seek an explanation of Edward?'

'Nothing is further from my thoughts.'

'But,' urged Lucy, ' it will be doing an injustice to Rose as well as to yourself. I consider it decidedly your duty to learn the contents of that letter, as it will either confirm your bad opinion of Rose, or clear all doubts from your eyes.'

'We differ Lucy very much in our ideas of duty.'

'Oh do be persuaded,' said Lucy, earnestly, ' to alter your determination this once; do not I beseech you let pride stand in the way of doing an act of justice to one who is not here to say a word in her own defence. I know, I am certain, that letter, if read, would cause you to have a very different opinion of Rose to what you now entertain.'

'I cannot tell, Lucy, how you can know anything of the sort; you are I believe, as well as myself, perfectly ignorant of it's contents.'

'Dear Marian, do not be angry with me. But Rose is innocent of all you suspect her of. What would I not give could I make you think as I do! and once more at the risk even of seriously offending you, I ask, as a favour to myself, if you will not open the letter, at least seek an explanation of it from Edward. Pray, pray do as I wish!'

Marian was silent.

'You consent,' continued Lucy; ' oh thank you a thousand times!'

'You mistake,' replied Marian, with an air of offended pride; ' nothing shall induce me to pry into the secrets of another. The letter remains where it is till Edward's return, when, if there is nothing in it objectionable, he will, I am certain, offer it for my perusal; but to ask it of him I should consider lowering my own respect, which Lucy, you should not desire me to do.'

Lucy saw that it was useless to persuade her further, and therefore said no more, though she was by no means so sure as Marian seemed, that if the letter from Rose only contained some slight request, or kind inquiry after the welfare of her London friends, he would unhesitatingly show it her, or even mention its purport; no, she entertained very different thoughts concerning Edward; and it was impossible to urge anything against her husband to Marian; but Lucy was of a kind and noble nature, and she determined, as Marian would not, herself to seek of Edward Trevors an account of the letter, and, if possible, make him do Rose justice.

In accordance, therefore, with this idea, she prolonged her stay with Marian, in the hope that Edward would return while she was there, but after remaining till the latest moment, she was obliged to leave without seeing him.

On taking farewell of Marian, she reminded her of her engagement to spend the following day with her.

'I shall not forget, Lucy; give my kind regard to your mother, and tell her she may depend on seeing me.'

'And Edward too, I hope,' said Lucy.

'Yes, he has given you his promise to come, and when he has done so, he rarely breaks it.'

Lucy returned home thoughtful and uneasy. Oh! could it be possible that Edward had succeeded in leading such a noble heart as Rose possessed astray? that he had striven hard—that he had done his best to do so, she did not doubt; and Edward was a dangerous character to one so innocent, who knew so little of the world as Rose. He was handsome, fascinating, and certainly insinuating in his manners, or, at least, she deemed him so—and then the letter. Oh! she fully believed that Edward had induced Rose to write to him to inform him of her safe arrival, and poor Rose had in very innocence complied: she knew no thought of sin, and, consequently, regarding him as a friend, she had, at his desire, written to him as one. But, alas! thought Lucy, what a shocking thing it is that men should be so eager to lead a woman into guilt! They are all alike, wicked, base, and deceitful; and poor Lucy judged the whole sex from what she had seen of one; but at the same moment she thought of her brother and inwardly exclaimed—'I was wrong; there is at least one man who, instead of endeavouring to plunge a woman into sin and shame, would extend a ready hand to protect and aid her, and, if need be, revenge her wrongs upon his fellow-man. But then,' and she sighed, 'Henry is an exception to the general rule—he is, indeed, all that is generous, noble, and good.'

Marian and Edward Trevors met at dinner alone, and, seated opposite each other, all smiles and politeness, a stranger would have deemed them happy and blessed in their mutual love. Edward addressed her with the tenderest concern for her welfare, and manifested the greatest desire for her comfort, while Marian, in return, entertained him with all the gossip of the day, lavished on him her sweetest smiles, and in short did her best to amuse and entertain him. At length, when the cloth was withdrawn, and the wine placed on the table, Marian said carelessly, 'There is a letter for you on the sideboard, Edward. John, hand it to your master.' The servant complied.

Edward gazed on the hand-writing and post-mark with an air of surprise which quickly changed into one of pleasure; but, placing it in his waistcoat pocket, without any apparent emotion, pursued the conversation which had been thus interrupted. She considered herself far too well bred to offer any question or remark concerning his correspondent, and they continued their discourse with as much interest as before.

'Lucy Melville was with me this morning,' said Marian, 'and desired me to remind you of your engagement for to-morrow evening.'

'Oh! indeed,' said Edward, smiling. 'Well, I had almost forgotten it; but I was about to inform you that I called on your brother, who has just received a letter from Rose.'

'And what may she say?' returned Marian.

'It is but a few lines, which he desired me to bring for your perusal;' and Edward presented the letter. Marian took it from the hand of her husband, read it with a smile that might almost be termed a sneer, and without a word of comment returned it to him.

'What do you think of it?' said Edward, as he placed it again in his pocket.

'Cold,' replied Marian, 'and quite at variance with the romantic love I have frequently heard her express for Albert.'

'Well, I must say that I was rather surprised myself,' said Edward, with an apparent air of candour, 'when Albert gave it me to read. I expected to find it, in every sense of the word, a love-letter.'

'Which it most certainly is not,' replied Marian; 'however, she takes care to let him know that she is already in better spirits than when she left home. I suppose Albert was delighted to hear it?'

' He seemed so, indeed, and expressed a hope that she would not be in a hurry to return, as the country appeared to agree with her constitution so much better than town.'

' Indeed !' returned Marian. ' Well, I was not aware that her health had suffered in any respect since her residence here ; but of course, she must be the best judge, and I dare say Rose will be willing to remain with her friends for some time, especially as they are to have a wedding in the family. She has not paid Albert the compliment to ask him to be present, not that I think that he would have gone, still it would only have been respectful to invite him ; but then, Rose never thinks of that, and never will become a fasionable woman : were she to live in town for years, she would still retain all her country ideas and prejudices. I think it a pity Albert ever transplanted her ; for though a pretty mountain flower, when blooming in her own native scenery, yet, placed amongst the belles and beauties of London, she sinks into insignificance.'

' Think you so ?' said Edward with evident surprise. ' Why, Marian, I always gave you credit for being one of Rose's greatest admirers : before I had the pleasure of seeing her, you wrote, I well remember, in the highest terms, in praise of what you styled her rare beauty.'

' Well, perhaps I did, and I certainly then thought her very handsome, but her beauty is of a a kind that you weary of, after becoming used to it.'

' I do not agree with you, Marian ; for the more I see of Rose, the more handsome I deem her ; but women are very short-sighted as regard each other's beauty, and are seldom competent judges : of the opposite sex I allow them to be infallible.'

' And therefore, I suppose, I must allow you to be of ours.'

' Exactly, Marian ; that is what I consider fair.'

' Well, be it so, but do you not think, Edward, that Albert would have been happier had he never married Rose ? she is certainly not the woman calculated to make him happy.'

' Why, Marian, without wishing to hurt your feelings, if I speak the truth I must say that I do not think Albert would be happy had he at once a woman of the greatest beauty and rarest talent for his wife ; he is naturally of too moody and melancholy a temperament.'

' Not naturally, Edward ; I remember when he was gay and light-hearted as yourself, or even more so ; it was the sad and ever-to-be-lamented affair that changed him into what he is, and of which I do not know the exact truth, though I am confident one day (it may be far distant) I shall arrive at the knowledge of that secret which has cast a shadow over Albert's life, and which he shudders to impart even to his sister ; and I shall again see Charles, whom I so dearly loved, and indeed still do, for never have I forgotten his slight boyish form—it is as present to my recollection as though it were but yesterday I saw him on the deck of the vessel, waving a farewell adieu, which even at the time my heart misgave me would be a longer one than he thought for ; but it will not be for ever—no, we must, we shall meet again.'

' You speak, Marian,' said Edward, filling his glass from the decanter, and motioning for her to follow his example, ' with as much enthusiasm as if it were a lover's loss you deplored, and so eagerly anticipated the return ; but, however, Marian, we will drink to his safe and unexpected arrival, though I think it all but impossible that he will do so while Albert is living ; so, unless you wish to mourn the death of one brother, do not hope to rejoice at the return of the other.'

' You may be mistaken, Edward. I know not what you think.'

' I think,' interrupted her husband, ' that circumstances have occurred to them abroad which would make them particularly desirous to avoid meeting each other, which, depend, they never more will in this world. But this subject, I have ever observed, affects your spirits ; so let us, for Heaven's sake, dismiss it. You are already beginning to look sad, and you know I have assured you frequently that it does not become you half so well as your own natural gaiety ; so pray, Marian, bid it adieu for ever. Life is not so long that we can afford to waste any part of it in sighs. We know not how soon it may close, and should therefore make the best of it, and enjoy ourselves while we can.'

Marian smiled at her husband's remarks, for she was used to them, and, consequently, did not feel shocked at the want of feeling they displayed. And, alas ! many think and reason as he did, till they actually persuade themselves they are sent into this world for no other purpose than to enjoy the good fortune that may happily fall to their share, pluck the fairest flowers and richest fruits, and then die. Yes, wonderfully formed as we are, there are many who fully believe, or profess to do so, that when we close our existence with this world, it will be for ever. They dream not, in their selfish enjoyment of this life, (and they are generally persons who have the means of gratifying their tastes, and often their whims, who hold this creed,) of a fairer world, wherein we shall awake to a renewed and sweeter existence, where none shall know what sorrow means.

We think our readers will have no objection to take a peep into the privacy of Albert's study, where they will behold him seated in front of his desk, where, indeed, we last left him ; and before which the greater part of his time was spent. He appears to be suffering from some great anxiety, for his brow wears a deeper shade than usual, and his hand, which holds an open letter, trembles violently. Occasionally he raises his eye from the paper, and glances round the room, as if half afraid of encountering some object he dreads to meet. Presently a cold perspiration stood upon his forehead, and pushing the letter from him, he covered his face with his hands. Then, rising hastily from his seat, he ignited a taper, and seizing the letter he had been perusing, committed it to the flames.

'Would,' he exclaimed, as he did so, 'that I could so easily erase from my memory the awful event that letter conjured up before my mind's eye! Though years have passed, yet every

letter I receive brings it as fresh to my memory as though it had occurred but a day ago; and yet I feel that I must receive them. I can no more help doing so, than I can help the beating of my heart, or bid it stop at my command. No, this is doomed to be my punishment, and I can do nothing but submit, and I would not if I could, feel less wretched. Oh, no! I gladly welcome and encourage this anguish of heart. Yes, this terrible emotion, that would drive others mad, is the only solace I can ever know—a bitter one it is true, but still a solace; for it convinces me that I repent of the blood that has been shed—blood——'

And, as he repeated the word, he shuddered, and seemed well-nigh overcome with the

No. 7.

thoughts that pursued him like some awful phantom, that ever forbade him to be acquainted with peace; and then trying to find a corner wherein to screen himself, he sought refuge in his favourite doctrine—a doctrine that never afforded him the slightest consolation; and yet he constantly recurred to it, expecting comfort and finding none.

'I am,' he exclaimed, endeavouring to recal his wandering thoughts, 'but a creature of destiny, and as such cannot be accountable for the deeds I have committed: if God has ordained that I should be more vile than the generality of my fellows, it would be unjust—unjust do I say?—it would be worse than injustice to require an account of it at my hands: I am not a responsible agent—I but fulfil what is allotted for me, and were I to have striven to the utmost, I must in spite of all, have done what was destined for me by fate, and fate alone can be blamed for the actions it has forced me to do, against my better reason and my will; and yet there are persons who refuse to believe in this doctrine; but then they are those whose lot is bright and happy, and consequently arrogate to themselves that it is the work of their own hands—that fate has had nothing whatever to do with it; and us poor wretches who are doomed to a darker destiny, they hold, might, like them, have been blest, had we so chosen—that man alone rules his own fate, and is equally capable of doing a bad or good action: but alas! they understand it not, their fortune dazzles their eyes, so that they cannot see clear; but!let them, for a short time be placed under the shadow of our destiny, and they will soon give us their acknowledgment that we are correct in our views; but it cannot be: some are doomed to good and some to ill, and it is utterly impossible for us to change the order of things—we might as well attempt to make the sun stand still, or prevent night ever drawing its dark curtain around us; if any ever strove to effect this they would be laughed at and treated as madmen. But is it not more absurd, more like a proof of want of reason, for a man to declare that God has given us power to alter the course of our lives, and bid it flow in what direction we please? Can we withstand the hand of Death, when he lays upon us his icy grasp? or will sickness depart and health return at our bidding? If this (which all allow is entirely out of our power) cannot be done, how then can it be supposed that we are responsible for the every-day actions of our lives? If we live or die, suffer under the effects of disease, or are blest with health and strength, utterly regardless of our own will or desire, surely the most common-place observer will allow that we can no more withstand the current that bears us along either smoothly, calmly, in happiness and peace, or boisterously urges us to the committal of deeds that bring with them sorrow and anguish of heart. Oh! were it possible for us to order our lives, every one would be naturally anxious to pursue that course of conduct which is universally considered to be the means of obtaining what all desire—happiness. No one would be wicked wantonly because sin is hateful, and ever endeth in disappointment and sorrow, which all are desirous to avoid by every means in their power; consequently, they would choose the best and brightest lot which is that the most remote from guilt. All know this and all feel it; and those who, like me, are doomed to sin and sorrow, would, Heaven knows how gladly (did we possess the power) change our fate into one of innocence and bliss. None would wilfully, with their own hand, cut themselves off from happiness. It is folly for any one to entertain so absurd an idea, and yet people do and will encourage such ridiculous fancies; and I,' he continued, with increased bitterness 'must learn to be content: it is useless to struggle against destiny; and, though I suffer in this world, never will I believe that I shall be called to account hereafter, when once I lay down this troublesome burden—for to me it is nothing more; then at last I shall have fulfilled my destiny, and henceforth be at peace. I know my doom it is to suffer on for years and then die; and knowing this, I have nothing to do but to sit quietly down and fill it up. Alas! alas! I could, I have borne it with without murmur or complaint; but that another's fate should be linked to mine—that I shall ere I close my own existence, be doomed to see that other sicken, droop and die—oh when I knelt with her at the altar, I saw it all—I felt that fate had selected her as the unhappy victim that was to wither beneath my blighting influence—that was to sink her to an early grave, when she might have lived for years, caressed and loved by those around her, had she not been ordained to become my wife. Almost on my first interview I felt urged by an irresistible impulse to gain her affections—I, who had ever disclaimed marriage—who had reason above all others to shudder at the very word, and she all but a child in years and knowledge. Yet, yet it was to be; fate, and fate alone brought me to her father's house, and induced me, notwithstanding all my wretchedness and gloom, to hide it in a measure from those around me, and seek her for my bride; and what else but fate would have made that young, light hearted girl ever consent to be mine? And oh, the saddest thought of all, the most akin to wretchedness, is, she has assured me that I am likely to be a father—that I shall have been the means of bringing into existence one whose lot may be—what do I say? it must be; I feel the doom will o'ershadow not only me, but mine; and should the unhappy babe ever live to breathe the breath of life, its destiny will be cast in the same sad mould as mine. Already has Rose begun to droop, even before her child has seen the light; and if it should be decreed to close its little existence ere it feels one pang, oh! what a load of misery it will escape—what anguish, what bitter tears, what sorrow and contumely! And I! oh, how thankfully will I submit to all else, and bless, at least, that one decree: there will be a solitary well of comfort springing up in the desert, where all is parched and scorched with the heat, and from that well I may draw some sweet, refreshing draughts, which will fortify me to pursue my sad career to the close; even though before my own I shall be forced to watch the slow, wasting decay of another, and feel that it is my work, conjointly with that of fate, which impetuously forces me to certain acts I would thankfully, gratefully have been spared.'

Thus conversed Albert with himself, and which, we think, must give the reader a better insight into his character than any description of ours. He was indeed a truly unhappy man, and we are sorry to be obliged to say that there are many, who, like him, ascribe their bad actions to the workings of what they call destiny, instead of repenting of their sins and seeking to amend their lives—which all may do, for Albert reasoned most erroneously: they declare themselves irresponsible of their actions, and regard themselves almost as martyrs in being obliged to follow the decrees of fate—though what fate is we have never yet been able to learn; we have sought an explanation of many, but have not found one that could give us a satisfactory answer to the question. The ascribing to God, that he has so ordered it that some of his creatures should have come into the world purposely to commit some great and horrible crime, is too awful and wicked to be listened to for an instant, and we have never failed to stop the mouths of those who would give utterance to such, we had almost said, blasphemy. The developing of Albert's character is extremely painful, and we are induced to do it only as a warning to others, to guard against such erroneous doctrines as Albert had taken up, and which only had the effect of hardening him in his sins, and not, as he foolishly hoped, affording him comfort or happiness; for, with all his determination to look upon what he had done, and what still remained in store for him to do, as being removed far beyond his own control, it would be difficult to find a man more miserable or wretched than Albert We will now, for the present, leave him, and turn with pleasure from one so moody and confirmed in error, to a favourite with ourselves, and, we hope also, with our readers—Lucy Melville. It is the evening of the day on which she expects Edward and Marian Trevors, and, conscious of the explanation she intends seeking from Edward touching Rose's letter to him, an unusual flush sat upon her cheek.

'What am I about to do?' she said, communing with herself. 'To ask of Edward Trevors why Rose has written to him, and on what subject. He may, alas! think I am actuated by feelings of—but no, he cannot, he dare not think so now,' and her eyes, usually so mild, flashed apparently with indignation. He may,' she continued, still communing with her thoughts, 'refuse my request, even though I ask it as a favour; and I once thought I could never ask a favour of Edward Trevors—should, indeed, have looked upon myself with contempt, had I thought it possible; but now, if I do not interfere on behalf of one I cannot speak to on the subject, she being at a distance—and it is by far too delicate a subject to trust to to a letter, —if I do not interfere, there is none else to extend a helping hand to save her from destruction. Oh! if she be innocent (which, indeed, I firmly believe) it becoms my bounden duty to use every exertion to make it clear in the eyes of Marian, who, unfortunately, thinks her guilty; and if I can by any means, no matter what sacrifice of feeling it may cost myself to do this, I shall truly deem myself blest.'

Thus argued Lucy in her own mind; and if one woman would, like her, feel it a duty to aid and protect another more frequently than is the case, and not judge her guilty merely because appearances are against her, this world would approach more closely to Eden, and we should hear much fewer tales of scandal and calumny than we are pained by doing now. It is, indeed, we believe, beyond a doubt that the bitterest enemies women have are far too often of their own sex. This is a very mournful reflection, and calculated to make us very sad; but it is no less true that a woman, especially if she possess what is unfortunately, very frequently, a great bane, good looks, had need guard her conduct very closely and narrowly, and, even then, will rarely escape the slander of her female neighbours: they are so ready to take advantage of the least carelessness on her part—so eager to make the most of every little indiscretion, that a woman (with shame we say it) is often hunted down, her conduct misinterpreted and calumniated, all her actions ascribed to a totally wrong motive—that there are cases in which she has been actually driven into the very guilt which she was before falsely accused of. How very seldom, if a woman is spoken ill of, do we find any of the sex hardy enough to urge a single word in her defence: this is a very wrong state of things, and should induce us to be very cautious how we give heed to anything that is said to another's prejudice, more especially if it be a woman, for, if we once stamp her as guilty, she loses all caste in society, is thrust out as unworthy to mingle with the virtuous of her sex, and, indeed, is beyond the hope of a return; let her future conduct be ever so pure and free from sin, she cannot, were it even possible for her to shed tears of blood, wash out the stain that is affixed to her character—she is regarded as utterly irreclaimable, and forbidden ever again to mix in that society women were especially intended to adorn.   And how sweet it is to hear a fair and lovely woman defending another from the scorching breath of calumny! Oh, were she even plain-looking, how lovely she appears in the eyes of her auditors; and if she possess personal attractions, how greatly they are heightened by her assuming, unasked, the tender office of defender of the weak! Men seldom love a woman well and truly for her mere beauty; there must [be something more to attract a man worth having; and though a woman possess, which is very rarely the case, perfect beauty, yet, let the man she most wishes to love and admire her—for you seldom find one without the other—let him, we say, hear her speaking unkindly, and imagining evil against an absent one of her own sex, and ten to one, he feels much less admiration for her beauty; and, of course, the unfeminine loveliness of her character cannot escape his detection. Weak and short-sighted indeed he must be who could marry a woman he has heard wilfully calumniating another. We hope, therefore, for human nature's sake, that there are many who, like Lucy Melville, would do their best to free the character of another from the aspersions which have been cast upon it.   After having fully confirmed herself in her original intention of speaking to Edward concerning Rose's letter, Lucy descended to the drawing-room, and anxiously awaited the arrival of him and Marian.

'I fear you are not quite well, dear Lucy,' said Henry, gazing upon her unusually flushed cheek.

'You are mistaken, Henry,' she replied, ' for I am perfectly well.'

And her brother thought she rather avoided meeting his looks: he could not account for it, and yet he felt certain there was something more than usual which agitated and confused her; she had never been so open, so not only willing, but apparently anxious to confide in him, and now he was certain, from her manners and appearance altogether, that she nourished some secret thought, that she either could not or would not impart to him. Being fully persuaded of this, he determined to watch her closely, not from motives of idle curiosity, for he loved her most tenderly, and guarded her happiness and innocence beyond all else on earth, and consequently was ever alive to, and fearful of its being endangered. He was naturally of a mild and gentle nature, and could himself bear patiently as much, or indeed more, than most men; but let any one injure Lucy, his dear and only sister, even by a look, and the iron within him which had been laying dormant was roused to the highest pitch of fury, and he was capable of almost any act, and which, at another time, he would himself have looked upon with horror. It was the knowledge of this, and also the expressed determination to revenge any wrong done to Rose, that prevented Lucy making her brother acquainted with the fact of Rose having written to Edward; she deemed that it would be best to conceal it from him, at least, till she had herself spoken seriously to Edward about it, and though, had it been possible to avoid doing so she would gladly have yielded her self-imposed task, yet, seeing no better way of getting at the precise truth, she shrank not from her first determination.

Though not exactly a ball, there was dancing at Mrs. Melville's, and Edward (who, with Marian, had arrived at an early part of the evening) engaged, as Lucy thought, most fortunately, her for a partner. It was certainly very unusual for them to dance together, for it had been often remarked that they in general avoided each other, but no, Edward seemed in excellent spirits, and delighted at having secured her; and Lucy, too, smiled upon him more sweetly than she was wont, and did not appear at all dissatisfied with having him for a partner. This did not escape the notice of Henry, who, not dancing himself, leant against the wall in an obscure part of the room, where, unobserved by others, he was himself a close observer of all.

At the close of the dance Lucy, under the pretence of seeking refreshment, led Edward into an adjoining room. After ascertaining they were alone, and not likely to be interrupted, Lucy, making an effort to speak, calmly said—

'Edward, I have a favour to ask of you, and which I hope you will not refuse to grant.'

'My dearest Lucy,' he returned, 'for the sake of our long acquaintance and past days of happiness, I will not hesitate to do anything, for you, that lies in my power.'

She shrank instinctively from his hand, which, in speaking, he had laid on her shoulder.

'Do not be so cold, Lucy,' he returned; ' I thought you were kind to me this evening.'

'Only,' she returned, 'because I had a request to make to you, and wished to induce you to comply with it, in any way not dishonourable to myself.'

'You were not, Lucy, always what you are now—so cold and calculating. There was a time, if I mistake not, when you confessed a mutual affection.'

'Name it not, Edward; it is a profanation of all I hold sacred to speak thus lightly of feelings which you have trampled on—of a love which you sought only from the basest motives; and never can I forget the advantage you would have taken of my affection had I not been more than cautious.'

'Well, Lucy, I think you should not speak thus bitterly. You know I offered you all the reparation in my power.'

'And which, you would say, I refused to accept of?'

'Most certainly you did.'

'Yes, Edward, when you could so forget the respect due to me as to endeavour to gain me on easier terms than marriage',—and the colour mounted to her cheek,—'I could never after regard you with the respect I would wish to feel for the man I called "husband," and consequently did refuse to give you that title; but all this is nothing to the purpose. I have sought your company to-day, in order, if possible, to persuade you to an act of justice to another.'

'What is it you say, Lucy? An act of justice to another?'

'Exactly.'

'You speak in enigmas, then,'

'Which are very easily explained. Listen, and I will solve them to you. You yesterday received a letter from Rose?'

Edward started, and exhibited evident signs of surprise.

'How know you that, Lucy?'

'It is sufficient that I do; and all I require of you, Edward, is to allow me to peruse it. I am very confident there is nothing whatever in it that she would object to my seeing; but others are aware of her having written to you, who judge not so charitably—nay, who do not hesitate to regard it as a positive proof of guilt, and affix it as a stigma to her character. Now, Edward, you surely will not refuse to show me the letter—not to satisfy me, for I am perfectly satisfied there is not one word in it she need blush to have it known to all the world she has written; but that I may be able to refute the calumnies of others.'

'I am sorry, Lucy, you should have asked the only favour of me I cannot grant; but though Rose might not blush to have it know that she has written to me, yet I can truly say she would not wish the contents of her letter to be made public.'

'Neither do I, Edward. I only desire to have it in my power to state it was merely a letter of business, inquiry, or friendship, accordingly as the case may be.'

'But it is neither,' returned Edward; 'in fact, it is on a subject that Rose herself desires to be a secret between us; and, knowing that such is her wish, I cannot satisfy your curiosity.'

'Call it not curiosity. Edward, for it is no such thing. Were you and she single, I, you may depend, would be the very last to make inquiry concerning any letters that passed between you; but the case is very different, and I have heard poor Rose—who I am confident is innocent in all but appearance—spoken of as being base, designing and deceitful: you alone can clear her of these insinuations, and it is an act of imperative justice, and which I shall regard you as bad, indeed, if you refuse to perform.'

'I have told you, Lucy, it is entirely out of my power to do so; but when will a woman listen to reason?'

'Such reasoning as that, Edward, I hope no woman will ever be satisfied with, and least of all myself. But am I to understand that you absolutely refuse to allow me to see that letter?'

'Most undoubtedly; it contains, as I before said, a secret, which I am not at liberty to disclose even to you.'

Lucy paused a moment, and then said, with marked emphasis,—

'Will you, Edward, give me your word that there is nothing in Rose's letter to you that, as a wife, she need mind having it known to me, or indeed any one, that she had written?'

Edward made no reply.

'You answer not,' said Lucy. 'Do you refuse to do her even this slight justice?'

Still no answer.

'Edward,' she continued, earnestly, 'I must have a reply to my question: say at once, yes or no.'

'Lucy,' he began at length, 'you have no right to ask this question, or demand an answer of me. I am accountable to no one for my actions, and least of all to you. If Rose chooses to correspond with me, it is no affair of any but ourselves; if it pleases us, depend we shall give no heed to what busy, meddling fools think proper to say. I am perfectly at a loss to understand how you or others came to know anything about the letter, but hope you came by the knowledge in no underhand manner.'

'You do well,' said Lucy, her eyes lighted up with an unusual fire, while her cheek flushed to a still deeper crimson—'you do well to accuse me of underhand dealings. You are yourself so entirely open and free from the least suspicion of such a thing, that I cannot be surprised you should be so ready to note it in another; but let that pass. You have absolutely refused to give me the least account of the letter—have indeed endeavoured to make me think Rose guilty; so now I give you warning—an explanation of the letter I am determined to get, and therefore shall unhesitatingly apply to Rose, and I am certain, when I tell her of the attacks made upon her character, she will thank me for the part I have acted, and clear away all the aspersions cast upon her.'

'Write to Rose by all means,' said Edward, 'I would wish you to do so; indeed, I was going to propose it myself. In the mean time her letter shall not be destroyed, but remain safe in my keeping; and if she desires me to let you see it, depend she shall be obeyed. I will afford you every facility for writing.' Saying which he wrote Rose's address on a card, and presented it to Lucy, who, accepting of it, thanked him coldly, once more reiterated her intention of writng, and left the room. Her brother was the first person she encountered, who had, indeed, watched her withdrawal from the company, and anxiously marked the time she was engaged with Edward. What could he think wrong of Lucy? No; it was impossible! a girl of such uncommon excellence and right appreciation of men and things could never be thus suddenly led into error; still it was his duty to inquire into the subject of her conversation with Edward, but not then; he resolved to defer it till the following morning, so merely making some remark on the warmth, as he observed her flushed cheeks, he drew her arm in his own, and kept her by his side the remainder of the evening.

They parted for the night without any allusion to what was uppermost in both their thoughts, and Lucy congratulated herself that the conversation she had held privately with Edward had escaped her brother's notice, and when, breakfast being over in the morning, he asked her to accompany him in a walk, she complied without a thought that he intended to make any inquiries respecting what she fully believed had not been observed by him, and was, therefore, quite unprepared for the serious manner in which he begged her, immediately after they left home, to acquaint him with what had passed between herself and Edward the previous evening—she was so taken by surprise that for a moment she hesitated, not knowing what to say. It had been her greatest desire to keep the knowledge of Rose having written to Edward from her brother; but now that she possessed, as she considered, the means of learning from Rose herself the purport of her communication with Edward, she considered there was no longer any occasion for secrecy, and therefore confided to him every paticular, both concerning Marian's opinion of Rose, and the result of her own conversation with Edward. Henry heard her to a close, without a single word of interruption or comment till she concluded her relation by saying,—

'I think, dear Henry, after all, Edward has acted tolerably fair; for I could hardly expect him to exhibit Rose's letter without her consent.' When he replied,—

'I scarcely know what to think, Lucy; it is very strange she should have written to him, and so soon, too, after her arrival. She must,' he continued, musingly, 'have been in haste to communicate some intelligence; and yet, why not have written to Marian? As to what Edward says about it being a secret, I give no heed to it whatever; for what I have seen of him lately, I should say he was just the man to make the most of a letter from one so lovely as Rose. I myself should, indeed, have felt proud at being honoured with her correspondence, though it were only to ask me to execute some trifling commission; therefore cannot so much blame him.'

Seeing he paused, Lucy added mildly, 'And now, Henry, that I have Rose's address, and can write to her myself, I have no doubt all will be very speedily explained.'

'I hope so, dear Lucy; and yet, at the same time, I fear.'

'You can have nothing to fear, Henry; Rose, I am certain, will be glad of an opportunity of clearing herself.'

'Yes, Lucy, if she can, or if Edward will allow her.'

'Dear Henry, be not unjust to poor Rose—her whom you once so ardently admired.'

'And do still, Lucy, as much as ever. Although she has wounded my feelings by treating me with marked discourtesy, yet I attribute it not to her, but the infernal machinations of Edward, who, alas, has too easily succeeded in turning her feeling of friendship for me into something little short of hatred; and may he not, also, have succeeded in—'

'No, no; stop dear Henry, whither are your thoughts leading you?' interrupted Lucy, in a tone of reproach.

'There is nothing, Lucy,' replied her brother, looking down into her face, 'makes a woman appear so lovely as to hear her pleading the cause of another, especially when more than a doubt may be thrown upon that other's conduct.'

'And do you, Henry, also deem Rose unworthy, I did not think you would so soon have abandoned her cause.'

'I abandon her cause!' exclaimed her brother energetically: 'you mistake me, Lucy; I never have nor will. Still I think it possible that Edward has obtained his desire, and succeeded in alienating her affections from Albert; but if he has,' he continued, in the same warm strain, 'he goes not unpunished—he who presumed to talk to me, and pretended to doubt my intentions towards Rose, when I only expressed (and what man would not have done the same?) the warm admiration I felt for her beauty. My eyes, at the very moment, were opened, in a great measure, to his real character; for he who, upon such slight grounds, suspected another, must himself be entertaining bad designs towards the object he so eagerly feigned to protect. I thought so then, and have since had opportunities of confirming my opinion; but as I said before, let me once prove him to have acted basely, and as I warned him, he will find to his sorrow that he has no light foe to cope with, but one who would willingly sacrifice his life rather than let him go unscathed to exult in his villany.'

'Dear Henry, you absolutely alarm me,' replied Lucy, trembling, 'and almost make me repent having confided all to you, and yet I know not how I could have done otherwise.'

'Compose yourself, my dear girl,' replied her brother, kindly; and then resuming his usual mild tone, he said, 'You have nothing, Lucy, to fear; you have acted nobly towards Rose, and I hope she will feel and appreciate your kindness.'

''I am confident she will,' returned Lucy, though I have only done what I believe most other women would, had they been placed in my situation.'

You judge other hearts by the truth and honesty of your own; and, although it is kind and, generous of you to do so, it is at the same time a mode of judging which will very frequently lead you into error.'

'Not in this case' she replied warmly; 'and I did not think, Henry, I should have occasion to plead in her favour to you.'

And Henry thought the tone she spoke in sounded like reproach, and he therefore answered to it immediately—

'Do not dear Lucy, think that I suspect Rose without sufficient reason. I have observed a great freedom in her manners and conversation to Edward. You remember the day we dined there last?'

'Yes' returned Lucy, ' when Rose first treated you with such disrespect.'

'The same; and when the ladies retired from the dining-room, Rose was the last to pass out, and exchanged, as she did so, a look with Edward, who held the door open—a look that I should be sorry to have misinterpreted.'

'And yet how easily you may have done so!'

'I confess it; but it is not all. The last time I was in the company of Rose, and which you know was just before she went into the country—'

'Yes,' replied Lucy, 'go on.'

'Well my suspicions having been aroused by what I had previously observed, I noticed both her and Edward very closely, though without allowing them to see I did so.'

'Proceed,' said Lucy impatiently, as her brother paused for an instant.

'Well, my dear girl,' he returned, smiling, 'I will as fast as I can. I was saying that I watched them very closely—yes, and in course of the evening saw Edward give Rose a letter, as he thought unobserved by any, and which she in a very timid and confused manner concealed about her person.'

'Is it possible!' said Lucy.

'The simple truth,' returned her brother; 'and putting this in connexion with what you have communicated to me this morning, I hardly know how we can acquit Rose, though ever so desirous of doing so.'

'But Rose was so very innocent, so almost child-like in her simplicity!'

Which would only render her more easy to be ensnared. Edward knew this, and regarded her from the first I am convinced, as one that it would require but a slight effort to to gain to his wishes, and consequently marked her as a victim.'

'Men are indeed base, if they can so contemplate a sweet and virtuous woman, and more especially one who was devoted to her husband, to whom she had been but recently married.'

'That is the only thing, Lucy, that makes me hope we may yet find Rose innocent; she was surely attached to Albert?'

'She loved him with the best and purest affection a woman can bestow; and although his station in society was far above her own, I am positive *that* never induced her to become his wife. No, had Albert been poor instead of rich, her love of him would have remained as true and constant as I do and must believe it is now,'

'And the belief, Lucy, does you credit: ever cherish, my girl, such pure and exalted opinions of your own sex.'

'I will, dear Henry, for I should lose all my self respect could I suppose men found such easy prey in women as you imagine they do.'

'Not at all, Lucy; there are some whom I firmly believe would withstand not only all the fascinations and temptations of the opposite sex, but what is still more, their own love and inclination, if it is wrong to indulge in it.'

'You do us but justice, Henry; and it is unkind of you to except Rose.'

'I do not except her—I only fear that her country education, together with her natural openness of character, have rendered her wholly unfit to cope with such a man as Edward.'

'I think, indeed,' returned Lucy, 'that he is about the worst person she could have to contend against; not that I think Rose has fallen, but he may have motives for wishing us to think so, and certainly his conversation with me yesterday was calculated to make me believe it ; yet I cast back the falsehood in his face, utterly refusing it my credence.'

'And it was bravely done, said her brother, gazing on her with proud affection; 'and I see, Lucy, you have got a dash of my fierce spirit mingled with your own feminine softness, and never could it be called forth on a nobler or more worthy occasion; but leave Edward to me, and see if I fail to call him to account, sooner or later, If I remain quiet for a while, it is only that I may gain stronger evidence against him. And yet,' he continued, speaking to himself. 'I once called this man friend'; fully, indeed, believed he was what he appeared, frank. generous, and sincere; confided to him my every thought and hope, as to a brother's breast. Oh ! is it not enough to turn us completely against our fellow-men—to make us regard them with suspicious coldness, and cautiously to guard, and in most instances prevent, their approximating to anything resembling friendship? I was, indeed. blind to have been deceived by him so long ; how carefully he must have hidden his real character ! and Marian, doubtless, still deems him worthy.

'Oh, yes, in every respect,' said Lucy, replying to her brother, who remained so deep in thought that he appeared not to notice her, till they had nearly arrived home, when, starting from the reverie he had fallen into, he said,—

'You intend, Lucy, to write to Rose—'

'Immediately on our return,' replied his sister, not giving him time to conclude his sentence.

'That is right; and, till you get a reply, we must suspend our judgment.'

'Most certainly; and now, Henry, mind, I have always said Rose is innocent; see if I do not prove perfectly correct. I am generally accurate in my ideas, and this time I have more confidence in my opinion than usual, and I shall certainly not fail to rally you on the erroneous judgment you have formed, though I suppose I must excuse you on the ground that you cannot be supposed to understand a woman so well as I.'

'I shall only be too glad if you have the opportunity of laughing at me, dear Lucy,' said her brother, kindly; ' and if Rose proves what you expect, I will cheerfully bear your raillery.'

'Still suspicious,' replied Lucy, smiling; ' well, they say women are difficult to convince, unless you can bring good proof of your assertions; but I think it is a far more arduous task to endeavour to bring a man to your way of thinking, especially if he has taken into his head an opposite idea.

'At any rate, the fault is not yours, for you can argue, dear Lucy.

'Yes, even though vanquished, as Goldsmith says; but I am not vanquished yet, Henry, nor do I ever expect to be, on this one argument at least, whatever I may be in others.'

As she finished the sentence, they ascended the steps of their own residence. The door opened to receive them, and exchanging a kind greeting with her brother, Lucy flew up the stairs, eager to lay aside her walking dress, and commenced her letter to Rose—a letter she intended in all kindness and charitableness of heart; and yet it was a delicate thing to write to a woman, and tell her she was calumniated and spoken ill of in her absence from home, and beg of her, for her own sake, to send an immediate explanation of all that had occured between her and Edward. Lucy felt this more than she had expected to do, and also found a difficulty in expressing herself in writing, so as not to give offence or hurt her pride. Could she have conversed with her, it would have been far different. It is easy enough, kindly and affectionately, to seek an explanation, during a friendly chat, of one we feel certain is falsely accused: we can introduce the subject in a manner that is impossible for any to take offence at, much less the one we are desirous of righting in the eyes of the world ; we can gently lead to the topic, glide from commonplace observations, so to speak, smoothly into the subject, without appearing to make it a matter of business inquiry, as we must in a great measure do, if we sit down to write a letter, especially for the purpose of having all doubts removed. Lucy felt this so much that, once or twice, she threw her pen down, half determined to wait till Rose returned to town before she sought of her what she was anxious to learn; but then the thought arose, that during the interval that must necessarily elapse, Marian would most probably grow more confirmed in the bad opinion she now entertained of Rose; and also Henry had acknowledged that he himself was doubtful whether she possessed the power of clearing herself; and she again took up her pen, and, after much hesitation, and great caution in her choice of words, so as to make no allusion that would sound at all like reproach, or even unkind, she at length succeeded in writing a few lines to Rose, in which she assured her she was perfectly satisfied herself, and only applied to her that she might be able to make others so. After Lucy had concluded her letter, before securing it in an envelope, she sought her brother, and placed it in his hands for perusal.

'Well, Henry, do you think it will do?' she said rather impatiently, as her brother, she fancied, seemed a long time considering its contents.

'Yes, Lucy, you could not have written more kindly, or, I may say, more to the point, than you have; and, if Rose is as good and innocent as you deem her, you will soon have a satisfactory answer; indeed, anyhow, she cannot do otherwise than return a polite reply.'

'Then I will send it off at once,' said Lucy; and, taking the letter from her brother, she sealed and directed it, and giving it to the servant, with many cautions not to lose it by the way —which made her brother smile—bade him take it to the post-office.

'Now it is off my mind,' said Lucy, 'and I feel to breathe easier, and must wait with all the patience I am mistress of, till I gain her answer.'

'Which is not a great deal, Lucy, I think,' said her brother, still smiling; 'if you have one fault, I think it is impatience.'

'Do not flatter me, I beg,' replied Lucy, laughing; 'instead of possessing but one fault, I must even plead guilty to a dozen.'

'There is nothing like candour, I suppose you think, Lucy?'

'Nothing whatever,' and she laughed again.

'You are very merry, Lucy,' said Mrs. Melville, speaking as she entered the room.

No. 8.

'Yes, dear mamma,' she replied; 'you will scarcely believe that Henry has taken upon himself the office of censor, and been reproving me for what he has been polite enough to term my only fault; can you guess what it is?'

'I think not, Lucy, unless it be the feminine one of curiosity.'

'Oh dear no, mamma; that, at least, would have been excusable, would it not, Henry?'

'Not more so than the one I have attributed to you, dear Lucy, especially under the present circumstances,' replied her brother, kindly.

'You surprise me, Henry,' returned Mrs. Melville, 'and induce me to suspect that you and Lucy have some secret I am not to participate in.'

'We have no secret, dear mother, that we desire to keep from your knowledge; on the contrary, it is the wish of us both ever to confide in you. Lucy, my love, you will oblige me by relating all that has passed between us this morning.'

Thus appealed to, Lucy explained to Mrs. Melville, all that had occurred, both concerning Marian Trevors' opinion of Rose, especially as regarded the letter, and her own conversation with Edward, together with his refusal to do Rose justice; and at length, having obtained from him Rose's address, she communicated the fact of having herself written to her that morning, and also the contents, as near as she could remember, of her letter.

Mrs. Melville, without any apparent surprise, attentively listened to her relation, and when she concluded, warmly applauded her conduct, and, like her daughter, entertained no fear for the result. All that seemed inexplicable in Rose would, she felt certain, be satisfactorily accounted for, and never for a moment doubted that Rose was pure, and, as far as it is possible in this world to be, entirely free from sin; and it was a great satisfaction to Lucy to find her mother's opinion coincided so completely with her own. It removed every little doubt that would, in spite of all her efforts to suppress it, occasionally flit across her mind, and perfectly reassured her that all would end well.

'And,' said Lucy, smiling triumphantly, 'all is well, you know, that ends well.'

She waited, with more patience than Henry had given her credit for, Rose's reply.

Who has not felt the anxious, nervous restlessness of expectation—the constant, feverish excitement, that swallows up every other thought, forbids us for one moment to indulge in any hope or feeling unconnected with that one deep anxiety that engrosses our whole being? and yet we are doomed to wait a certain time before we can see the accomplishment of our wishes, perchance, even in the end, have to suffer the pangs of disappointment; and, if a letter is to seal our fate—to assure us our expectations are realised—or cast hope for ever from our bosoms on the subject we have secretly nourished and encouraged the most—oh, how we tremble at the sound of the postman's knock, and when the letter is placed in our hands, how eagerly we gaze upon it! There it is, before us, containing what may overwhelm us with joy or plunge us into the deepest distress. Few, we think, have not, at one time or other of their lives, felt thus—have not gazed at the hand-writing on the outside—the seal, the very fold of the letter, even the post-mark, as if they could form an index to the inside, and yet deferred to open it, half dreading to meet with disappointment. At such a moment, how the heart throbs between hope and fear! for an instant it seems to suspend its movement, and the next how tumultuously it throws the blood to the brain, till we reel under the very intensity of our feelings; and, when at length, it is opened, and all is known, either what a gush of sparkling gladness rushes through our whole frame, or what a sad, cold shiver of disappointment chills our very heart, appearing to freeze up every emotion of pleasure that yet remains to make life sweet. A letter! The word conveys to the mind all, or at least much, that has ever brought to our eyes tears, be they of joy or sorrow. When merry, noisy children, driven and pushed about in the bustle of a public school, a letter from home would check us in the midst of the maddest revelry of holiday hours, and turning from the noisy group, we would seek out some quiet corner of the playground, and, with tearful eyes and throbbing heart, con carefully over its contents; not one word was ever lost sight of—often a more tender meaning put on the most trivial sentence than, perhaps, was intended by the writer; and, oh, with what unsophisticated feelings of joy did we learn all the little home news, of no interest whatever to another, and yet how sweet to ourselves! perhaps we were told that baby had begun to lisp our name, or that preparations were already going on to welcome us at the forthcoming vacation; or sometimes it would contain bad tidings—our dear mother was indisposed, or some little dearly loved sister or brother had met with an accident, or fallen ill. Either way, a letter had the effect of suppressing for the day our boisterous mirth, and making us thoughtful and reserved. And later in life, when surrounded by still dearer ties, and fortune hath, for a while, cast us asunder; oh, with what eagerness did we receive a letter that was to convey to us tidings of either their welfare or distress! with what a trembling hand have we broken the seal—with swimming eyes perused the well-known writing! With what sweet transport have we seen our own name coupled with words of tender regard, which told, though absent, we were still unforgot. In the joy of the moment we have oft dropped a kiss and a tear upon the insensible paper at the same time. We think there must be very few, if any, who have not known and felt all this, or who have not shed bitter scalding tears over a letter which has brought the painful news of the sickness of some treasured friend; perchance, it has even come bearing the insignia of mourning, and we have suffered the anguish of hearing of a death-bed we were too far removed to be summoned to attend. One we loved has passed from earth, and we not by to receive the parting blessing, which could only be conveyed to us by a letter when all was over. A letter! volumes might be written on that one one word, but we forbear. We fear, indeed, we have already tired the patience of our readers, so crave their pardon and proceed with the tale.

It is morning. Mrs. Melville, Lucy, and Henry, are conversing, over the breakfast-table. They were interrupted by the servant, who handed Lucy a letter: at the first glance, she felt it was from Rose, and joyfully held it up, as she said,—

'Now, brother Henry, to prove who is the best judge of a woman's heart, prepare yourself for my raillery, for I am determined not to spare you in the least; it is so seldom you afford me an opportunity of triumphing over you, that I am resolved to make the most of it now.'

'You had better, Lucy, make quite certain that I am in error before you begin to boast,' replied Henry, catching some of the gay humour that enlivened his sister.

'Well,' said Lucy, laughing, 'you still hold your opinion then; I expected the sight of this (pointing to the letter) would have forced you to recant your error, and humbly sue to me for pardon; but there is no convincing men, except by their own eyesight, so I suppose, to put an end to all doubt, I must even break this seal, and spread the contents of the billet before you.'

'Certainly, before I sue for pardon,' replied Henry, in the same strain; 'it is only justice.'

'Justice! you talk of justice, Henry?' resumed Lucy, laughing still more—'you who could entertain a wrong thought of the absent, merely because a few circumstances involved her in a little mystery. I am absolutely surprised at your assurance.'

'Never mind my assurance, Lucy; it is, you know, part of man's nature; so open the letter, there's a good girl.'

'Yes,' said Mrs. Melville, who had been quietly smiling at their playful remarks, 'open it, Lucy. I feel anxious to know the contents.'

Lucy complied; but, as she glanced over the writing, the smile with which she commenced gradually faded from her countenance, while a look of fixed sorrow took its place.

'Well, Lucy,' said her brother, noting with deep grief the alteration in her face, 'tell us what Rose says : does she, like Edward, refuse to give any explanation?'

'Alas! alas! you are right,' replied Lucy; and she was so overcome by the bitterness of her disappointment, rendered so much worse by being unexpected, that she burst into an involuntary fit of tears.

'Come, come,' said Henry, kindly taking her hand, and losing, in his anxiety to soothe her grief, all thought of the letter, 'it is unwise to give way to such sorrow for a trifling disappointment: consider, Lucy, had anything happened to our dear mother, you could do no more than weep; and tears should not be wasted on any trivial grief.'

Mrs. Melville likewise added her words of consolation to those of Henry, and Lucy, being a girl of strong mind, soon recovered her self-possession, and removed all trace of sorrow from her cheek, and, smiling faintly, said,—

'Forgive me, dear mamma; forgive me, Henry: it was wrong, I know, to give way to my feelings in the manner I did; but oh! I had such confidence in Rose's innocence—felt so certain that she could and would have cleared her character from all imputations, that I was more disappointed, perhaps, than you can imagine.'

'I can imagine it all,' replied Henry, pressing her hand; 'but as you have failed in all your endeavours to get an explanation, it is my turn to see if I can force one from Edward.'

'Oh no, dear Henry,' said his sister, the colour receding from her face and temples till it left them, white as marble; 'we have done all we well could, and may now let the matter drop; it would be useless to embroil yourself in a quarrel with Edward.'

'We shall see,' he returned; 'at any rate he goes not scot free to laugh at our futile attempts to right one who I judge, from what you say, has no longer a desire to stand well in the eyes of the world.'

'Hush, Henry!' said Mrs. Melville; 'We have not yet heard Rose's letter: allow Lucy to read it to us, and that may put Edward's conduct in a different light.'

'You read it, dear mamma,' replied Lucy, placing the letter in her mother's hand, who, receiving it, read aloud as follows:—

'MY DEAR LUCY,—

'I thank you kindly for the part you have acted in defending my character from the attacks of others, and am sorry to be obliged to refuse your request of desiring Mr. Trevors to show you my letter to him, of the contents of which, indeed, I can offer no explanation, as it contains a secret, appertaining not to myself but another. Such being the case, I trust you will not deem it necessary to make any further inquiries respecting it. With kind regards to yourself and Mrs. Melville, believe me, yours affectionately,

' ROSE MORELAND.'

After she had finished reading it, Mrs. Melville remarked, that she thought it very possible that it might be some little family affair on which she had consulted Edward, and which she might naturally desire should be communicated to no other party. There was certainly nothing very wonderful in supposing such to be the case, and she could not help thinking that Lucy had been rather premature in giving up the belief of Rose's innocence.

'Depend, my dear children,' she said emphatically, 'we shall yet have convincing proof that I am correct in what I say.'

'The only proof I ever hope to find is to force it out of Edward,' said Henry, in the same determined tones he had last spoken.

Lucy clasped her hands, but remained silent. Mrs. Melville resumed—

'I know not, Henry, what you could do, were you ever so desirous. If Rose wishes her correspondence to be private, how can you compel Edward to make you acquainted with it, when it would be dishonourable on his part to do so?'

'What mamma says is perfectly correct,' urged Lucy; 'and let me beg of you, dear Henry, to listen to reason. It would be madness, under the present circumstances, to quarrel with Edward, who, in withholding the letter, is only acting as you would, were you in his place.'

'Talk not so, Lucy,' replied her brother, almost sternly: 'Edward, I am certain, has tampered with Rose in some way or other, I am not prepared to say exactly what; but that that letter has emanated more from him than her, I am convinced beyond the possibility of a doubt. At the same time, make yourself easy; I shall not call him to account till I have better, that is to say, stronger proof of his villany.'

'Oh! thank you, dear Henry,' said the still trembling Lucy. 'I hope all may yet turn out better than we at present anticipate.'

'I hope so, indeed,' said Henry, 'though I think there is but little room to do so.'

'We cannot at present tell,' returned Mrs. Melville, 'not being in a situation to form an accurate judgment; and, therefore, it is best to allow things to take their own course for a while, and something may turn up that we little expect.'

'Will you promise us, dear Henry, not to say a word to Edward on the subject?' said Lucy, laying her hand on her brother's arm.

'I cannot do that, as I am determined to caution him once more; but do not fear that I will quarrel with him. I shall only calmly and coolly bid him beware how he acts for the future; and now, dear Lucy, bid adieu to all anxiety on that score, and let me see you smile with your accustomed cheerfulness.'

Lucy endeavoured to do as her brother desired, and strove to speak on some other subject. Her brother joined her, and, after a while, they apparently succeeded in banishing Rose from their thoughts. Yet, when Henry, taking leave of them for a time, stated his intention of walking out, poor Lucy again turned pale, and besought him to allow her to accompany him.

'You know, my dear girl, how pleased I ever am with your company, and therefore will not feel hurt that I decline it now, as I think of calling at the club.'

'The club!' re-echoed Lucy, turning still paler, 'you may then, perchance, meet with Edward.'

'Nothing more likely; indeed, I fully hope to do so. But what ails you, Lucy, after all my assurances to be thus foolishly alarmed? Why, I gave you credit for more courage.'

'I have such a dread, Henry, of your involving yourself in any disagreement with Edward—such an unaccountable foreboding that you may, unless you are very careful, sustain some injury at his hands; your life even may fall a sacrifice.'

'Hush, hush, Lucy! whither are your forebodings leading you? You must not, my girl, allow yourself to be thus carried away. If you encourage such idle fancies, your life will soon grow a misery to you; return to your mother, my love,' (for Lucy had followed him from the parlour,) 'and banish at once and for ever all such silly fears, which indeed, are unworthy of you. Let me have one kiss, Lucy,' he added, stooping to press it on her cheek; 'and now, for a little while, adieu!'

Lucy entered the parlour where Mrs. Melville was sitting, with a sad and serious air. It was easy, she thought, for Henry to bid her banish her fears, but it was no easy task to perform. Still she felt it would be unwise to encourage them, and consequently did her best to converse with her mother, and hide, at least as much as possible, from her the anxiety that dwelt in her own breast. And here it is worthy of remark, that Lucy, loving her brother most dearly, and dreading beyond all else on earth aught befalling him, yet never for an instant did her heart reproach him for so readily taking up the cause of another. No; so far from deeming him unkind towards herself, in being so willing (did occasion offer) to risk his own life in that cause, she, on the contrary, thought more highly of him, and treasured him in her heart as the very type of what an honourable and virtuous man should be. Some, perhaps, may smile at the term 'virtuous' connected with a man, but it is a word of very extended meaning, and virtues that adorn and elevate one sex are equally to be admired, and ought to be equally cultivated in the other. Men, unfortunately (and it is chiefly the result of a mistaken education,) think that, if they act honourably, and never take any unjust advantage of their fellow-men, their dishonourable conduct to women, and too often the breaking of their most solemn vows, is a matter of very slight import; and yet how unjustifiably wicked, how base and mean are such acts, to take advantage of the soft and yielding nature of woman—of woman, whom man was intended to protect and shield from every ill! so far from having the face to glory in such conduct, it is surprising that men should not blush to have it known. Still there are men who would, in all their dealings with their own sex, be most scrupulously exact, and would scorn to be thought mean enough to act with the slightest deceit; and yet these very self-same men think it a matter to boast of—the wrongs and injuries (to say nothing of the deception) they have heaped upon woman. An honourable man, in the strict sense of the word, was Henry Melville: he would have shrunk abashed at the bare thought of injuring another, much more if that other were a woman. His arm was ever ready to protect the weak, and his utmost abhorrence was a man who sought, by the most deceitful and dishonest conduct, to lead a woman into sin. The reader may, therefore, judge of his feelings towards Edward Trevors, who had for years so entirely succeeded in imposing on his credulity, that he deemed him a man of sound honour and morality. Why Edward should have desired his friendship, and thought it worth while to conceal his real character for the purpose of gaining and keeping that friendship, can scarcely be accounted for, unless we attribute it, in the first instance, to Lucy, whom he had most probably thought to obtain an easy victim: but deceit and cowardice pretty generally go together; and when, in the bitterness of heart at the discovery of his intended baseness, Lucy declared her intention of denouncing him to her brother, he offered her what he deemed the only reparation, and what he thought would have been eagerly accepted—marriage; but no! Lucy had a soul above, far above, such a low, grovelling nature as his; and though she had loved him, when at the same time she could look upon him with respect, yet it quickly vanished when she discovered his real intentions towards her, and, casting back his offer, and with it all the love she had ever felt for him, she in a tone and with a flushed cheek utterly at variance with the gentle, feminine softness that usually characterised her, bade him insult her no longer with his presence, and at the same time told him he need fear nothing from her brother, as, for Henry's own sake, she would conceal all that had taken place within her own bosom; and painful as it was to poor Lucy to be obliged still to receive him as her brother's friend, yet for that dear brother's sake alone she bore all patiently; and though, from the hour Edward threw off the veil that had previously concealed his deformity, a melancholy not altogether of an unpleasing kind dwelt a constant inmate of her heart, and a paleness sat upon her features, yet not even her mother knew the true cause, for Mrs. Melville placed it to the account of Edward having married Marian, which he did almost immediately after Lucy's refusal of him, and of which her mother knew nothing, and wrongly judged her daughter had entertained an affection for him which was not returned. Thus even a mother's instinctive acuteness may be deceived. And Lucy had conceived a sincere friendship for Marian, and, though opposed to each other in many respects, Marian prized and returned it: she confided to Lucy every thought and feeling of her heart, and not unfrequently received patiently from Lucy reproof she would not have borne from any one else. Marian's greatest fault was that of judging too hastily, and too much from outward appearances; while Lucy, on the contrary, weighed well in her own mind everything for and against, and often waited long ere she fairly balanced and gave her decision; but then she very seldom had occasion to recant it when it was once given; whereas, Marian, more often than not, was obliged to acknowledge herself in error, and yet for all this it had become so much her nature to judge in this manner of what was passing around her, that although often seeking counsel of Lucy, she very seldom bent to her opinion till undoubted proof was given in favour of it.

And this is not at all an unusual fault. Many, very many, there are who do and will, in spite of everything, judge in this hasty foolish way. We say foolish, but it is worse than foolish; for the injury we may do others by thus wrongly interpreting their actions, is often irreparable; and then when the harm is done, of what use is it for us to say 'I am very sorry, but I really thought I was correct in my judgment, or I never would have formed so erroneous an opinion, much less have so represented it to others?' None whatever; and if we possess right and proper feeling, the severest pang we can suffer is the consciousness that, through forming a rash and hasty judgment, we have been the cause of infusing some bitter drops into the cup of one which, perhaps, was already overflowing with bitterness. The young are generally most addicted to this fault, and it is but kind to caution them against giving way to it. It cannot be checked too soon; for, when once it grows into a habit, then, as in the case of Marian, it is almost impossible to eradicate it; in fact, it is the case with all faults, but of this one especially.

After Henry left Lucy he walked direct to the club, on entering which his searching glance was sent round the room, and immediately detected Edward, whom, indeed, he fully expected to see there. Finding himself unobserved, he took up a paper and commenced reading, waiting a favourable opportunity of speaking to him more apart from the others. At first he looked over it with a very listless air, but, glancing down the columns, he met with an article that interested him, and very soon became absorbed in its contents, to the utter exclusion of all that was passing around him, till the name of 'Moreland' struck upon his ear. He started and turned round, when he immediately recognised the speaker in Sir Charles Mortimer, who, with his back turned towards him, was standing between Edward and Mr. Fairford, to whom he was addressing some observations, which, though almost lost by Henry, certainly sounded to him like congratulation on some important event; and, although hating to be a listener to conversation that was not intended for his ear, yet, under the circumstances, Henry deemed it justifiable to resume his former position, and, while appearing engrossed with the paper, to give heed to what next might be said. He had no occasion to exercise his patience long, for Mortimer resuming, remarked,—

'Well, she is certainly a fine-looking girl, and her complexion does, as you say, match the white and red roses of her father's—what shall I term it?—parterre.'

'Oh! call it what you please,' replied Edward, laughing, 'so as you don't dispute the roses.'

'That would be impossible,' said Fairford, 'she is certainly a charming girl.'

'What a breadth of neck and bosom.' rejoined Mortimer.

'What, do you not admire it?' said Edward, in a tone of surprise.

'Yes, I admire it, but still it does not suit our London ideas of gentility; and then her foot is too large, and her gait savours strongly of a country hoyden.'

Henry heaved a sigh, and felt relieved; he was mistaken in supposing they were speaking of Rose, and smiled at himself for having fancied the name he had caught bore a resemblance to that of Moreland, and, again giving his whole attention to the paper, he became once more so interested as to have totally forgotten the circumstance that had previously interrupted him. Having read to the bottom of a column, he paused for an instant to turn to the top of the next, and was just on the point of commencing with it, when—certainly it could be no trick of the imagination—he again heard, or fancied he heard, one of the three, he could not tell which, mention the name Moreland; it was certainly very strange, almost unaccountable, for the person they had been speaking of bore no resemblance, except in complexion, to the charming face and figure of Rose;—a country hoyden, and wanting that which, in his eye, was everything—grace. Oh! it was certainly impossible they could be speaking of the graceful figure and light fairy tread of Rose—of a being he had regarded as scarcely less than Nature's masterpiece, and approaching so closely to perfection as to be pronounced all but perfect. He smiled at himself for having, for a moment, entertained such an absurd notion, and was preparing to give his entire thoughts to the oft-interrupted paragraph, when Mortimer, in a louder tone than before, said,—

'Well, I have told you my opinion of her; I think she would do very well for the country, and pass, may be, for a beauty, but I am not fond of your pudding women, nor an over great admirer of rosy cheeks, unless it is in their native element, the country: for, transplant them into our atmosphere, and the bloom soon withers, like an apple which, when suspended on the tree, looks all beauty and sweetness, but, gather it and shut it up for a while in a close cupboard, and see how soon all its beauty will disappear.'

'But think,' said Edward, 'how beautiful and rich it is when first gathered!'

'Yes,' added Fairford, laughing, 'I think the apple should be eaten while it is ripe and fresh, and not be consigned, on any account, to a close cupboard, there to waste its sweetness on the desert air;' and then they all laughed, and seemed to consider it an excellent joke.

'They cannot be talking of Rose thus; they would not dare to do it, and I must be a fool to have thought so for an instant,' muttered Henry to himself; still his thoughts were so unsettled that he could not refrain dropping the paper, and giving his undivided attention to what was going on. In the mean time, having expended their merriment on the jest, the trio began to talk afresh.

'You can think as you please, Mortimer; but though she may be rather of a full make, I'll defy you to know, as Byron says, where to pare without destroying some separate charm.'

'I have only given you my opinion, which is the truth. I am not very apt to flatter young ladies even to their face, much less then when I am not inspired by their presence.'

'That is the reason you gain so few favours from them. You take upon you too much the office of censor, and are also, if I mistake not, rather given to pointing out their faults, of which ladies can never bear to be told.'

'If a woman can give heed, and appear pleased with the fulsome adulation some men shower upon the sex, and which indeed is totally devoid of meaning, I should entertain but a very poor opinion of her—a woman of any mind should be above such absurd flattery.'

'I think,' returned Fairford, 'I know the sex a little better than you do; and though a woman may be deaf to what you call fulsome adulation, yet she is never displeased at being praised for beauties, either of person or mind, she is conscious, and what woman is not, of possessing.'

'You, Fairford, are a professed flatterer, and as such are no true lover to one particular woman, but a general admirer of the sex; and if you see a woman is but handsome, inquire no further, but are perfectly satisfied. Now I dive deeper, and not content with a fair outside, I seek the inner graces of the mind; and when I find one that assimilates with my own shall yield my whole heart to that one being, regardless of all others; but then if I see faults in her that stand in need of correction, I shall not hesitate kindly to tell her of them, and in doing so, I shall consider that I am giving her the strongest proof of my regard in thus treating her as a reasonable being; and if I once saw that she coveted flattery, I should say "Good bye" to her at once, for she would no longer be worthy of my love.'

'Well,' returned Fairford, 'I am convinced that, however much a woman may regard a man, or love him, if you will, and however patiently she may endeavour to bear reproof from him, and seek to alter what may be disagreeable to him, either in person or manners, she will, after a while, grow weary of being continually found fault with, and having every little error pointed out, while her numberless good qualities are looked upon as a matter of course, and for which it would be wrong in her to expect a little praise.'

'You are right,' said Edward; 'women are wise enough to prefer praise to reproof, admiration to wise counsel and sage remarks; and they like to have credit given them for virtues which they are themselves conscious of being deficient in; therefore I ever make it a rule to laud them to the skies—to pronounce them perfect, both in form and features; and above all let me know them to be ever so badly inclined, I never fail to address them as the most innocent and virtuous of their sex; and this is I firmly believe, the grand secret that has gained me so many laurels; for none, I think you will allow have ever been more successful in love than I.'

'But such success as that I would not give a pin for,' returned Mortimer, 'for any one, by adopting your plan, might be equally successful.'

'I hardly think so,' replied Edward, 'for it is not every one who has the knack of fascinating the sex. Now, for instance, what I may say to them shall be so said that they will firmly believe it comes from the sincere and overflowing love of an affectionate heart; and ladies are never displeased at possessing a lover who is so entirely devoted to them that he is fully alive to all their beauty and grace, but totally blind to all their faults.'

'By Jove! you are right, my boy,' said Fairford, slapping Edward heartily on the back, 'and I give you credit for knowing the sex well, and, what is more, for richly deserving all the laurels you have won: you must indeed have early made woman's heart your study.'

'I have studied love, and not, as Byron would have men make it,—" of their lives a thing apart." By St. George! mine, I verily believe, has approached nearer to what he says it does in women; at any rate, I have done my best to make it my " whole existence." '

'If you come to quoting poets, I shall say, with Moore, that you have roved liked the first bees of summer, thus rifling each sweet, and never loved, but the free hearts that loved again,' said Fairford, laughing.

'True, most true,' returned Edward; 'at least I have endeavoured to make the free hearts love again.'

'But suppose they were not free, what then?' said Mortimer.

'Why, then I have strove to make them so,' replied Edward.

'And a very wise proceeding,' returned Fairford, 'and worthy of more general adoption.' At which they all laughed again.

'Alas!' thought Henry, as he bent once more over his paper, 'how little I have known of Edward! To make a public boast of the wickedness and deception he has been in the constant habit of practising when it was least suspected! Poor Rose! she has indeed been exposed to more temptation than I thought for; and if she has fallen into the snare that has been purposely spread to entangle her, she will be far more an object of pity than of reproach, while such monsters as these' (and he threw a glance fraught with hatred towards Edward,) 'are constantly prowling about, using the most infernal arts and devilish machinations, that women need be made of stone to resist them. Oh! who then—knowing what, alas! I fear I only know too late —could harshly visit upon Rose the sin that more justly appertains to another? If she has fallen, her very innocence and unconsciousness of the world containing such men as these' (and he again glanced towards the spot where the three were standing) ' has been one of the chief instruments used in working her ruin. But oh!' (and he clutched the paper tightly in his grasp) ' it must—it shall bitterly recoil on the head of him who could thus villanously lead such a gentle and virtuous heart astray! Oh, God! that such deeds should ever be allowed to go unpunished!'

' At this moment they again began to talk; and Henry's reflections were interrupted by Fairford, who in reply to something Mortimer had said, and which had escaped Henry's observation, spoke as follows :—

' It is all very well, Mortimer, for you to talk, but were you to attempt to put your precepts into practise you would soon find that a woman would get tired of the company of one who was constantly acting the part of a monitor. None of ourselves care to hear of our faults; how much more unreasonable then, to expect a woman, whom we call the "weaker vessel," patiently to bear with our lectures on decorum! For my part I think a woman knows best herself what is correct in her conduct, and therefore, as a matter of course, should leave her to act as she deemed best. Flowers that grow wild ever look prettier in my estimation in an uncultivated state.'

' Our ideas are totally at variance, and never on this subject, I fear, will by any means approximate; and as we shall each keep our own opinion, in spite of all the other can say, I think it is useless for us to pursue the subject further,' said Mortimer, and then turning to Edward, added,—

' As your conquest is as yet incomplete, it would be premature to wish you joy; but her being the first as you say, to commence a correspondence, shows that you have advanced at least some few steps in her favour. And if I am any judge of hearts, I should say that hers was one that could never be taken by storm. If taken at all, it must be by a long and well sustained seige.'

' Which pleases me all the better. I am by no means enraptured with a woman that is willing on the slightest encouragement to throw herself into my arms,' said Edward.

' And yet, if I mistake not,' returned Fairford, ' your arms are ever open to receive them.'

' Yes; but then how very soon am I weary of such easy conquests!'

' You are uncommonly soon weary of all, I think,' replied Fairford, who seemed particularly disposed to laugh at everything.

' Not of Rose, sweet, charming, innocent, blushing Rose, stealing upon your senses, fresh and sweet, like the soft breath of spring. Of her, I think, I may reasonably expect to weary never, say what you will against her full round form, and the soft, carmine glow of her cheek; if I once win her, I will proudly bear her on my heart for ever.'

' Ever, is a long time,' said Fairford, laughing immoderately. ' You had better assign a shorter period, for I fully expect to see her after a while cast aside, and you, still keeping true to your butterfly character, pursuing some fresh and newer bloom; and then I perhaps, may stand a chance of filling the empty corner of poor Rose's heart.'

' Stop !' exclaimed Henry, in a voice of thunder, rising. and coming towards them at the same time; ' dare to breathe but one word more in the strain you did just now—and, by God I swear you shall bitterly repent it.'

' Repent it !' said Fairford, in a tone of unfeigned surprise, ' and who is it that will make me do so ?'

' I,' replied Henry in the same commanding voice; and then, without giving any further heed to him, he turned to Edward, who shrank abashed from his open manly look, and said,—

' The knowledge which I have gained from your conversation, that Rose is still innocent, alone prevents me inflicting that severe chastisement your villany so richly deserves.'

' You do well to speak of chastisement; it is easy enough to talk about it, but you would find yourself much mistaken if you attempted to put your threat in practice,' said Edward, with a sneer.

' I have made no threat,' returned Henry, ' I have only intimated what you might have expected, had you succeeded in your base designs; as it is, I deem it beneath me to take further notice of you—you need, therefore, fear nothing from me.'

' Fear,' said Edward, still speaking sneeringly; ' you had better take more heed what you say, or you will find to your sorrow that you have something to fear from me.'

' I fear no man,' replied Henry, evidently striving to speak calmly, ' much less you; and in your heart you know it well, though it answers your purpose just now to pretend to doubt me.'

' I have no purpose to answer,' returned Edward; ' and as regards Rose, you have no right to interfere.'

' I have the right which every honest man ought to feel, to defend the weak and helpless.'

'Rose wishes not your interference; indeed, I had thought the extreme coldness of her manner to you would have convinced you of it long ago.'

'You have played the villain in that as in every other respect: now, Edward, I will give you one caution—Rose, thank God, has so far escaped the machinations you weaved purposely for her destruction; had it been otherwise, you would not have come off so easily; as it is, you had better have a care for the future.'

'Do not think, Henry, to exasperate me into a quarrel with you; I have given Rose my solemn promise to avoid doing so by every means in my power, else depend I would not have

borne this insulting language from you so patiently; she foresaw, that if by any unfortunate circumstance you discovered the regard with which she favoured me, that you would endeavour to force me into calling you out.'

'It is a lie—a base cowardly lie!' interrupted Henry.

'Ah!' said Edward, 'you can use opprobrious epithets now I have told you that my solemn promise is pledged to Rose not to meet you, as I otherwise would, and punish your insolence at once and for ever.'

'I repeat,' replied Henry, 'it is a lie, and I am ready to prove my words to you or any one present,' and he glared fiercely round.

No. 9.

'Bold words,' returned Edward, 'but wisely kept back till you were assured that my hands, so to speak, were tied, and I was incapable of doing you an injury.'

'Again I say it is a lie,' replied Henry, 'and invented purely to shield yourself from the effects of your indignation.'

'Say on,' returned Edward, in the same cold sarcastic tone he had assumed from the commencement of the conversation; 'I have told you that you are perfectly safe from me. I hold, in spite of everything you may urge to exasperate me, my promise to Rose sacred and inviolable.'

'Safe from you!—rather say,' replied Henry, 'that you are determined to keep yourself safe from me. You fear me, and you know it; but, though you escape now, a day of reckoning will come, till when I put this down to your account; and, rest assured, when the time arrives for settling our differences, I will not forget to pay you in full of all demands. And remember that my eye is ever on you, and perhaps, when you least expect it, I shall require a reckoning at your hands. Well, indeed, is it for you that your base designs have fallen harmless to the ground, instead of ensnaring the young and innocent victim they were intended to desecrate to your vile passions.'

'I see very plainly how it is,' said Edward, leaning in a careless and easy attitude against the wall. 'You are annoyed at the preference Rose shows for me, and I can therefore pardon the violence of your language. You see I have not forgotten the warmth of your admiration, so loudly expressed immediately after your first interview with her.'

'Neither have I forgotten it,' returned Henry, endeavouring to calm his passion, 'nor the fear you manifested, or at least pretended, that I should in any way be induced to offer her any insult. You might well fear for me, when you were, at the moment, entertaining such base wishes, nourished so long, that they have at length assumed the appearance of hope.'

'Be it so,' replied Edward. 'You would be glad could you nourish the hope concerning Rose that I am proud to acknowledge I do and will entertain.'

'This to me?' said Henry.

'Yes, to you, or any man.'

'Then, mark my words, you do not entertain them long. Rose's eyes shall be opened, as mine have been, to your real character.'

Edward laughed scornfully.

'Rose will pay very slight attention to anything you may say, therefore make yourself quite easy on that score.'

'I intend to do so; yet, no stone will I leave unturned that may aid me in persuading Rose to look upon you with the detestation that I myself feel; I, who called you friend—who ever treated you as one—who believed you open, honourable, and upright. I am no longer surprised that you have so well succeeded in imposing on the credulity of a woman, when you could thus for years so completely deceive one of your own sex. And you pretend to love Rose?—a strange way of showing it, to coolly hear, nay more, to encourage, the bandying her name from mouth to mouth—to listen while others make her the subject of coarse jests, and even to participate in the mirth excited by turning her grace and beauty into ridicule.'

'Mr. Melville,' said Mortimer, 'you have made me completely ashamed of myself. I acknowledge we have all acted exceedingly wrong in speaking of Mrs. Moreland in the manner you appear to have overheard, and can only say for myself, that I, at least, am heartily sorry for the share I took in the conversation, and am willing to make any apology you may think necessary.'

'It is enough,' replied Henry. 'You, Mr. Mortimer, are the least to blame, and I accept your acknowledgment that you were in error, which is all the apology I would desire you to make to me; but for the future, be careful how you speak of a woman; although you have no sister, you have a——'

'Mother,' interrupted Mortimer, 'whom I dearly love and respect.'

'Then for her sake think charitably, and speak, at least, respectfully of all.'

'I will,' returned Mortimer, apparently affected by the other's earnestness. 'Fairford, you also, I am certain, will tender your apology to Mr. Melville.'

'Not I,' said Fairford, carelessly, 'or at least till he can prove he is the husband or brother of Mrs. Moreland; then, indeed, I might think it necessary to offer some little excuse, but, as it is, I conceive he has no right to expect me to humble myself, merely for speaking a few words in praise of one of the finest women I know.'

'No great crime, surely,' said Edward; 'even were she my wife, I could not expect such glowing beauty as she possesses to remain unadmired by others.'

'I wish to hold no communion with you,' said Henry, with marked emphasis on the personal pronoun, and turning contemptuously away.'

'I would punish your insolence,' said Edward, "if——

'You dared,' added Henry.

'What is it you say?' replied Edward, at length roused to something like indignation; 'you will have to answer for this yet; when I tell Rose all that has passed, she will, I feel certain, release me from the promise which now forces me to bear patiently with your insult.'

'You will find me not only ready but willing to respond to your call, if, indeed, it were possible you could ever have the courage to make one. In the meantime, be very guarded in your actions, for let me even have cause to suspect you of any further villany, and, by God! I swear you shall repent it to your latest day, if even you escape with your life, which I will do my best to prevent. Mortimer,' he continued, turning towards him, 'when that day comes, as come it will, I am perfectly convinced I may look to you as a friend who will stand by me and see justice done between us.'

Mortimer extended his hand, which Henry cordially grasped, as he said—

'You may, Mr. Melville, depend upon me.'

'I thank you,' returned Henry, 'and shall one day unhesitatingly apply to you; it may be speedily or otherwise, I am not at present prepared to say, but your services will be required by me.'

'And when they are so, you will find them at your command.'

Edward smiled, as he said—

'Well, Fairford, as the preliminaries are all being settled on the other side, I may as well engage you to officiate for me; though, as I said before, until Rose absolves me from my promise, nothing shall induce me to meet Mr. Melville.'

'All this puts me in mind of the old play "Much Ado about Nothing," replied Fairford, laughing; 'is not a man at liberty to admire a pretty woman, and gain her if he can, without submitting to the insult and interference of one who bears no manner of relationship towards her?'

'It seems not,' said Edward, sarcastically.

"Why, hang it, then! if I would for an instant put up with such interference; it is asking too much of a fellow to bear with such confounded impudence.'

'Treat it with the contempt it so well merits,' said Edward, changing his position to one of greater ease.

'Punish it with the chastisement it deserves, would be more to my way of thinking; said Fairford, 'and as you say it is impossible for you to do so under the present circumstances, delegate the task to me—let me be your proxy, and see if I do not teach them a lesson not quickly to be forgotten.'

'Take it coolly,' returned Edward, 'for a little while, and then I will take the reins in my own hand, for to none will I delegate the task that most properly belongs to myself.'

"Well, I suppose it must be as you desire; but if Mr. Melville is not satisfied to wait, I can only say I am willing to meet him on my own account, and the sooner the better. I am of too fiery a temperament to be fond of any dilatory proceedings.'

'So am I, in a general way,' replied Henry, who saw at least something to admire in the hot blood and courageous bearing of Fairford, opposed to the cold, scheming villany of Edward, 'but this time I am not only willing, but anxious, to wait till such time as Mr. Trevors will have his arms at liberty. I could force him on to give me satisfaction almost at the present moment, but I scorn to take advantage even of one I despise; and being bound by a promise, he would scarcely like to act otherwise than merely on the defensive, and so, as I said before, I will let my anger rest, not fearing for an instant that it will cool.'

Henry spoke these words with considerable bitterness, and in a tone of sarcasm he rarely assumed; but his provocation was great, and he felt more exasperated than he would have wished to be known, by Edward's cold contempt, and, without a single word more, he bowed to Mortimer and left the house. The thoughts that filled his breast, as he walked towards home, were mingled ones of joy and sorrow. Rose was still in a great measure innocent, for had not Mortimer observed to Edward that his conquest was still incomplete? Doubtless she had been so far led away as to entertain feelings of regard towards him, but she was not without the pale of hope; no, she might yet be snatched from the brink of destruction on which she was hovering, wholly unconscious of the danger that momentarily assailed her: it was this thought that shed a brightness over the otherwise dreary sadness of his heart—a sadness that sprang from the purest feelings of his nature, to think that the man he had so fondly cherished as his best and dearest friend, should have proved so totally unworthy of the affectionate regard that had been lavished on him, not by himself alone, but by his mother and sister. Thank God, he had done them no injury; but oh! for the future how cautious it would make him—how carefully he would scan his merits ere he introduced another to those dear friends. If Lucy had fallen a prey to his vile passions—if even, dazzled by his showy exterior and prepossessing manners, she had become his wife—the wife of one he could now only look upon with horror and detestation—oh! what anguish would have been his portion, to think that he was the means of her having become acquainted with such a character! God be praised! that misery at east was spared him, and it would have the effect of inducing him to watch more closely, and guard more vigilantly, the happiness of his sister: and when he reached home, and she flew with flushed cheeks and anxious face to welcome him, he unreservedly communicated to her all that had passed at the club. With clasped hands and tearful eyes she entreated him, as Rose had as yet escaped Edward's schemes, and was still innocent, to let him go unscathed from his displeasure; with kind and tender words he soothed her anxiety, and though by no means promising asquiescence in her desires, he put off the day of retribution he intended seeking with Edward to so indefinite a time, that she was all but satisfied with what she deemed would be the result.

We think that it is high time we return to Rose, whom we last left in the enjoyment of peaceful slumbers, and concerning whom so many hopes and fears were entertained, both by friends and foes. In the mean time poor Rose, happily unconscious of all, was innocently enjoying herself to her heart's content. Blessed in the society of those she loved, and who dearly loved and prized her in return, she rightly judged herself blest, and the only thought that ever cost her a pang was connected with Albert; but then she was storing her mind with useful lessons for the future, culled from the tender counsel and wise advice of a truly affectionate mother; therefore secretly nourishing the purest hopes for coming days, and with which were entwined sweet thoughts of her unborn babe, Rose gave herself up to the enjoyments of the present, without entertaining a fear for the future. Preparations were already far advanced towards the solemnization of the nuptials of her brother, and in witnessing his happiness, and the modest blushing joy that illuminated the pretty features of Agnes, Rose found a source of unmixed delight.

'May you be happy!' were words often and earnestly repeated, as she watched and assisted Agnes in preparing for the forthcoming event.

'I do not doubt it, dear Rose, neither should you,' replied Agnes, in a tone of slight reproach, 'I have given my consent to be united to your brother from no mercenary or unhallowed motive, but for the plain simple fact that I love him, and firmly believe that he loves me.'

'I know it, Agnes, and do not, I entreat you, feel hurt at my remark—but oh! sometimes love alone does not render wives and husbands happy.'

'Most certainly not; for unless the love is built upon a sure foundation, such as excellent qualities, and above all, a similarity of taste and feeling, it will undoubtedly, ere long, wear itself out.'

'I think you are right, Agnes; and as you love Henry, not for himself alone, but for the excellence of his character, and feeling an interest in all that concerns him, you may not unreasonably hope for happiness.'

'A love,' said Agnes seriously, 'such as I feel for Henry, would make me blessed in the lowliest cot; and to share his sorrows and anxieties would be to me far sweeter than to participate in every joy and happiness of another.'

'I doubt it not, dear Agnes, nor that Henry so loves you, and can only breathe the prayer I do so much wish to be realised—may you be happy!'

'Marriage is, indeed, a solemn thing,' continued Agnes, in the same serious tone, 'and should not be lightly entered into.'

'Indeed not,' said Rose; 'for oh! what a dreadful thing, after vowing at the altar to love one, and one only, till death breaks the bond, to have the affections estranged from that one being, and perchance (for such things have occurred) to meet with another we feel assimilated more to ourselves, and, doing so, our hearts involuntarily acknowledge that we give them the preference.'

'That would indeed be sad,' replied Agnes; 'but I trust, dear Rose, neither you nor I stand in danger of such a direful calamity.'

'Oh dear, no!' returned Rose—'for our best and purest affections are lavished on the one who has a right to claim them to the utter exclusion of all others, and loving once, we must love for ever.'

'Yes, even if it were possible in after years for that one to become unworthy of regard.'

It would make no alteration either in our affection or duty, having solemnly promised (without any stipulation) to love, honour, and obey them. We must continue to do so, no matter what their conduct may be; it can form no manner of excuse for an alteration in ours.'

'How exactly we think alike, dear Rose, your ideas completely coincide with mine; but then we have both learnt from the same kind teacher: having no mother of my own, yours has ever been ready to aid me both with counsel and encouragement, and knowing how highly she most justly stands in Henry's estimation, it will be my constant endeavour to mould my conduct and feelings from so excellent a pattern, and then I think I shall not fail to give satisfaction to the one I most desire to please.'

Thus did these two young girls converse, and open their hearts freely to each other; and it will be seen by the foregoing conversation that Rose nourished not in her innocent and virtuous breast even one thought or desire that it was wrong to cherish there; every hope and wish was centered in her husband, and to please whom alone—she was now at a distance from him—her own heart would have flown eagerly to soothe and share his solitude; but he wished and willed it otherwise. Misanthrophical feelings had taken entire possession of his breast, and he preferred to be alone.

The day was fixed for the wedding, for Rose was anxious to witness it, and return to Albert. All were looking forward to the event with joy, for Agnes was a favourite with the entire household, and the young farmers of the neighbourhood envied Henry the happiness of gaining such a girl as Agnes. Yet they liked and admired his frank and noble disposition so much, that while they envied his good fortune, they at the same time declared him worthy of it; and no unkind feeling mingled with the envy which they unhesitatingly confessed dwelt in their hearts.

'Your correspondents are rather numerous, Rose,' said Mrs. Sommerville, one morning as she entered the breakfast-parlour, where Rose was conversing with her brothers.

'A letter for me, dear mother! pray give it to me, it is doubtless from Albert.'

'Not one, Rose, but three,' returned Mrs. Sommerville, exhibiting them.

'Three for me, dear mother!' replied Rose; 'it must be a mistake.. I know of no one who could write to me with the exception of Albert.'

'It is, nevertheless, the case,' said Mrs. Sommerville; 'and one, I think, is from Mrs. Trevors—it is evidently a lady's writing.'

'Oh! I forgot,' returned Rose; 'she may have written.'

'I should think it most likely: you remember, Rose, you wrote to her the day after you came down, and it would be only common politeness to return a reply.'

The colour deepened on the cheek of Rose, while she endeavoured to hide her confusion by bending over the letters her mother placed in her hand; and making some slight excuse, she hurried to her own little room.

Who does not desire to read a letter from one they love best on earth entirely alone, where no prying eye can mark the inward workings of the mind? Be it the extravagance of joy or the soul-sickening effects of sorrow, we like to indulge in it alone. This was the feeling that prompted Rose to seek retirement before she broke the seal of what she deemed a letter from Albert; and filled with sweet expectation, with a tremulous hand she tore open the envelope and commenced reading. Alas! what could it be that so quickly drove the blood from her cheek ere she had perused many lines, and then sent it rushing again tumultuously to her very temples? Still she paused not, but went on reading, line after line, till she came to the close. It was a long letter, and evidently designed purposely to rouse her indignation against some person whom the writer expected would also address her by letter: for, when she had finished her perusal, she quietly laid it aside, and turned to one evidently written by a female hand, which she opened with a listless air, as if already apprised of its contents, and read it with a still flushed cheek; and at length, bursting into tears, she hastily crumpled it in her hand, as if desirous of crushing with it the emotion it had caused, and then, striving to check the tears, she exclaimed, half aloud—

'I am very, very unfortunate! I thought, at least, Lucy Melville was a friend to me; and' had I not such convincing proof to the contrary, would have deemed her far above the mean curiosity of wishing to pry into a secret, that even I felt I was acting wrong in desiring to become acquainted with, and sent the letter back to Edward unopened; consequently, it was folly in her to suppose that I would give my consent for Edward to exhibit it to her; however, I can but thank him for the part he has acted. I feel that I have at least one true friend, and on this advice I may. ever depend, and, to show him that I feel it, I will write just such a letter to Lucy as he has in sincere friendship expressed a desire for me to do I am determined for the future to follow his advice, for how much more he knows of the world than I! Had it not been for his letter, how innocent I should have been of Lucy's real desire in writing to me! I should unconsciously have taken it all in good part, and been drawn into a web, from which it would not have been so easy to extricate myself; but this letter is a complete explanation of her's, and it is indeed kind of him to take the trouble of writing, and putting it in a proper light to me; very few would have taken sufficient interest in my affairs to have been at all the trouble he has. Well, if some whom I was short-sighted enough to consider my real friends, have proved the reverse, one whom I looked on with cold distrust has acted towards me nobly, generously: it all proves, what I am more and more convinced of, how very unfit I am to combat with the world, —it is not my element; how gladly I would, could it be, remain for ever at a distance from its noisy strife; but no, for Albert's sake I must again mix in it; but I will endeavour to be but a spectator, and not an actor in the scenes I shall be obliged to mingle in.

As these thoughts passed through her mind, she sat at her little dressing-table, with her head resting on her hand, when her eye suddenly caught sight of the third letter her mother had given her, and which the engrossing interest of the others had caused her to overlook: she gazed on it for a second with a listless aspect, but, as she became acquainted with the hand-writing, her look changed into one of intense joy—it was from Albert. Oh yes! she knew his writing too well to be deceived, and she had allowed that to remain unheeded while she was reading, thinking on, and even weeping over the others; and now that she was certain she held one from him in her hands, the other two seemed to sink into a mere nothingness: what mattered it if persons, almost strangers, certainly unconnected to her by any tie, chose (to answer some bad purpose of their own) to pretend to think ill of her, even to declare she was calumniated. Oh, nothing, nothing! if he she so dearly loved and treasured still thought of her with kindness, still knew her heart to be pure and unsophisticated, as in truth it was. He had not forgotten her, amid the studies that so intruded on his time, as to swallow up almost every moment; she had hoped, earnestly hoped, he would write, and yet she had hardly dared to expect it, and thus she had judged wrongly of him, for now she held in her hand a letter from him, how fondly she pressed it to her lips, even covered it with kisses, till she smiled at her own folly in thus delaying to open it, and resolved to do so at once, to turn every hope into sweet certainty to read, perhaps, that he was desirous again to have her with him, and beg her to hasten her return home. While thus thinking, she broke the seal and commenced reading : the letter was short, being as follows :—

'MY DEAR ROSE,—I was much pleased to hear that your health and spirits were improved, as you seemed sadly to lack both when I last saw you. I hope a further continuance from town may be the means of procuring you a complete restoration, to which end I think it would be advisable for you to remain where you are for at least some weeks longer ; but, however, I am only desirous of rendering you happy, therefore consult your own feelings, without any reference to me. In the country, I am well aware, you meet with kindred spirits, who do their best to amuse and enliven you ; whereas in town, I know I am but a very poor companion ; and, if I understood you rightly, you have wearied of the gaieties that I thought would have been the means of preventing you feeling the want of a more lively companion, and Marian assures me that you have lately rather avoided her than otherwise, or else I could have hoped that she might occasionally have dispelled the *ennui* under which it sadly grieved me to observe you were labouring. Do not think, my dear girl, I mean for an instant to chide you, such being very far from my intention ; I am only anxious for your welfare ; could I feel assured of your happiness, it would tend greatly towards my own. Give my kindest regards to your parents and brothers, and wish Henry joy : I hope you will spend a right merry day at the wedding. And, now, my dear Rose, farewell! Your affectionate husband,

'ALBERT MORELAND.'

Rose scarcely knew how it was; but, after perusing this letter, and endeavouring to put a tender construction on every word, she felt dissatisfied with the contents, and yet she knew not what to complain of, unless it were separating himself so entirely from her ; she would rather, much rather, he would have spoken less of her and more of himself; he meant to be kind, she was certain, and thought more, even than she desired, of her happiness; but he had said not one word of his own health or spirits—had expressed no desire to see her again—he wished her to be happy—but it was to be a happiness totally unconnected with him, with which, in fact, he was to have nothing whatever to do.

'He knows not my heart,' exclaimed Rose, inwardly, 'and, indeed, I sometimes fear he never will; he looks upon me wholly as a spoilt child, and deems I shall be pleased at being thus allowed to study my own will and pleasure without reference to him ; but, alas! it is far, very far otherwise ;—how sweet, how blessed it would be to resign my own gratification in obedience to his wishes! to show him, by my ready acquiescence to his lightest desire, how dearly I loved and treasured in my heart each little thought of him! Oh! had he been poor, instead of rich, in becoming his wife, he could not have suspected me, as I now sometimes fear he does, of being actuated by mercenary feelings, and then, indeed, being his equal in station and birth, I could have freely offered him those little endearing attentions that make poverty so pleasant when shared with those we love, and which the rich can never know ; they are too much hemmed in my forms and ceremonies, which forbid a wife performing those duties which are so sweet, and which bind the ties of relationship more close and firm ;—but no! a menial must attend to the rich man's comforts, and supply his every want, while the wife sits idly by, and when, as in my case, of inferior birth and breeding, almost afraid to speak before the servants lest she betray her want of acquaintance with those things the rich consider a mark of extreme ignorance not to understand. Poor Rose had indeed paid dear for the luxuries Albert had profusely scattered round her—dear, if they had even brought with them a something like commensurate amount of happiness; but when, instead of that being the case, they wearied her, and kept back the sweet ebullition of spirits that had previously made her beloved by others, and blest within herself, the reader may judge that her's was indeed a sad exchange, and only made endurable by the tender love she cherished for Albert—a love that, had it been returned with equal warmth, would have caused her willingly to brave all things else, to trample on her pride, and endeavour to re-mould her entire character, till she has become what he most desired her to be. As it was, she resolved to return to him, as soon as she had witnessed her brother's nuptials, and, keeping aloof from all scenes of gaiety, strive to convince Albert that all she wanted to make her happy was his love and affection. Blest with that, she cared for nought beside, therefore, placing his letter in her bosom, and destroying the other two, she descended to the parlour. A sadness she could not wholly conceal sat upon her fair countenance, and was immediately perceived by her anxious mother.

'I trust, my love, you have heard no bad news; Albert, I hope——'

'Is quite well, my dear mother; at least,' replied Rose, recollecting herself, 'he does not say a word to the contrary.''

'Then, of course, you draw an inference and conclude that he is,' said her mother, smiling.

'Yes,' returned Rose, rather confused and avoiding Mrs. Sommerville's earnest look.

'He desires his kind regards to you all, and wishes Henry joy.'

'Very kind of him, my love; and I suppose he is anxious to have you back again, and though desirous of complying with his wishes, you are still sorry to leave us.'

'No, he would rather prefer my remaining here some time longer, on account of my health, but still at the same time he begs me to consult my own wishes.'

Mrs. Sommerville, although born and educated entirely in the country, without having ever strayed from her native place, was nevertheless a very shrewd woman, and none were quicker in reading that mystic volume, the human heart; few characters were ever inscribed there that she failed to unravel, and in the end entirely understand. A few questions adroitly put, and in such a manner that none ever suspected her motives, and she knew almost as well as the possessor what thoughts and feelings had found a resting-place in their hearts. Thus, she said no more to Rose; but she knew as well as if her daughter had intentionally imparted to her, that the letter she had received from Albert was unsatisfactory, and though seeming what some women would perhaps have deemed exceeding kind in allowing her entirely to consult her own pleasure, yet, as a proof of love, a sensitive mind like Rose's would have been far more delighted by his expressing a desire for her return, though, at the same time, she was willing to believe that Albert meant it, in all kindness and affection; at all events, as she had derived her knowledge from the ingenuity and facility she had acquired in marking the expression of Rose's countenance, and drawing from that conclusions she had never failed in finding correct, she deemed it best to offer no comment, and turned, therefore, to the second letter.

'Mrs. Trevors, I hope, Rose, is in the enjoyment of that richest blessing, health?'

'Yes, I believe her, dear mother, to be perfectly well.'

'Why, your correspondents, Rose, do not seem much given to egotism,' replied Mrs. Sommerville; 'did Marian say how Mr. Trevors was?'

Poor Rose was conscious of looking very foolish and confused, and for the nonce would have been glad to be anywhere but on the chair she now occupied, directly facing her mother; but there was nothing for it, but to answer, with as little show of agitation as posible; and she replied—

'Mr. Trevors. Oh! yes, he is in excellent health.'

Mrs. Sommerville laughed.

'Marian, it seems, Rose, resembles you, and thinks more of her husband than herself.'

Rose's confusion increased tenfold, so much so, that she could not trust herself to reply, and inwardly hoped her mother would allow the subject of her letters to drop, although she could not herself introduce another topic, though assuredly most desirous of changing the conversation to some more trivial subject. Mrs. Sommerville marked her confusion, and for the first time in her life entertained a fear for her daughter's moral conduct, and it cost her the severest pang it had ever been her lot to feel. Oh! could it be possible that Rose, hitherto all innocence, had, amid the gaieties and wickedness of London, been unhappily led into sin. Alas! it is indeed the severest torture we can ever know, to tremble for the virtue of one we love. Mrs. Sommerville had arrived at an age that seldom retains much of the bloom of youth, but what time had left her; the anguish of the moment when the first doubt of her only daughter, who had been educated in the strictest virtuous principles, crossed her mind, was quickly chased away, and she sat confronting her, without the slightest vestige of colour.

'My dear mother,' said Rose, recovering from her own confusion at sight of the agitation of her parent. 'You are ill, what can I do for you?'

'Do not alarm yourself, my child,' said Mrs. Sommerville, endeavouring to calm the violence of her emotion, 'it was but an involuntary spasm, and is now gone.'

"But, dear mother,' urged Rose, 'I never saw you thus before, and it has made me very uneasy.'

'There is no occasion for uneasiness, my love, for I assure you that I am perfectly recovered,' replied Mrs. Sommerville.

'Well, then, dear mother, I will endeavour to dismiss my fear."

They then conversed on different topics for some time. After dinner Rose excused herself to her mother, and again sought the privacy of her own room, to reply to the letters she had received; and first, she drew from her bosom Albert's letter, and perused it again, determined, though unsolicited, to write an answer. She could not, even on this second reading, think it otherwise than cold; but then she argued with herself. 'He does not intend it to be; on the contrary, he deems he is studying my happiness in preference to his own, therefore it is my duty to write to him kindly and affectionately;' which she accordingly did, stating the day which was fixed for her brother's wedding, and naming the third day afterwards as the one on which he might look for her return; her health, she assured him, being fully re-established, she would much prefer returning to him, to remaining longer from home; this done, she wrote also to Lucy, which letter the reader is already acquainted with, therefore any remark upon it is needless, as, connecting that with the letter Rose received from Edward, it is easy enough to draw a conclusion. The third letter Rose appeared to think required no answer; for laying aside her pen, she took those she had written in her hand, and left the room. Her mother's eye watched her closely as she gave them to the servant, and failed not to observe that there were but two; consequently one of the letters she had given to her daughter in the morning must still remain unanswered. Mrs. Sommerville felt anxious, and would have been glad could she have known who it was who had written to her daughter. One letter Rose had acknowledged came from Albert, and one of the others she was certain was written by Marian Trevors, or some other female acquaintance; but the third, she was equally sure, came from a gentleman, and to which letter Rose had made no allusion whatever. She could not, on such slight suspicion, think ill of her daughter Rose, who, up to the time of her marriage, was universally admired for her modest manners, and which, even now, after mixing for a season amid the fashionable follies and gaieties of London, had by no means worn off; on the contrary, it had only given place to a pretty becoming matronly air, that suited well her charming features. But, alas! she had heard so much of the dangers to which the young are exposed in the bustle and strife of London, of such terrible temptations that were spread to ensnare young and innocent females, that she began to tremble for Rose. Hitherto she had safely rested, not alone on the virtue of her child, but in the guardian care and protection of Albert; but now it seemed, from what she had gathered in her conversations with Rose, that he delegated the task that so properly and exclusively belonged to him, of watching narrowly the steps of his wife and keeping all temptation from her, to another; and that other a gay and volatile female, unfitted, from her very position in life, to have the guardianship and care of so tender a charge. And here, alas! we are obliged to remark, that many, very many virtuous women have fallen low, both to their own and their husband's dishonour, through being most unnecessarily exposed to temptations, that they need be almost more than human to be capable of resisting. For example, a man of moderate ability and personal attractions marries a woman, who, in addition to the most fascinating manners, and a pretty face and figure, possesses rare and uncommon talents in literature, which makes her company eagerly sought for, and universally delighted in. Such a man as we have described, naturally feels very proud at having gained such a woman; and, to gratify his vanity, (innocent enough in itself,) he introduces her to men, whose minds and pursuits assimilate more closely with hers than his own, and consequently she feels pleasure in their company, which she expresses to her husband, and, instead of a kind word of caution, or a gentle withdrawal of her from society that may become dangerous, he encourages her in it, with the boast—

'I am not jealous—I love to see you admired—nothing affords me so much gratification. I am well aware that my disposition is in many respects at variance with yours, and cannot be so selfish as to desire to exclude you from society that you feel a pleasure in—enjoy it by all means —I know I can trust you, I have not the slightest fear of your betraying me.'

Did we not know the very words we have quoted to have been used by men when addressing their wives on this subject—wives, too, whose very beauty and talents rendered them attractive, and sought for in no common degree—we say, did we not know of ourselves such to be the case, we could scarcely have thought it possible that men would thus wilfully, as it were, place their wives on the very brink of destruction; especially when they know, as they must, how ready men are to take advantage of a woman. A moment's betrayal into an undue familiarity, misconstructs (perhaps purposely) into more than was really meant. Sometimes even a tender look, and all is lost. It is, indeed, worse than folly to expect a woman so cautiously to guard her looks and words, as never, at any time whatever, through being on terms of intimacy with men, whose company she acknowledges is pleasing to her, to give them the lightest opportunity, which, doubtless, they are constantly on the watch for, eagerly to improve it to their own advantage, and the ruin of her. It was utterly impossible for a woman (as some husbands appear to expect) to say to herself, so far will I go and no farther. She may entreat; she may think to do so; but while men are ever seeking to win women, by any means, honourable, or dishonourable, no matter so the end is gained, we repeat it as a downright impossibility. And men who know their own sex better than a woman can, especially if (as is not unfrequently the case) she has been, up to the time of her marriage, rather excluded from their society, should carefully protect her from temptation, and not thus thrust her into it, but if they will be wilfully blind to the consequences, let them not, after the mischief is done,

blame aught but their own want of caution. No one can pity such a man for having his wife's affections seduced from him; any one who knows the world would only say, 'It serves him right! Suppose a man to be possessed of some rare treasure which he knows to be coveted by others, and feels assured they will not hesitate to deprive him of it on the first opportunity that may offer, that, in fact, they are watching for that opportunity. What would any unconcerned spectator say if he carelessly laid it about; and at length, actually threw it in their way? They would, of course, smile at his folly, and think that he desired to lose it; and, if afterwards, when it was irretrievably gone, he made bitter complaints and accusations against the parties who had possessed themselves of it, would not everybody laugh at his absurdity in not taking

No. 10;

proper care of it while it was his own property?—of course, there cannot be a doubt of it. How much more, then, does it behove a man to guard the best and dearest of all treasures, his wife—the one that makes home so sweet and pleasant—whose cheering smile is his sure reward, and sweet incentive to renewed exertion—who lavishes on him all the warm outpourings of an affectionate heart, one whom he had honourably won, and whom he should proudly wear in his bosom, throwing around her, by his constant and endearing attentions, and wise counsels, a shield, from which all temptations will harmlessly rebound, having no power to penetrate the inward recesses of the heart. Some may perchance deem these remarks totally uncalled for; but, we doubt not, there are others, who know, by sad experience, that wives are often left entirely unguarded by those whose duty it is, and pleasure it should be, to watch over them.

Mrs. Sommerville felt, as indeed she had from their first acquaintance, that Albert was not at all the man she would have chosen for the husband of Rose, and now that she began to fear for her innocence, she also began to blame herself for having so readily given her consent to their union; yet it was excess of kindness towards Rose alone that had prevented her offering any objection. But oh! if it should prove to have been mistaken kindness; for rather, a thousand times rather than see her she had so tenderly watched over in infancy, and exulted proudly in her ripe years, as a perfect pattern of excellence and purity, seduced from her high estate, would she have laid her in the quiet churchyard while yet she were innocent.

'You have written to Albert, my love,' said Mrs. Sommerville, inquiringly.

'Yes; and named the day for my departure from here,' returned Rose, 'for, though grieving much to leave you, dear mother, I am most anxious to return to Albert. It is, you know, the first time we have been separated, and it is therefore natural I should wish to see him again.'

'But does he not, my love, also desire to see you. I thought I understood you to the contrary.'

'He only mentions his wish for me to prolong my stay, out of a desire for the restoration of my health, which, you knew, dear mother, was really out of order on my arrival.'

'It was, my love, but then your situation might in a great measure account for it.'

'Not altogether, dear mother,' returned Rose, 'for how much improved I am now, both in health and spirits.'

'True, my love, you certainly looked very poorly when you first came amongst us,' said Mrs. Sommerville, musingly; 'and I am delighted to observe, as you say, such an improvement, especially in so short a time; indeed, it is almost more than we could expect.'

'And what is better,' added Rose, 'I do not fear a relapse.'

'You will forgive me, Rose,' returned her mother, anxiously, 'for what I am about to say; it arises, I am sure you will believe, wholly, from a desire to see you happy.'

'Dear, dear mother,' interrupted Rose, 'you know how happy I have ever been, and I may truly say I still am, to receive instruction, counsel, or reproof from you—therefore, I entreat of you to say on, and do not, oh! do not, think it for a moment necessary to offer any apology to me. I feel troubled at the bare idea of such a thing; a child should be always thankful to attend to what a parent may suggest.'

'Still, my own dear girl,' replied Mrs. Sommerville, folding Rose to her bosom, 'I feared, I must confess, that having passed to another's care, you would no longer be so eager to receive my counsel, especially as it would bear upon a subject that may, perhaps, be painful to you.'

'Fear it no longer, dear mother; although married, I am no less your child, and possessing a husband does not cause me to forget I have a mother.'

'I see, dear Rose, that I should have known you better, and will at once proceed to open my mind to you. You love Albert as dearly and fondly as when you were first united?'

'I do, indeed,' returned Rose, with an air of surprise. 'What could induce you, dear mother, for a moment apparently to doubt it?'

'I scarcely did,' replied Mrs. Sommerville, 'and yet——'

'What!' said Rose, 'I entreat you tell me all that has transpired to throw even a shadow of a doubt upon the subject of my love for Albert?'

'It was not, Rose, that I so much doubted your love for him, as I feared it might become estranged. Do you think, my child, that he still entertains the same affection for you?'

'I can most unhesitatingly answer, yes,' replied Rose; 'but I will not conceal from you that I have, since our marriage, discovered that Albert is unhappy.'

'And have you no clue to the cause of his unhappiness?'

'I have, dear mother, but it is a subject on which I am not at liberty to disclose aught that I know, even to you.'

'Such being the case, Rose, I would not ask it of you; but what he has confided in you, you should do your best to remove, or if that is impossible, at all events to make him forget his uneasiness.'

'Pardon me, dear mother, I did not say he had confided in me; in truth, indeed, he has done no such thing.'

'Did I then, Rose, misunderstand you in saying you were in possession of a clue to the secret cause of Albert's grief, or am I to infer that you have gained your knowledge of it from others ?'

'I am perfectly ashamed of myself, and yet will not seek to hide from you that such is the case; I now feel it to have been wholly unjustifiable on my part, but must own that I not only gained the clue to my husband's unhappiness, but have actually sought it from others, and when I obtained the knowledge I so eagerly desired——'

'It had only the effect of plunging you into sorrow,' said Mrs. Sommerville; and depend, my child, that this will ever be the case with any secret that is gained in any unworthy manner; think not, dear Rose, that I am angry with you,' she continued kindly, as Rose hung her head at her mother's reproof; 'although you have acted wrong, at the same time I consider it was very excusable; it was certainly but natural that, seeing your husband unhappy, you should desire to know the cause, and not being able to obtain it from him, you innocently applied to others. Had you seriously thought on the subject for a short time, you would doubtless have acted differently.'

'I should indeed, dear mother, and in proof of it, allow me to tell you, that I had an opportunity of pushing my inquiries much farther, but recollected myself in time to decline doing so at the very moment when the secret (for there is a secret connected with Albert's grief) seemed about to be unravelled to me.'

'Did you indeed, dear Rose? Then I am sure I need not tell you that I highly applaud your conduct. Rest assured, Rose, that it is not only wrong, but foolish towards themselves for wives to seek an acquaintance with things that their husbands manifest a desire to keep from their knowledge; but this is foreign to what I was about to observe at the commencement of our conversation. You received, Rose, three letters this morning, and when I conversed with you about their contents, I observed an agitation, not to say a confusion, in your countenance and manners, that (you must not feel hurt, Rose, at my remark) created a fear in my mind I had never previously entertained towards you.'

'Dispel it instantly, dear mother,' said Rose, the rich blood suffusing much her face with crimson; 'I am willing, anxious to explain to you everything concerning them : one,' she added, trembling with eagerness to banish all doubt from her mother's mind, 'was, as I told you, from Albert, another from a young lady I was introduced to by Marian Trevors while in London.'

'And the third?' said Mrs. Sommerville.

'Was from Mr. Trevors,' replied Rose, with a slight blush, 'and was in reference to the very secret concerning Albert that I have already told you I am not at liberty to explain.'

'Rose,' said Mrs. Sommerville, seriously, 'it was that letter which awakened fears in my mind that I, for a moment, supposed it possible you could be easily led astray, but connecting your husband's apparent carelessness of you with your receiving a letter from another, about which there hung some little mystery, I was puzzled to account for it otherwise than by fearing (I feel certain now unjustly) that he might be endeavouring to wean your affections from Albert.'

'You are indeed mistaken; Edward is devoted to Marian, and would, I have reason to know, be the first to shield me from the attacks of others.'

'You greatly relieve the anxiety I was labouring under, dear Rose, and will, I am sure, make every allowance for the fears of your mother; till lately you have never been exposed to temptation, and though I know you to be amiable, virtuous, and good, yet, when I saw you receiving letters from one of the opposite sex, about which you observed an air of concealment and mystery, I must confess I began to tremble for my child; especially when I connected it with the want of attention from your husband, and in a great measure your exclusion from his company.'

'Oh! dear mother, do not ever entertain such fears again even for a moment; Albert is my first and only love, and never, never can I by any possibility be brought to regard him with less affection than I now feel, which, indeed, is as fondly devoted to him as on the first day he called me wife.'

'You make me very happy, my love, by this assurance; it is a great source of pleasure to have our affections fixed on the object who has a right to claim them, and I feel, my Rose, as if I had wronged you in harbouring a suspicious feeling of you even for an instant; yet one word more, my child, before we dismiss this subject from our conversation, I hope, and fully believe, for ever; it is this—never allow anything to induce you to make a confidant of your secret thoughts and feelings to any one but your husband; if you find a difficulty in imparting all to him, you had far better allow them to remain concealed in your own bosom, than unburden your heart to others.'

'Thank you, dear mother,' returned Rose, 'this visit to you will be of unspeakable benefit to me, and I shall ever reflect upon it with satisfaction; and when I return to town how improved shall I be, not alone in health—that will be but a secondary consideration—but I feel that I shall be enabled to study more the happiness of my husband, and by constant and unwearying exertions I may at length become the means of securing it, and oh! then what pure, unmingled joy will be mine.'

As she spoke these words, she raised her eyes, beaming with the ardour of her mind, to her mother's face. Mrs. Sommerville gazed upon her with the rapture a parent alone can feel, and as she looked full into her lovely countenance, now lighted up with the smile of hope and radiant with joy, the expression was so full of innocence that it gave her the appearance of almost infantile beauty; and, while her mother gazed upon her, a pang, by no means for the first time felt, mingled with the natural pride and delight of a mother. 'She is innocent, I am confident, and will ever be so,' was Mrs. Sommerville's secret thought: 'and I have wronged her by encouraging a doubt of her purity, and never more will aught on earth induce me to entertain a suspicion of the innocence of one who can thus look and speak; her whole heart and soul is, I am convinced, devoted to Albert; a treasure she is in herself, and should be doubly treasured for the sweet and unselfish devotion with which she regards him. But, alas! I fear he knows her not, nor the fond, trusting love she so lavishly bestows upon him, the chosen of her heart. Poor Rose! who would have thought that you, so tenderly nurtured, ever reposing on the love and care of others, would thus, while yet so young, have nobly resolved to rise independent of all obstructions, and stand as it were alone, endeavouring, likewise, to support and cheer your husband; but oh!' and a sigh heaved from her breast, 'should your generous efforts prove unsuccessful; and Albert, unmindful of your love, still remain the moody, gloomy misanthrope, I fear this sad disappointment of your fondest hopes will be too much for you; that the recoil will be more than thy tender frame can bear, and I may be doomed to see thee sink into an early tomb. Oh! just God, forbid that this should be the end of my maternal love and care. Grant that the pure and trusting love of this fair child may be rewarded by the fulfilment of her proudest hopes.'

Busily engaged in these thoughts, Mrs. Sommerville had sunk into silence, and Rose likewise followed her example: but her thoughts were not tinged with the painful melancholy that marked her mother's—her visions for the future were painted in rainbow tints: she felt as if she were about to begin life anew, and in a manner that could not fail to ensure happiness, both to herself and him she loved best on earth. She was so young, and had known so little of disappointment, that she could encourage hope without experiencing the feeling which in after years creeps over our minds, and tells of fairy hopes destroyed, and sweet expectations blasted. In youth we are all hope, nor doubt not the accomplishment of our desires, be they ever so ardent, or to others even unreasonable; but as we approach to middle age, we begin to hope with trembling, and to desire, rather than expect; and when we reach to length of days, we look back upon the past, and smile at the folly of our youth; often, indeed, even at the vain hopes too fondly clung to of riper years; and yet how gladly would we, if we could, recal that sweet friendship of the heart, that fond, deep faithfulness with which we willingly trusted in, and leant upon our ellow-man.

Oh! not all the wisdom we may have culled on our onward progress towards the grave; not all the talents we may have the ability to display; not all the tact we may have acquired to induce our company to be sought for and our advice thankfully received; not any, or all of these can make amends, in the slightest degree, for the loss of that sweet, though oft illusive feeling, hope. It is hope that cheers us under the saddest trials, that dries the mourner's tear, and repels the burning sigh; and lone, indeed, must be the heart which hope has entirely forsaken.

There is nothing on earth so delightful to look upon as a child—how sweet to hear him ere he has learned what sorrow means, discoursing on the future—how fair and bright is everything to his young eye—how pleasant to behold the confidence he reposes even on an entire stranger; never dreaming that there is one heart in the world less pure than his own. It is wrong, decidedly wrong, to check this guileless feeling, and force him to entertain an ill thought towards another: we should rather encourage the trust he is so willing to repose, for, the moment he begins to suspect, one great charm of life is lost—let none teach a child the rough lessons he will have to encounter as he grows to manhood: he will find it quite soon enough of himself, and buffets that come unexpectedly ever trouble us the least—the looking for painful events is often worse than the reality: how often do we hear the remark, 'I have borne it far better than I thought I should.' Why, then, have thought of it at all? It is a true and wise saying, that we should never go forth to meet trouble, as trouble is ever ready to come to us: and childhood should be a happy time, remote from care or sadness: no thought for the future should ever be allowed to throw a shadow o'er that bright and sunny path: far less, then, should any purposely (as some parents most mistakingly do) wilfully expose their children to disappointment, under the idea that it will inure them to bear the troubles and vexations at will beset them when forced to mingle in the world. Oh! rather let them paint their future career, as they would most desire to have it realised, and, though, as they grow older, they will most probably be doomed to see one hope vanish after another, yet they will still hope on, and when they gather roses, will little heed the thorns that may pierce and wound them, for they will have learned that no pure, unmixed joy is to be found on earth; but when we grasp the sweetest pleasures, we must, with them, also, take the briers. It is, undoubtedly, a wise ordination, that the richest joys are ever obtained at the greatest cost, for we never prize what is very lightly obtained; while, on the contrary, we regard as dear and precious what it has cost us so much trouble and anxiety to procure; this is a truth that every one has known and felt.

The days that intervened previous to the wedding, flew rapidly by; all were happy, and all busily engaged in preparing for the important event. Joy beamed on Henry's countenance, and happiness reigned supreme in his heart. Yet, this did not prevent him pursuing his usual avocations. He accompanied his father and brothers daily, as had been his wont, in their walks and rides round the farm; conversed with his mother and sister, with the same affectionate interest in their welfare, as he had ever manifested.

This happiness was not the intoxicating bliss, which the possession of the one he so dearly loved might soon be the means of restoring to his senses, and with them, perhaps, a weariness of the object, and a too quick perception of her faults.

Agnes Forster was not, in his eyes, perfection; he thought not extravagantly of her beauty, nor loaded her with flattery or praise; he expected not to find an angel in the woman, but knew she was not exempt from faults and failings any more than himself; but for those faults and failings he was prepared to make every allowance. He was sure she would do so as regarded him; and it was no less his duty to look with a tender eye upon her failings. He had known and studied her long, and felt certain that she possessed an excellent and amiable disposition; that her heart was in the right place, and that her many virtues and good qualities overbalanced the few weaknesses she had in common with her sex. This had determined him on making her his wife, if by constant and affectionate attentions he could succeed in winning her heart; without that, were she even ten times more lovely both in person and mind, Henry would never have knelt with her at the altar, but his efforts were not disappointed; in the course of time he had drawn from the lips of the blushing girl a confession of a reciprocal affection, and they were now about to be united to each other, to share one common fortune, be it good or ill; and Agnes, like her lover, went round the little household, overlooking the dairy and the farm, as observant as ever that all were fully employed; she indulged in no childish exultation over her promised happiness; on the contrary, a more serious air than usual sat upon her fair countenance; no snatches of song might be heard, that used to announce to all the part of the house where Agnes might be found; she seemed to perform all her duties with a more matronly air, as if preparing, unconsciously, for the new character she was so soon about to assume. The evening before the day appointed for the wedding she sat alone, with her father fondly holding his hand in her's, as she gazed tenderly, and with tearful eyes, in his face.

' What ails thee, girl?' said the farmer, bending down to kiss her cheek; ' ye are not sorry ye have promised to marry the lad, eh, girl?'

' No,—no, dear father,' replied Agnes, hurriedly.

' Then ye must not look sad, Agnes. Ye know that ye are not going to leave me and the old house; no, no, that would never do,' he continued, shaking his head and smiling, ' under this old roof ye were born, Agnes.'

' I know it, dear father,' she replied, seriously, ' and here I hope to live and die.'

' Ye must not talk of dying, girl; ye are far too young and blooming to think of death; and yet,' continued the old man, ' your mother was as young and fair when it pleased the Lord to call her away; it seems, indeed, but yesterday, that I brought her home to this very house, and she looked so merry, Agnes, and skipped about from room to room, just like you, my girl; and we never thought that we should be obliged to part so soon, but laughed, and sang, and talked as though we were certain of living together for many, many years to come, instead of only one short one, which was all that was allotted to us of happiness.'

' It was indeed, dear father, but a very short space of time to spend with each other,' said Agnes, and the tears which had been gathering in her eyes, rolled slowly down her cheeks.

' Ah!' replied the old man, mournfully, and as if musing on the past, ' it is years ago, now, Agnes; you were not then born, and now ye have grown into a woman; and so like your lost mother, that, as I look upon ye, I can almost fancy it is her returned to me, fresh and blooming as when we plighted our faith in yon church, where to-morrow I hope to witness the bridal of our child.'

And as the thoughts of past years came thronging back to the farmer's mind, connecting the whole circumstances of his courtship and marriage with the mother of Agnes, even to the slightest detail, linking event to event with occurrences that had long been forgotten till now the chord was touched in his heart which awoke thoughts and feelings that had so long slumbered; he had deemed them buried in oblivion, but now they were roused once more to renewed life, and, overcome with the rapidity with which one circumstance followed upon the steps of the other, without allowing him time to separate or examine them apart, the old man, who had weathered many a rough storm, and had ever been hale, hearty, and generous, leaning his head upon his bosom, wept like a child.

Agnes, unable to utter a word of consolation, could only throw her arms round his neck, and mingle tears and sobs with his. 'Precious relief,' as the poet Bloomfield sings—

> 'Sure friends that forward press
> To tell the heart's unutterable distress.'

And oh! something there is, something sweet and holy in mingling our tears with those we love —to rock on the bosom that would ever be ready to receive us, and there be safely shielded from all temptation, to fold our arms round those who are dearest to us on earth, and while tears run down our cheeks, to know that theirs mingle with our own.

'Oh! if it be, as some men say, a foolish weakness to indulge in tears, it is a weakness so dear and sacred, that none need be ashamed of thus giving their feelings vent; when too proud to tell how deeply we feel hurt at the supposed coldness of one we love, a tear speaks all the pent-up feelings; it at once reproaches, and promises forgiveness; and if it is answered by a tear, all is known. Oh! language is nought to this; not the most glowing, passionate words can convey to a sensitive mind one-half what is told by a single tear; and this belongs alone to virtue; it is consecrated and hallowed to the best feelings of our nature. Guilt would only scoff at it; the hardened regard it as a positive proof of childish weakness in a man to indulge in tears; but oh! it is a luxury they can never know, and we fully believe it to be far beyond a doubt, that the man who can, on an occasion, be softened to tears, is ever the bravest in battle, the most daring and reckless in danger.

'Dear Agnes,' said the farmer, after an interval of silence, striving to subdue his emotion, ' we must not, my girl, give way to such useless regrets; thy mother is far better where she is, she died innocent. God be praised, she knew no thought of sin; and oh! if it is possible for the blessed to observe what is passing on earth, she will look down from her abode in heaven upon her child to-morrow; thou wert indeed, Agnes,' he added, folding her to his breast, ' a precious treasure, which she, dying, bequeathed to my love and protection.'

'And well, dear father, hast thou taken care of thy motherless child—motherless almost from her birth.'

'It is true, Agnes, as thou sayest; she but lived to press her lips to thine, and then placing thee in my arms, more by looks than words, committed thee to my love and keeping—and now, Agnes, my girl, in giving thee to Henry Sommerville, I think, had thy mother been living, she would have approved and blessed thy choice, otherwise I never would have given him my consent.'

'And without it, dear father, I never would have wed him; no, had you desired me, I would have striven against my love, and if I could not have overcome it, I would have so subdued it, that none save my own heart should have known I cherished a single thought of him.'

'Good, brave girl,' returned the farmer, ' I am thankful that, in placing your affections on a worthy object, you have spared yourself this trial. Girls are too apt to be dazzled by the first ad that courts them, even should he be ever so unworthy of their regard, but this is not the case with you, girl; you refused so many lovers that I began to think ye had determined to live and die an old maid. Ye are, indeed, a good girl, Agnes, and God will reward ye for your kindness in refusing to leave your poor old father, and he is a good lad ye have chosen, for he willingly agreed to your desire to come and live with us, and that is not what every one would have done: I trust ye may both be happy, my child, and may God bless ye with good and dutiful children like yourselves.'

'This is the last night, dear father,' said Agnes, ' that we shall enjoy unrestrained intercourse with each other alone, and though in studying my husband's happiness, yours, my father, will never, for a moment, be forgotten by your Agnes, yet I can never more be so entirely your own as I have been up to the present time; it is this that has ever induced me rather to avoid marriage—the fear that you should deem yourself less cared for, or feel your comfort and happiness more incomplete; and did I not think, and I may say, fully believe, that Henry will rather add to your cheerfulness and contentment, than diminish it, I would even now, late as it may appear, retract the promise I have given him, and refuse to become his wife.'

'I know the goodness of thy heart, my Agnes; it is the exact counterpart of your mother's; you resemble her, my girl, not only in person, but in disposition; and I can only repeat what I have often told you, that I believe Henry to be a good lad and worthy of ye, and may God bless you both.

While this conversation was taking place between Agnes Forster and her father, Mr. and Mrs. Sommerville, Rose, Henry, and their brothers, were seated together, conversing thoughtfully and seriously on the morrow. No loud laughter or coarse jokes were bandied round, as is too frequent on such occasions; they were serious, but not sad; hope dwelt in all their breasts, for the union that was so soon to take place was founded on good qualities and mutual esteem; still they could not think or speak of it lightly. They felt that marriage was a sacred and holy thing, and as such should never be profaned with boisterous mirth.

Mrs. Sommerville felt for Agnes as though she were her own daughter, and exhorted Henry to study her happiness above all things else.

'I know you dearly love her, Henry,' said this excellent woman; 'but men often wound the feelings of a sensitive woman like Agnes, by a want of those little attentions, dearer than a thousand words of affection. And her father, too, Henry,' she continued: 'I know that Agnes would feel grieved beyond everything if you should be unmindful of his comfort, who thinks more of his happiness, I am convinced, than she does of her own, having not a relative in the world but him; they have been all in all to each other. I mention this, my son, because I know that men are apt to be forgetful of what they deem trifles; whereas, trifles make up a woman's life—not that I for a moment doubt the goodness of your heart.'

Henry received this counsel from his mother in submissive silence, and at the close, kindly thanked her for the interest she had manifested in Agnes.

'I can never thank you enough, dear mother, for the affection with which you regard the one I have chosen for my wife, and in return for your love for her, rest assured I will ever consult the happiness and welfare of Mr. Forster.'

'He is of a most noble and generous disposition, my son,' said Mr. Sommerville, 'and, moreover, entertains a sincere regard for you; therefore I should think the duty that is incumbent on you of studying his happiness will also be a pleasure.'

'It will,' returned Henry, 'and more especially when I know that in doing so, I am likewise pursuing the course that will make my Agnes happy, and in her happiness I shall ever find my own.'

'With such united feelings,' said Rose, 'you must—you will be happy.'

This affectionate party then separated for the night; their hopes and wishes were all in unison, each anxious to hail the morrow that was to add another member to their family, who was already acknowledged one in their hearts.

The morning dawned soft and fair—all things looked bright and beautiful; the grass was fresh and green, and the summer flowers cast their rich perfume upon the balmy air, and seemed to wish them joy. Rose was amongst the first who awoke from their slumbers, and throwing open her latticed window, looked forth upon the lovely scenery that surrounded her childhood's home; it was yet so early that few were stirring, and Rose, seating herself at the open window, fell into a long train of thought. It was but natural that at such a time she should recur to the morning that had witnessed her own betrothal to Albert, it was just such a lovely day as this, and all had concurred to make her heart light and joyous, yet much had occurred since then to sadden it; but now she hoped all would be changed for the better; in two more days she should again leave these peaceful scenes, where her best and happiest years had been spent. How much seemed crowded in the short space of time that had elapsed since her marriage; she appeared to have aged years in knowledge of the world, and her own heart had become acquainted with characters hitherto undreamed of, among which, she thought with horror of Henry Melville, and her heart swelled with gratitude towards Edward Trevers, who had enabled her to avoid one so dangerous. Dearly as she loved Albert, and anxious as she was again to see him, yet a sad, melancholy feeling mingled with her desire to return to town: here she possessed at least a peaceful asylum, where nought had power to injure or oppress her; there she knew not on whom to repose, even Marian and Lucy, of whom she was perfectly unconscious of ever having offended, seemed to have turned against her; Albert and Edward, she felt with something of a mournful satisfaction, were the only two she could number as her friends, out of the many to whom she had cordially extended the hand of friendship. In the country she was surrounded by loving and tender hearts, who, like herself, knew nothing of deception, and consequently, never feared it from others; but in town she scarcely knew who were her friends or who her foes. Alas! that one so young and gentle should have had cause to suppose the earth held one who would desire to injure her; yet such undoubtedly was the case. But now that she had determined for the future to live in strict retirement, though in the very midst of gaiety, she trusted that none would trouble her more.

She had been so absorbed in her thoughts, that hours had fled unheeded by, and she was aroused by the entrance of her mother.

'What, dressed my love!' said Mrs. Sommerville, smiling; 'I thought to find you still in the enjoyment of sleep.'

'Not this beautiful morning, dear mother,' replied Rose.   'I have been at my window for hours; I have not much longer, you know, to enjoy this scenery, and am willing to seize every opportunity of doing so now, instead of wasting my hours in bed.'

'You look, indeed,' said her mother, as she surveyed her lovely countenance with a smile of gratified pride, 'as fresh and beautiful as the morning itself; but come, dear Rose, let me call your maid to put those ringlets into a little more form, as the air from the window has taken the liberty of blowing them about, till they have assumed rather too careless an appearance to be suitable for a wedding, even though it is a village one, and Henry is anxiously waiting for you to join us.'

Rose was soon attired—her natural grace and loveliness needed but little aid from the toilet, and her dress, always simple, was on this morning, if possible, more so than usual; with a sober, serious air, as though they felt the solemnity of the occasion that called them within its hallowed walls, they entered the church, where they were soon joined by Agnes (and her father), attired in plain white muslin; her only ornament a rose she had plucked from the garden, and placed in her bosom.   Agnes leant on her father's arm, her eyes modestly cast towards the ground; she raised them for a moment as she entered the church to greet Rose, who flew to her side, but quickly cast them down again, while a soft blush suffused her cheek, as she became sensible of her lover's ardent gaze, who, pressing her hand in his own, led her to the altar; their friends closed round, and the clergyman, the same who had united Rose and Albert, commenced in a deep, impressive voice, reading the marriage service.   Henry replied to the few simple interrogatives in a firm, manly voice, in which joy and exultation strove for the mastery over the solemnity of the bond he was now entering into, and Agnes, in her turn, spoke the vows in a tone of voice, which, while it trembled at the responsibility she was taking upon herself, yet breathed purest love in every word; tears stood in the eyes of each dear relative, and also in many of the friends and neighbours who had come to witness the betrothal of two hearts that had long been given to each other; when the clergyman pronounced the last benediction that closed the ceremony, all stood in silence for some moments, breathing an inward prayer for the happiness of the youthful bride and bridegroom.   Mr. Forster was the first to break it, by catching the still kneeling Agnes in his arms; and at the same time, extending a hand to Henry (who grasped it cordially in his own), he uttered an ardent aspiration for their happiness, and while he endeavoured in vain to twinkle away a tear, that would, in spite of all his efforts to conceal it, force its way down his cheek, said,—

'Agnes, you are young and beautiful as your mother, when she plighted her willing faith to me; I cannot wish ye happier than she was, the short time she was permitted to remain on earth; may your lot be as bright, but God grant that it may extend over many, many more years; take her, boy,' he continued, turning to Henry, who willingly received so fair a burden from her father's arms, 'and be to her all my fondest wishes could make you; she is worthy of all your love and devoted affection.'

'And she has it all,' replied Henry, solemnly pressing a kiss upon the lips of his young bride; 'and ever will, Agnes,' he added in a lower tone; 'my own dear Agnes, bless me at least with one smile on this day, ever to be treasured in my memory as the brightest of my life.'

These tender words recalled her scattered thoughts, and doing as he desired, she fondly returned the pressure of his hand.   Mr. and Mrs. Sommerville, with Rose and her brothers, now also offered their warm greeting, and breathed wishes and prayers for those so newly married; on their return home, the young maidens of the village hastened before them to strew flowers on their path, expressing, in this sweet manner, their fervent hope that their path through life might be thus soft and fragrant.   Oh! it was, indeed, a happy bridal; and when they arrived at Mr. Forster's farm, and seated in the clean and comfortable parlour, where a goodly array of the young farmers and their sweethearts were assembled to do honour to the wedding, though all were eager to offer congratulations to Agnes, yet, not a word was uttered by any present that could call a blush upon her cheek; on the contrary, all seemed to feel the newness of her position, and endeavoured by every means in their power to relieve the embarrassment a young bride naturally labours under: this is a delicacy of feeling not always found among even the more refined class of persons on such an occasion; indeed, we have been too often pained by remarking that at a wedding persons frequently think themselves authorised to indulge in a liberty, very improper, and certainly unpleasant to all concerned.   Many regard the whole affair as a pageant, and appear to think mirth not only allowable, but absolutely becoming to the occasion; but we trust none, who have officiated as principals at such an important ceremony, have regarded it in that light; it is one of the most—we may say the most—solemn and holy bonds upon which a person can enter; they are taking upon themselves vows, and making a covenant, not for weeks, months, or years, but which death alone should ever break; and though, when two have long loved each other, like Henry and Agnes, and at length, with the willing consent of their parents and connexions, sanctified that love by kneeling at the altar, and, in the presence of God, making a vow, too sacred to be broken by any right-minded individual, to share each other's weal or woe; a little innocent mirth may be indulged by those who have thus witnessed the happy accomplishment of their mutual love, yet, neither the bridegroom or the bride, we think, will feel disposed to join in any noisy merriment. Happiness, such as they must feel, with a fond trusting confidence in each other that their love will not give way before that sad despoiler, Time; but, when the rose has flown from the cheek, and the lustre from the eye, and the rich tresses no longer depend over the soft, sunny brow of youth, that the love which binds them so closely and fondly may, now then still live on,

and, having passed the light and gladsome days of life together, they may, hand-in-hand, descend peacefully and happily into the vale of life's decline, assisting and upholding each other's tottering steps. It is pleasant and cheering to look upon an aged couple that have braved life's ills together; and their love yet surviving, in spite of all that years and trouble could do to annihilate it, still fondly clinging together, in the full confidence that, when their days on earth are over, they will only for a very short time be separated, and then meet again to spend a blissful eternity, never more to know what sorrow or parting means. We say that happiness, such as two persons feel, who have but just plighted their faith, must be of a calm and thoughtful kind, utterly at variance with boisterous revelry; and we should tremble for the future

No. 11.

happiness of a bride whose newly-made husband joined in the exciting mirth that some person actually look upon as part and parcel of the ceremony.

Agnes and Henry preserved a serious and thoughtful demeanour throughout this, the first day of their married life. Mr. Forster had resolved to be gay, and strove hard to keep faith with himself; yet his daughter's marriage recalled so forcibly to his mind his own gladsome bridal with the fair and blooming mother of Agnes, that he found himself frequently more inclined to cry than laugh; this he deemed very vexatious on a day that he had determined on being unusually merry. After they had partaken of the good cheer which was provided in such profusion that the villagers were indiscriminately invited to eat and drink whatever they pleased, a dance was proposed on the lawn in front of the house, and heartily agreed to by the farmer.

'Come, Rose,' he exclaimed, 'you know you promised me your hand as a partner. Why, what ails thee, girl?' he continued, looking at her. 'If thee ain't every bit as bad as Agnes. I can't think what is come to the girls. Rose used to be the merriest little puss that ever footed it on the green, and now I can scarcely look at her but she is in tears. Well, times are altered;' and the remembrance of other days came back so forcibly on his mind that the big tear gathered in his eye, and then rolled, unheeded by himself, slowly down his cheek. Rose was at his side instantly, wishing to conceal her father's feelings from Agnes; and, drawing her arm through his, said kindly, 'I am not only willing, but anxious to redeem my promise of dancing with you; come, let us go at once, they are already preparing to begin, and I shall expect you to set me an example of gladness, and then, I have no doubt, my joy will keep pace with yours—this is, indeed, a happy day for us all.'

'Ay, ay, girl, I think it is as you say; but Agnes does not look so happy as I would wish to see her, and you, too, you little rogue, had tears in your eyes just now.'

'Agnes, I am certain,' returned Rose, 'is as happy even as your fond desire would make her; but she feels the sacredness of the new tie with which she is bound, and that necessarily keeps her thoughtful; and, for myself, I was thinking how soon I should be obliged to quit these peaceful scenes, and the near and dear friends by whom I am now surrounded; and that is the only excuse I can offer for the tears that did, as you say, come unwillingly to my eyes.'

'Say no more, girl,' returned the farmer, 'I was wrong to chide thee, but thou'lt forgive me, I know.'

'Forgive you, my dear, dear old friend, with whom in childhood's happy days I have spent some of the brightest hours of my existence! Have you forgotten how I used to climb to your knee, and even sometimes have the audacity to push Agnes off one side, that I might have the first kiss when you returned from the plough?'

'No, no, girl; I have not forgotten it, nor many more things, which, though told again, may seem but trifles; yet they have given me almost a father's interest in thy welfare. I wish thou hadst never left us; thou wert never formed, Rose, for a fine lady. A simple country girl should blossom in her own native bowers.'

This was touching on a subject that Rose felt was too delicate to enter upon; she had long known the truth of the farmer's remark, but it was a truth that she had never acknowledged to any but her own heart; therefore, leading her old friend towards the dancers, who had begun to foot it on the soft green grass to the merry sounds of the tambour and pipe; they were all glad to receive Rose and the farmer among their number, and not a few of the young men envied Mr. Forster so fair and sweet a partner as Rose. Who that has ever known the innocent delight of joining on a summer's eve, in the merry, light-hearted dance of the villagers on the soft green sward—nature's carpet, and which is spread alike for all—no matter how humble they may be, they are at liberty to rest their weary limbs on this luxuriant carpet—softer, sweeter, fresher, than any of man's invention: yes, on that the poorest may recline, and view as they do so, the wondrous works of God; lovely, incomparable nature, thy rich blessings are scattered profusely for all; none are forbidden the dear enjoyment of roaming far away from the busy haunts of man, and seeking out some sweet solitary spot, where they are surrounded by the beautiful, where all conspire to raise their thoughts far above this sublunary sphere; then all the cares of life vanish from our minds, and our soul seems to take wing and soar away, until we feel ourselves no longer an actor in the world, but look down upon it, as it were from a height, and smile at the strife and efforts after minor things, which engage our fellows.

Oh! it is good to roam o'er solitary and sequestered nooks, to gaze on nature's smiling face, and feel there is nought can match its loveliness, when we return, if return we must, to cares and temptations that strive hard with us for the mastery; we feel ourselves strengthened to combat and overcome them; a holy feeling dwells in the heart, which the wear and tear of life cannot entirely cast off; we seem to have drank from a pure stream, which has refreshed and invigorated all our faculties, and we are more ready, patiently and cheerfully, to bear the ills that we cannot prevent. Oh! then, how sweet the thought, that this pure, unalloyed delight is open free to the enjoyment of all who choose to avail themselves of it.

But we were saying, that who has participated in the pleasure of a dance on the village-green, where fair and unsophisticated maids, blooming gracefully like the wild flowers of their own native valleys, have given their hands, without a thought of coquetry, to the honest, open-hearted, and those roughly good-tempered young farmers. Who has witnessed and joined in this, without drawing a comparison greatly in disfavour of the fashionable London balls, where a large and mixed assembly meet together, in hot and crowded rooms, not so much to enjoy the exercise of the dance, as to show off their own faces and figures, and criticise those of their neighbours ? We may, perhaps, be thought censorious, but yet must confess, that we have never gazed round a ball-room, and saw the bright eyes and pretty faces that surround us, without thinking how few would guess the anger, mortification, and envy that lay beneath that smiling surface ; but we have had experience that convinces us how often that is the case: all young ladies desire is to procure good partners; and, if they see others more fortunate in this respect, their mortification and anger is greater than many would suppose ; consequently, we deem a ball-room a dangerous place for the young, not only on this but other accounts. Girls are too often fascinated by the insidious attentions of a young and handsome partner; and are flattered into the belief, only too easily, that he means something serious in his attentions ; and then, when their hearts are more than half gone, and they are fluttering between hope and fear, he totally neglects them, and pays his *devoirs* to some other beauty; and then, again, there are many professed coquettes, who laugh, flirt with, and flatter a man till he is, or fancies himself, in love with them; and when he summons up courage to tell his tale of love is treated with cold contempt. This is a very unhappy state of things, and it is unknown the injury a coquette may do the rest of her sex—especially if the man whose love she has won by a system of unpardonable duplicity, is very young—if this should unfortunately be his first insight into the female heart, he will naturally judge of others by the one he has proved to be false and unfeeling, and thus the whole sex will suffer for the heartlessness of one; and the beautiful attributes that belong exclusively to the female character are entirely lost sight of, by a man who has been duped by a coquette ; he from that moment regards women as made up of deception and artifice, and fancies they are constantly endeavouring to ensnare hearts for the mere pleasure of refusing them when offered to their acceptance ; the knowledge of this should make women very wary, lest by any oversight they forfeit not only their own claim to the good opinion of men, but through their folly, and oftentimes worse than folly, the claim of the best and most amiable of the sex. It is bad enough to cause any one to think ill of ourselves, but to a person of good feeling, it is still worse to make them think ill of others.

Farmer Forster and Rose danced together to the delight of all present.

'She is a bonnie lassie, and a good one,' said an old man, who was seated under a tree, with pipe and jug in hand, viewing, with almost the hilarity of youth, the festive scene before him.

'She is, indeed,' returned another, who was seated by his side, and whose silvery locks, hanging loosely over his shoulders, spoke to his having seen at least some eighty summers. 'Ah!' he continued, shaking his head, 'I have known her from a baby, and she is by no means so happy since she married that melancholy-looking stranger that came so suddenly amongst us. It was a bad day for the poor child when she first set her bright blue eyes on him—a bad, a very bad day.'

'You must not think so, neighbour,' replied the other. 'You knew that he has made quite a grand lady of her ; they say that in London she has a house so large and fine, that it is fit for the Queen herself to live in.'

'That may be, and I am not going to dispute it,' returned the elder speaker ; 'but, for all that, it was a bad day. You remember the stranger well—he who is her husband now, worse luck, poor child ?''

'Yes ; and he was, as you say, a melancholy-looking sort of a body; but then, you knew, he was given to books, and could write them, too, equal to any of the great men whose books used to fill one's heads with wonder. Well, it is an uncommon fine thing to be able to write ; and one need not be surprised at it making a body rather melancholy and strange-looking.'

'Ah, neighbour, if that were all, we need not care much for it; but that man has a bad conscience, which the Bible tells us is a continual torment. I have seen him often, when he first came down here, wandering among the tombs, and muttering to himself in such an awful way that I have felt I would not change situations with him, were he even Prince Albert himself.'

'It might be the effects of what they term over study,' replied the first speaker.

'I think not,' returned the elder one, 'for I came upon him once unawares, and he had such a wretched, woe-begone look as I never shall forget; and he was talking, or as, I said before, rather muttering to himself, and, as I passed him, said something about his having caused the death of some one, and then he smote his breast and looked so wildly round, that I was glad to pass on without his observing me.'

'Good God!' replied the other, gazing upon the fair and innocent face of Rose, 'can it be possible that sweet child is married to a murderer?' and horror sat upon his features at the bare idea.

'I have told you nothing but what I myself saw and heard; but he may not be exactly what is termed a murderer in the law; mayhap, he has killed a friend or relative in a duel, and that, you know, is seldom looked upon or treated as murder.'

'More shame that it is not,' replied he who had first spoken; 'to my mind, he who takes the life of another, unless it be by an unavoidable accident on his part, commits murder; and if a poor man takes away life, it is considered in that light by judge, jury, and indeed the whole court; but when gentlemen fall out, they think it no harm to shoot each other, and it is generally looked upon as a very light offence by man, but God, I am sure, does not so regard it; but as to the husband of Rose, bookish men, I have heard say, often talk to themselves, especially when they are going to describe any particular character, and this might have been the case with him when you saw him in the churchyard.'

'I can't think it, neighbour. His misery appeared far too real to be feigned, and the expressions he gave utterance to seemed to come from his heart. I hope, poor child, she may never have cause to rue the day she first beheld him; but she does not look happy. I fear she already regrets having left her childhood's home.'

'I hope not, neighbour. She is soon, I hear, to leave us again; but wherever she goes, she will carry the blessing of an old man, who dandled her on his knee when a baby.'

'Say two old men, neighbour, and ye will be nearer truth. God Almighty bless her!' he added, bowing his white head.

'Amen,' returned the other, uncovering his head.

At an early hour the visitors took leave of the bride and bridegroom, and with many hearty expressions of good-will and wishes for their happiness, sought their own homes. Rose had agreed with Agnes to remain at Mr. Forster's that night and part of the following day, when she would return to her mother's to prepare for her departure to town. The wedding day was over; it had passed in harmony and peace, and Rose, thankful and happy at having witnessed the happiness of her brother and Agnes, and breathing a prayer for their welfare, laid her head on her pillow, and soon sank into a calm refreshing sleep. She was up betimes in the morning, and wandered out among the well-known corn-fields, ruminating as she went on the sadness of being so soon obliged to leave the spot dearest to her on earth, as containing hearts she knew beat in unison with her own. Having extended her walk some distance, she turned homewards, and was met by Henry, who had come in search of her.

'Why, Rose,' he said, drawing her arm through his own, 'Agnes is positively quite uneasy; she could not conceive where you had got to thus early, and has been looking for you all over the farm, and not finding any trace of you, at length enlisted my services to seek out the truant, and, having found you, I must now convey you back in triumph,' he continued gaily.

'I am glad to see you so cheerful this morning, Henry,' replied his sister; 'and I am sure you have good cause to be so. Such a girl as Agnes, is not always to be obtained.'

'Indeed not, Rose; but, if you are not weary, let us hasten our steps back—we shall be keeping Mr. Forster without his breakfast, and that will be a bad beginning for me.'

'Is it, indeed, so late!' said Rose, with an air of surprise. 'I had no intention, I assure you, of remaining out so long; the air is so pure and fresh this morning, that it has kept me loitering about much longer than I was aware of, and I shall not be able to enjoy this sweet breeze many mornings more.'

'I am sorry, Rose,' said her brother, kindly, 'that we are so soon to lose you; yet at the same time I could not be selfish enough to desire to keep you longer from Albert, who must be very dull without you.'

Rose sighed. What would she not have given to have entertained the same opinion regarding her husband as Henry did! but no; she did not think he was any more dull without her society than he was with it. She felt with sorrow that Albert was a melancholy man, and she trembled as she thought that, from what she had heard, he had too painful a cause to be so; but now she had resolved to banish all such thoughts, to look upon and feel for him, only in his relative character to her as her husband, chosen of her own heart; he was entitled to her best love and confidence, and this she determined to lavish upon him, and to give no heed for the future to aught that might be said to his disadvantage.

On their arrival at the farm-house, Agnes, fresh and blooming, with a modest blush upon her fair brow, came forth to welcome them, and gently chided Rose for stealing out unknown to her. Breakfast was all in readiness, and partaken of in front of an open window, through which peeped in the blushing rose, and mingled its perfume with the sweet-scented briar.

'Oh! who would live in the dusty town,' thought Rose, 'when there are such sweet spots as this to live and die in.'

And she sighed to think that Albert should give the preference to what she herself so much disliked. The short time she had now spent in her native place had enamoured her still more with a country life. Since she had lived in London, and became acquainted with the formal, dull routine with which her days there glided on, she was so much the better enabled to appreciate the thousand enjoyments and delights of the country.

After breakfast the young girls spent a quiet and happy morning together, opening their hearts freely to each other, and imparting the sweet hopes they nourished for the future.

'I shall miss you sadly, dear Rose,' said Agnes, hanging fondly over her; 'but you will write to me often, very often, will you not?'

'It will be one of my greatest pleasures,' returned Rose; 'and you, Agnes, will find time to answer, at least, some of the letters I shall send to you when far away; and believe me, in fancy, I shall frequently be sitting at this window gazing out on those dear native hills, sacred to me by a thousand hallowed recollections that hover round them; but we will not, dear Agnes, afflict ourselves with useless and unavailing regrets. Let us speak on some other subject."

Agnes gladly acceded to this suggestion, and the hours flew rapidly by till Rose deemed it time to retire to her mother's. Agnes and Henry walked with her, and it was one of the pleasantest walks they had ever taken. Rose determined, on leaving her friends, to think only of the pleasure she should experience in returning to Albert, and this, she judged would spare her much of the pain consequent on parting. As they drew near Mrs. Sommerville's, they saw her coming out to meet them, and hastening their steps, they soon joined her.

'I am very glad you have come!' was the first exclamation; 'I am so soon to part with Rose for an indefinite time, that I am anxious to have as much of her company as possible, now she is with us.'

'And Rose,' said Agnes, smiling, 'has been not the less anxious to return to you, otherwise, I assure you, you would not have seen us here so soon.'

Relinquishing Henry's arm, Rose took that of her mother's, and, drawing her on one side, inquired if any letter had arrived for her in her absence.

'No, my love,' returned Mrs. Sommerville, 'neither was I aware that you expected any.'

A shade of disappointment passed over Rose's expressive face as she replied,—

'I thought perhaps Albert might have written.'

'Expecting so shortly to see you, he doubtless considers it unnecessary,' said her mother.

Rose made no reply, but walked on in silence. She had endeavoured to persuade herself not to expect a letter from Albert, but yet, nevertheless, she did expect one, and felt sadly disappointed at not receiving any.

'I should have returned to town with a much lighter heart if he had but sent me one line to say he was pleased with the decision I had come to, of being with him again so soon,' thought Rose, as she once more entered her father's dwelling.

But, alas! the morrow came, but brought with it no letter from Albert; and this, the last day she was to spend with her relatives, for she knew not how long. She was saddened by anxiety concerning him she expected to meet so soon; thoughtfulness was too plainly marked on her brow not to be observed by her mother, who watched every change in her expressive countenance. Sometimes Rose wished she had not so definitively determined on returning to town; as, after Albert had kindly intimated a desire for her to remain in the country some weeks longer, he might feel hurt at her not acceding to his request, and that perhaps was the reason of his not writing to her, as she had (in spite of all her efforts to the contrary) fondly anticipated. She knew in her own mind, that in resolving to join him again so speedily, she was actuated by the tenderest affection, and the desire, if possible, to promote his happiness; could she feel certain that would be best obtained by her absence from him, she would gladly have sacrificed her own desire to see and be with him once more—this she was confident of herself. But oh! if he judged her differently; if Albert felt he was happier without her, and was grieved at her determination to return; if, when she did so, she found him far from manifesting any pleasure at her arrival; he certainly had seemed very desirous of sending her into the country, of hastening her away from him, scarcely allowing her sufficient time to make a few preparations that were necessary for her departure; and then came the oft painful thought, that she was not by any means a suitable companion for one so clever, so highly gifted in literature as Albert. Oh! how much she was conscious of coveting a little of that talent so liberally bestowed upon him.

'If,' she exclaimed inwardly, 'I could only converse with him on subjects that I know he loves to talk on, I should be able to win his esteem, as well as his love; I fear, indeed,' she continued, musingly pursuing the train of thought she had half unconsciously fallen into—'I fear he loves me but for the few charms of person he may fancy I possess; and, oh! if it is founded on nothing more, by what a slight thread do I hold his affections; the lightest thing may sever it at any moment, and the eye wearies of beauty that is constantly before it, till at length we wonder that we ever deemed it such.

Rose stopped herself suddenly; she was conscious of being unjust to Albert, in thus judging of his love for her, and thought it proceeded entirely from an humble opinion of herself; she felt he had no right thus to think of his affection for her, and calling to recollection every kind sentence or word of love he had addressed to her, endeavoured to persuade herself his love was as true and constant as her own.

'True,' she said, half aloud, 'he cannot admire in me the wonderful talent, that can express in such beautiful language the feelings of the soul, that I so love and admire in him; but after seeking and mixing in the company of many, very many handsome, and doubtless, also clever women, both in England and abroad, yet he chose me out of them all, for his nearest and dearest friend and companion, and told me—yes me, a simple, uneducated, village girl, that he loved me; how many high-born ladies would have been proud to have now such a man as Albert, and shall I then repine, because I feel myself unworthy of the happiness of being his wife? No,' she continued exultingly, 'rather let me use my earnest endeavours to encompass his happiness, and then, (and the tear swam in her eye at the thought,) I shall indeed be blest.'

Thus did Rose reason herself into composure, and, looking forward to coming events, as though they threw, were it possible, a bright outline before them, she felt perfectly satisfied with her determination to return to her husband.

Her mother followed her about the whole day with tearful eyes and pallid cheeks. The morrow, she knew, would rob her of her child, and to part from her—even if she were confident that Albert's whole study was to ensure her happiness, and guard her feet from every snare—but Rose had unconsciously imparted to her mother, during her visit, or rather Mrs. Sommerville had drawn from her much that made her dread her child again 'breasting a stormy world,' her who had, previous to her marriage, been safely housed and shielded from the lightest wind; still her faith was strong and unshaken in Rose; she knew she could trust her, and wept, not for fear her feet should deviate from the right path, but for the buffets and trials she would have to encounter; and this last day they were to spend together for she knew not how long, she kept Rose constantly by her side, whispering, ever and anon, some words of affectionate counsel for her future guidance. Nor was her health forgotten in the anxiety she felt for her only daughter, who was thus unfortunately about to be separated from her.

'Be sure, my dear Rose, to write often and freely; do not fear to impart aught to your mother, and especially be explicit regarding your health. I wish,' she added, and a tear forced its way down her cheek, 'that I could have kept you with me till after your confinement, as there is no one, Rose, that can watch over your health with the assiduous care and attention of a mother.'

'Do not fear,' returned Rose, cheerfully; 'I shall follow your advice in everything, and have no doubt but all will go well.'

'I hope so, indeed,' replied Mrs. Sommerville; 'were it otherwise nothing should induce me to be parted from you, or rather than be obliged to do so I would return with you to town.'

'Dear, dear mother,' said Rose, affectionately throwing her arms round her mother's neck, 'how happy should I be were such a thing possible! But no; I could not for so long a time deprive my dear father and brothers of your company.'

'But you will promise me, Rose, to send for me should (which God forbid) any unfavourable symptoms manifest themselves?'

'Indeed, indeed I will, dear mother; but do not allow your anxiety for me to render you unhappy; for myself, I assure you, I nourish no apprehensions.'

'You must retire early this evening, Rose, for you will have to start soon in the morning, and will require rest to strengthen you for your journey,' resumed Mrs. Sommerville, after a pause; 'for if Albert sees you looking fatigued, he will think this visit has been of no service to you; and as for leave-taking, my child, I shall allow but very little of it; let us part in the full hope of a happy re-union, perchance more speedily than we now dare hope for.'

'That is exactly my wish,' replied Rose, 'for I entertain a hope that we may ere long be more closely united, for if (as I mean earnestly to endeavour to do) I win Albert from the close seclusion of his study, we may, dear mother, both of us visit you again after my confinement. I shall of course be anxious to show all of you my child, and Albert will not object to my coming to you again, even if he should not accompany me, which I hope to induce him to do.'

The tears gathered thick and fast in Mrs. Sommerville's eyes as Rose spoke thus: she knew not why, but she had a foreboding that the hopes her daughter so fondly entertained, and so ingeniously expressed, would never be realised; it was a difficult task to conceal from Rose the emotions of sorrow that filled her breast. But oh! she would not for worlds check one fairy dream of hope that had so brightly illuminated her daughter's destiny. Alas! she feared the reality was doomed to be utterly different from what she had so fondly painted it. It was difficult, we said, to hide these from Rose; but she did so—nay more—joined her in speaking of that happiness they should experience when they again met.

It is a great thing to be able to command our feelings, to hide from others the anguish and sorrow, and sometimes the joy and delight, we experience; those who have attained this have accomplished a great object. We do not like every prying eye to see the inward workings of our mind—some, perhaps, who have designated us as proud and cold. Oh! it would be adding wormwood to our gall for them to witness the excess of anguish which will sometimes threaten to overwhelm us; if we must suffer, it is sweet to be allowed to indulge in sorrow alone, to carry ourselves before the world with the outward bearing we have ever assumed, and which affords no index to the state of the heart. And then again, as in the case of Mrs. Sommerville, by being unable to command our feelings, we may give pain, and indeed, render miserable one who, had we concealed them from observation, would have been happy in the unconsciousness of sorrow. Mrs. Sommerville was, fortunately, completely successful in her endeavour to hide from Rose the deepfelt anxiety she inwardly nourished.

'I shall have time enough,' she thought, 'when the dear child is gone, to give way to my feelings, and shall, at least, have the satisfaction of knowing that she is unconscious of it. Why should I shade her young brow with fears for the future, which, after all, may only arise from the excess of my maternal affection? And yet, oh! that she had never married Albert—that she had never left the innocent enjoyments which, upon trial, she herself holds dearer than all the wealth and gaiety with which he surrounds her; her heart, I know, is lonely amidst them all.' But she felt her thoughts growing too painful, and forbade to pursue them further.

Rose occupied her little room for the last time; the morrow, she knew, would waft her back to him with whom her heart had dwelt the whole time of her absence. This she had proved by the constant recurrence of her thoughts; for round him was twined every hope and wish, so entirely did he form a part of herself—that never did a thought or desire cross her mind with which he was not more or less connected. He was indeed the centre round which revolved every feeling of her young heart, and the thought that she was again so soon to be with him was fraught with bliss—it was painful to leave those she loved, but oh! they sank into nothingness when compared with him, and, in the joy she felt at his not replying to her last letter; and when remembrance forced it on her mind, she argued,—

'Had he been less engaged in his study, I might have expected him to write; but knowing how valuable he deems every minute, it was wrong of me to think he would write to me again, especially as he will so speedily see me. Under the circumstances, it was really absurd in me to to expect a letter.'

Thus endeavouring to excuse Albert, though at the same time she could not help feeling how much better satisfied she should have been had he but sent her one line, signifying the pleasure he anticipated in beholding her again.

Rose fell asleep, and awoke in the morning to the joyful certainty that, ere night again closed in, she would be with her husband. So taken up was she with this thought, that not till she descended to the breakfast parlour, and observed the sad faces that were already assembled to bid her farewell, did she think of the kind hearts she was about to leave behind her.

'How selfish I have been thus to forget the dear friends who I know will grieve for my departure,' thought Rose, as she glanced from one to another.

Farmer Forster, with Agnes and Henry, had walked over thus early on purpose to bid her adieu, and tears of self-reproach filled her eyes for being so pleased at the thought of leaving them all. She was at the breakfast table, between her father and mother, holding a hand of each, which she frequently carried to her lips, while the tender affection of her mother still manifested itself in the anxiety she constantly betrayed for her health and comfort.

'Be sure to write, Rose, the morning after your arrival, as we shall be so anxious to know how you have borne your journey.'

'I will, I will, dear mother,' replied Rose, and her thoughts recurred to the morning she had left Albert; and she remembered with a pang that no such tender request had fallen from his lips on the eve of her departure, and the sigh escaped, unrepressed, from her bosom at the recollection; but even then, excusing him to herself, she said, inwardly,—

'This would have seemed very unkind in another, but he is so different to most men that I cannot deem it so in him; indeed, I am certain he never meant, even in thought, to be unkind to me. He is much too anxious concerning my welfare. I wish, indeed, he would think more of his own happiness, and less of mine.'

Entertaining these thoughts, and fondly picturing to her mind the pleasure of again beholding her husband, Rose remained during breakfast time profoundly silent—silence which no one seemed disposed to interrupt. All eyes were tearfully fixed upon Rose; each felt that it might be long before they could again gaze upon her sweet, ingenuous face; and what might not occur in the interim to dim its brightness? Hers was a face upon which none ever gazed without a feeling of pleased satisfaction, which was not alone derived from its extreme beauty, but also from the sweet, fresh look of innocence, wherein the hope-beaming countenance of the child contended with the softest dignity of the woman; and oh! to think that ere they again gazed upon it sorrow or sickness might perchance

Eclipse e'en light like hers;'

that Care might set his stamp upon her sunny brow, and chase the bloom from that cheek, upon which they joyed to see it dwell. Rose was beautiful and good. Oh! that she might also be happy, was the inward inspiration of each dear relative, that had now assembled to bid her fare-well. 'Farewell'—oh! what a heart-stirring word; how much of anguish and pent-up emotion does it contain; it is hard to breathe it, save in—'an utterance faint and broken;' with a soul-sickening desire, a heart yearning 'for the time when it shall never more be spoken.' It was thus that all Mrs. Sommerville's family felt, as they fondly clung round Rose, to press on her lips the parting kiss oft given, to be again renewed, till at last her brother, fearing the effects of this sad scene on Rose's delicate frame, gently, yet firmly, withdrew her from their circling arms, and tenderly bidding her a last adieu, ordered the coachman to drive on, and in a few minutes the vehicle was out of sight.

'And is she really gone!' exclaimed Mrs. Sommerville (now giving full vent to the feelings she had held in constraint, while Rose was there to witness them). 'My dear, dear child, oh! if we should never meet again on earth, would that I had insisted on accompanying her; alas, alas! I fear she will never visit us more; my heart misgives me, that she will not survive her approaching confinement; and if she should breathe her last, and I not by, to soothe and comfort my dying child, what bitter sorrow and anguish will be mine!'

Mr. Sommerville was himself too sad to offer consolation to his beloved partner, and his sons felt her grief too sacred to allow them to intrude upon it with any common-place expression of sympathy. Farmer Forster could only twinkle away the tears as they gathered fast in his eyes; but Agnes gently glided to Mrs. Sommerville's side, and taking her hand affectionately in hers, while she whispered a few tender words of hope and comfort, entering into her feelings as none but a woman can, she kindly pointed out the very few fears that could be reasonably en-tertained—while, on the contrary, how much room there was for hope.

'It is natural, my dear madam,' she continued, as Mrs. Sommerville evinced signs of returning composure, 'that you should feel unhappy about Rose, especially as she will be removed so far from you, that you cannot day by day watch over her health; and that being the case, fears arise in your mind, and are magnified into real ills, that, had you been differently circumstanced, would never have occurred to your imagination.'

Mrs. Sommerville was a sensible woman, and, when Agnes thus placed her feelings regarding Rose in a proper light, was speedily made to perceive that Agnes was perfectly correct, and, clasping her to her maternal bosom, poured blessings on her head.

'My dear Agnes, my second daughter, I shall still retain you near me; then let me not repine if one daughter is removed to a distance from me; rather should I thank God for having thus given me another in Rose's absence; you, my Agnes, shall supply her place.'

Affectionately returning her embrace, Agnes replied—

'My mother! you will then allow me to call you so? how sweet does the name sound in my ears, who never have breathed it before, save to mourn the loss of one I never knew; but oh, my mother, on you will I now lavish that warm affection which has been treasured in my bosom as sacred to one, who gave her own life in exchange for mine; but oh, if it is permitted her to view me at this moment, my heart tells me she will ratify the sacred bond I have now entered into.'

'Sacred indeed, my child,' returned Mrs. Sommerville, 'is the offering of parental love you have this day made me, and which, indeed, I accept as such, and receive thee to my arms as an affectionate and dutiful child. You are now, my Agnes, as much as my own Rose; and it shall be henceforth my joy and happiness to love and care for thee conjointly with her.'

'I thank thee,' returned Agnes, solemnly; 'and am now in truth thy child. Yes,' she continued, changing her tone to one of exultation, 'I have now a mother, and one that I may well feel proud of possessing! Oh! for how many years hath my heart longed, nay, yearned for so dear a tie? When, in childhood's years, my playfellows have spoken of their mother, how the name has struck upon my heart, and tears, even in the midst of mirth, have gathered to my eyes, to think that I alone, of all I knew, was motherless.'

'But not fatherless, girl,' said Farmer Forster, pressing to his daughter's side, and prisoning one little hand in his.

'Oh, no, no!' she replied, throwing her arm around his neck; 'think not, my father, that I for a moment forgot you, or missed even one night or morning to thank God in my prayers for having spared to me so good and dear a father. You have,' she continued earnestly, and kissing his sun-burnt cheek, 'supplied to me till this hour the place of my lost mother, in so far as you were able to do so; but you will not feel hurt that I rejoice in possessing a mother and a father too?'

'Hurt! no, no, my girl; I am proud that others should know and feel the worth of my Agnes.'

'And we do know and feel it, all of us,' said Mrs. Sommerville, 'Agnes is well worthy of being the sister of my Rose : you will forgive me, my old friend, if my maternal affection will not allow me to say more.'

'Ye have said enough,' replied the farmer. 'Rose, ye know, was always a pet with me when I used to sit outside the old house yonder (pointing in the direction of his residence),

with Rose on one knee and Agnes on the other, ye know I used to call them my cottage flowers. Ah! how the little rogues would coax me, with kisses from their cherry lips, to tel them tales about the fairies, or sing them some old songs of days gone by. Ah! well-a-day many's the happy afternoon I have spent in that manner. I sometimes fear I shall never see such happy days again.'

This was touching a chord Agnes was desirous of keeping silent, and she hastened to reply,—

'Oh! no, dear father, you must not think that we shall not yet spend many, I hope, happier days together ; for are we not now more closely united than ever? Methinks,' she added, smiling, to cheer the spirits of Mrs. Sommerville, which she saw her father's remark had caused.

No, 12.

again to flag, 'methinks, that when Rose next comes among us, we shall have nothing but merry-making, You forget, father, that she will bring a little play-fellow for you, whom I know you will be proud to dance upon your knee.'

'Ay, indeed, my girl, that I shall; and you, my Agnes, may also, in the course of time present me with some little images of yourself and Henry. God bless them! I shall dearly love them for your sakes,' exclaimed the warm-hearted old farmer.

Agnes averted her blushing face from the ardent gaze of Henry, whose eyes lighted up with joy at the farmer's remark. Never had his young bride—no, not even when, at the altar, she freely pledged him her faith—looked so transcendently beautiful, as at the moment he beheld her bending over his mother, performing, unasked, the sweet office of consoler to the aching heart. Had she been anxious to make her new-made husband more satisfied and delighted with the heart that had so recently become his own, or desirous to have him think more highly of her charms, she could not have taken a surer course than the one she pursued, though from no such thought or motive—no, Agnes was actuated alone by the kind and gentle feelings of her bosom, and the love and respect she nourished for the mother of her husband.

The last parting with Rose was most painful, and more fraught with anxiety to Mrs. Sommerville, than when she first left her parental roof. All was then new to Rose, and her mother fondly hoped and endeavoured to believe, that in the love of her husband, and the kind affection of Marian Trevors, she would find an equivalent for the tender and trusting love of the friends she left behind her. But now, alas! that hope had vanished; there was nothing, Rose had herself acknowledged, in the gaiety and pleasures of London, that could recompense her for the want of kindred spirits on whom she could rely—for hearts, which beating in unison with her own could understand and appreciate her character. Albert, her mother had gathered from the conversations she had held with Rose, was too closely wedded to his studies to take much heed or care of his wife. He desired to see her happy, but not endeavouring to make her so; and Marian, from some unaccountable cause, had of late shunned her society; it was strange how one so gentle and confiding should have given offence, without being herself in the slightest degree aware of it; but such was the case, and, consequently, poor Rose was almost without a friend in the midst of the gay metropolis Had her husband been to her all that the name implies Mrs. Sommerville would not only have been satisfied, but happy, for he alone would have supplied the place of all others; but such not being the case, she felt anxious and unhappy concerning the welfare of her child, which, when we take into account her present delicate situation, was not to be wondered at. But oh, if Mrs. Sommerville could have known that not only was Rose without a friend, but what was far worse, surrounded by foes, who are anxious to catch at any little oversight on her part, and magnify each trivial thing into a crime, who had already deemed her guilty, and branded her as such—oh, had it been possible for Mrs. Sommerville to have known this, what would her feelings have been? But no, at present she was happily ignorant of all, and, sustained by the kind consoling affection of Agnes, looked forward to the future with a comparatively light heart. In the meantime, Rose was once more fast approaching her husband's abode: the mingled feelings of joy and apprehension that filled the heart with such contending emotions were so great, that she could scarcely support them; sometimes joy would predominate, and then, again, anxiety and fear would usurp its place; and near and more near as she approached the well-remembered spot, the more her agitation increased; and yet, in the midst of her emotion, hope for the future was fondly nourished. Oh, when she could reduce to practice the excellent advice she had received from her mother, all would surely be well. Albert would —must be happier than she had hitherto beheld him; his sorrows, that now so closely environed him, would vanish before her tender, loving care, and a gentle withdrawal of him from the close seclusion of his study. How sweet a task would be hers to minister to his comfort, to console his anguish, and whisper words of hope and love. This—this would indeed be happiness— pure, ecstatic bliss, the most perfect that life can know. Buoyed up by these thoughts, that lighted her eye with an unusual brilliancy, and flushed to a deeper crimson her glowing cheek, she was scarcely aware that she was so near the end of her journey when the carriage stopped in front of the house that owned her for its mistress. She threw a hasty glance at the door, half hoping to see the form of him whom she loved waiting to greet her, and then as hastily looked up to the windows, but no trace of him she most desired to see was visible; the door was opened, the steps let down and an obsequious servant stood in readiness to assist her to alight, but no friendly eye bade her welcome back, or kindly inquired after her welfare. This, thought Rose, was but a poor greeting after an absence of some weeks, and far different to the joyous welcome she received from her parents and brothers.

'Is your master at home?' were the first words she uttered as she entered the drawing-room and beheld it vacant.

'He is in his study,' was the reply.

'Tell him I have arrived,' said Rose, in rather faltering accents.

The servant left the room to obey, and Rose carelessly threw herself on one of the seats How dull and dark the room appeared; how dusty the streets; and yet, though it was in the middle of summer, and a lovely day, how very little sunshine, Heaven's richest gift, found its way into the confined atmosphere of London! Rose felt this the more from having just left the pure, invigorating air of one of old England's most salubrious villages, and having parted with such fond, warm hearts. She also felt more keenly the apparent want of kindness that thus left her waiting, anxiously waiting, to see her husband, while a servant formally announced her arrival. Had it been him who was thus returned, even after a much shorter absence, Rose felt she should have flown to welcome and receive him back. At this moment the servant entered with a message to the effect that Mr. Moreland would be pleased to see her in his study.

Rose hastened to do his bidding, and with a throbbing heart, knocked timidly at the door.

'Come in,' was repeated in the well-known voice, whose lightest tone was ever music to her ears, and in another instant Rose stood in the presence of her husband.

'I am glad to see you back, my love, he said, rising, and extending his hand, 'though, for your own sake, could have wished you had profited by my advice, and prolonged your stay in the country for some weeks more; but, however, you know, I am only desirous of your happiness and health,' he added, after a short pause—'that you are aware, my love, is dearer to me than aught else on earth.'

Rose could scarce make any reply. Her heart was too full for utterance; she could only gaze upon Albert's face and repel the tears that strove to find their way to her eyes. She thought, as she looked upon him, that a deeper shade of sorrow than heretofore sat upon his features, and care had stamped still stronger lines upon his brow; but this might arise from her being used of late to gaze upon happy, merry faces, all of whom bore the strong impress of innocence in their light and sunny smile.

'You think you are in better health and spirits then, my love,' continued Albert, drawing her close to him, and imprinting a kiss upon her cheek; and as his eye fell upon her lovely beaming countenance, he heaved a sigh, and a dark shade of melancholy passed over his own face. Rose hastened to reply.

'Oh! yes, dear Albert, I am much better; but how have you been all this long while?'

'I, Rose,' he returned, in a manner, as if half musing to himself, unconscious of her presence; 'oh! I have been as usual, that is as well as I can ever expect to be; memory, memory will still pursue me; it is in vain I endeavour to escape from the pangs that it does, and ever will recal, with a vividness but little removed from reality; but this is my portion, and it is useless for me to rebel against it: for years I have drank of this poisoned cup, and yet live on, for I am doomed to drain it to its dregs; there is much of bitterness left for me yet, but I am forced to taste it, drop by drop, and may not at once drain off the draught, that would be mercy: but oh! I must not speak of mercy—I who showed none. I might have pitied, and have spared: but no, I thought not of it, till it was all too late, and a life that should have been to me most precious, and treasured of all things else! but forbear my heart, forbear, nor conjure up the awful scene too strongly, already fixed in my mind, never to be erased!'

Rose shuddered, as these words fell from Albert—this was the first proof she had ever had from his own lips, that a dreadful secret was involved in his early life; but now he spoke of a life that should have been treasured, implying that such had not been the case, and to none other but the ill-fated Florence could he allude. Transfixed with horror at this, as she considered it, acknowledgement that he had deprived a fellow-creature of life—one too, whom he himself felt ought to have been pitied and forgiven—Rose could only fix her eyes on the ground, and preserve an impenetrable silence. Albert, too, seemed lost in thoughts—deep, and, to judge from his countenance, painful thoughts. Rose was the first to recollect herself, and with a strong effort, and in a tone of voice that tremblingly bespoke the feelings of her heart, said,—

'Dear Albert, you must endeavour to forget the past, at least so far as to prevent it making you miserable.'

He started at the sound of her voice, which appeared to recal his scattered senses, and answered with emphatic earnestness,—

'The past, Rose! what know you of the past? It has ever been to you a bright and sunny dream! Oh, that you may never know the stern truths that have been taught me in the rugged school of sorrow,' and here he checked himself and stopped abruptly.

'Speak not sadly of the future, Albert,' said Rose, 'for I feel certain it will be to us both bright and happy.'

Albert sorrowfully shook his head. 'It is useless for me to encourage such thoughts, Rose; but oh, could I know, could I feel that you were blessed, I would gladly submit to all that may be allotted me of ill.'

'Think so, then, Albert,' returned his young wife, 'for I am determined not only to be happy myself, but if possible to make you so.'

He laid his hand kindly on her head. 'God bless you, my dear child! you will, you must be happy, for are you not innocent in every sense of the word? You know, I am sure, no thought of sin; and, therefore, will never know its curse, or how heavily it hangs over the head of the guilty.'

He spoke these words with impressive earnestness, and Rose felt too awed by his manner to reply. At length he gently led her to a seat, kindly inquired after each member of her family; listened, apparently with interest, while she related to him the particulars concerning her brother's wedding, hoped she had enjoyed herself, and finally begged, if she felt comfortable, where she was, she would remain in his study the rest of the evening.

'I have a little writing that I wish to do; but you, my love, will be no interruption,' he said smiling on her more kindly than was his wont. Rose felt gratified beyond her most sanguine expectations; all fatigue was forgotten, and, with a smiling face, she watched him as he wrote, and as she marked the lines that sorrow had traced with no light finger on his manly brow, and saw the habitual look of suppressed sadness that hovered over every feature, a deep sympathy arose in her mind, and blended so tenderly with her love for him, that, for the time, she thought that she would not desire to see him, if she could, more gay. There is, surely, something endearing, not to say pleasing, to a young and sensitive mind in melancholy; we feel a holier affection for a subject round whom is entwined an appearance of sadness; it seems, as it were, to raise them above the common worldly feelings of man, and consecrate and hallow them; they are beings that ask not only our love, but tenderness and compassion, and this binds them doubly to our hearts.

Thus felt Rose as she watched her husband's countenance, and though her heart swelled, and her eyes swam with tears, yet never since her marriage had she felt more happy; he seemed pleased with her company, had asked her to remain with him—a thing he had never done before—and poor Rose was overjoyed at the prospect of spending many happy hours by his side. Their absence seemed to have had the effect of binding them more closely together; and now Rose felt she would never consent to leave him more; they should for the future, she hoped, be one—one in thoughts, hopes, and pursuits. It was, to be sure, sad to think that his hands had been imbrued in guilt; but oh! she knew that one dark act was terribly repented of—had been for days and years. And oh! he might surely hope for pardon—for pardon was denied to none, not even the guiltiest; and therefore he might deem himself forgiven, and, though he never could forget, yet might find peace, and, perchance, happiness; at least nothing should be wanting on her part that could in any way tend to it.

After he had concluded his narrative and put it on one side, Albert kindly renewed his conversation with Rose, evidently desiring to hear her talk, and frequently smiled at the innocent and ingenuous manner in which she expressed herself. The evening passed away in peace and concord, and Rose retired to rest with a light and thankful heart. She awoke the next morning with a sense of cheerfulness that, of late, had been a stranger to her bosom, and with much of the buoyant spirit of her childhood, after breakfast, sat down to write to her mother; for, when we are happy, how sweet it is to be enabled to communicate it to those we know will rejoice with us, will shed tears of gratitude over the warm outpourings of our heart, and will join with us in sweet thanksgivings for the present, and hopeful aspirations for the future! And Rose communicated to her fond and tender parent the warm and affectionate reception she had met with from her husband; and over this letter, which was carefully hoarded, how many tears were shed, how many a kind prophecy for the future cherished! It was, indeed, a sweet relief to Mrs. Sommerville's maternal fears; for it conveyed the glad tidings that Rose had safely reached her home, and was, when she wrote it, in the full enjoyment of health and happiness.

Two days had glided smoothly on since Rose's return, and she was seated at her work-table, busily engaged in preparing some little article of clothing for her expected infant; she had as yet seen not one of the many whom she had been used to call her friends, none having inquired for her, or were aware, so far as Rose knew, that she had returned. Having remained ever since in strict seclusion, her thoughts were now divided between the work she was engaged on, and the husband that she loved, picturing to herself the joy she should feel, when she presented to him her child. 'Oh, surely he will be pleased, he will feel the affection for it that I shall, it is surely impossible that it can be otherwise;' and yet Rose felt a sense of pain shoot across her breast, as she remembered that he had not made the slightest allusion to her situation since her return, and her own natural delicacy had forbade her to be the first to mention the subject, consequently nothing had passed between them concering it since the day before she quitted home; and then she recollected with sorrow, that he had seemed for more disappointed than pleased, when she communicated what she deemed he would consider pleasing intelligence. 'But how foolish I am to allow this to make me sad,' argued Rose to herself; 'how kind and affectionate he is these last two days! when I think of that, I am sure it ought to prevent anything making me unhappy. When my infant arrives, I cannot, will not doubt that he will gladly and proudly welcome it.   I must remember what my dear mother said, that no doubt his sadness, when I told him of my expectation, arose in a great measure from anxiety concerning me.

'Dear mother, how much am I indebted to you for your tender counsel, and wise construction of all I communicated to you ; how plain you made things to me that, of myself, I could not understand.'

Rose was, at this moment, interrupted by a servant, who handed her a card.   Rose receiving it, read, ' Mr. Edward Trevors.'   ' Oh ! let him be admitted,' said Rose, with evident pleasure. He was immediately introduced, and warmly received by the unsuspecting Rose, who saw in him one she deemed her best and truest friend.

'How delighted I am to see you once more!' said Edward.   When the first greetings were over, he seated himself by her side.   ' How very suddenly you left, without even saying good-bye.   I thought it positively unkind of you, Rose.'

'Oh ! do not say so, Mr. Trevors,' returned Rose, ingenuously ; ' I assure you, that the last time we met, nothing was farther from my thought than leaving home.'

'It was very suddenly determined on then,' replied Edward.

'It was, indeed,' returned Rose ; ' Albert thought I seemed very unwell, and persuaded me to try the effect of my native air, without any longer delay than sufficed to prepare for my departure, and you may judge the benefit I have derived from it, by seeing me thus returned in the enjoyment of perfect health.'

'You do indeed, look well,' said Edward, gazing rapturously on her glowing face ; ' I do indeed think, Rose, that time, which carries the bloom away from so many, only adds to the lustre of yours.'

'You make me smile,' said Rose, good humouredly, ' for you speak as though you had known me for many years, whereas our acquaintance can only be dated, you know, by months.'

'But, oh ! how much, Rose,' he replied warmly, ' of friendship, esteem, and regard, may be crowded into the space of a few months !'

'It may, indeed,' said Rose ; ' and this reminds me to thank you for the advice contained in your letter, which I implicitly followed.   You have indeed, Mr. Trevors, been a true and sincere friend to me, and as such I shall ever regard you.'

'Thank, you, Rose, for your good opinion ; I thought you would one day deem better of me than you once did.'

'Mention it not, Mr. Trevors, I beseech you.   I am covered with shame whenever the idea occurs to me, but I was then a weak and silly girl, and knew not my friends from my foes.'

'I am aware, Rose,' resumed Edward, ' that you wrote to Lucy Melville, and which letter both her and Henry deemed very unsatisfactory.   I am glad that you approved of me not showing them the letter you enclosed to me, which, of course, I refused to do without your sanction.'

'I did, indeed, approve of it, and thank you for so acting, and should have written to you to say so, only knowing that I was about to return so soon, I deemed it unnecessary, more especially as my former letter got known to the Melvilles, and for which, I suppose, you cannot account.'

'Oh, since writing to you, I have remembered that the morning your letter arrived it was during my temporary absence from home, and also while Lucy Melville was in company with Marian, consequently I can only suppose that Lucy must have examined it and recognised your handwriting, which awakened her curiosity to become acquainted with its contents ; and though, when she applied to me for a solution, I candidly told her under what circumstances you had occasion to communicate with me, she positively refused me credence, and insisted on my showing her the letter.   I had then no resource, without compromising you in the matter, but to give her your address, and with a promise, that if, on appealing to you, you desired me to yield to her request, I would most readily do so ; but if otherwise, nothing should induce me to break the trust you reposed in me.   In consequence of your non-compliance with her wish, Henry has attacked my character in every way, irritating me to a degree that it required all my patience to bear without calling him to account for it.   Even now, dear Rose,' he continued, taking her hand in his, which he carried respectfully to his lips, ' I have sought you this morning as much to ask a favour of you, as to express the pleasure I feel at thus beholding you returned with renewed health and strength.   Say will you hesitate to grant it me ?'

'Not if I can possibly do so without.—'

'Make no exceptions, dear Rose, this time ; my honour imperatively calls on me to pray of you to retract the promise you extorted of me that I would not meet Henry Melville, and punish him for his villany.'

'Oh, no, no, Mr. Trevors,' replied Rose, her fears instantly chasing from her cheek the rich glow that had previously mantled there leaving in its place a deadly paleness. ' Oh, no, no, ask anything of me but that,'

'But Rose, dear Rose,' murmured Edward, in his softest and sweetest tones, 'I have borne much, very much from Henry; I have even heard myself called a coward, which I would not have borne for a moment from any, but for your dear sake; that indeed stopped the arm which would have been otherwise raised to wipe away the stain from my honour in the blood of him who dared to deface it.'

'Oh, talk not so, I beg of you, Mr. Trevors,' said Rose, raising her hands imploringly, 'your promise to me is sacred, and never, never will I release you from it; ask me anything but that,' she continued, looking earnestly and beseechingly in his face.

'Yet, think for a moment, Rose, to what you doom me by this refusal. I tell you, Henry Melville has stigmatised me as a liar and a coward in the presence of others, and to which no man of honour can possibly submit. I know my promise to you is sacred, but you will, I am convinced, release me from it, when you consider the provocation I have received, and which imperatively calls upon me to make it recoil on the head of him who uttered it; now, dearest Rose, I am confident you will absolve me, if I break the promise I have given you.'

'I cannot,' replied Rose, 'under any consideration. Oh! to think for a moment that I should be the cause of bloodshed is too awful a thought to think upon: if you ask Henry Melville, he will probably apologise for the warmth into which he was betrayed.'

Edward shook his head.

'Henry is far too vindictive against me, Rose, to offer any apology; it would be perfectly useless to seek it of him, unless I was at liberty to challenge him if he refused.'

'Tell him then,' urged Rose, 'that you would not bear his insults, only that you are bound by a promise to me, not to meet him, as you would otherwise wish to do.'

'I have told him so, dearest Rose, but he casts it back in my teeth, and refuses it his belief, and even has the impudence to accuse me of inventing it as a shield, behind which I can escape unscathed, though in his heart he must know that, were my arms at liberty, I should bitterly revenge the wrongs he has heaped upon me.'

'Then,' said Rose, with dignity, 'he shall hear it from my lips.'

'It would be perfectly useless, dear Rose, neither could I allow you (even were it possible it could have the effect you desire) to lower yourself by speaking to him on the subject; say at once, dearest,' he continued, pressing the hand he held to his lips—'say that if you cannot absolve me from the promise you will at least forgive me for breaking it.

'Alas! alas! I cannot; if you challenge him he will most likely accept it?' said Rose, in a tone of inquiry.

'Undoubtedly he will; for I must give him credit for possessing courage in no small degree, and to apologise, when he deems himself right, would never be the case with Henry Melville.'

'Then, if you meet him, which I unfortunately may not be able to prevent?'

'Say not unfortunately,' interrupted Edward; 'the thought of Melville's dishonourable desires towards you will animate my arm, so that I am convinced he will not leave the ground uninjured. He shall indeed,' he added, half aside, 'pay dearly for his conduct.'

'Forbear, forbear!' cried Rose, 'you fill me with horror at the thought of bloodshed. If, Mr. Trevors,' she continued, turning her tearful eyes full upon his face, and, in her earnestness, laying her hand upon his shoulder—'if, as you have told me, you entertain any feelings of regard towards me, you will bear with Mr. Melville, even if he should (which is certainly improbable) offer you any further insult.'

'For your sake, dear Rose,' he said, bending fondly over her.

'Oh, yes, for my sake,' she returned.

'For your sake, Rose, dearest, I would cheerfully bear anything,' and, in the excitement of his feelings, he passionately kissed her lips.

Rose started, and endeavoured to free herself from his ardent embrace, but before she had time to recover from her surprise and confusion, the door of the room in which they were sitting, and which communicated with an adjoining apartment, opened, and Henry Melville and Marian Trevors presented themselves to her astonished gaze.

Henry's brow was contracted, and his mouth closely set; but no other appearance of unusual agitation was apparent in his demeanour, as he strode forward with a firm step into the middle of the room, where he stood, for a few moments, confronting Edward with a fixed and earnest look. Anger was plainly depicted in the countenance of Marian, which she vainly endeavoured to conceal under an appearance of feminine dignity; unlike Henry, she moved not from the threshold of the room, but drew herself up to her full height, while her dark eyes flashed fire in the expressive glance she threw upon her husband, which comprehended at once anger, reproach, and shame.

Rose was she first to overcome her confusion; for being innocent, even in thought, of wrong, she consequently felt she had nothing to be ashamed of, and, rising from her seat, she approached

Marian with the intention of welcoming her, but, without scarcely deigning her a look, with a cold wave of the hand, she forbade her further approach. Rose stopped and looked from one to the other for an explanation of Marian's conduct.

'Come hither, Rose,' said Edward, rising, and drawing her towards him; and then, as if some fresh thought had suddenly occurred to him, he said, 'You had better, Rose, retire, while I speak to Mr. Melville, as, I suppose, the honour of this unexpected visit is meant rather for me than you.'

Rose hesitated, and looked from Edward to Marian, from Marian to Melville, and from Melville back again to Edward, with an expression of fear he well understood.

'You will go, Rose,' said Edward, persuasively, leading her to the door opposite to where Marian stood.

'But you,' she said, and then catching Melville's louring look, 'oh, I dare not leave you with him.'

'Marian will take heed, Mrs. Moreland, that I do him no injury,' said Henry, in a voice that was thick and husky with emotion; 'would, indeed, that he had never done you any!' he added in a tone of bitterness, as he gazed upon the lovely face and form of Rose.

'You hear what he says,' urged Edward, 'now do not hesitate to leave us; I will see you again this evening, till then, farewell; do not, I entreat of you, allow any fear for me to make you unhappy.'

While speaking he drew her from the room, and gently disengaging himself from her, returned alone, and folding his arms upon his breast, said, addressing Henry,—

'I have this morning informed Rose of the impossibility of my keeping the promise I made to her of not accepting any challenge from you, and consequently am now at liberty to meet you when and wherever you may desire.'

'Desire,' replied Henry, 'you know well how much I have desired it; but when I tell you that myself and Mrs. Trevors have overheard the latter part of your conversation with Rose this morning, you will not be surprised if Mr. Moreland, himself, should desire to avenge the wrongs you have done him; should he, when he is made acquainted with what has passed, refuse to call you to account, depend that I will gladly avail myself of the opportunity of doing so, for never did any man succeed in leading a more gentle or innocent heart astray.'

'You have played the spy,' replied Edward; 'and—but it matters not; if you have any message for me, I shall be at the club this evening,' and without taking the least notice of Marian, Edward turned and left the room.

'Mrs. Trevors,' said Henry, relaxing the sternness of his demeanour, and approaching her with an air at once of kindness and pity, 'I little thought, when I accompanied you here this morning at your request, that we should prove the fears you entertained to be so sadly realized. I must acknowledge that I more than suspected Edward's designs towards your brother's wife; but I deemed Mrs. Moreland to be far above all guile; she seemed, indeed she was, till he contrived, by some infernal art, to rob her of it, all innocence and virtue.'

'Your eyes have borne witness, what she is now,' replied Marian; 'you suspected Edward, but I more than suspected her, and have for some time done so; mine is a sad task, to have to communicate to my brother, that she, upon whom he has lavished his affections, and raised from comparative poverty to wealth and splendour, has proved herself utterly unworthy of his love and affection—it is a truly painful office, but must nevertheless be done; I cannot allow him to nourish in his bosom, a being who has thus repaid all his tenderness, and yet my poor, poor brother, I fear it will be almost too much for you! you have so garnered up your affections on that unhappy girl, that to cast her from you will be like rending thy heart-strings asunder; and Marian, spite of all her pride, and uncommon self-possession, allowed a tear or two to steal unheeded down her cheek.

'I beseech of you, Mrs. Trevors, not to give way to such painful emotions,' replied Henry, who could never bear to see a woman weep, 'recollect yourself; you were famed for possessing firmness in no slight degree, let me see you exercise it now, for if ever you needed it, this is surely the time.'

'I am firm,' said Marian, recovering her composure, 'and rest assured, Henry Melville, that it was the thought of my brother's anguish that forced the tear, not any of my own,' and she drew herself up with an air of pride that surprised even Henry, accustomed as he was to see her exercise it.

'It is necessary, Marian,' he resumed, after a pause, 'however painful it may be, that either your brother or myself should challenge Edward, and much as I am desirous of being the one to inflict the chastisement on him he so well deserves, yet I feel at the same time that this office most properly belongs to Albert. I shall, therefore remain in the house till you have communicated to him the sad intelligence, and then I shall be glad to learn his intentions towards Edward.

Do you, Marian, feel equal to speaking to your brother at once? From no one can he better hear the story of his disgrace than from you.'

' And yet how I dread to acquaint him with it; still he must know all, and, as I shall gain no confidence by delay, I will go at once;' saying which she left the room, and ascended the stairs to her brother's study. Contrary to his custom, it was half open, and looking in she beheld him seated at his desk, with less of sadness visible in his countenance than usually sat there; she hesitated a moment before entering. ' Alas!' she thought, ' how unfortunate that his appearance should be so cheerful (he is seldom otherwise than wretched) on this day when I have to communicate such overwhelming news; and now I would gladly have found him sunk in despondency, he is apparently buoyed up with hopeful pleasure to a degree that I have seldom witnessed. Were it possible to avoid casting him down, how thankfully would I do so!' and for an instant she wavered in her determination, and seemed inclined to return to Henry without speaking to her brother; but murmuring to herself, ' No, no! it would be dishonourable to allow him to remain in ignorance of what I myself have witnessed,' she summoned up courage and entered the room. Albert turned his head as she did so, and greeting her with a smile, begged she would be seated.

' You have seen Rose, Marian, how do you think she looks—better than when she left us?' said Albert, in a tone of kind inquiry; and then noticing, apparently for the first time, her earnest and anxious look, he continued, ' You are yourself indisposed, Marian, either in mind or body, I am convinced; tell me, I entreat of you, what it is that ails you.'

' Alas! dear Albert,' replied his sister, ' I am wretched both on your account and my own; there is something which I deem it a sacred duty to impart to you, and yet, in doing so, I shall be the means, I fear, of plunging you into the very depths of despair.'

' Say on, Marian,' returned her brother, moodily, ' it cannot make me much more wretched than I am; the canker has long been in my heart, and I feel that it is impossible for aught to make me more unhappy than I have been for many long years.'

' Would that I could think with you; mine were then an easy task—but no, when you have heard my tale, you will acknowledge yourself wrong.'

' Nevertheless, speak,' said Albert; ' let me know what renders you unhappy without more delay.'

' I will begin at once,' replied his sister; ' but prepare for sorrow from a source you little deemed would ever cause you any: Rose is unworthy of your regard. Yes, she who owes so much to you, has repaid you with base ingratitude, and has taken advantage of the confidence you placed in her, basely to betray it.' Marian's eyes had been fixed on the ground while speaking; but as she warmed with the anger she felt at Rose's supposed cruelty, she raised her beaming eyes with indignation to her brother's face; she was prepared for, and fully expected to encounter in him severe distress and anguish of heart at the intelligence she had communicated, but never for a moment had she dreamed of beholding the convulsive workings of his features, that now spoke of misery too bitter to find vent in words. He sat in his chair stiff and erect; his hands were firmly clenched, and his eyes intently gazing on vacancy, while grief, not anger, was plainly depicted on his pallid countenance, which assumed an almost ghastly hue. Still not a word, or even a sigh escaped him, and he listened while she communicated all she desired to him as though he was entirely insensible to all around. How long he might have remained thus it is impossible to say; for Marian, terrified by his altered and death-like appearance, laid her hand upon his arm, and besought him to calm his emotion, or at least to give it outward vent. He started, momentarily, as it were, with renewed life, and casting her hand roughly from him, said, in a voice that sounded harsh and discordant in her ears,—

' Leave me, I desire to be alone.'

' Brother,' replied Marian, ' my dear and only brother, do not bid me leave you thus—indeed, indeed I cannot do it.'

' Brother!' said Albert, hearing apparently only the first part of the sentence, and pausing for an instant, repeated again, ' Brother!' with a bitter emphasis; ' who speaks to me of a brother?' and his eye rolled wildly round the room. ' A brother!—years have past since I last breathed the name, and yet it seems but yesterday that my father gave him to my keeping, and well have I repaid the trust. How carefully have I watched over his happiness, how tenderly guarded him from sin and sorrow!' and then, bursting into a wild and bitter laugh, he smote his forehead, and exclaimed, while a chill apparently ran through his veins, and his satirical manner changed into one of agonized terror, ' Oh, God! his blood wilt thou require at my hands—a brother's blood—it is an awful thought.'

And again he relapsed into silence. Marian, ever alive to, and desirous of hearing of Charles, could not resist even now the desire that impelled her to inquire concerning a brother she so well and tenderly loved. No; though sunk in the deepest distress, both on her own and Albert's account, she for a moment forgot it all in her anxiety to learn the fate of the absent Charles.

'Albert,' she began, approaching closer to the chair he occupied, and speaking in an earnest, though hurried manner—' Albert, if you have spoken your real sentiments, and feel, as you say, that should your brother (and she laid deep stress upon the words) come to harm, his blood will be required of you—of you, to whom a dying father bequeathed the precious trust, made still more so by the gentle, loving disposition, and endearing tenderness, that so peculiarly characterised the youthful Charles—oh ! Albert, of which I cannot doubt, you know and feel

all this—let me beseech you to do him the late justice of once more bringing him beneath your roof ; and whatever his sins may be, tell him that a brother, an elder brother, that stands to him in the place of his dead parent, can pity and forgive them all.'

As she spoke, Albert buried his face in his hands, and sob after sob heaved from his bosom with such bitterness, that they seemed to rend his very heart-strings. Feeling for her brother's anguish, and yet thankful that she had made an impression on him, and anxious to follow up the effect of her words, she leaned over the back of his chair, and placing her hand upon his shoulder, spoke again.

" We are now, dear Albert, both of us brought low. We had confidence in the love of those upon whom we had placed our affection and chosen for our nearest and dearest friends and companions; but they have, alas! cruelly deceived us, and we can only depend on each other for comfort and consolation in this our deepest affliction. Let us not forget there is one also in sorrow who has, who must, long have drunk of the cup of bitterness—yes, one who shared with us in childhood's joys, and mingled with us tears of childish sorrow, who laughed when we were gay, and wept if we were sad, and who shared with us one blessed and happy home, and the love of a fond and tender parent—we called him brother. Oh! let us not forget that he bears in truth that dear relationship, and now that we, too, know what sorrow means, recall the wanderer home, and take him once more under our fostering love and care. Let us again mingle our tears together; and when time shall have partially healed the wounds that throb and smart, oh! may we not again be blessed—blessed, at least, in sisterly and fraternal affection. We have all of us proved how hollow and false is the love of others; then let that unite us more closely and tenderly to each other. It will be sweet in after years to know that out of sorrow and bitterness came forth some sweet springs of consolation—that if we had forgotten our brother while] possessing faith and confidence in the love of others, yet when grief came thick upon us, threatening even to overwhelm us with anguish, that we then remembered there was another who sorrowed even as we sorrowed, and that then we sought him out, and in soothing his grief half forgot our own.'

She paused, but still Albert spoke not. He had succeeded in suppressing his sobs, and now remained in the same position as when she had commenced speaking—perfectly motionless; and as Marian leaned over him, the tears that mingled feelings had brought to her eyes, unusual visitants there, rolled unheeded over her brother's forehead and trickled slowly down his hands which concealed his face. The two remained thus for some time, Marian's hair drooping over and mingling with Albert's, which, long and now dishevelled, matched hers so closely in colour that you could not tell them apart, or say which belonged to which, and Marian's face was entirely hid from view by the thick and confused mass of curls that hung before it. Each of them were insensible to all that was passing around, or they would have heard a gentle footstep at the door, which, hesitating for a moment on the threshold, while a timid voice pronounced the name of Albert, and receiving no answer, the lovely face of Rose peeped in. There is, undoubtedly, a solemnity in grief, a hallowed feeling, that even the most degraded will respect and retire from the presence of, as from something sacred, that they are conscious it would be profanity in them to meddle with. Grief is a holy feeling, and no stranger desires to witness it or intrude upon its privacy; no, rather in solemn silence would they retire from its presence, and leave the hearts that feel it to indulge in their sorrow apparently unheeded. Thus felt Rose, who was ever most alive to the best feelings of our nature, and though astonished at finding Albert and Marian giving way to such an abandonment of sorrow, and of which she could not guess the cause, yet feeling it was almost wrong to witness, though unseen herself, their agonised feelings, was on the point of retracing her footsteps with the utmost caution, that no sound should arouse them to the consciousness of her presence, when Marian raised her head, and all trace of sorrow vanishing instantly from her countenance at the sight of Rose, while anger shone conspicuously on every feature at the presence of one whom she considered had so deeply injured both herself and Albert.

'Leave us instantly,' she exclaimed; 'how dare you intrude upon the sorrow you have caused?'

'I—I caused!' stammered out poor Rose: 'I know not what you mean. I was not, indeed, even aware that you were in this room; I came merely to speak a few words to Albert, not knowing any one was with him, or, I assure you, I would not have intruded; and, seeing you together in such apparent sorrow, I would have left the room directly, had not surprise, and I can truly say grief at witnessing yours, kept me for a few moments stationary; and being here, Albert, I think, will not feel displeased at my inquiring into the cause of his sorrow, and, if I cannot relieve, I may, at least, desire to share it with him.'

At these words, Albert raised his head, and casting a look of bitter reproach on Rose, which went to her very heart, said, 'Oh, Rose, Rose, I thought you would have been the last to forsake me.'

'Forsake you, dear, dear Albert!—what is it you say?' replied Rose, running with outstretched arms to his side.

He motioned her back, and replied, 'For *forsake* I should have said *betray*, and then you would have been at no loss to understand me.'

'Understand you! Oh, Albert, Albert, be cautious, and give no heed to aught that may be urged against me by persons who know not how devoted my heart is, and has ever been to you.'

'Which is shown by submitting to the embraces, nay, more, encouraging the love of another, and that other should have been the last to find favour with Rose Moreland, as in doing so she not only betrayed her husband, but his sister, and whom, at one time, she called her friend,' said Marian.

'And would still. Oh, Marian, is it my fault that you have avoided me in every possible way, treated me with marked coldness, though, at the same time, with an appearance of politeness that forbade my noticing the change?'

'Or is it mine,' replied Marian (with a tone of satire, that so often marked her converse), 'that you used every means to wean Edward's affection from me, and fix them on yourself, and at last succeeded so well, that, gaining them by little and little, you at length have monopolised the whole? Truly, I give you credit for the conquest, for his was not a heart easily fascinated.'

Rose seemed literally bewildered, and knew not what answer to make; this springing entirely from her innocence was construed by Albert and Marian into a proof of guilt; and making an effort to subdue the emotion, which was palpably depicted in his countenance, he addressed her as follows:—

'It is useless, Rose, to upbraid you for what is past. I was wrong to expect faith and constancy from woman, after the bitter experience I have already had of their frailty; yet, nevertheless, I did place confidence in you, which, alas! I have only too convincing a proof you have betrayed; surely,'' he said, with increased sadness, as he gazed upon her beauteous countenance, now flushed to a deep and crimson glow, 'surely guilt never dwelt in a more lovely form, or vice hid itself beneath so winning an exterior.'

'Albert,' returned Rose, 'you do not, you cannot think I have wronged you even in thought?'

'I have told you, Rose, that I am in possession of proof: my sister Marian and Henry Melville were both eye and ear witnesses of your interview with Edward this morning; this surely must convince you that concealment is now out of the question, after all that has passed. Were it even possible that I could forget the wound my honour has received, and still keep you beneath my roof, happiness, even for yourself, would be totally out of the question—return, therefore, to your parents in the country; for your sake, I will conceal from them my dishonour. I bitterly repent having withdrawn you from them, and placed you in society which has proved too dangerous; but I could not, at least I did not, foresee the consequences that were likely to accrue from so doing, although I feel that I ought to have done so; but now, alas! it is useless, all is over, and I trust you may yet find happiness on earth—You were innocent when I first knew you.'

'And am so still,' interrupted Rose, in a voice and manner so energetic, that it startled her companions; 'who dares to accuse me of guilt?'' and, at the moment, her eyes encountered those of Marian's. Had any unconcerned spectator been there to witness it, he would have been pained to observe the two confronting each other—both young, both lovely, and both women; and yet they bore the relative characters of accused and accuser. Marian's hair was pushed from her forehead, and hung loosely down her neck, affording a chilling contrast, by its shining blackness, to the face and neck, now perfectly colourless with excitement; her large black eyes seemed to dilate even beyond their ordinary size, and sent forth such deep anger in their glance that they really appeared to flash fire; her whole bearing appeared characteristic of wild and unearthly excitement, and the likeness which, at all times, she bore to her brother, was now so heightened that no one could for an instant have failed to recognise it. On the other hand, Rose's fair hair hung in rich profusion over her neck and shoulders, and her soft blue eyes, now lighted up with an unusual fire, quailed not before the angry glance of Marian; and the form of Rose was emblematic of retiring and modest beauty, blended so sweetly with innocence, that had not Albert been prejudiced against the sex, he could never have believed her guilty, had even the entire world branded her such.

Marian had made no reply, save by an angry glance of indignation, to Rose's question, 'Who dares to say I am guilty?' And, after a short pause, Albert began afresh:—'Concealment, as I before said, is no longer of any service to you; I had rather see you own your sin, yet none shall know the story of your disgrace through me. I cannot send you anywhere better than to the friends who, I am sure, love you, and will do their best to secure your happiness: attribute the whole blame of our separation to me, tell them that the incompatibility of my temper to mould itself to yours is the entire cause of your being under the necessity of returning to them. I pledge you my most solemn assurance that I will never breathe to them, nor to any one else, one word to the contrary: should any appeal be made to me, I will confirm them in their error. This, Rose, should prove to you that, though you have added bitterness to my sorrow, and misery to my grief, yet I still remember past days, when you were guileless as fair, as innocent as lovely.'

'Am I to understand,' said Rose, bending forward with clasped hands, in a beseeching attitude, 'am I to understand that you intend to send me from you—to turn me from your doors? Oh! never, never will I go; you will not, surely, remove me by force, and nothing else shall tear me from you. Guilty as you deem me, unworthy as I may be by birth and education to share your wealth and splendour, yet, knowing in my heart that I am innocent, I will cling to you through good and ill report,'

'Stop, Rose,' said Marian, angrily, 'and do not by your rash and unthinking speech, urge my brother to denounce you to your parents and friends as the guilty thing you are ; rather thank him for the kind and affectionate consideration he has shown for your feelings, but which you appear too hardened to appreciate.'

'Talk not thus to me,' replied Rose, roused to indignation even beyond what she herself was aware of, for her bosom was the seat of every gentle virtue that can adorn a woman—' talk not thus to me!' and then, turning to her husband, and subsiding instantly into her own natural softness, said, in a voice whose sweet and touching notes spoke more than the words, ' I am innocent, indeed I am innocent. Oh! no one on earth should induce me to think ill of you! Do me, oh! do me the same justice, and believe nothing that they urge against me! You relent, I am sure you do,' she added, springing forward, and making an effort to take his hand, which was stretched out on the table before him.

'It is perfectly useless, Rose' he said, coldly withdrawing it ; ' you must return to your parents. I do not forget that you have lately been accustomed to luxuries and enjoyments that they cannot procure, neither am I forgetful that you are shortly to become a mother ; and believe me, you shall want for nothing that money can procure.'

'Alas! alas!' said Rose, clasping her hands in agony, ' and is it possible that you think me mean enough to desire to remain with you for the sake of your wealth and splendour ?'

'To what else can I attribute it ?'

'Attribute it wholly and solely to the love I feel for you.'

Albert laughed bitterly, and then, checking the mockery of mirth, he said,—

'At one time, Rose, the knowledge of the frailty of one I loved could nerve me to the wildest revenge, and I was capable of any crime ; but the memory is so fraught with horror that I would gladly forget it. Oh! Rose, what thoughts hast thou not conjured up in my heart the last few minutes! I seemed to have lived over again years of agony!' and he rose and paced the room in very bitterness of heart.

'You will kill my brother,' said Marian, turning to Rose, and striving to speak calmly ; ' and to talk to him of love is indeed a sad and bitter mockery ; rather prepare at once for your departure than keep him thus tormented with your presence. He has behaved most handsome and honourably towards you, and, had you the least spark of feeling left, you would go at once ; for in thus boldly expressing your determination to set Albert's desire at defiance, we can only think you are actuated by a wish to remain near Edward.'

'Edward can have nothing at all to do with my desire not to leave my husband,' said Rose, still keeping her eyes which, spite of all else, were beaming with affection, fixed on Albert.

'Rose, Rose!' said Albert, suddenly stopping in his hurried walk across the room, ' you wring my heart with anguish, and force me to entertain a still worse opinion of you ; but as you seem so much to dislike returning to the country, you may choose your own residence, and, if you still persist in remaining in London, I will break up my establishment and go abroad for some time, perhaps never to return. It is now late in the morning ; I will give you till to-morrow to come to a decision, and expect by that time you will be prepared to leave this house. In the meantime I trust you will not intrude on my privacy ; I wish not to see you more ; the sight of beauty such as yours, joined to the knowledge of your degradation, maddens me. Whatever your wishes are, therefore, let me know them through the medium of another ; and be assured that, let them be ever so unreasonable, they shall, if possible, be complied with.'

Saying this, he was about to leave the room, but Rose, anticipating his intention, placed herself in front of the door,—' Oh! do not, pray do not leave me in anger. I am innocent in everything but appearance ; and I shall, I am confident, one day be able to prove to you the truth of my words. Oh! were I the guilty degraded being you think me, I should shrink abashed from your gaze—would gladly hide myself from your just displeasure. Should I not, think you, thankfully avail myself of your kind proposal and return to my parents, from whom I have just parted, to their sincere regret? Oh! Albert, my dear, dear husband, how little, how very little do you know of my heart! Did I not love you with the strongest affection that was ever nourished in the breast of woman, the thought of returning to the pleasures of a simple country life would be fraught with bliss ; wealth has no charm for me ; and for gaiety I have long had a distaste. God in heaven well knows that no thought or feeling, save my ardent love for you, prompts me to beg of you, even on my knees, who never knelt to man before, to allow me to remain near you, even in the same house, if it be only in the capacity of a servant ;' and she threw herself in the attitude of a suppliant before him.

'Rose, Rose,' he replied, with a firmness bordering on anger, ' kneel not to me again—I say it is useless ; you cannot move me from my purpose. Nothing shall induce me to tamper to my own dishonour—if even a brother were sacrificed ;' and his lips trembled convulsively, and he seemed unable to proceed.

'Oh, yes!' said Marian, earnestly, ' think of that, always think of that, and be not moved by her tears; she should have thought how dear you were to her before she betrayed your confidence.'

'Oh, my God!' exclaimed Rose, raising her clasped hands and streaming eyes to Heaven, 'thou alone knowest I am innocent. Oh! that thou wouldst make it clear in the eyes of him whom alone on earth I love!'

'Let me pass,' said Albert, evidently overcome at the sight of her distress.

'Oh no, no!' replied Rose, turning her eyes, which were almost blinded with tears, full upon his face; 'if not for my sake, for the sake of our unborn baby, pity my distress. Oh! while I kneel in this tearful agony, remember, that, had I been guilty, I would never have sued thus; but,' and she dashed away the tears from her eyes, 'I am innocent, God knows I am innocent!'

'Oh! can it be that she speaks truth, Marian?' said Albert; 'give me but a hope that it is so, and I will bless you for the same.'

'Ask Henry Melville,' she returned, 'he is still below, and will only repeat what I have already told you. I am not, I assure you, over anxious to believe ill of Edward, were there a possibility of a doubt; I came here this morning, and brought Henry purposely to satisfy myself whether there existed aught more than friendship between him and your wife.'

'Twice deceived—miserably, wretchedly deceived—my own eyes witnessed my dishonour, or then, fool, that I was! I had never have believed the base deception; but oh! Florence, thou wert so fair and lovely, and to all appearance as free from guile; but thou wert false, of that I had most damning proofs, and yet thou knelt to me and declared thy innocene—spoke, too, of thy unborn babe. Oh, God! my God! my brain is on fire—I am surely going mad!'

'Rose,' said Marian, endeavouring to raise her from her knees, and induce her to quit the room, 'we pity your distress, but you have brought it on yourself; be persuaded then to retire to your own apartment, you are now killing my brother and yourself.'

'No, no,' said Rose, casting Marian from her, with a strength that was truly astonishing. which, at another time, she might have endeavoured in vain to exercise, 'I will not, will not leave this room, till Albert assures me that I may remain with him. I ask for nothing more than to be allowed to be near him, to see him, to hear him speak, though he never breathes a word, save of bitterness. Oh! this, this is surely not asking too much?'

'It is, it is,' said Albert, moving and coming towards the door; 'I tell you, it must not, shall not be. I am proof against all you may urge, but desire not to be tormented with your presence; therefore, either leave the room, or make way for me to do so.'

'Never!' replied Rose, firmly, 'you may kill me, but you shall not drive me from you; you may forcibly turn me from this house, but I will, so long as I have strength to do so, return and watch by the door, till I die upon the threshold, pleased to know that I draw my latest breath within the sound of thy footstep, and perchance, e'er I do so, catch one last glimpse of thee.'

'Then stay,' replied Albert, sternly; 'but, Marian, you and I must to-morrow prepare to leave this country, perhaps, for ever. It contains nought now to make it dear; let us then, my sister,' and for a moment he melted to softness, 'let us hasten to go; you,' and he drew her to him with more of kindness that he had ever shown, 'are now all the world to me.'

'And you to me,'' said Marian, sobbing on her brother's shoulder.

'Then let us wander hand-in-hand, no matter where, so that we can together seek out some lonely nook, and there, forgetful and forgetting, pass the rest of our days, if possible, in peaceful serenity.'

'Yes, yes! let us go,' said Marian, twining her arms round her brother; and, mutually supporting each other, they essayed to leave the room; but Rose, whose head, whilst they were speaking, drooped upon her bosom, like a sweet-scented flower bending meekly to the blast, now suddenly started to her feet, and scarcely knowing, in her anger of mind, what she did, clasped her hands tightly on Albert's arm, so tightly that he strove in vain to cast her from him, while she exclaimed,—'Kill me! kill me; if you will; now, indeed, it would be almost a mercy; but, while life and health remain, thus I will cling to thee. You cannot, Albert, release yourself from my grasp,' she added, as he endeavoured, rather roughly, to tear her hands from him; 'it is despair that nerves me with strength to hold on; say that I may follow you wherever you go; that I may at least see and hear you; and, though forbidden to speak one word, I will humbly follow you at a distance. If my presence is hateful to you, I will endeavour to conceal myself from your gaze. You shall not even know for certain that I am near you. Oh! let me at least have the poor satisfaction of watching over you secretly!'

Rose's energies were beginning to give way—a mist seemed to gather before her eyes, yet she still clung to him with the wildness of desperation. Taking advantage of her loosening grasp, Albert, with a sudden effort, freed himself from her, and, still clinging to Marian, they together left the room. Rose, half unconsciously, made an effort to follow, with outstretched arms, but, finding herself incapable, and feeling that on him she had now looked her last, with one prolonged shriek, so shrill and piercing that it rang in the ears of those who heard it like a death-knell, fell lifeless to the ground.

As Albert and Marian were about entering an adjoining apartment, they met Rose's maid, who, hearing her shriek, was hastening to inquire the cause, and, not thinking it proceeded from the study, with bewildered looks was descending to the drawing-room; Albert touched her on the shoulder, and, pointing to the study, said, in a hoarse and broken voice, 'See to your mistress;' and then, closing the door on himself and Marian, threw himself on a chair, and still enfolding Marian in his embrace, bowed his head and wept—yes, wept long and bitterly.

For awhile Marian allowed him to indulge his sorrow, and when his bitterness was, in a measure, past, they conversed long and mournfully.

' Oh! Albert,' said Marian, ' we may yet be blessed,' and her voice trembled as she gave utterance to the words.

'We may—we may,' replied Albert, veiling his face; 'in solitude we may pass the remainder of our days, be they few or many, in peace; never again will we mingle with the world; we must henceforth live alone—apart from all others.'

' Let one share our solitude, and our days will glide on in peaceful serenity.'

' Whom would you desire to be with us? surely, after all we have experienced of the love of others, there can be no being in the wide world you wish to share our lot?'

' Yes, oh yes, Albert, there is one for whom my heart yearns—has long yearned; I spoke of him but now; it is one who is bound to us by no common tie—it is our brother.'

'Oh, name him not, Marian, for God's sake name him not,' and Albert's face assumed a ghastly hue, and his eyes rolled around the room in evident terror.

' I know, Albert,' resumed Marian, endeavouring to calm his agitation, ' that his very name recals to your recollection a frightful event, too frightful to dwell upon, yet, oh, let me entreat of you to forgive him the deed, consider the youth, the ardour of his affection, his over wrought feelings.'

' I have, Marian, considered all,' interrupted her brother, ' and have long felt that I was the most to blame.'

"Oh, then you will forgive him?' said Marian eagerly.

' I have forgiven him,' replied Albert solemnly; 'would that I could as easily forgive myself!'

' God be praised,' returned Marian; ' then you will consent to my desire, and we shall meet again. Yes Charles, my brother, I shall again embrace you, again gaze with rapture on thy face. Oh, will not this be bliss?' She turned to look on Albert's face, and was shocked to observe a look of fixed horror on his countenance: his eyes were intently bent on the ground, his mouth was closely shut and contracted, and his whole frame shook as with some convulsive struggle, and large drops of sweat stood upon his forehead; to look upon him, any one would have thought that some appalling sight met his gaze.

Marian shuddered as she witnessed his appearance, and would have spoken, but her tongue seemed to cleave to the roof of her mouth, and refused to give utterance to the words she would fain have spoken.

Alas! she was now sure that something more than she was aware of was connected with the fate of Charles, else why should his very name conjure up apparently such direful thoughts as now agitated the frame of Albert? True, she looked upon him as the murderer of Florence—Florence, who was tenderly beloved by both her brothers; and awful enough it was that one brother should, through his inability to command his affection, be the means of the other committing such a dreadful deed; but then Albert declared he had forgiven him; and now that years had passed, he surely might hear his name mentioned without horror; but then she thought again, they had never, she fully believed, met since the tragical occurrence, and, per-chance, the idea of again being face to face with Charles brought back the remembrance of the past so vividly to his mind, as to cause the horror and anguish now visible in his counten-ance: yes, that must be it, she was surely right in her conjecture, and, throwing her arms around her brother's neck, with mingled tears and kisses sought to win him back to peace and hope. He was insensible to her caresses, and endeavoured to repay her kindness by smiling, which was, indeed, an effort, for he felt as though his heart were breaking.

Time passed on, yet no one intruded on their privacy; they ceased to speak, but each com-muned in silence with their own thoughts. Marian, though severed she felt for ever from a husband upon whom she had cast her earliest affections, and with whom she had lived in harmony for several years, yet was now plunged into the depths of misery, and Albert acknowledged for his portion. Marian was differently constituted, and most certainly made up of strange contrarieties; her affection for her brothers, and especially for Charles, was the most predominant and amiable feature in her character; her love for Charles had from her infancy been tinged with romance, which after years and a mysterious separation had greatly increased, and, in proportion as her hopes of beholding him again grew stronger, so did the romantic affection she felt for him increase ; we do not mean to say that she was wholly devoid of anguish at her husband's conduct, on the contrary, she undoubtedly felt it severely; but hers was a proud nature, and she felt more of indignation against Rose than bitter grief for the loss of Edward's affection; and, feeling herself deeply injured, she deemed it far beneath her dignity ever again to consider him in the light of a husband. No : a barrier from henceforth she felt was placed between them—a barrier that it would be worse than weakness in her ever to allow (even if Edward desired,) to be broken down, and it is strange how eager we all are to supply a vacant place, if we have one in our hearts! Thus, Marian turned he thoughts and affections solely on her brothers, and in the eager anticipation of again beholding one she so dearly and ardently loved, endeavoured to forget the wound her pride and self-love had received; Albert, ever moody and full of painful thought, dwelt bitterly upon the workings of what he deemed fate, that was his scape goat, and he loaded it well and heavily with the sins he committed. 'There is a fatality,' he inwardly exclaimed, as busy wandering thought, free as the pure air from the mountain, roved over scenes and days long passed—'there is surely fatality in all that concerns me ;' and Albert certainly possessed a rare faculty for remembering every trivial ill that had occurred to him, even in the days of childhood, while all the sweet green sunny spots, that live in most men's memory, and which all have know more or less in early youth, and which come forth, fresh and warm in our recollections, of what we feel proud to term, 'Auld lang syne.' How sweet it is to hold converse with some old play-fellow, and the merry lightsome frolics in which we used to indulge; each mirth-roving adventure of our early days is counted o'er and o'er again with renewed zeal, till we seem to live once more in days gone by ; to be again the happy careless child, looking only on the bright and fairest side of life, building afresh our castles in the air, and laughing as we see them tumble to the ground, eager again to uprear them, forgetful of our first mishap. All this, that is so precious and delightful to others, was completely sunk in oblivion to Albert. He could only remember each little trouble that had ever cost his bosom a pang, and he would rake up everything from the ashes of memory, that had at any time caused him any annoyance, and then, blindly attributing it to fate, would declare that his lot was cursed above his fellows—that he was singled out as a being upon whom trouble upon trouble, wound upon wound, was to be heaped without mercy, while other more fortunate individuals, were to go through life pleasantly and smoothly, with scarcely anything to annoy, much less to trouble them. Truly, misanthropes have a curious power of magnifying all their own ills and misfortunes, whole those of their neighbours they view in a very different light. We ourselves cannot help thinking that misanthropy arises, in the first place, from a very selfish disposition, which, growing discontented, because they cannot enjoy all the blessings of life, but find that they must take the thorns and briers as well as the sweet-scented rose-buds, fret their proud spirits into a state of mind that they dignify by the name of misanthropy—a fine sounding, dignified word, it is true ; but if we trace it to its real source, and are correct in our ideas on the subject, all must necessarily acknowledge that there is nothing at all dignified in the state of mind that it implies—it being in our opinion, far more dignified to bear the ills of life bravely, to make the most of the flowery paths which are spread alike for all, and when we get entangled in the briers and hedges, which occasionally spring up between us and some fair spot, all fresh and green, fight our way good humouredly through them all, till we reach the goal that tempted us to brave all difficulties, and throw our wearied spirits down to rest. Oh! is it not wiser—is it not far pleasanter to pass through life with smiles upon our lips and sunlight on our brow; to pluck the flowers that are strewn profusely around, and lighten our journey by choosing some dear companions and friends to pursue it with us ; to drain long draughts from the cup of happiness whenever it is proffered to our lips—instead, as gloomy, moody misanthropes do, of sitting down and bewailing every little scratch we may receive in forcing our way through the envious briers which will sometimes endeavour to stop our paths? Oh! let us rather dwell long upon and keep fresh in our memory all the bright and happy hours we have ever known; for even the retrospection will ever afford us delight. And let us, at the same time, ' wipe from the tablets of our memory' all the darker shades of our existence ; for oh! it were foolish to give one thought to the circumstances that pained us at the time of their occurrence. Oh! when they are past and gone, let them be for ever forgotten.

Albert and Marian had been for some time buried in deep thought; they knew not well how long—it might have been for some hours for aught they could tell, when they were aroused by a tap at the door. They both started; silence had for a long time reigned supreme, and this was the first intimation that they had received that others were in the house, and the knock was repeated before either of them made an effort to attend to it. Albert then, releasing himself from his sister, gently opened it, and, to his surprise, beheld Henry Melville.

' To what do I owe this unexpected visit?' said Albert, drawing back with on air of cold surprise.

'This is no time for ceremony, Mr. Moreland,' replied Henry, evidently endeavouring to speak calmly, ' or I would not have intruded upon you.'

'Come at once to the object of the visit,' said Albert, with increased coldness; ' had I known you were here, I should have refused to see you, as my greatest desire is to remain undisturbed by strangers.'

'Mrs. Moreland,' replied Henry, giving no heed to Albert's observations, ' is very seriously indisposed, so much so, that it is absolutely necessary that some female relative should attend upon her.'

'I told her own servant to attend upon her,' returned Albert; ' what more can I do?'

'What more can you do!' replied Henry, indignantly; ' I tell you she is seriously ill. God only knows, indeed, whether she will ever recover.'

'What would you have of me?' said Albert.

'Mrs. Trevors,' said Henry, advancing a little within the room, and taking no notice whatever of Albert's last words, ' your sister is entirely insensible, and evidently in a very dangerous state; such being the case, I should think your own desire would prompt you immediately to send her all the assistance in your power.'

'I am perfectly at a loss,' replied Marian, ' to know in what way I can render her any assistance; there are plenty of female servants in the house.'

'Servants!' interrupted Henry; ' and would you leave so near a relative, in almost a dying state, entirely to the care of menials?'

'I am myself,' replied Marian, ' totally unfit to watch by a sick bed, and, though grieved for Rose's illness, yet I can but remember she as brought it all on herself: she insisted, in spite of our united endeavours to the contrary, in giving way to the most violent passion, although my brother, so far from upbraiding her with her guilt, made her the most handsome offer of returning her to her parents, and at the same time concealing from them the knowledge of her shame, yet she resolutely refused to leave this house, and threw herself into such emotions, that I am by no means surprised to hear of her indisposition; indeed, it is no more than I fully anticipated.'

'It is useless to speak of that now,' returned Henry; ' Mrs. Moreland is very ill, and the only question is, whether you will, or will not, cast from you bosom all bitter feeling against her, and perform the office of a kind and tender nurse.'

'I stated but now that I was unfit for the task; neither do I think, were Rose capable of choosing, she would be pleased with my attendance.'

'Very well,' returned Henry; ' but Rose shall not, I am determined, be left to the care of a servant;' and then turning to Albert, he added, ' were Rose in a fit state to be removed, I would convey her to my mother's house; but, as I fear she is in far too dangerous and critical a position to admit of that, you will not, I think, object to my fetching my sister here; and Lucy, I know full well, will be only pleased, if she can be of service to one in distress.'

'Do as you will,' replied Albert, ' I am anxious that Rose should have every assistance: guilty and deceitful as she is, I would not on that account she should be neglected.'

'I will go immediately, then,' said Henry; ' I have already sent for medical advice and shall not be long before I return with Lucy, and then, if you will grant me a private interview of a few minutes, I shall take it as a favour.'

'Well, then, be it so,' returned Albert, with evident reluctance; ' you will find me here, and after that interview is over, I trust you will not disturb me more.'

'Fear not,' replied Henry, ' that I will again intrude myself an unwelcome visitor into your presence. I would not even ask the few minutes I now seek to converse with you alone, did I not consider it my duty to do so; but I am now as anxious to go as you are for me to leave you,' and, without a word more, he left the room.

When Rose uttered the piercing shriek we have before mentioned, Henry was patiently waiting in the drawing-room, to hear the result of Marian's interview with her brother. Startled at this sound of distress, without a moment's hesitation he hastened to inquire into the cause, and arrived at the study door at the same instant as the maid whom Albert and Marian had met in their passage from the room; and bending over the prostrate form of Rose, Henry was the first to raise her from the ground, when, horror-struck at the havoc grief had in so short a time made in her fair countenance, but lately beaming with hope and health, he tenderly conveyed her to a sofa, and, with the assistance of her servant, endeavoured, by every means, to restore animation to her lifeless frame.

'She will die,' exclaimed the poor girl, wringing her hands in agony, for she was tenderly attached to Rose.

'No, no, my girl, do not thus alarm yourself, or you will be incapacitated for attending upon your mistress; and yet,' he added, half unconsciously, ' it is sad, it is dreadful to see her thus let some one,' he continued, in a louder tone, 'run directly for the nearest surgeon, and then, my good girl, remain here while I acquaint Mrs. Trevers and Mr. Moreland of her illness.'

We have seen the result of Henry's kind intercession with Marian on the behalf of Rose, and also heard the resolution he expressed to fetch his sister, the kind and gentle Lucy, to watch by Rose's couch. Getting into the first vehicle that offered itself, Henry soon reached his mother's abode, and finding Lucy fortunately at home, lost no time in making her acquainted with all that had passed at Mr. Moreland's, and the services he required of her, and truly did he find he had not overrated the excellence of his sister's character, when he said,—'He knew she would be happy to be of service to one in distress.'

Willingly, nay, gladly, did Lucy return with him to Mr. Moreland's, and her gentle bosom heaved with anguish as she gazed upon the altered face of Rose. During Henry's absence, she had been removed, under the doctor's orders, into her bed-room, and by the bed-side Lucy now took her station, receiving information from the doctor as to the treatment of his patient, which she assured him she would see was rigidly attended to.

'In that case, my dear young lady, I will for a time take my leave; but should any change take place, do not fail to send to me immediately.'

Poor Rose! a change had indeed 'come o'er the spirit of her dream.' It is strange and painful to think what a terrible alteration a few short hours may work; that morning Rose's heart had been light, and free from care, her spirits more buoyant than usual, for her fondest hopes seemed on the point of being realized. Yes, Albert had relaxed the sternness of his brow, had conversed with her in a tone of tender familiarity he had never before assumed, had manifested a cheerfulness totally unusual to him, and her most anxious desire had long been to win him from the melancholy which so constantly surrounded him, and her heart had danced with joy at the prospect of happily accomplishing her wishes: but all her hopes were suddenly dashed to the ground, and she had heard (oh! with what direful bitterness of heart) herself accused of unfaithfulness toward the being upon whom she so fondly lavished every thought and feeling of her young, pure heart. None can know, or for a moment even conceive, the heart-stirring anguish that wrought so awfully on the frame as to steep every sense in forgetfulness: none can form an idea of the maddening intensity of her anguish but those who have themselves been falsely accused, and trembled lest those they love dearest on earth should give credit to their calumniators. It is oftentimes so difficult for the innocent to clear themselves of the vile aspersions cast upon their spotless names, that even their just indignation, which should be a proof of their innocence, is more often held as a proof of guilt. Thus it was with poor Rose, who could only exclaim, 'I am innocent, indeed I am innocent.' These were almost the last words that escaped her ere her senses forsook her; and the first exclamation that burst from her lips when, once more awakened to renewed life, she became conscious of surrounding objects; and as her eyes, all dim and lustreless, fell upon the form of Lucy, who, kindly bending over her, inquired how she felt, the touching and earnest manner in which she repeated ' I am innocent,' went to Lucy's very heart; and, turning away to hide the tears that choked her utterance, she could only press the dry and feverish hand Rose presented to her, in silence to her lips.

' You must keep yourself quiet, my dearest Rose,' she said, after she had succeeded in calming a little her own emotion; 'you have been, indeed still are, very ill, and I have come purposely to nurse and attend you. Think me your sister, Rose; as such, indeed, I am at heart.'

' My sister,' repeated Rose earnestly, 'come here purposely to nurse me! I thought——'

' Hush, dear Rose; you must not talk now. I know all you would say, but you have mistaken us. Yes, you judged wrong both of myself and Henry; for, though you thought ill of us, we have ever been entirely devoted to you.'

Rose made an effort to reply; but Lucy motioned her to be silent, saying at the same time, ' suffice it for the present, Rose, that we know and understand each other, when you are perfectly recovered, we can mutually enter into an explanation.'

Rose shook her head mournfully, and with an expression of countenance that seemed to say she had no desire to recover. It is a pleasing, and yet a painful task to watch by the sick bed of some dear relative or friend, to administer to their comfort by a thousand little tender offices that are sweet and precious to the sufferer, and are valued tenfold more than the strongest protestations of love or friendship, and the tenderest manifestations of regard shown when we are in the enjoyment of health and vigour. Oh! sorrow and sickness will soon prove to us who are and who are not our real friends. We have all of us plenty of self-styled friends, who buzz about like summer flies in our prosperity; but wait until a winter's day of storm and cold draws nigh, and then, perchance, we may deem ourselves blessed if one heart remains true in misfortune."

Lucy was, indeed, truly attached to Rose; and though, of late, repulsed in her effort to serve her, yet, knowing it proceeded from the guileful influence Edward had obtained over her, and not from any wrong feeling nourished in the bosom of one who, she felt certain, was herself free from all sin, so far as it is possible to be so in this world; knowing and feeling all this, she was only too happy to avail herself of the opportunity of showing Rose how sadly she was mistaken in her character; and now, as the invalid sunk into a quiet sleep, she remained perfectly motionless by her side, fearful that even her breathing might disturb her repose. Rose slept for several hours, and still Lucy stirred not from the position she had assumed; but, tenderly gazing with tearful eyes upon her face, remained in deep thought. She had much to render her unhappy, and afford her matter for sad reflection: she was well aware her brother intended seeking an explanation of Edward concerning her who now lay helplessly extended before her, and she shuddered as she thought to what that explanation would lead. She knew the temper and bearing of both of them too well to doubt for a moment that the end of it would be bloodshed; perhaps she had even now looked her last upon that brother who from infancy had ever been her dearest friend and companion—one upon whom she could lean for succour and consolation in every trial—who was ever ready to bare his own bosom to the storm, so that he might shield and protect her. She thought that she might be doomed to lose this, her best and dearest friend—that his days might be cut short by the hand of Edward, of one to whom she had paid her first and earliest vows of love—the bare thought blanched her cheek to a deadly white, and curdled the life blood in her veins; still she moved not, though thought had become so dreadful that she was sick and faint, till towards midnight when Rose suddenly roused. In an instant Lucy cast from her mind the chain of ideas that the moment before had seemed rivetted there, and giving every thought and feeling at once to Rose, was shocked to observe that she seemed decidedly worse. Her eyes, that were before dull and lustreless, were now lit up with an almost unearthly brightness; a burning crimson spot sat upon either cheek, and the palms of her hands were parched up and dry with heat. She became also dreadfully restless, tossing from side to side, and now and then giving utterance to sentences that showed her mind was wandering.

Inexpressibly pained by these alarming symptoms, Lucy immediately sent a messenger for the doctor, who, on his arrival, confirmed her worst fears.

'If she has any relatives or friends,' said the doctor, 'it is but right that they should be made acquainted with her situation, as she is certainly in great danger.'

'She has a mother,' replied Lucy, 'and I will send for her at once. Alas! alas!' she ejaculated, still gazing on the face of Rose, 'I fear it will break her heart!'

Nothing could induce Lucy to leave the sick room for a minute, but she desired the maid to give the necessary orders for a messenger being immediately despatched to fetch Mrs. Sommerville to the bedside of her daughter, from whom she had so lately parted, in the very bloom of health and beauty, and now so suddenly brought low.

Rose continued in the same state of fever and insensibility all night, and towards morning prematurely gave birth to a still-born son: thus the poor babe fell a sacrifice to its mother's bitter anguish, before it ever saw the light.

Till this moment, Lucy had not once left the room since she first entered it; but now, pressing a kiss upon the burning cheek of the still unconscious Rose, she crept slowly from it, and, ascending the stairs, knocked gently at the door of the room which the servant had pointed out as the one wherein Albert and Marian were sitting: a voice bade her enter, and, doing so, she speedily communicated the intelligence of the birth of the child.

'It is well,' exclaimed Albert, as soon as she had ceased speaking, 'it is better thus; I would not have it otherwise.'

Lucy looked at him with an expression of countenance that appeared to doubt his reason, and then, turning to Marian, she said,—

'Rose is still very ill; I have sent for Mrs. Sommerville, who, I trust, will arrive in the course of a few hours, or, indeed, she may be too late to see her daughter alive.'

'Is she indeed so ill?' said Marian, apparently touched.

'So ill,' returned Lucy, 'that I think all her troubles will soon end. It is sad to think of one so young and beautiful descending so suddenly to an early grave;' and the tears she had previously restrained gushed in torrents from her eyes.

'I had fully intended to have left England with Marian this very day,' said Albert, 'but I cannot go while Rose remains in the state you describe—I will therefore wait the termination of her disorder; I do not forget she is my wife, though she can apparently forget that I am her husband.'

'Oh, believe it not,' said Lucy, looking up in the midst of her tears, 'nothing on earth should induce me to believe it but her own avowal, and, so far from doing so, she has repeated, even in the height of her delirium, "I am innocent!" and she is innocent, I am convinced she is.'

'You would not even then give credit to your own eyes and ears, I suppose?' said Marian.

'Henry has told me all that you saw and heard concerning her and Edward, and, though I entertain the very worst opinion of his designs towards poor unfortunate Rose, yet, so far from deeming her guilty, I acquit her even of a knowledge of his desires; he has induced her, by the most artful and specious manners which he has assumed, to gain if possible his own ends, I say he has in this way induced her to regard him in the light of an affectionate brother, who has her welfare and interest at heart; at the same time, he has done his best to make her entertain a bad opinion of myself and Henry, has not indeed hesitated to affirm the most direct falsehoods as regarded us, and thus he has succeeded most unhappily in imposing on Rose's credulity.'

'You forget the letter which she sent Edward from the country, and of which she refused to give you any account,' said Marian.

'No,' replied Lucy, 'I do not forget that letter, nor do I forget that I have since ascertained, no matter how, that Edward wrote to her by the same post as I did, and undoubtedly advised her how to reply to mine.'

'Well, it is useless to argue about it more,' returned Marian, endeavouring to assume an air of indifference.

'Worse than useless,' replied Lucy, 'for it is detaining me from Rose, to whom I am anxious to return.'

Lucy found her in much the same state as she left her, and, resuming her position by the side of the bed, did her best to cool the fevered brow of the patient, and moisten her parched lips—a blessed and holy task, and one in which woman shines pre-eminent: it is her alone that can noiselessly move through a sick room, and, with light and skilful hand, apply the cooling lotion to the forehead, or offer with prompt exactness the medicine that is intended to relieve pain, subduing the violence of her own emotions, shedding no tear, unless she turn away and drop it unheeded by the sufferer: at such a time self is totally forgotten by her—all her energies, hopes, and fears are excited for another. With what eagerness does she anticipate each little want, arranging and smoothing the pillows, so as they shall be soft to the aching head, administering a cooling beverage, ere the patient hath time to express a wish for it. Oh! these, and numberless other gentle and loving offices, doth a woman perform in the sick chamber; and these were never more tenderly or lovingly performed than by Lucy Melville.

When Henry had brought his sister and placed her as nurse in the sick room of Rose, feeling that he himself could be of no further use, he proceeded to the room occupied by Albert, and demanded the interview with him that he had previously promised to grant.

Albert, leaving his sister alone, led the way into an adjoining apartment, and then, closing the door, turned round, and, confronting Henry, said,—

'You must be well aware that it is exceedingly painful to me either to see or converse with you. You have witnessed, Marian informs me, what can only be interpreted into almost convincing proof of my dishonour, and, consequently, your presence is anything but agreeable to me. Tell me at once, therefore, what is your desire in seeking this interview, that it may the more speedily be brought to a close.'

'I have,' began Henry, 'as you rightly observe, been a witness of the great familiarity that exists between Mrs. Moreland and Mr. Trevors, and it is that I have been a witness of that, and also of much more—of Edward's villany—that has brought me here this evening. I desire,' continued Henry, raising his voice, and looking steadfastly at the other's countenance—'I desire to know if, after what you have heard of Mr. Trevors' conduct towards your wife, you intend to allow him to go unpunished?'

Henry ceased speaking, but continued to gaze on Albert's countenance, which exhibited signs of evident discomposure.

'To what end do you put that question?' replied Albert, after a pause of a few seconds. 'I know not what right you have to do so; but perhaps you will be kind enough to explain your motive?'

This was spoken in sentences, with a pause after each, as though he were musing on something partly foreign to the subject.

'My motive is this,' replied Henry, with firmness, 'Edward has behaved in the most dishonourable manner towards myself as well as towards you, and dishonour can only be wiped out in the blood of him who caused it.'

These words seemed to recal Albert's scattered senses, and, with a shuddering that appeared to affect his whole frame, he, with difficulty, contrived to speak with at least something like the appearance of calmness.

'There was a time, Mr. Melville, when I thought and felt as you now do, but that is long ago. Blood,' and he spoke the word with a tremor, 'may never more be shed by me! the very thought turns me faint and sick.'

'That being the case,' replied Henry, with a contempt that he could not conceal from the other's observation, 'I will take him in hand myself, and, believe me, I applied to you with the utmost reluctance, doing violence to the wish, I can truly assure you, lay uppermost in my breast —that of revenging the wrongs he has heaped upon your unhappy wife, with my own hand; thank God!' he added, as he turned to leave the room, 'I have no womanish horror at the sight of blood.'

The handle of the door was in his hand, but, at the moment he was about to turn the lock, he was arrested by the voice of Albert, who cried in a tone at once of sternness and command,—

'Stop!'

Henry immediately loosened his grasp, and, turning round, once more faced Albert, and folding his arms, waited what more he had to say.

'I thought,' began Albert, 'that I had attained to that degree of dignity and firmness with myself, that I cared little or nothing what others thought; that, in short, being well satisfied with myself, I could afford to allow others to entertain a bad opinion of me.' He paused, but Henry making no reply, he again went on: 'You have just now convinced me that my idea is erroneous, for I cannot allow you to leave this house, carrying with you a mean opinion of me; you think I am actuated by cowardly feelings in not availing myself of the opportunity you have just afforded me of sending a challenge to Edward.'

'I should have thought,' replied Henry, 'that you would have required no opportunity; your own desire would have prompted you alone to seek for instant revenge for the foul dishonour that shall hereafter rest upon your shield, and which, as I said before, nothing but the blood of the injurer can wipe out.'

'You can calmly speak of blood,' returned Albert, shuddering; 'but,' and his face assumed the hue a spectre is supposed to wear, 'you have never shed any.'

'Before this time to-morrow,' he replied, 'I hope to do so! and shall account blood so shed as nought but an acceptable sacrifice, which will lie very lightly on my conscience. What!' and he turned his open manly countenance full on the pallid features and sunken eyes of Albert, 'would you allow this man to go free— to practise fearlessly some further villany on the young and unwary? Oh, never! never shall it be so, while I have an arm and strength to use it.'

'You, you are different,' replied Albert. 'I was once the same: to know myself deceived, and recklessly to seek the wildest revenge, was one and the same thing. But oh! I have seen, have felt—what, God forbid, you should ever see or feel—the thought even now, at the distance of years, drives me almost to madness. Oh! blood, blood lies heavily on my heart —the bloood of one that was nearest and dearest to me on earth—to whom I was bound by every tender tie. Henry Melville, when I tell you this, the heart burning secret that is daily, hourly consuming me—that pursues me like the memory of a horrid dream, saddening even my lightest hours, crying perpetually aloud for vengeance—oh! when I tell you this (and let this care-worn brow, these hollow cheeks, and these sunken eyes vouch for the truth of my statement), then say, can you attribute my horror to the very name of blood to cowardice?'

'No, no,' said Henry, frankly extending his hand, which Albert met with more cordiality than he generally showed; 'no, no; I can understand and appreciate your feelings; they must indeed be dreadful.'

'They are,' returned Albert, and he bowed his head upon his breast. 'You are the first to whom I ever breathed a word of this; but I know I can depend on your secrecy.'

'Be assured that your secret will die with me. Should it be my fate to fall in the duel that will take place between myself and Edward to-morrow, you will, in remembrance of the tender care she is now manifesting for Rose, do your best to fill my place to Lucy. I would choose you above all men as her guardian and protector, for I know, if you give me your word to be kind to her, you will hold it sacred.'

'I give you my most solemn promise,' replied Albert, ' that in case (which God in his mercy avert!) your life should fall a sacrifice, that so long as I live will I take Lucy under my most especial protection; nought that I can avoid by the most watchful care shall ever cause her bosom even the slightest pang.'

'I thank you,' said Henry; 'your words have relieved me from an anxiety I only felt on account of her. To-morrow, if I live, you shall hear from me again, till then——'

'Farewell!' said Albert, emphatically.

'Farewell!' re-echoed Henry, as he left the room.

Once more alone, Albert, with anguish imprinted on his countenance, with hurried step paced the floor of the room, muttering to himself from time to time—'Another victim—oh! when will this cease? where, alas! where can I turn—ruined in my fondest hopes, doomed to see all around me, all who can by any means claim kith or kin with me, hurled recklessly from the very pinnacle of happiness down, down to the depths of despair! And oh! if my heart forebodes aright, ere another day shall close o'er my luckless head, this warm-hearted young man, now in the very prime and vigour of manhood shall no longer breathe the breath of life; and I—oh, dreadful thought!—I alone the cause. And her, his gentle sister; alas, alas! who will be equal to the task of soothing her distress? Oh, misery! that I, fiend-like, should thus wither and destroy the happiness of all within my reach, and yet fate has so ordained it; I am compelled, not only to suffer myself, but to cause, and then calmly look on, the sufferings of others. Would that I could avoid this! but no, it is my destiny—a sad and fearful destiny it is true, and yet I can do nothing but fill it up; it is useless to strive against it, God knows how much and vainly I have striven, and yet would that this last stroke had been spared me!'

Marian had remained alone while Henry conversed with Albert, but having heard him leave the room, and her brother not returning to her, she now ventured to open the door, and take a peep inside. Seeing her brother pacing the room with evident anxiety depicted on his countenance, she pronounced his name; he turned, and in the next moment was again clasped to her bosom. Neither of them thought for an instant of retiring to rest; their minds were too absorbed by the events of the day, to allow them to think of repose, and they remained (seated side by side, each clasping the other by the hand, though but few words escaped them) the entire night undisturbed save by the entrance of Lucy, who came to communicate the painful tidings of Rose's illness, and the premature birth of her child. When Henry Melville left Albert, he proceeded direct to the hotel where Sir Charles Mortimer resided, and, sending up his card, was immediately admitted.

'I am afraid you have come on no pleasant business,' said Mortimer, as Henry entered, and he noted his harassed and care-worn appearance.

'I have come,' replied Henry, 'to claim that service of you, you promised to grant whenever I might require it.'

'And you find me ready and willing to fulfil the promise; but help yourself, my good fellow,' he added, pushing a bottle towards him which stood on the table.

'I thank you,' replied Henry, 'but I cannot drink to-night; I must even, I fear, stop your libations, at least for a time, as I am desirous of your carrying a message to Mr. Trevors immediately: he is now at the club, expecting to hear from me; and I would not,' he continued, with a satirical smile, 'keep him longer in suspense than I can well help.'

'I am at your service now—therefore, give me your instructions at once, and I will be off.'

They then conversed for some time, after which they left the hotel together. As soon as they were in the street, Henry said, addressing his companion, 'There are a few things I wish to arrange at home, in case it may be my lot to fall; but, in two hours from the present time, I will again join you here;' and, mutually wishing each other good evening, they pursued different roads, Mortimer took that which led to the club; upon entering which, and casting a hasty glance around, he discovered Edward and Fairford seated at one of the tables; approaching nearer, he heard singing, and Edward, with goblet in hand, he found had arrived to about the middle of the popular melody,

'When glasses sparkle round the board.'

Not wishing to interrupt him, he remained concealed from their notice, till, with a full, clear voice, he concluded the last stanza,

'If life's a pain, I say again,
    Why, drown it in the bowl.'

'Bravo!' exclaimed Fairford, smacking the foot of his glass vehemently on the table; 'that's the song for me; come, fill yourself a bumper, and let's be happy while we can, and merry while we may.'

'Yes,' replied Edward, as he drained off the contents of his goblet, 'a short life, and a merry one for me.'

'So say I, old boy,' returned Fairford; 'what is the good of a long life, I should like to know, if we are to spend it in dullness and care? for my part, I'd rather bid it good-bye at once, and take my chance of finding some more congenial clime elsewhere.'

'As to that,' replied Edward, 'I can't say I have much faith in the popular doctrine of heaven and hell; it may be some comfort to a weak mind to suppose that when he leaves this world he may be fortunately installed into a better; but, for myself, I am well content with my present situation, and have no desire to leave it; but come, Fairford, you must give us a song; let us spend the evening as merrily as we can.'

'With all my heart,' replied Fairford, and he immediately commenced 'Friend of my soul this goblet sip.'

'Surely,' thought Mortimer, who remained still unobserved, 'Mr. Trevors cannot be expecting the challenge I have come to bring him. Mr. Melville must be labouring under a mistake. At any rate, I will take advantage of the next pause to break in upon their merriment.' Accordingly, as soon as Fairford had finished his song, and before Edward had time to make any observation, he stepped up to the table, and said, by way of apology for the interruption, 'I am sorry, gentlemen, to be obliged to put a stop to your hilarity, but I come on business that is at once painful and pressing. Did it admit of delay, I would not, I assure you, have intruded at the present time.'

'No apology is necessary,' returned Edward; 'you come, I presume, from Mr. Melville: we have been expecting you a long while.'

'Had I known that,' returned Mortimer, 'I would have spoken sooner, as I have been waiting some time, in hopes of having the opportunity of taking advantage of a break in your conversation, not wishing to disturb your mirth.'

'Of course,' said Edward, carelessly, 'you bring a challenge. Fairford has received instructions from me to arrange everything with you: only appoint an early hour for the meeting, as, in things of this sort, I hate delay.'

'You but anticipate the wishes of Mr. Melville,' returned Mortimer; 'he charged me to insist upon its taking place to-morrow morning.'

'That exactly meets my wishes,' replied Edward; 'Fairford, you will oblige me by proceeding to arrange everything necessary at once, and then we can conclude the evening as we have begun it, in merriment.'

Mr. Fairford immediately withdrew Sir Charles Mortimer to a distant part of the room, where they soon settled the preliminaries, and then, with a word of caution to be particular as to time, Fairford returned to Edward, and commenced the festivities of the evening afresh, and with renewed vigour after this interruption. They drank long and deep—song after song was given and applauded, till day began almost imperceptibly to dawn, when, pledging each other in a farewell cup, they sallied forth into the cool fresh air, disturbing the calm silence of that early hour by rude shouts and snatches of songs. Arrived at Fairford's apartment,

Edward threw himself on a couch, in order to seek that repose, which was absolutely necessary to refresh his exhausted frame, while Fairford examined his pistol-case. to see that all was ready for immediate use. Time wore on, till the sound of wheels announced the arrival of the coach Fairford had ordered to convey them to their destination; awakening Edward, he informed him all was in readiness, and, in a few minutes, they were seated in the vehicle, and hastening rapidly towards the ill-fated spot. They conversed together during their journey on things and subjects totally foreign to the object they had in view in thus taking an early drive, till they had nearly reached the place appointed for meeting, when Edward suddenly exclaimed,—

'I will not conceal from you, Fairford, that I have not yet succeeded in gaining Rose; still I do not repent having resolved to accept Melville's challenge, as it may serve to help my suit with her; though, at the same time, I would, had it been possible, much sooner have preferred deferring this duel till she was entirely my own; I should then have had the satisfaction of knowing, that if I fell, it would be in the moment of victory; but now, if I lose my life in this encounter, it will be sacrificed without obtaining aught that made it worth the cost.'

'Think not of falling,' replied Fairford; 'the first fire is yours by right, and you have ever been famed for a clear eye and a steady aim; therefore you may make sure of disabling him, in a manner that will put it out of his power to do you any serious injury.'

'You say right,' returned Edward; 'I have, indeed, ever been famed for possessing a clear eye and a steady aim, and if they ever did me good service, I hope they will do so this day; and then see if I do not succeed in winning the fair and lovely Rose: she has already given me good proof that she regards me highly, therefore, with that sweet reward in prospect, I will not, even for one moment, despair.

Henry Melville slowly retraced his steps to his mother's residence.

'My dear Henry,' she exclaimed, as he entered, 'how very indisposed you look; you must absolutely take some refreshment and retire to rest immediately.'

'No, no, my dear mother,' replied Henry, 'I am, I assure you, perfectly well, and have only now come home to arrange a few trifling things, and shall then return to Mr. Mo eland's, as my services may perhaps be required by him. I know, my dear mother, that it is hardly right for both myself and Lucy to leave you at the same time, but your own kind heart will, I am sure, prompt you to forgive us, for you are ever ready to succour the distressed.'

'Certainly, Henry; I should be the last to prevent you affording assistance to any that might require it, and shall therefore most gladly resign you.'

And Mrs. Melville, though a most kind and anxious mother—even apt to be, if anything, over solicitous for their health and comfort—did not now say one word concerning her fear of their over-fatiguing themselves. This is worthy of remark, as showing how a really good and feeling heart will forget all connected with self, and think only on the sorrows and distresses of others.

Retiring to his own room, Henry wrote a kind and affectionate letter to his mother and sister, and having disposed of a few other things, in anticipation that the forthcoming duel might prove fatal to him, he placed the letters in his bosom, and with a heavy heart prepared to bid his mother farewell, perhaps for ever. It was a hard task to conceal from his tender parent the suffocating emotions that filled his breast, and when he affectionately kissed her cheek and bade her be careful of herself in his absence from home, she was somewhat startled by his earnest manner.

'Henry, my dear child,' she said, as she gazed with maternal pride upon his open, manly countenance, and pushed from his forehead the thick, clustering curls, that she might press it with her lips, 'did I not know that it was impossible that you could leave me for any length of time without informing me of your intention, I should imagine, from your serious and almost melancholy leave taking, that you were contemplating a much longer absence than that of a few hours only.'

'Honoured, dear mother,' replied Henry, 'please God I am still living, we shall meet again.'

'My dear boy,' returned his mother, 'I never saw you so sad before; to what can I attribute it?'

'Attribute it,' replied Henry, kindly, 'to the sad events that have so recently taken place at Mr. Moreland's. Poor, unfortunate Rose, is, you know, dear mother, stretched on a bed of sickness, from which, it is more than improbable she will ever recover. Is not this enough to make me, who knew, admired, and loved her as a sister—oh! is it not enough to make me sad?'

'It is, it is, my Henry,' returned Mrs. Melville, tears filling her eyes; 'and I would not at the present moment wish to see you more gay.'

'Thank you, dear mother, for saying so; and now let us hope that our best wishes may speedily be realised—that we may have the unbounded delight of seeing Rose, not only restored to health, but also to her good name.'

'God grant, my child, that may yet be the case.'

'And now, dear mother, for the present, adieu.'

'Farewell, dear Henry; mind you forward me early intelligence of Rose in the mornin"

Henry promised to do as she wished; and, once more in the street, pursued his way to the hotel. He found Sir Charles Mortimer already returned from the club, and who, in a few words communicated to him all that had passed. They spent the night together—but oh! far different from Edward and Fairford. No noisy revelry characterised this, perhaps the last night that one of them should live—no quenching of bitter thoughts in the maddening bowl. No; they passed the night in serious converse. Henry delivered the letters he had written to his mother and sister into the keeping of Mortimer, with a charge to him to safely give them to those dear friends, should the engagement he was under unfortunately prove unfavourable to himself.

'This is the first encounter of the sort I have ever been engaged in,' said Henry; 'and I cannot cast from my mind a—I will not say fear, for fear is unknown to me—but a foreboding.'

'Stop,' replied Mortimer, ' I know what you would say; it is always the case when a man first enters upon a duel. I felt it myself, I assure you; yet I returned home sound and whole, without even a graze of the skin.

'You were fortunate,' replied Henry; ' but, nevertheless, a man will die none the sooner for making preparations for it.'

'Not a bit,' returned Mortimer; ' I am glad you view it in that light; and depend, dear fellow, that to-morrow morning all I shall have to do on our return will be to give these letters back again to yourself.'

'Well, I hope so,' replied Henry; ' yet think not, Mortimer, that I fear death on my own account, for I know full well it is a debt we must all pay, and it would be of little consequence, as regards myself, whether it was paid now or some years later; but I have a mother and sister who cling to me as their dearest earthly friend, and when I think of the bitter grief I am well assured they would feel at my loss, I must confess it unmans me.'

'Think no more about it,' returned Mortimer, ' you will need all your coolness. Mr. T e ors is, I have heard, an excellent shot.'

'I believe so,' said Henry, 'and yet I think we are very nearly matched; for we have not unfrequently, in our days of friendship, tried our skill against each other, and I think I may say with truth that he has missed the target as often as myself.'

'That is fortunate,' replied M r imer, 'although you b ing the challenger, Fairford, I have no doubt, will endeavour to procure him the first shot, but I shall most strenuously oppose it.'

'Oh no,' said Henry, 'let him have fair play.'

'I shall,' returned Mortimer, ' but shall see that you have fair play, too.

'Well, you understand these sort of things better than I,' said Henry, ' so I am sure I cannot do better than leave all to you.'

The morning broke fair and fresh, the sun rose majestically, pouring forth it's rich flood of light o'er the soft green valley, and the rich clad mountains; all nature seemed in harmony: the air gently rustled the rich foliage of the trees; and, gathering from each modest flower some sweet perfume, flung it softly on the ambient air; the grass was yet damp with the pure refreshing dews of night, and lay so enshrined in the blushing rose and modest lily, that now the sun shone fully on them, it gave them the appearance of so many precious stones. The lark rose from his lowly bed, and, uprising towards the heavens, his clear and melodious note sounded far and wide; and, taken up and re-echoed by others, the whole air resounded with this enchanting music. The spot chosen by the seconds for the duel was a quiet, secluded valley; one of those pretty, tranquil spots which are to be found at a short distance from the metropolis, and which are valued by the lovers of nature, as affording all the fairy sweetness of the country, within a moderate drive; and here it was that, on this soft, early morn, the grass gave signs of being trodden down, and in a minute more Sir Charles Mortimer, Melville, and a third person—evidently from his dress and bearing a surgeon—made their appearance.

'We are first on the ground,' said Mortimer, as the trio withdrew, and placed themselves under the shelter of a few trees that skirted the open meadow; and, laying the pistol-case by his side, he threw from his shoulders a large cloak that had previously completely enveloped his form.

'You will excuse me,' said the third person, following Mortimer's example, and allowing the cloak he also wore to fall to the ground—'you will excuse me, but I trust when the other party arrives, this affair may be settled without bloodshed.'

'I do not think it can be,' said Mortimer, speaking to the surgeon, and looking at Henry, who stood with his arms folded on his breast, leaning, in a pensive attitude, against a tree.

As he took no notice of this mute appeal, the surgeon, who appeared a man possessed of strong feelings of humanity, blended with the upright bearing and character of a gentleman, stepped to his side, and, gently touching his arm, said,—

"Mr. Melville, you are the challenger; consequently you should be the first to offer tokens of reconciliation. Let me entreat of you to do so. Think, sir, how awful it is to take the life of another, and especially of one whom you once called your friend.'

'I pardon, sir, this intrusion on my feelings,' replied Henry, with dignity, ' for I believe you to be actuated by honourable and praiseworthy motives; but, had you seen,' Henry continued,

in a voice, hoarse, and broken with emotion, ' the devastation, the utter wreck of hope, o
health, perhaps even life, that this man, whom I am here now purposely to punish for his villany,
has caused to one young and lovely beyond what your fairest ideas could picture—I say, had
you seen this, you would not speak to me of reconciliation. Still, in spite of all this, I am
ready, for the sake of others, to receive from him an ample confession of his infernal acts, and
a solemn promise that he will quit this country immediately after he has made in writing a
contrite apology for the part he has acted. Can you wring this from him, I will be content
to allow him to depart uninjured; but no other satisfaction will I receive.'

The surgeon bowed; and, turning to Mortimer, expressed a hope that these terms might
acceded to by Mr. Trevors.
' Do not, my good sir,' returned Mortimer, ' flatter yourself for a moment with such a hope, I
am myself so certain of their being scoffed at, that I do not think it advisable to offer them.'
' Oh! surely, surely,' urged the surgeon, ' you will do so; it is, indeed, your bounden duty to
leave no stone unturned that may lead to a reconciliation between the adverse parties.'
' As you think so, I will do as you wish, though I warn you, before trial, that I know it will
be useless.'
' You will, at least, have the satisfaction,' replied the other, ' that should either of the un-
No. 15.

happy men lose their lives, of knowing that you did your best to avert so awful a calamity.'—While this conversation was going on, Mortimer was engaged in loading and preparing for use his weapons. Henry maintained his position under the tree, while an air of stern resolve sat upon his usually gay and handsome countenance. He looked around him on the hills and valleys, all fresh decked in Nature's livery, and above him at the cloudless morning sky and glorious sun, shedding its elegant and refulgent beams so brightly on hill and plain. He felt the soft, pure air fanning his fevered brow, and invigorating with its freshness his harassed frame. He heard the song of the birds blithely carolled, as borne up with lightsome wing, they poured forth their morning hymn of praise—he saw, felt, and heard all this, as one who saw, felt, and heard it for the last time. Henry had ever been, even from his earliest youth an ardent admirer of nature; but never before had she seemed half so beautiful as now, and as his eye took in at one glance the wide expanse of heaven, thoughts long forgotten came back afresh to his mind, as though they had occurred but yesterday—scenes of childhood, when he lisped the morning prayer, and was first taught that beyond the blue sky of heaven lay a land where holy spirits dwell, enshrined in bliss, where tears and sorrows were forbid to enter, and where the weary are at rest; and he wondered if there was any truth in those doctrines that, till now, he had long ceased to think of, and rivetted his gaze upon the sky, as though he could pierce through the clouds, and view all that lay beyond. He steadfastly avoided giving even one thought to his mother or Lucy. He had done his best to provide for their comfort and mitigate their grief, in case he fell; and to think of them at such a moment as this, he knew, would melt his whole soul to softness; and Henry would not for worlds appear otherwise than stern and cold. Oh! no, he would avoid, by every means in his power, showing any outward signs of softness, and consequently, he resolutely resolved to fix his thoughts entirely on what was passing around him; but, even then, we have seen him led back to days and years, long since past and gone. He was startled from his meditations, by the voice of Mortimer, who exclaimed, aloud.—

'Here they are at last, having kept us waiting a good ten minutes by my watch.'

Henry and the surgeon simultaneously turned their eyes in the direction of Mortimer's, and observed Edward and Fairford quickly advancing. As they drew near, they raised their hats—a salutation which was returned in a similar manner by their party, and then Edward withdrew to a short distance, and Fairford joined Mortimer alone. Like him, he carried a pistol case, from which he now began eagerly to draw the weapons destined for use.

'I desire to inform you,' said Mortimer, 'that Mr. Melville, in order to save bloodshed, is willing to receive from Mr. Trevors a written apology; with that, and his promise to quit this country immediately, he will withdraw his challenge.'

'All apologies are out of the question, unless they come from your side,' returned Fairford, haughtily; 'then, indeed, we might be willing to listen to them, though certainly with reluctance.'

'Mr. Melville is the aggrieved party,' returned Mortimer, mildly.

'We think differently,' said Fairford, 'therefore, it is useless to waste time in bandying words. Are your pistols in readiness.'

'Quite ready for use,' said Mortimer, 'and Mr. Melville is, I assure you, ready, and anxious to use them.'

This being settled, and the distance walked over by the seconds, nothing remained but to place the opponents in their respective places.

'Mr. Trevors, of course, can claim the first fire,' said Fairford.

'I believe, in the strict principles of duelling, he can do so,' replied Mortimer, 'but I think it would be more honourable in him to waive it; indeed, it is an observance that I have never myself found adhered to, as it is certainly taking an undue advantage of another; Mr. Trevors is I know, an excellent marksman, and if he perseveres in his claim to the first fire, he will at least maim Mr. Melville, and so deprive him of the power of retaliating. Therefore, in justice to him, I desire that both parties shall be allowed to fire at the same moment, this will place them on an equality; and were Mr. Melville the challenged instead of the challenger, I should not hesitate an instant to do as I now wish to be done by.'

There was so much truth, as well as excellent reasoning, in Mortimer's remarks, that Fairford felt himself obliged in a manner to accede to his request. This the seconds communicated to the principals, as they placed them opposite to each other. Melville and Edward were both tall, fine men; indeed, they were much of the same figure and height, and were both dressed in a plain suit of black, with nothing about them that could afford a mark for the other. Henry was deadly pale, but not from fear, for his hand was steady, and not a muscle about him moved, Edward's cheek, on the contrary, was flushed, and he seemed endeavouring to assume an indifference he did not feel; and oh! how sad, that hands which had oftentimes been clasped in friendship, should now be raised in an attempt to take each other's life. It was an awful pause, though only for a few seconds, that intervened after the weapons were placed in their hands, and they stood confronting each other, waiting for the signal which had been agreed upon. Oh! words cannot tell the multiplicity of thoughts that crowded on their minds during those few seconds, and which were suddenly driven away by the voice of Mortimer, who cried in a loud and distinct tone, 'Fire.'

In an instant both the pistols were raised, and the report of the two blended so closely together, that it almost seemed but that of one. Ere the smoke had time to clear away, Mortimer, Fairford, and the surgeon ran to ascertain the result: Edward they discovered stretched upon the ground, and to him they instantly proffered their assistance, partly raising him from the ground: Fairford supported him on his knee, while the surgeon hastened to stop the blood, which was flowing copiously from his right side.

'Is there any danger?' said Mortimer, with anxious countenance as he bent over Edward, who was perfectly sensible, though weak from loss of blood.

The surgeon shook his head, and motioned with his hand that he and Melville should consult their own safety in flight. Mortimer turned away, intending at once to seek Melville, and induce him to leave the ground, when to his surprise he found him by his side.

'Thank God, you have escaped, my dear fellow,' said Mortimer, grasping him cordially by the hand, 'but I fear it's all over with Mr. Trevors, and consequently we had better be off at once.'

'Stop a moment,' said Henry, and his voice was faint, 'I have not wholly escaped; my right arm, you see,' he continued, pointing to it.

'Why, God bless me! you are wounded,' interrupted Mortimer, now, for the first time, perceiving his arm hung powerless by his side, and that the blood was flowing freely from a wound in it.

'It is but slight,' replied Henry, 'and yet,' he added, 'I feel sick and faint, I must even sit down on the grass to refresh myself, and perhaps, Mortimer, you may be able to obtain me a drop of water. I think we passed a small brook on our way here this morning, not far from this spot.'

Mortimer hastened to the place indicated, and found, as Melville had said, a small running brook, whose water was as clear as crystal; dipping some out with his hat, he quickly returned with it to Henry, but found that, during his absence, he had fainted. In the meantime Edward's wound had been hastily dressed, and Fairford and the surgeon were now conveying him in their arms to the coach, which had been drawn up a short distance off. Mortimer summoned the coachman to aid them, and then, whispering to the surgeon he should be glad of his attendance on Henry, returned to the side of his friend, and endeavoured, by throwing water over his hands and face, to restore him to consciousness.

'This is bad,' said the surgeon, who, as soon as he had placed Edward in the coach, and given the man strict orders to proceed slowly, returned to offer his assistance to Henry; and then looking at his arm, he aded, 'Well, I do not think there is any danger, it is certainly a bad wound: the shot must have entered at the elbow, and travelling up the arm, escaped at the shoulder, and it has certainly bled very profusely, and that alone has caused him to faint.' While speaking he proceeded to bind up the arm, and Mortimer, relieved of the fear he had begun to entertain for his friend, inquired what opinion he had formed of Edward's wound.

'I think it is impossible he can ever recover,' replied the surgeon, seriously; 'it is a sad affair, a very, very sad affair.'

'In that case,' returned Mortimer, 'we had better get Mr. Melville into the coach, and proceed at any rate some litte distance from London, immediately.'

'Yes, I think that would be the best we could do, at least for the present.'

They then raised Henry from the ground, and, placing him in the coach, got in themselves, ordering the man to drive in an opposite direction to London.

Thus the quiet, tranquil spot we described previous to the duel was once more left in undisturbed repose; but oh! the sad evidence they left behind told its tale to all, that some lamentable affair had taken place during the last half hour. The soft grass that had, in the early morn, been sprinkled o'er with the most refreshing dews of heaven, was now reeking with blood—blood shed in the defence of what men call their honour—and though, in this case, Edward's villany well deserved the chastisement, yet could no other way have been found of inflicting on him the punishment he so richly merited, than thus for the guilty and the innocent to stand face to face, and calmly point the fatal weapon in a cold, reckless desire to take each other's lives? Oh! surely, surely, such sacrifices as these to wounded honour are utterly the reverse of acceptable to God, and should never be deemed so by men. How very often does it happen that the life of the innocent is sacrificed by that of the guilty! and one perchance in the bloom of manhood, the hope and comfort of a widowed mother and orphan sisters, who are bound to him by the dearest and noblest ties, in his endeavour to right what is sometimes a fanciful wrong, is suddenly—in the very midst of life and joy, without time to seek for that pardon which we all, more or less, stand in need of—oh! oftentimes, indeed, without being able to give utterance to even a single prayer—deprived of that life which God gave, and which God alone should ever take away. Sudden death is at all times melancholy, even when we are conscious that it is the omnipotent will of God alone that ordered it; then how much more so when man, in defiance of God's holy law—'Thou shalt not kill'—to avenge some trifling wrong, wilfully deprives a fellow-creature of life, and thereby not only incurs the awful sin and consequent punishment of so doing, but frequently plunges a whole family into the very depths of affliction. Oh! if they would but consider that not only their own lives depend on the issue of the duel, but the happiness, also, of all that are near and dear to them, and which they ought to feel themselves bound to consult, even at the price of lowering a little their own dignity, and endeavour by every means in their power to avoid the awful onset which they are well aware will render those they love unhappy, no matter which way it may terminate!

Mrs. Sommerville had greatly regained her spirits, and succeeded in dissipating much of the fears she had entertained concerning her daughter, since the receipt of Rose's letter, which was all that her fondest wishes could have desired, and was read with rapturous delight by the whole circle, and many fond anticipations for the future were warmly indulged in by all—how sweet and pleasant it would be to greet Rose amongst them again? when restored to perfect health, she would present to them her infant babe; how loved and treasured it would be by those who so truly loved and treasured her, especially her fond and doting parents, who had tenderly nurtured her in infancy, and carefully watched over her early-budding charms! How sweet it would be to them to fold their child with rapture to their parental breasts—to trace the fresh, warm beauty of the mother in her infant's face, to mark the soft roundness of its little limbs, and know that in time they would attain to the polished fulness of hers. Oh! this would indeed be transport to their truly affectionate hearts, and much and long they dwelt upon the promised joy, and these hopes were fully participated in by the warm-hearted old farmer Forster, and his good and amiable daughter Agnes. It is true that Mrs. Sommerville had occasionally a little of that gloomy and unaccountable foreboding, which all have felt before any dire misfortune or heavy calamity—foreboding of ill, which we cannot cast from our minds, but sadden our hearts even in the midst of mirth, which comes we know not how or where, ' like warning ghosts,' and give us a mournful presentiment of sorrow, which is afterwards only too truly realized. But Mrs. Sommerville was not a woman to give way before the presentiment of misfortune, and the presages she now felt were comparatively trifling: so, buoying her mind up with the hope that all would yet be well, she pursued her accustomed avocations with the peaceful serenity of countenance that so peculiarly marked her usually unruffled brow. And in Agnes she daily found increased comfort, for not a day had passed since Rose's departure without finding Agnes a visitor at their farm. It was indeed a pleasure to this amiable girl to devote an hour or two of each day to mutual converse,—' always friendly, and always sweet,' with Mrs. Sommerville; and on the afternoon of the day, when at early morn the duel took place between Henry Melville and Edward Trevors, Agnes tied on her straw bonnet, and hanging her little work-basket on her arm (for though Agnes found time to visit Mrs. Sommerville, she could not afford to be idle while there) tripped across the fields on her way to Mr. Sommerville's farm. The morning of this day was, we have already said, fair and beautiful as ever beamed upon this earth, and the afternoon was worthy of so sweet a beginning. It was the delightful time of harvest, and Agnes occasionally lingered on her road, to view with beaming eyes the golden store which the reapers were gathering in against the forthcoming winter, relieving their toil by snatches of song, or pausing to quaff the nut-brown ale, and then pursue their task with renewed vigour. Agnes was well known to all the labourers, and they lifted their straw hats, and bade her good afternoon as she passed, which she returned with that affability which made her so universally beloved; and, after she had passed through the corn-fields, her road led through some beautiful meadow land, where the tinkling bell of the sheep sounded drowsily on the ear, inviting the toil-worn wayfarer to repose, who, stretched upon the grass, slept sounder than many on their luxurious beds of down. Not a single fleecy cloud was to be seen in the heavens; no, all was transcendently blue, and just that soft breeze stirring which prevents the weather being styled sultry.

Agnes, though used to the beauties by which she was surrounded, from her very birth, yet still looked upon them with an unwearying delight. Cowper has said, and we think truly, that scenes 'must be beautiful, which, daily viewed, please daily;' and this well applied to the fair landscape on which Agnes now cast her delighed eyes. ' Sweet spot!' she inwardly exclaimed, as her eye took in the wide expanse of hill and dale; ' here surely is to be found all that heart could wish. Oh! here may I live and die, surrounded by those I love!' and she sighed as she pursued her walk, for her thoughts involuntarily had fled to Rose. 'She writes as though she were happy,' she continued, musing to herself; ' and yet how her heart must pine amidst the dusty, bustling streets of London, for the fresh air that blows from these her native hills. Poor Rose! would that, like me, your choice had fallen upon one who loved these rural scenes, and would have been content to abide amongst them—then, indeed, we should not be separated from you, but together could rove o'er these fair hills and valleys, visiting, as in childhood, hand in hand our favourite spots—together could draw around the fire of a winter's eve, and sing the songs we loved again. And oh! it would have been sweet mutually to have soothed the declining years of our beloved parents—to assist their tottering steps, when age shall have bowed them down, and thus gratefully pay back the debt we owe them for their love and tenderness shewn to us by many years of anxious solicitude for our welfare. But, alas! it is ordered otherwise: the greater part of Rose's life must be spent at a distance from all that are dear to her; she will be obliged to have her cares and anxieties (for from these none are free) totally unconnected with us, and it is useless to repine. Let me rather bear in mind that I have, consequently, a double duty to fulfil. Yes, I must endeavour so to supply Rose's place that her parents may not miss her affectionate care, and, in doing this, I am confident I shall gain, if possible, still more the love and esteem of my husband.' Husband! how sweet and dear a tie! It was new to Agnes; and the very word possessed a charm that was truly precious to her; and, though Agnes knew and felt herself blessed, yet she determined carefully to guard her happiness. Her happiness, she knew, proceeded chiefly from the mutual love of herself and Henry; and love, she felt convinced, was a delicate plant—one that required constant care and attention, or it would wither and die; therefore, she wisely resolved not to neglect it in these her early marriage days, but carefully to cultivate it, day by day, till at length she hoped to have the unbounded delight of seeing it grow into a strong and vigorous plant, which should be able to withstand the rude blasts of adversity, should such ever-threaten to overwhelm it. Wise resolve! would that others of her sex would act in the same praiseworthy manner! It is the only way of securing their own and their husbands' happiness, which we naturally suppose to be the greatest desire and highest aim of every woman who becomes a wife. Women, unfortunately, are too apt to think that, if a man loves them at the time of their marriage, he will continue to do so as a matter of course, and never dream that it is their duty, their most solemn duty, by every tender and winning grace, by a constant and unremitting attention to even his slightest wish, to make him feel blessed in and proud of the choice he has made. Instead of all this, it, alas! too often happens that—

> ' Eyes forget the gentle ray,
> They were in courtship's smiling day;
> And voices lose the tone that shed
> A tenderness round all they said.'

The new made wife will forgive us, we are sure, for strenuously urging her to avoid falling into this fatal error—this rock against which so many have had their happiness wrecked. We fear not for Agnes; her mind was completely divested of all romantic notions of love; she saw all in its proper light; and, though she was confident she now possessed the entire love and affection of her husband, yet she did not on that account look forward with certainty to his never changing; on the contrary, she felt that it rested entirely with herself, either to unloose the chains that now bound him to her, or to rivet them more firmly on him. And oh! she felt it would not only be an easy but delightful task to study his wishes and happiness before all else on earth, and, by commencing thus early, she should so accustom herself to think and act only in accordance with his desires, that it would become so habitual that she could not, if she would, throw it off. There is little or no medium in marriage: persons are either happy or miserable, and it is all but optional with themselves which they will be. More, we are ready, to grant, belongs to the wife in the way of happiness; for it is certainly more in her power to render both herself and her husband blessed: it is she who can make his home so happy that he will never desire to be absent from it longer than he can help. A woman is by nature so constituted that her power over man is almost unbounded: she can mould him to anything she pleases, direct his tastes and pursuits in accordance with her own, and so fix his affections upon herself that he will never so much as think of another. Of course, it requires tact and knowledge of his natural disposition to enable her to do this; but it is easily acquired by one who really and truly loves her husband, and desires to make him at once love, admire, and respect her. A wife, nevertheless, should avoid appearing to rule, or even lead her husband, as her doing so makes him contemptible in the eyes of others; she should, therefore, appear to the world rather to follow the bent of his inclination, and never, by any means, seek to deprive him of the liberty of a single, while she procures him the comforts of a married, man.

When Agnes arrived at the farm, where she was ever received with the warmest welcome, she found Mrs. Sommerville rather indisposed.

'Why, how is this, my dear mother!' she exclaimed, as she entered the usual sitting-room, and observed her pale and languid appearance; 'you are surely unwell; why did you not send for me this morning, you know how gladly I would have come to you?'

'I do, indeed, my dear Agnes,' Mrs. Sommerville returned, folding her in a warm embrace, 'but I was sure I should see you this afternoon, and my indisposition being very trifling, I would not alarm you unnecessarily! now you have come to talk to me, I shall soon be well; I declare I feel better already.'

Agnes was not long in laying aside her bonnet and scarf, and seating herself at the window, which looked out upon the London road, drew forth her work, and, while plying the busy needle sought to amuse and interest Mrs. Sommerville by her conversation.

'I cannot so much complain of bodily illness,' said that good lady, 'as I think my indisposition arises from mere disturbed repose; I last night was troubled with a painful dream concerning Rose, and I cannot divest myself of a fear which has taken possession of my mind, that we shall hear bad news of her.'

'Do not, I entreat of you,' replied Agnes, 'allow that to make you unhappy; it would grieve Rose much if she knew that you suffered anxiety concerning her to disturb your repose.'

'It would,' said Mrs. Sommerville; 'and yet, though I have never been a believer in dreams, this one has made such an impression on my mind, that I cannot cast it from me. I thought I saw Rose with a dead baby in her arms, and while tears——such tears of anguish as I have never seen her shed——poured from her eyes, she begged of me in broken accents, to come to her.'

'It was, indeed, a painful dream,' replied Agnes, and she could scarcely repress a convulsive shudder; 'still, my dear mother, it was but a dream, and as such should not claim any attention, though at the same time I am not surprised that it has affected your spirits; yet,' she continued trying to assume a more cheerful tone, 'had Rose been ill, we should be certain to have heard of it without delay; you know, dear mother, when she parted from us, she voluntarily promised to forward us early intelligence, should she be at all indisposed.'

'She did,' returned Mrs. Sommerville, 'and would, I am certain, redeem it; no,' she continued, seriously, "I do not apprehend she is now ill, but may not this dream be ominous of the future?'

'I do not think so,' replied Agnes, 'there are many ways of accounting for your dream; for instance you know how anxiously you have been thinking of her lately; your dream has but taken the same shape as your waking thoughts.'

'You may be right,' said Mrs. Sommerville, 'God send that you may; and though I am willing to hope that this dream arose from nothing more than my over anxiety concerning my beloved child, still I cannot wholly cast from me the fear of ill befalling her, that has taken possession of my mind; when I awoke, the impression of it was so strong on my memory, that it was impossible for me even to attempt again to sleep, and I half resolved that the morning should find me preparing for a journey to London.'

'I am very glad, dear mother, that you altered your resolution, as if, on your arrival you found Rose perfectly well, you would have been puzzled to account to her for your appearance without arousing her fears; and, as she evidently looks forward to the future without the slightest fear for the result, it would be wrong needlessly to alarm her.'

'It would, my Agnes, and I am thankful I did not act so rashly, and we will no longer converse on this painful subject: it is certainly unwise, as well as useless, to anticipate misfortune.'

'It is,' replied Agnes; 'for it will neither prevent nor mitigate it.'

And then, with that ready tact she so well knew how to use when occasion required, she adroitly turned the subject, relating some little anecdote concerning her father and Henry, which she knew would be pleasing to Mrs. Sommerville, and in a short time succeeded in recalling the smile to her countenance, and was gratified at seeing her regain, apparently, her usual spirits.

It was, as we have said, a lovely afternoon, and it being now the hour at which the family usually took tea, Agnes, putting away her work, began to arrange the repast in front of the open window, and, tripping out of the room, and across the farm, presently returned with Mr. Sommerville and his two sons.

'I am quite afraid,' said the farmer, as he stooped to kiss the polished brow of Agnes, 'that Henry and your father will grow quite jealous, if we monopolise you so often.'

'Oh, never fear,' returned Agnes, smiling; 'if I have two fathers, you must remember that I have but one mother,' and she cast an affectionate look on Mrs. Sommerville, 'and it is but right I should spare some of my time to her.'

'Well, dame, and how are you now? I must confess you look better than you did at dinner-time.'

'I am, indeed, much better, both in health and spirits,' returned his partner, 'and you must thank our dear Agnes for it, for to her alone can I attribute the change.'

'It is indeed kind of thee, Agnes, to come to us so often; and God I am sure, will reward thee.'

'Do not praise me, or at least not yet; for many years,' said Agnes, smiling, 'I hope to be able to give you much stronger proofs of my love than merely taking a pleasant walk——to spend a pleasant afternoon with those I love.'

'Thou art too modest, Agnes; but we know well thou leavest two behind who are dearer to thee than all else on earth.'

'We do, we do, indeed,' rejoined Mrs. Sommerville; 'and though you wish us to think but little of the sacrifice you daily practise in leaving your husband and father to spend some hours with us, yet we know and value it highly.'

'More highly than it deserves,' said Agnes; 'for I assure you, so far from being a sacrifice it is a real pleasure to me. And then,' she continued, archly, 'it is quite essential that I should leave them to shift by themselves sometimes, or they would not know the worth and value of my society; so you see, my visits are not entirely disinterested; and though I hold long absence to be the greatest foe love can have, yet short ones, I think, make the heart grow fonder.'

They had by this time commenced the social meal, and Agnes, seated at the table, dispensed the refreshing beverage, and handed round the seed cake, made by her own hands, and brought with her as an humble offering; and sweet smiles and kind words seasoned the repast, and all cheerfully joined in the conversation, and did their best to entertain the others.

How pleasant it is when friends in friendship meet, and partaking of the frugal fare together, converse over the tea table with light and happy hearts, when, free from all constraint and form (which so encircle the great), they can pass the merry jest and laugh at the little ills of life which, perhaps, have at one time caused their annoyance, but are now only remembered to afford mirth to themselves and others.

Oh! is not this pleasant? We pity the man, be he whom he may, whose heart does not throb with delight at the memory of some happy hours spent round the tea-table, where each, gay and blessed, has added his modicum of mirth for the amusement of the whole.

The present circle were so happy that they still lingered over their tardy meal, and were indulging in unrestrained laughter at some witticism of Mr. Sommerville's, when Agnes, who from her position at the window could see right down the high road to London, thought she perceived a great cloud of dust quickly approaching, and called the attention of the others to it.

'It must,' said Mr. Sommerville, 'be caused by a carriage or some other vehicle.' Nor were they kept long in suspense, for scarcely had he pronounced the words, before a post carriage made its appearance, and drove rapidly up to the house; the horses were covered with foam, and had evidently been put upon their mettle. 'It surely must have come from London,' said Mr. Sommerville, with increased astonishment, as the vehicle stopped short at their door.

His wife sank back upon her chair, pale and spiritless, without the power for the moment to speak or move. Mr. Sommerville's two sons rushed to the door, and received from the hands of the postilion a letter addressed to their mother; to hurry in and give it her was but the work of an instant. Breathless with impatience, she tore it open, glanced her eye hastily over the contents, and then giving utterance to an almost heartbroken shriek, she exclaimed,—'Rose, my dear, dear Rose, alas! my heart forboded this;' she let the letter drop from her hands, and gave vent to her feelings in a burst of agonised tears.

Agnes endeavoured to console her, but it was in vain; she could only wring her hands, and exclaim, in piteous accents, 'Rose, my darling Rose! why, why did I allow you to leave me?'

Mr. Sommerville picked the letter from the ground, and, having read it himself, made the others acquainted with its contents; it was but a few lines, and ran thus:—

'MY DEAR MADAM,—

'It is with deep and painful regret that I am compelled to acquaint you of the severe and dangerous illness of your daughter. Rest assured, till you can come to her yourself, she will receive every care and attention from, my dear madam,

'Yours, most respectfully,
'LUCY MELVILLE.'

Agnes instantly, on reading this, crept from the room, and with hurried hands began to prepare for the instant departure of her mother in law. In a few minutes all was in readiness, and returning to the room with the necessary articles, she hastily assisted Mrs. Sommerville to put on her travelling dress and bonnet.

'Thank you, my dear Agnes,' said that lady, affectionately kissing her cheek; 'what should I do without you, ever thoughtful and kind, even in the midst of sorrow!'

'You will allow me to accompany you,' said Agnes, mournfully, 'indeed I cannot allow you to go alone.'

'Oh no! not for worlds,' replied Mrs. Sommerville, 'you must, dear Agnes, remain to comfort those behind; you will, I assure you, serve me more by doing so.'

'But are you, indeed, equal to travelling alone?'

'Yes, yes, my child; give me one kiss, and let me go. Rose may, perhaps, be better when I arrive.'

'You will write to us, dame, immediately,' said Mr. Sommerville, brushing away the tears that dimmed his eyes.

'Oh, yes, I shall remember your anxiety,' returned his partner, throwing her arms round him in a farewell embrace; and then, breaking from him, she tenderly kissed her sons, and then turning to Agnes, she exclaimed affectionately, 'Farewell, my child, I entrust to you this parting kiss for Henry; tell him he was not forgotten, nor your father either, Agnes: once more farewell, my dear husband and children.' And, in the midst of kisses and tears, she entered the vehicle, which, driving rapidly off, was soon out of sight; and Agnes, with Mr. Sommerville and his sons, again returned to the parlour, where late they had been so merry—but dull and lonely it seemed now. Alas! it was a sudden and a mournful change; and oh! how often does it happen that our flower of happiness is, 'in flushing, when blighting is nearest.' Mr. Sommerville had never been separated from his wife since their marriage. No, they had lived together for nearly thirty years without having once to pronounce the word 'farewell,' till now; and he not only deeply and bitterly mourned her absence, but the sad cause which occasioned it. He felt as one suddenly bereft of all that was near and dear to his heart, and it was not till Agnes had thrown her arms round his neck, and kissed off with her ruby lips the tears that fell in torrents from his eyes, that he remembered he was not entirely alone. Clasping her to his bosom, the bitterness of his emotion gradually subsided, and he could speak of his wife and daughter with renewed hope.

'I will not despair, my Agnes; Rose may yet be restored to us,' he exclaimed in answer to the words of comfort she whispered in his ear; 'to-morrow we shall hear of her. It seems a long time to wait in anxious suspense, but there is nothing for it but patience. It is a sad dispensation of Providence, but we must endeavour to bear it as meekly as possible. I have a blessing, a rich blessing in thee, my Agnes, let what will happen.'

In the course of the evening, as had been previously arranged, Henry and Farmer Forster walked over to fetch Agnes home. Great, indeed, was their surprise, and severe their distress, to find, instead of the gay and light-hearted family, where peace and happiness made their home, one sunk in the depth of affliction. They were soon made acquainted with the mournful cause of their sorrow, and they mingled tears and sighs with them. The night that followed was long and sleepless to them all, and when the morning dawned, fair and beautiful, its beauty was for the first time unheeded by them. Oh, how drearily the day passed on! but it went at last, and evening again closed round them; and, with throbbing hearts, and anxious, fluttering breasts, they received a letter from Mrs. Sommerville. It was given to Agnes, and her hands trembled so that she could scarcely open it. It was written almost immediately on her arrival. She had found Rose very ill, but the surgeon gave her some hopes that she might yet recover—that was all the letter contained. But oh! the hope that she might be spared filled them with rapture; still they hoped with trembling, and mingled tears with their aspirations to Heaven on her behalf.

We left Lucy in attendance upon the insensible Rose, and thither we return. The morning on which the duel took place found the unhappy Rose in a high state of delirium. Unconscious of the birth of her infant, she yet retained in her memory much that had passed previous to her illness. Sometimes she apparently fancied herself in the country, and, addressing her parents and brothers, would express in touching language her desire to return to Albert.

'Why,' she would exclaim, 'do you desire to separate us? Oh! nothing but death should ever part husband and wife. Let me—let me go to him. Oh, why detain me so cruelly here! You would not keep me, did you know how dearly I love him;' and then, remaining quiet for a few minutes, she would suddenly make an effort to get out of bed; and, clasping her hands, exclaim in accents of the tenderest devotion, and earnest supplication, 'Do not, pray do not send me from you. I will submit to anything, if you will only allow me to remain near you. Oh! do not look upon me with that dreadful frown—your anger pierces my very brain;' and then again she would fancy herself conversing with Edward; and calling him by his name, would say, 'You know I am innocent of all that is wrong; you alone can make it clear to Albert. Do me justice in his eyes. What! you refuse? Oh no! it cannot be; he will listen to you; he will believe you; I shall die if he sends me from him. Indeed—indeed, I cannot go.'

Thus did poor Rose rave till her strength was wholly exhausted; she sank back into a deep sleep, disturbed only by the convulsive sobs that occasionally heaved her breast. Lucy, seated by her side, watched her slumbers with a grateful heart. After having witnessed with intense agony the wanderings of Rose's thoughts from one thing to another, but always with the same sense of misery weighing her down—oh! it was sweet indeed to see her sunk at least for a time into an oblivion of her sorrows; and she took every precaution to prevent aught awaking her.

Marian and Albert still occupied the room above that in which Rose was. They had, as we before remarked, never once thought of retiring to rest; but Marian, towards morning, had fallen asleep on a sofa; while Albert, restless and unable to keep the same position for a moment together, now trod the floor with hasty strides, and anon seating himself at a table, buried his face in his hands; and then suddenly starting up, would clench his hands, and seem on the point of leaving the room, and then, checking himself, would mutter between his closed teeth, 'No no; things must take their course; I cannot alter them; Fate will work its own way; and yet, if that one life might be spared, he is a brave and noble youth, beloved by his mother and sister. Oh! my life would be as nothing in the balance weighed against his, and gladly would I have yielded it to save his; but oh! blood to me is too awful to allow me for an instant to think even of shedding it; and I felt from the first that it would be perfectly useless to attempt to persuade him not to challenge Edward. Well, it was to be; and if he falls, it will only be in the fulfilment of his destiny.

As hour after hour passed on, his anxiety but increased. His impatience to know the result of the duel, he felt assured had taken place, was so great, that he knew not what to do; touching the bell with a light hand, he asked of the servant who obeyed the summons, if any letter or message had arrived for him; he was answered in the negative.

'The moment one arrives, bring it to me, or should Mr. Melville call, admit him instantly.'

The servant bowed, and inquired if it was his pleasure he should bring breakfast in.

He was about to say, 'No,' but his eye falling upon Marian, who was just rousing from her slumber, he replied, 'Yes.'

The morning wore on; still no news of Melville till towards mid-day, when the servant brought in a letter for Marian.

'Who can it be from?' she said, glancing at the direction; 'the hand is totally unknown to me.

'Open it,' replied her brother, with a quiver of the under lip, which Marian could by no means account for: but, however, doing as he bade her, she, not without some misgiving, began to read it.'

'Good God!' she exclaimed, turning pale, 'Edward has been shot, in a duel, by Henry Melville.'

'How say you?' said Albert, quickly. 'Is Mr. Melville injured?—does he live?—speak at once!'

'Yes, he still lives,' she replied, mistaking him, 'though the surgeon pronounces the wound dangerous; and he expresses a desire to see me; of course—I—must comply with his request and go to him immediately.'

'And does he say nothing about Lucy?' returned Albert.

'Lucy!—oh dear no!—what should he?'

'I thought he might desire to have his sister with him.'

'His sister!—of whom do you speak, Albert?'

'Why, of Henry Melville, of course.

'Henry Melville! it is Edward, not him, that I told you was wounded.'

'Did you?' replied Albert, with a ray of hope upon his countenance, that surprised his sister, 'there is, then, no allusion to him in that letter?'

'None whatever, beyond the mere statement of his having shot Edward, who has been conveyed to his own residence, where he now lies in a dangerous state.'

'May I ask who is your informant?'

She gave the letter into his hands. It was from Fairford, and merely contained what Marian had acquainted her brother with.

'I should think,' said Albert, after he had perused it, 'that as no mention is made to the contrary, Melville must have escaped unhurt.'

'God grant that it may be so!' returned Marian; 'it is enough that one is dangerously wounded.'

'More than enough,' replied Albert, solemnly, 'would they had both been spared!'

'He may yet recover,' said Marian, who, now that she was assured her husband's life was in danger, had lost much of the resentment she had previously nourished against him, and was all eagerness to obey the summons which called her to his side. 'It is with sorrow that I leave you, Albert,' she continued, gazing intently upon his anxious countenance, 'but do not allow yourself to be sunk in despondency; no one, I assure you, but Edward should induce me to part from you—nor he,' she added after a pause, 'were he not dangerously ill; I cannot think what right Henry had to seek a quarrel with him; if you did not choose to challenge him, he certainly had no business to do so; but he is himself a great admirer of Rose, and thought it his duty to revenge any injury done to her, though I cannot myself conceive he was by any means authorised to do so.'

'What is done cannot be undone,' said Albert; 'troubles seem to gather more closely and thickly around us. It was not enough that Rose lies in a very precarious state, but another—what do I say? perhaps two, for we know not how Henry has come off—is added to the number It is not improbable even that they may all die.'

'Oh! do not talk so,' said Marian; 'you absolutely frighten me! Let us rather hope that all may recover.'

'I do hope it,' replied Albert; 'no one hopes it more than I; but, alas! it is more than I can expect; one kiss, Marian, and then adieu!'

'Adieu, Albert, my dear brother! remember, though I leave you for awhile, my heart still abides with you;' and with a sad and tearful face she left the room, and Albert was alone once more, with nothing but his perturbed thoughts for a companion. The servant, as a matter of form, brought in dinner, but it was taken untasted away.

'Inquire how Mrs. Moreland is,' were the only words he addressed to the servant, who, hastening to obey, returned with the answer that she had for some time been in a quiet slumber, from which they trusted she might awake a little better.

'Is Miss Melville still with her?'

'Yes; she has not left the room for an instant since she communicated to you the birth of the child.'

'And she has received no letters?' said Albert, pursuing his inquiry.

'None; she wrote a few lines to her mother this morning, which were taken to Mrs. Melville according to her request, but which required no answer.'

'That will do,' replied Albert, seeing the servant waited. 'You may go; but forget not, should a letter or messenger arrive for me, to let me have it without delay.'

Mrs. Sommerville travelled as fast as it was possible to urge the horses, which indeed they changed frequently, and with as little hindrance as possible; for the man had given orders to have horses ready harnessed at every stage; so they had nothing to do but to take the tired ones out, and put the fresh ones in, and yet how little, how very little did the speed keep pace with the impatience of a mother hastening to the sick bed of perhaps a dying child.

'Oh! if I should be too late to receive her parting breath,' inwardly exclaimed Mrs. Sommerville, as she wrung her hands in agony. 'Oh! that I could fly to her side, could even, at this moment know that she was still living, it would be some little relief,' and then burying her face in her handkerchief, she sobbed and wept like a child.

Oh! how long and dreary the miles appeared; it seemed as though she would never reach her journey's end; but everything must have an end, and so at length did that mournful and tedious journey. As she approached the residence of her daughter, known to her only by description, her heart beat almost to suffocation; and, when the carriage stopped at the house she felt contained her, her agitation was so great, that she was scarcely able to support herself. The door opened, and a middle-aged gentleman dressed in black, whom she at once knew as the doctor, proffered his arm to assist her in alighting; and, kindly supporting her into the house, placed her in a chair, without a word having been spoken on either side. Mrs. Sommerville then turned her eyes full upon him, with an expression he knew well how to interpret, and he instantly replied to it,—' Your daughter, my dear madam, has had some refreshing sleep, and though she still remains in a state of insensibility, yet she is certainly more quiet, and the fever is a trifle subdued.'

Mrs. Sommerville drew a deep breath, and then exclaiming, ' Thank God ! you will conduct me to her, doctor,' immediately rose from her seat, and moved towards the door.

'Are you prepared, my dear madam, to see her ill—very ill?'

'Yes, yes, doctor, only let me see her; I am prepared for all.'

' Then, follow me,' and he led the way to the sick room.

Mrs. Sommerville had thought herself prepared to see Rose sadly altered, but the sight of her fevered cheek and pallid brow, where so late had revelled every charm of health and beauty, had almost proved too much for her, and she sank, well nigh fainting, on a seat. And she now for the first time, became aware of the presence of Lucy, who, gliding gently to her side, besought her to seek rest and refreshment after her journey, before she commenced her attendance upon Rose. ' I will, myself,' she added, mildly, ' do everything for her that can possibly be done, and, as she is insensible of your presence, it cannot, at present, benefit her in the least.'

'You may safely leave your daughter under the care of this young lady,' said the doctor, ' for she has, indeed, unmindful of fatigue or anxiety, been constant and unremitting in her affectionate care and solicitude for her.'

Mrs. Sommerville raised her eyes, overflowing with tears of gratitude, to Lucy's face, and then, complying with their united request, she suffered herself to be led into an adjoining chamber. After a few hours' rest she arose, and seeking Lucy, learned from her the particulars of Rose's illness.

Lucy dwelt as lightly as possible upon the supposed improper familiarity that existed between Rose and Edward Trevors; yet it deeply affected Mrs. Sommerville, and when she heard of the premature birth of the child, she gave way to a bitter flood of tears, exclaiming,—

' I know, I am certain my Rose is innocent; but they will kill her with their unjust suspicions.'

' Compose yourself, my dear madam,' replied Lucy. ' I feel with you, sure that she is innocent; indeed, none who heard her, as I did, say pathetically declare it, could doubt her assertion for an instant, and it will yet, I am sure, be made clear in the eyes of every one. My brother intends seeking an explanation of Mr. Trevors, and if possible force him to do Mrs. Moreland justice.'

' Dear, generous young lady,' said Mrs. Sommerville, ' Heaven will reward you for your goodness, and your brother too : noble family, thus to espouse the cause of the suffering and distressed !'

Indeed, Mrs. Sommerville regarded Lucy in the light of a ministering angel, come to succour and soothe her in affliction, and they now conjointly directed their every care and attention to the truly unfortunate Rose.

      *   *   *   *   *

After the carriage which contained Melville had driven for some distance, he gave signs of returning animation, and in a feeble voice inquired whither they were going? On being informed of the necessity that existed for their seeking, at least for the present, concealment, he at first strenuously opposed doing so.

' I am ready,' he exclaimed with deep earnestness, ' to answer, even at the bar of my country, for the wound I have inflicted on Edward, and which I think he richly deserves. He has (in a more underhand manner, I allow) destroyed the happiness, perhaps even the life of one young, lovely, and innocent—one whose very loveliness should have pleaded with him to pity and to spare so sweet a flower; but he heeded it not, and with fell ruthlessness sought to wither and to blight it.'

' Hush !' said the surgeon, ' this earnestness will injure you; be content to follow our advice for a while. You are yourself badly, though I trust not dangerously, wounded. Still it is absolutely necessary that you should keep yourself perfectly quiet.'

' Yes, yes,' urged Mortimer, ' you will, I am sure, listen to reason.'

Henry signified his willingness to abide by their decision, and, feeling very weak and faint, leaned back in the carriage, and maintained silence the rest of their drive. When they had got, as Mortimer considered, a prudent distance from London, they stopped at a road–side inn ; and assisting Henry into the house, he was, by the advice of the surgeon, immediately put to bed, and his arm, which had been only superficially dressed, was now properly bandaged. The surgeon evidently considered it badly wounded ; indeed, he appeared to entertain doubts whether he might not ultimately be obliged to have it amputated. But this he prudently concealed from Henry, who began to be uneasy concerning his mother and sister.

'What is to be done, Mortimer ?' he said, anxiously. If you write to inform them of the duel, they will certainly think I am dangerously wounded, and will be suffering an agony of suspense on my behalf. I really cannot think what we had best do.'

The surgeon, who was one of the most humane and kind hearted men living, replied to Henry's interrogatives,—

'Undoubtedly, by this time, they are acquainted with the fact of the duel having taken place ; for Mr. Trevors' second purposed conveying him to his own residence, and that being so very near Mrs. Melville's, she cannot fail to know of the duel. Now I propose, if agreeable to you, to go myself and convey a message from you to Mrs. Melville, and at the same time relieve her mind from the fear that your life is in danger, and I can also learn how Mr. Trevors is going on.'

'A thousand thanks,' exclaimed Henry. 'You cannot possibly serve me better than doing as you propose, and, if you will call on Mr. Moreland, you will add still more to the obligation.'

The surgeon promised compliance, and all being arranged, both as regarded Henry's treatment in his absence, and his own mission, he bade Mortimer and his patient a short adieu, and set forth on his praiseworthy errand. On reaching Mrs. Melville's residence, he found that good, lady, as he had anticipated, already apprised of the duel, and fluttering between the hope of Henry's safety and the fear of his danger. A few words sufficed to acquaint her with the truth, and amidst tears of gratitude to Heaven for her son's preservation, he learned from her that Mr. Trevors had received the best surgical advice, and their opinion was unfavourable to his recovery.

Mrs. Melville was at first very solicitious to be allowed to go to Henry, but upon reading a note from him, which the surgeon placed in her hands, and in which Henry assured her that she would more serve him by remaining in town and forwarding to him from time to time, an account of the health of Rose and Edward, and not thinking his arm had sustained so much injury as it really had, she consented cheerfully to comply with his request.

Having thus happily fulfilled the chief part of his mission, the surgeon next proceeded to Mr. Moreland's, and, using Henry's name, found no difficulty in gaining access to him.

Albert was, as the reader will readily believe, delighted to hear that Henry had escaped with so little injury ; his gloomy imagination, which ever caused him to look at the darkest side of everything, had induced him to think, with a feeling bordering almost on certainty, that his life would fall a sacrifice to his revenging the wrong done to Rose ; consequently he was rejoiced, as far as it was possible for him to be, at the fortunate result of the duel, as far as Henry was concerned ; still he considered he had sufficient cause to justify him in being miserable, and for the nonce he certainly had.

Rose, his young and lovely wife, was stretched upon a bed of sickness from which she might never again rise ; Edward, his only sister's husband was, he deemed, the whole and sole cause of that illness, and for which he would doubtless shortly pay the penalty of his life—events sad and startling, and melancholy enough to plunge the gayest into gloom. No wonder, then, that Albert's brow was darkened with intense sorrow ; but instead of humbling himself before his Creator, and attributing all that had occured to the wise dispensations of His omnipotent will, he regarded himself as a creature singled out from the mass, to have all the fury of the elements let loose upon him—to be cursed above his fellow-man, and never sought, as he might have done, to avert the storm when he saw it impending over him. On the contrary, he rather invited its approach, and then blamed it all to destiny.

'Yes,' he exclaimed, as he thought upon the sorrow and sickness that encompassed those who were nearest and dearest to him, 'it was to be ; no power on earth could have prevented it. Fate alone can be blamed for all.'

Directly the surgeon left Albert, he hastened back to Henry, whom he found better than he had dared to expect, and consequently hesitated not to inform him of Edward's danger.'

'It is entirely of his own seeking,' said Henry ; 'he well knows that I repeatedly warned him what he might expect, if he persisted in his endeavour to draw Rose from the path of virtue, but he gave no heed to the warning voice, and consequently his blood must be on his own head.'

At a slow and gentle pace, the carriage which contained Edward and Fairford proceeded along the streets of London, till it reached his residence. The hour was yet so early that few persons were stirring, and Fairford entering, the house, summoned Edward's own servant, and with his assistance conveyed his master up stairs, and, undressing him, managed to get him into bed. By this time Edward was quite exhausted, and the surgeon having arrived, whom Fairford had despatched the coachman to fetch, proceeded to examine the wound in his side which he immediately pronounced to be of so dangerous a nature as almost entirely to preclude the hope of discovery. Fairford received this intelligence in an adjoining room, and which had the effect of so saddening his countenance that for a while he could not again trust himself in sight of his friend, for fear his anguished face should reveal the truth. Still, he omitted nothing that could by any possibility tend to his recovery, and to this end desired the attendance of the highest medical skill; and, having succeeded in partially subduing his emotion, ventured once more into the sick room. It was, indeed, mournful to observe the strong man so suddenly brought low—he who at dawn was all activity and vigour, whose muscles and sinews seemed to bid defiance to sickness and death, whose full and strong manhood evidently promised length of days. Yet, here he was, bowed down to the very verge of the grave. The healthy colour from his cheek had flown, and a deathly paleness had usurped its place, and the convulsive workings of his frame betokened intense pain.

'How do you feel?' said Fairford, kindly, as he seated himself by the bedside, and took Edward's hand in his.

'Devilish bad,' he returned; 'they say every bullet has its billet, and the one which I received this morning in my side, plagues me horribly. I begin to fear, Fairford,' he added, after an interval of extreme pain, 'that I shall lose my life for the lovely Rose, without having the satisfaction of knowing that I have won her.'

'Speak no more of that,' said Fairford, earnestly; 'rather think, is there anything I can do to add to your comfort?'

'No, my good fellow, you cannot relieve me of this abominable pain, and there is nothing else I desire at present; by the bye, I wonder how Melville gets on! I think I heard Mortimer say he was wounded?'

'But very slightly,' returned the other, 'merely a trifling wound in the arm,'

'Ah! he is fortunate; but this pain terribly increases; hand me that draught Dr. Wilcox said I was to take, in case I found the pain become more intolerable; and it surely cannot be worse than it is now.'

Fairford poured it into a glass, and then, gently raising him in the bed, administered the sedative

'I thank you; that will do,' said Edward, as he again placed him in a recumbent position; 'and, now that I feel a trifle easier, I will endeavour to sleep, and I may, perhaps, be better when I awake.'

Fairford re echoed the wish, and drawing the curtains round the bed, so as to exclude the least ray of light, was soon thankfully convinced, by his breathing that he had obtained, at least a transient relief from pain; and alas! it was doomed to be transient, for he shortly awoke to renewed agony. The surgeon, who was in attendance, endeavoured in vain to assuage his pain, or mitigate the unfavourable symptoms which manifested themselves; he could only have recourse to laudanum, and that only for a short time deadened his feelings.

'Would you not like to see Mrs. Trevors?' said Fairford, during an interval of ease.

'I scarcely think she would come, were I even to desire it,' replied Edward: 'she thinks I succeeded with Rose to the extent to which my wishes carried me, and infidelity is a wound to her pride I think she will never forgive.'

'Oh! she will surely come to you, when she hears how ill you are. Let me entreat of you to allow me to send for her, in your name.'

'Well, do as you wish;' and Edward relapsed into silence, while Fairford hastened to write the note to Marian, which speedily brought her once more under the roof of the house, which had for several years owned her as mistress. The moment she arrived, Fairford hastened to acquaint her with the extreme danger of Edward, and also the intensity of his sufferings. She wept, as she exclaimed,—

'Oh, Mr. Fairford, how much misery do our uncontrolled passions cause not only to ourselves, but to all who are connected with us. My brother I have just left, sunk in the deepest affliction; his wife is, I fear, stretched upon her death-bed; little hope, you tell me, is entertained for Edward; and all, all this misery, is caused, merely from Edward being unable to control the unfortunate passion he entertained for my brother's wife; and now alas! not only his own, but, most probably, the life also of the misguided girl, whose affections he has estranged from her husband, and has only too surely succeeded in seducing from the paths of virtue, must fall a sacrifice to the indulgence of that ill-fated passion.'

'Is it indeed true,' replied Fairford mournfully, 'that Mrs. Moreland is seriously ill, and that her illness has arisen from Mr. Trevors' partiality for her?'

'Perfectly: I have told you the exact truth, and it shows the sad consequences of sin.'

'I think you are labouring under a mistake as regards Mrs. Moreland,' said Fairford mildly, 'for Mr. Trevors has himself frequently avowed her innocence.'

'Rose innocent! why, why then was Edward shot? but no, it cannot be! for when in my presence Mr. Melville accused him of entertaining bad feelings towards her, he never attempted to deny it.'

'Neither, my dear madam, does he now. On the contrary, I am compelled to acknowledge that he regrets not having succeeded to the extent he desired.'

'Can it be possible, then, that we have falsely accused and wrongfully judged Mrs. Moreland   Alas, alas! if it be so, we shall have her death to answer for;' and Marian cast a look of bewildered agony on Fairford

'I entreat you to compose yourself,' he said kindly, leading her to a seat, and, pouring out a glass of wine from the decanter which stood on the sideboard, he respectfully handed it to her.

'If I have wronged Rose,' said Marian, with anxious countenance, 'it is my duty to repair the error I have unintentionally committed, and use my utmost endeavours to re-establish her innocence.   Do not, Mr. Fairford, I beg of you, think that I acted rashly in depriving her of her good name; for never did I breathe a word against her purity till I possessed, what I deemed, absolute proof of her guilt.   Even now, to think her innocent, I must doubt the evidence almost of my own senses.'

'I know too well the goodness of your heart,' replied Fairford, 'to think for an instant you would willingly injure another.   But I will acquaint Mr. Trevors of your arrival, and then return and conduct you to him.'

Saying which he left the room, to apprise Edward of Marian's wish to see him   He faintly gave the required permission, and in another minute Marian was by his side.   At sight of his pallid brow and countenance, which was contracted with bodily suffering, she was so overcome, that she could only clasp the hand he held out to her on her entrance, and bedew it in tears; resentment against him was totally forgotten, as with swelling bosom and agonised heart she beheld him thus helplessly stretched on the bed of death. From the first moment her eyes fell upon him, and marked the hue of death upon his features, she felt it was impossible he could ever recover.

'I am glad you have come, Marian,' he said at length. 'I was afraid you would refuse me this favour.'

Tears so choked Marain's utterance, that though she attempted to do so, she was unable to reply; but pressed the hand she held, in silence, to her lips.

'Are you still in so much pain?' said the surgeon, who entered at this moment, addressing Edward.

'Indeed I am doctor; can you give me anything to afford me relief?'

'I am afraid not,' said the surgeon, shaking his head.

Edward paused for a few moments, and then collecting his strength, said with more of energy than he had before spoken, 'As, on quitting this world, we all of us have accounts we would gladly get settled beforehand, I should like to know, doctor, whether you think my time has come; because, if so, there are a few things I should like to arrange as quickly as possible.   I trust to your candour, therefore; to answer me truly the following question—"Do you think it improbable that I shall survive the effect of this wound, which is now causing me such torment?"'

There was a pause of a few seconds—a painful and a solemn pause—it was broken by Edward, who, impatient at not receiving an answer, said, 'Do not fear, doctor, to tell me the truth; I am fully prepared for your answer—I know you think my present situation a critical one.'

Thus appealed to, the surgeon replied, 'I am thankful that you have spared me the pain of informing you that your wound is, certainly, a very dangerous one.'

There was another and a longer pause, during which the sobs of Marian were distinctly audible.   It was again broken by Edward; but his voice was faint and weak, and it seemed an effort to him to speak with a degree of calmness.

'I heard from your answer, doctor, as well as my own feelings, that I shall never rise from off this bed again; but how long do you think I may reasonably expect to live?'

'If your unfavourable symptoms do not abate,' returned the surgeon, 'your time, I fear, is short; more indeed to be numbered by hours than days: therefore, I would advise you to settle all your worldly affairs without delay, and then prepare your soul for another and, I hope, a better world.'

Edward made no reply, but buried his head under the bed clothes, in order to conceal the emotion that evidently shook his frame; still his bodily sufferings were so great, as to drown in a measure the sufferings of his mind.   And when the lawyer whom he desired to see had arrived, the agony he endured was so great, that he could not converse with him.

'It is impossible for me to talk at present,' said Edward, addressing the surgeon; 'cannot you give me some opiate to lull this pain?'

The doctor did as he desired, and in a short time it had the effect of causing him to sleep. Marian and Fairford, seated on either side of the bed, watched his slumbers, while the surgeon took his station at the foot.   For nearly an hour the most profound silence prevailed, broken only by an occasional half-suppressed burst of anguish from Marian.   Now and then, the surgeon felt the pulse of his patient, and numbered its beats by his watch; and each time with an increased anxiety of countenance, which was noted by Fairford and Marian with inward agony. At length,

Edward awoke, and, gazing for a moment vacantly around, apparently became gradually conscious of his illness, and the sorrowful faces of his attendants.

'Do you feel any easier?' said Fairford, gazing anxiously on him.

'Yes, much easier—I am almost free from pain; but where is Rose? I thought I saw her face bending over me. but oh! so altered, so dreadfully changed, that I scarcely knew her; and she whispered to me that Albert and Marian had accused her of guilt and shame, and then she appealed to me, that, knowing her innocent, I would do her justice before I died, and declare it; and, when I promised to do so, she stooped and kissed my lips—the kiss thrilled through my whole frame and awoke me, but now I see her not—I fear my sight is already failing me; but at any rate, guide my hand to her that I may die pressing it in my own; one more such kiss, sweet Rose, and I shall die blest.'

'Edward,' said Marian, solemnly, 'listen to me, while you have the power; it is your wife Marian that speaks.'

'Then is not Rose here?' inquired Edward, faintly.

'No, would to God she were! but she is like you, struck down in the bloom of youth and health.'

'What is it you say?' replied Edward, eagerly, 'Rose ill! oh tell me, tell me I have mistaken your words?'

'I cannot, Edward; it is, alas! only too true. After myself and Henry Melville had discoverd you together yesterday morning, I deemed it my duty to make Albert acquainted with what we saw and heard, when, believing Rose guilty, he denounced her as such, and desired her to leave his house: this she refused to do, declaring herself innocent in everything but appearance; he still persisted, urged, alas! I must own, by my persuasion, in giving no credit to her assertions, and the violence of her emotions having brought on premature labour, she last night gave birth to a stillborn child, and now remains in a state of insensibility and imminent danger.'

Edward heard her through without any interruption, save by his groans, and now, having requested to be raised and supported in the bed with pillows, spoke as follows:—

'I feel my life to be ebbing fast, and nothing now could add to the bitter agony I endure, at learning the unhappy position of the innocent and unsuspecting Rose. God is my witness, at this solemn moment, that I never breathed a word to Rose that could call a blush to her cheek. I spoke to her only as a kind and affectionate brother, and in that light she regarded me, I am certain, with sincere affection. I do not mean to say that my wishes or intentions went not, on the contrary, beyond a brotherly regard; I loved her passionately, and hoped in time to gain her to my desires, and often I longed to break the bonds that enchained me, and tell her my true feelings towards her; but though often, when away from her, I resolved to do this, I never in her presence had the courage to do it; though the words were frequently on my lips, I was deterred from giving utterance to them, by the certainty of her anger and scorn—of losing the kindly feelings of friendship with which she regarded me; and never till yesterday had I ventured to approach her lips; but I was then carried away with the ardour of my love, and thought not of the consequence; though, had you not interrupted us at the moment, you would, I am sure, have been witness of her severe displeasure. The only letter I ever received from her you will find in my writing-desk, together with another I had sent her for perusal, but which she returned me unopened. I am too exhausted to say more now, but bear witness, all who are present, that with my dying breath I declare Rose innocent even of the knowledge of my desires towards her.'

Having with much difficulty and frequent interruptions from pain and shortness of breath, given utterance to these sentences, Edward sunk back exhausted, and remained for some time motionless. At length, whispering to Fairford, he called in the lawyer, and gave him the few directions that were required, as to the disposition of his property. This done, he gradually dozel off again to sleep. It was now night; and he who lay dying there, and one who watched in anguish by his side, had spent the previous evening in rude mirth and drunken hilarity. Oh! it was an awful thought, and came with deep and solemn feeling on the mind of Fairford, forcing tears from his eyes that had not been wet since early youth. Oh! it is a solemn and a holy task to watch by the dying bed, to know, as the minutes fleet quickly on, they bring the departing spirit closer and closer to the confines of another world; that the life-breath is quivering the frame, threatening each moment to desert it for ever, and yet lingering a few more seconds ere the immortal spirit is let loose, free to take its flight to worlds unknown, to wander we know not where. This is, as we have said, a solemn task, and calculated to fill our minds with awe, especially when we remember that a few more fleeting years, at most, and we shall be compelled, prepared or otherwise, to lay down this mortal life, while our disembodied spirits waft away to scenes and realms unknown, where we are assured we must give an account of the actions, be they good or ill, that we have performed while sojourning here. It was these thoughts and feelings that weighed down and oppressed the trio, who were now gathered round Edward's couch. When they spoke, it was in whispers, as though dreading to trust their voices in the stillness of that chamber. Edward suddenly opened his eyes, and, with an almost supernatural strength, raised himself without the slightest assistance, upright in bed; and, gazing round the room, while his sunken eyes, and the cold, damp sweat upon his brow, gave tokens that his dissolution was close at hand, exclaiming, in broken sentences,—'I was wrong—I feel it now —Melville, Rose—forgiveness!' sunk back again for the last time upon his pillow, and, making an effort to smile as Marian pressed her lips to his bloodless cheek, which faded for an instant into one of pain, and next stiffened into the fixed look of death, and all was over: Yes! his spirit had flown to the footstool of his Maker, there to render an account of the sins done in the body. Marian's anguish was beyond description: borne from the room in a fainting fit, in the arms of Fairford, it was long before she gave any signs of returning life.   When she did so, it was to an agony so dreadful, that few could bear to witness it.   'Oh, Edward, Edward!' she exclaimed, 'wretch that I am! it was I who caused your death.   Had I not been mad enough to take Melville to my brother's house, to witness the interview I was aware you intended seeking with Rose: oh, had I been content to have harboured suspicious feelings in my own breast—this, this would not have happened.   But no; wretch that I am, this was not enough!   I must communicate all I suspected to Melville; had it been otherwise, Edward would have been still living; but now cut off in the prime of manhood, and I, I alone answerable for it all!'

In vain Fairford essayed to comfort her; it but increased the anguish of her mind, till he accidently made some allusion to her brother,—this recalled her wandering thoughts, and, demanding pen and paper, she traced the following lines :—

'DEAREST ALBERT,—Rose is innocent, entirely so, and we have done her grievous wrong in suspecting her for a moment to be otherwise than affectionate and true to you.   Edward is no more; but with his dying breath he called God to witness the truth of what I now tell you. I can write no more, my very brain seems on fire.—Your heart-broken sister.

'MARIAN TREVORS.'

'This,' she said, giving what she had written open into the hands of Fairford, 'this may, perhaps, be the means of preventing another life from being sacrificed; at any rate, it is an act of justice that cannot be too speedily accomplished, and, though it is now night, yet, undoubtedly, there are persons up at my brother's residence: will you entrust this to some one you feel assured will safely deliver it?'

'I will,' replied Fairford, affixing to it a seal, and leaving the room, he gave it in charge of Edward's valet, and bade him go with it at once.

Mrs. Sommerville had, as we have recorded, refreshed her worn-out frame with that repose which is so needful to the body, and afterwards heard from Lucy the sad cause of her daughter's illness, and they were now, at the dawning of another day, watching over the unconscious Rose.

The doctor we have mentioned, who was in attendance upon Melville, had obtained an interview with Albert, and made him acquainted with Henry's wound; but of this, and, indeed, of the duel altogether, they were happily unconscious.   Day was just struggling to obtain the victory over night, and, casting its pale beams through the window, began to make the lamp that was burning unnecessary, when a light tap at the door was answered by Lucy, who received a message from the servant to the purport that Mr. Moreland wished to speak to her immediately in the room above.   Tremblingly she obeyed the summons, with a sort of ominous fear that some fresh calamity was about to break over her devoted head.   Albert was pacing the floor with those rapid strides that characterised him when any unusual emotion painfully affected him; he stopped abruptly in his hurried walk as she entered, and, forgetful that she was yet unacquainted with the duel, said, pointing to the letter he had just received from Marian, and which was lying upon the table, 'Read that.'   Lucy complied, and as she did so, he watched her countenance. At the commencement. 'My dear brother,' it wore a puzzled expression, as she was not aware Marian had left the house.   At the next sentence, 'Rose is innocent!' it was radiant with a smile of joy; but as she proceeded an universal trembling seized upon her frame, the letter dropped from her hands, and her face, ever pale, but now unusually so from anxiety and watching, yet gave token that it was capable of being blanched even more, for every vestige of blood now forsook it, leaving her countenance of a deadly hue.   She strove to speak—it was useless; she could not give utterance to the slightest sound, and she would have sunk to the floor, had not Albert caught her in his arms.   To call the servant, without disturbing Rose, was impossible; therefore, conveying her to a sofa, he sought the only remedy that was at hand—cold water, with which he plentifully bedewed her face.   Lucy was not a girl easily overcome, but when the reader remembers that she had for many long and weary hours been in close attendance upon Rose, without even once closing her eyes in sleep, he will not be surprised that the shock she now received on hearing thus suddenly, without one word of preparation, of the death of Edward —of one to whom she had once been fondly attached—to whom her heart had beat responsive to that first warm love which neither years nor estrangement can make a woman entirely forget —we say, we think it not astonishing that the surprise at thus unexpectedly hearing of his death acting upon an already weakened frame, should have caused the fainting we have already described.

It was not of long duration, and Albert speedily had the joy of seeing her restored to consciousness. 'Pardon me, dear Lucy!' he exclaimed, kindly bending over her; 'in my anxious desire to communicate to you Edward's confession of Rose's innocence, I forgot.'

'Edward Trevors is dead!' said Lucy, interrupting him, and speaking with a calmness more painful to witness than the agonised expression of grief.

'He is,' returned Albert.

'Then tell me at once what caused his death.'

'Alas! and are you not aware that a duel took place yesterday morning, between ——'

'Edward and my brother!' exclaimed Lucy. 'Oh, no, I knew it not! Then Edward has fallen by his hands? Alas! alas! this is dreadful! But oh! for mercy's sake, tell me how my——'

'Your brother,' interrupted Albert, 'fortunately escaped with only a slight wound in his arm.'

'You are sure it is but slight?' said Lucy, her countenance expressive of alarm. 'Do not —pray do not deceive me!'

'The surgeon who was in attendance upon him, was here not long ago, and repeatedly assured me his wound was but trifling.'

'Thank Heaven!' ejaculated Lucy, fervently; 'but to Marian, poor Marian, this is a dreadful

No. 17.

blow ; then, picking the letter from off the floor, where it had remained since it had fallen from her hand, she added—

'Mrs. Sommerville is with Rose, and as I was under the painful necessity of communicating to her the suspicions you entertained regarding Rose, it is but right that I should immediately show her this letter, which so completely acquits her daughter.'

'And,' said Albert, ' let Rose, as soon as consciousness returns, know how deeply I have injured her, and the desire I feel to make every amends in my power.'

'I will,' returned Lucy, as with tottering footsteps she left the room.

On returning to Mrs. Sommerville, she placed the letter in her hands : she read it calmly through, and then laying it on the table, merely said, apparently half unconscious that she did so—

'I knew it,' and silence again reigned in the apartment.

Towards the middle of the day, Mrs. Melville called, and with an exclamation of pleased surprise, Lucy ran into her open arms. For awhile, they mingled tears and embraces, without a word being spoken by either, but when their emotion was a little subsided, Mrs. Melville inquired after Rose.

'She remains to all appearance much the same,' said Lucy, ' yet I am thankful to say, that though we cannot see any change, the doctor pronounces her better.'

'God grant,' said Mrs. Melville, fervently, ' that her life may be spared !'

Lucy then showed her mother the letter Albert had received from Marian.

'This is, indeed, a treasure,' exclaimed Mrs. Melville, ' and I think Mr. Moreland cannot object that I should inclose it in one I intend writing to Henry, on my return home, as it will afford him sincere delight, and be an antidote to the painful intelligence of Edward's death.'

'Take it, mamma ; I am sure Mr. Moreland will be perfectly willing for you to do so. But, oh ! it is dreadful to think of the death of Edward.'

'It is, my child; and we know not yet how it may fare with Henry, if he is called to answer for taking away his life.'

'Oh! but mamma, that must not be. Henry—all of us, must go abroad. But, oh! poor Marian, what will become of her ? have you seen her ?'

'No, my love. I called, but, as I anticipated, was not admitted. The sight of either of us must too forcibly recal Henry to her memory to allow her to have any desire to see us. But I saw Mr. Fairford, and he assured me she was as well as under the distressing circumstances, we could expect. But I think, Lucy, that as Mrs. Sommerville is with her daughter, you had better lie down and endeavour to get a little sleep, or you will be so worn out as to incapacitate you for future exertion.'

'I believe, mamma, you are right, and will, therefore seek a few hours' rest.'

'Then, farewell ! my child. I will return home, and write to Henry.'

'Farewell, mamma.'

Lucy then acquainted Mrs. Sommerville with her intention of retiring for a short time, which, meeting with her cordial approbation, she threw herself on a bed, and was soon locked in the arms of sleep. After sleeping for a much longer time than she intended, she awoke greatly refreshed, and hastening into the sick room, found to her great joy that Rose had, during her absence, awoke to sensibility, but in so low and reduced a condition both of body and mind, that they had not dared acquaint her with the contents of Marian's letter, fearing that the excess of joy, on learning that Edward had done her justice, would be too much for her weakened frame to bear. The sight of her mother, indeed, had nearly overcome her. The doctor, who was unremitting in his attention, had ordered some gentle restorative, and she was now more composed.

On Lucy's entrance, her eyes filled with tears, and when she stooped to kiss her cheek, Rose clasped her white arms round the neck of the dear and true friend, who had clung to her through good and ill report. Lucy gently disengaged herself from her embrace, fearing to allow her to indulge in her feelings in her present weak state. And while Lucy felt a weight of sorrow removed from her own bosom, she was not unmindful of others ; but stole up stairs to communicate the glad tidings to Albert. He received them with that subdued emotion, which made so strong a feature in his character, and merely expressed his desire to see Rose, when the doctor considered he might do so with safety to her.

'She still thinks you believe her guilty, and we desire, before admitting you, to break to her the knowledge you possess of her truth and virtue.'

'Yes, it will be advisable to do so,' returned Albert, ' and I think if you withhold the death of Edward, all else might safely be imparted to her.'

'Well, I will endeavour in the course of the evening, if she recovers a little stronger, to do as you wish.'

Rose did seem stronger, and was enabled to converse with her mother and Lucy, though still exceedingly weak. Lucy was carefully watching for an opportunity to introduce the name of Albert ; and when Rose, in alluding to the cause of her illness, said, with an earnest look at

her mother, 'You, I know, believe me innocent,' Lucy took advantage of the opportunity to say—
'Yes, dearest Rose, we all of us know and believe you are innocent, even Albert.'

'Albert!' said Rose, catching eagerly at the name most dear to her on earth; 'nothing, nothing, I think, will ever induce him to love, or even allow me in his sight again. Forgive, me, my dear mother and kind friend, for saying what I know will grieve you; but oh! I had rather, a thousand times rather, have died than lived to be despised by him.'

'But you will not—you are not,' said Lucy kindly; 'he is now sensible that he has wronged, deeply wronged you, in suspecting you of aught but loving him with the fondest and most enduring affection.'

'Oh! what is it I hear? but no, it cannot be. It is kind of you, Lucy, to endeavour to reassure my fainting spirit; but it is hopeless for me to expect even ever to behold his face again. I did, as you say, indeed still do, love him with the most ardent affection—would be content to suffer anything, if he would only allow me to remain near him.'

'It is not hopeless,' replied Lucy, affected even to tears; 'he himself only a few hours ago, expressed to me his earnest desire to see and sue to you for forgiveness for his unkindness towards you.'

'Oh! Lucy, you would not, I am sure, be so cruel to intentionally deceive me; but may you not have been mistaken?'

'No, dearest Rose, there is no mistake, Edward has done you the justice to declare, in the most solemn manner, that you are perfectly guiltless.'

'But,' interrupted Rose, with as much eagerness as her strength would permit, 'does Albert believe him?'

'He does, and is anxious to hear you pronounce his pardon, for having brought you by his unkindness to this sick bed."

'Oh! Lucy, suffer him to come; let me hear from his own lips that he still loves me. Oh! what transport it will be. Mother dear, plead; bid them let him come.'

Mrs. Sommerville, who had remained perfectly silent during the foregoing conversation, now kindly and gently persuaded Rose to wait till the morrow, before she had an interview with her husband—an interview which would undoubtedly be painful, as well as pleasing to both: and Rose was perfectly willing to sacrifice her own wishes, in obedience to the desire of her mother, who she was convinced had nothing but her welfare at heart.

'And now, my dear child,' said Mrs. Sommerville, 'you had better endeavour to compose yourself to sleep, while I write a few lines, to acquaint your father and brother with the delightful intelligence, that you are now surely mending.'

'Oh, yes, dear mother, I feel that I shall now quickly recover; my heart is so light that I feel to have lost the heavy burden of sorrow that lately pressed upon it. These tears you must forgive, for they are, I assure you, tears of joy.'

'Yes,' said Lucy, 'I am convinced they are, but joy is sometimes as fatal as sorrow; therefore, dear Rose, for all our sakes, compose yourself to rest. I am going to leave you for a short time; and if, on my return, I do not find you asleep, I shall be disposed seriously to chide you.' Saying which, she pressed a kiss upon her cheek, and closing the door behind her, once more sought Albert.

There was something in the kind and gentle disposition of Lucy that had in the last two eventful days greatly won upon Albert, and he now welcomed her with a smile of pleasure, and when he heard from her of Rose's continued improvement, he thanked and blessed her for her kindness, and suffered Lucy to persuade him to retire to rest that night.

'Rose is no longer in any danger,' urged Lucy; 'for two days and nights you have watched, and never even sought repose; now do promise me that you will to-night take that rest and refreshment which is absolutely necessary if you desire to see Rose to-morrow, for unless you look much less harrassed and exhausted, I cannot permit you to enter the room.'

'I promise you, Lucy, that I will do as you desire, though I do not feel much inclined to sleep with that promise!'

'I will leave you at once; so good night.'

'Good night, dear Lucy; Rose and myself will never forget your tender care of us both. God bless you!"

Albert spoke these words with an earnestness quite foreign to his nature, and Lucy, thankful at having won from him the promise she had purposely come, if possible, to extort, once more resumed her place in the sick chamber. Rose slept the greater part of this night, but it was a long and solemn one to Lucy; her thoughts were filled with the lamentable death of Edward, and the consequent distress of Marian. All that had taken place during the last two days passed in review before her; and oh, how much they appeared to resemble the fancies of a troubled dream! but oh, the knowledge that what had occurred was no idle imagination of the brain, but sad and awful realities. Oh, how palpably came back to her imagination the days past and gone, when she confessed to Edward a reciprocal affection—when she believed his heart the seat of honour and virtue; and then came the deep and burning thoughts she had nourished when she first discovered his intended baseness towards herself, and many other circumstances, long forgotten, returned to swell the train of thoughts that now filled her heart; and then to know that he was dead, killed by the hand of her brother—a brother whom she loved, and knew to be upright and honourable, beyond the generality of his sex, who ever made the cause of the oppressed his own—indeed, it was the noble feeling of his heart which leading him to espouse the cause of the truly unfortunate Rose, had made him the destroyer of Edward, and well she knew how bitter must be that brother's feelings, who had never before injured even a worm. Oh, sad and lonely must now be his heart! Her bosom heaved with anguish as she thought upon his sorrows; and while she thanked Heaven that he was spared, she bitterly deplored the untoward death of Edward. Thus passed the night, and the early part of the following day. Rose was refreshed with her slumbers, and after the doctor had seen her, he pronounced her decidedly improved.

'If you go on like this, my dear madam,' smiling, you will soon be restored to perfect health.'

'It is the earnest hope of us all,' said Mrs. Sommerville, "and you must allow us to offer you, sir, our sincere thanks for the kind attention you have shown to Mrs. Moreland.'

'You must rather thank this young lady,' he replied, pointing to Lucy; 'without her tender care and good nursing, I fear my skill would have been unavailing.'

'We are, indeed, indebted to her,' said Mrs. Sommerville, her eyes filling with tears—'indebted to her in an amount it is utterly beyond our power to repay.'

Lucy and Rose exchanged glances of sincere affection, and as the doctor left the room, Rose said,—

'Now, dear Lucy, you will not refuse to fetch Albert; I am sure I have waited patiently.'

'I can no longer refuse you, dearest Rose,' replied Lucy, moving toward the door, and she presently returned leading Albert by the hand. Rose endeavoured to calm her feelings, but it was impossible. When Albert advanced to her bed side, she started up, and throwing her arms lovingly round him, sobbed out her joy upon his bosom: he was nearly as much overcome, and for some minutes neither could command themselves sufficiently to speak. Rose was the first to break the silence by whispering in almost inaudible accents,—

'You will not bid me leave you?'

'Leave me! Oh, Rose, dearer in this hour than you have ever been, say, can you, will you forgive me.'

'All, all is forgiven and forgotten,' sobbed Rose; 'you still love me—you have given me that blessed assurance, and I care for nothing else.'

'And you, my Rose, will live to bless and cheer my wayward spirit.'

'Sweet task!' exclaimed Rose, holding him closer to her, 'dear and sacred task; for that alone I live.'

Sweet indeed was this reconciliation; but it was also fraught with deep and overcoming emotion—so much so, that Mrs. Sommerville and Lucy, themselves affected even to tears, deemed it right to interfere, and begged Albert to calm his own feelings, on account of the weakened state of Rose's health.

'You had better now retire for awhile,' said Mrs. Sommerville; 'Rose seems already exhausted, and I fear a continuance of this emotion, consequent on again beholding you, may have even a fatal effect upon her.'

Albert gazed upon the pallid cheek of Rose, whom he had so cruelly injured by his unjust suspicions, and in a voice of agonised entreaty, said, as he clasped her to his bosom, 'Oh, do not part us!'

'Rose is so very ill and weak,' urged Lucy, 'that it is absolutely necessary for her mind to be perfectly composed; indeed, the doctor particularly desired she should be kept as quiet as possible, and nothing whatever allowed to excite her, at least for the present.'

'Dearest Lucy,' said Rose, disengaging herself from Albert's arms, while an almost heavenly smile played over her face, 'I am so happy—so blessed! I feel—I know that I shall live, if only to cheer and comfort him. Let him but remain with me, and we will not speak a single word, if you fear it will retard my recovery.'

'Oh, no!' said Albert; 'I shall be content to sit by her side, and, holding her hand in mine watch her returning health with silent gladness.'

'You hear what he says, and cannot, I am sure, refuse him that slight satisfaction, dear mother,' said Rose, appealing to Mrs. Sommerville.

'Well then, dear Rose, I must for the present enforce silence on you both.'

Thus blessed in the returning love and confidence of a husband she adored, Rose each day grew stronger. Nothing could induce Albert to leave the room night nor day. What repose he took was in a chair by her side; they conversed together but little, for the feelings of both were tinged with melancholy, and whenever they spoke of the future, tears gathered in their eyes. Rose's hopes and wishes were still buoyant, and she looked forward to happiness with the being she so tenderly regarded; and yet, mingled with this, there was a vague sense of fear. Frequently would she check herself in the midst of painting some bright vision of forthcoming bliss, and, bursting into tears, would hold Albert to her bosom, and, as though she dreaded him being snatched from her embrace, would beg of him to assure her that he would not leave her—that nothing on earth should part them.

'Nothing, my Rose,' said Albert, soothingly, 'but death shall ever again part us for a single hour.'

'Nor that,' replied Rose, tenderly, pressing her lips to his forehead, 'for when you go, I shall shortly follow. I live but for you alone; and when you no longer require my love to cheer and bless you— when I shall have performed for you the last tender office, then, Albert, my husband, I shall join you in another, and I hope a better world.'

Mrs. Sommerville, with deep and heartfelt sorrow, marked the sad change that had come over the once gay and light-hearted Rose. In vain she strove to infuse an air of joy and gladness into the spirits of her daughter. The kind and gentle influence of Lucy was likewise ineffectual; her spirits and feelings seemed entirely to have taken the sombre hue of Albert's: to sit clasped in each other's arms for hours, without a word being spoken by either, seemed the greatest delight of both.

At first, Mrs. Sommerville and Lucy hoped and believed, that as Rose regained her usual health, she would with it also regain her lost cheerfulness, but in this they were disappointed; not that Rose was unhappy; on the contrary, she constantly declared herself blessed beyond what she had ever once hoped to be. But the merry laugh, that sounded like music on the ear; the light and playful gaiety of her conversation, that used to charm every one who came in contact with her; they were obliged to acknowledge with heart-wrung anguish, was irrecoverably gone. It cost Mrs. Sommerville many, very many bitter tears to feel that her daughter had lost that sweet charm which had rendered her so universally beloved; and to see, in the place of that lovely bloom which had sat so sweetly on her once happy countenance, a melancholy paleness, broken only by an occasional hectic flush. Ah! how utterly unlike the bloom of health, and nothing unconnected with Albert appeared visibly to affect her, or engage her thoughts, beyond the passing moment: thus, when she was so far recovered, that they deemed they might with safety communicate the death of Edward, she was by no means so overcome as they expected. In the meantime, Henry, naturally possessed of an excellent constitution, recovered from the effects of his wound far more rapidly than the surgeon anticipated. He was much shocked at the untoward fate of Edward, but in spite of the earnest entreaties of his friends, declared his intention of appearing to take his trial for having caused the death of Edward.

'I am not ashamed of, neither do I repent the part I have acted: then wherefore should I seek to conceal myself, as though, like a midnight assassin, I had taken him at a disadvantage, and deprived him of life? No, while I know that by open and honourable means I called him to account for his base conduct, I shall not shrink from answering for it at the bar of my country, and if (which I cannot believe) it will think fit to punish me for the part I have acted, I will endeavour meekly to bear it.'

Though this resolution, of course, grieved and pained Mrs. Melville and Lucy, yet they could not do otherwise than applaud it.

'It is so like himself,' said Lucy to her mother, 'our dear, noble Henry; I knew from the first he would act thus—I was certain of it, though I endeavoured to persuade you to the contrary.'

'But alas!' said Mrs. Melville, 'if this resolution should cause him to be torn from us! The coroner's jury have brought a verdict of wilful murder against him; if the jury on the trial should do the same, what, oh, what will become of us!' and Mrs. Melville was so overcome with her feelings, that she burst into tears.

'Oh! think it not, dear mother,' said Lucy; 'I am certain we shall be spared so awful a calamity;' and yet, buoyed up with hope to a feeling of certainty, that the jury empannelled to try her brother would regard the death of Edward in the same extenuating light as she did herself, for all this, it was with a palpitating heart, and an aching, throbbing breast that Lucy beheld the day draw nigh.

The assizes came on a week after Edward's death; and it being generally known that Henry Melville and Sir Charles Mortimer, together with William Fairford, intended to surrender themselves to take their trial, the court was crowded to suffocation. Rose was now sufficiently recovered as not to require the attendance of Lucy, who had returned to her mother; neither of them had seen Henry since the occurrence of the fatal duel, and though strongly urged to afford them an interview, Henry had often replied, in answer to their reiterated request,— 'Wait till my country has freed me from the stigma that now attaches to my name; then I can meet the two dearest to me on earth without a blush upon my cheek. I know that you acquit me of all but honourable motives; let my countrymen do me the same justice and then we shall meet with pride and joy.'

The trial occupied many hours—hours past in anxious suspense by Mrs. Melville and Lucy; even Albert, and consequently Rose, were anxious, and forgetful of all else but the fate of Henry; Marian likewise could not be indifferent to the issue, for Fairford, who had watched her husband with unceasing love and attention in his dying moments, had soothed her anguish with the kindness of a brother, had performed the last sad office of following the remains of Edward to the tomb, and returned from that mournful ceremony to dry her tears; or, if that could not be, at least, to mingle his with her own. Oh! he who had done all this, and more, was also taking his trial, for having caused the death of his friend, for whom he had performed so many tender offices. Yes, when he heard of Henry's noble resolution, he immediately announced his own intention of doing the like; and consequently, his fate also hung upon the issue of this trial. During the day, Albert and Rose sat side by side, her head resting on his bosom, while her arm encircled his neck; their features wore an expression of deeper melancholy even than usual, and a knock at the door had the effect of causing the blood to rush tumultuously to their faces, thus mutely giving evidence of the anxiety of their minds concerning Henry. Marian sat alone in her splendid boudoir, surrounded by every comfort, even to luxurious profusion, yet this yielded her nought of joy. She glanced for a moment at the opposite mirror, and beheld the widow's cap, and the bombazine and crape, of which her dress was composed; and then came the sad and bitter memory of Edward's death-bed, forcing afresh the tears in torrents from her eyes; though she could not, would not doubt that Fairford, at least, would be acquitted, yet a restless anxiety filled her mind, especially as hour after hour passed on, without the trial coming to a conclusion. Mrs. Melville was plunged into sorrowful distress, which Lucy, in spite of her own feelings, strove by every means in her power to assuage. It was indeed a long and weary day to all concerned, with the exception of the parties themselves: in them no anxiety was visible, except in the first moment of meeting, which of course forcibly recalled Edward to the remembrance of all three; and as they politely exchanged greetings, an expression of sorrowful regret sat upon their features. After which, answering as their names were called over, they took their places in the dock, and when called upon to plead, Henry particularly, in a loud and firm voice, said 'Not Guilty;' and though there was nothing whatever approaching to levity in their manner or appearance, still less could there be discerned anything like anxiety. No they seemed perfectly conscious, and satisfied as to what would be the result. We have said the trial lasted for hours, but it at length came to a happy conclusion, for when the judge had charged the jury, they, without leaving the box, or consulting together for so long as five minutes, gave in their verdict, 'Not guilty'—a verdict which gave entire satisfaction to the whole court, so much so, indeed, that an effort was made, on the part of the numerous persons assembled to witness this trial, to applaud it, but which of course was suppressed.

Words cannot do justice to the joyful meeting that took place between Henry, Lucy, and Mrs. Melville. Hurrying from the court, and the numerous friends who pressed round to give him joy, he was the first to announce to those dear friends the favourable result of the trial. Clasping his mother and sister alternately in his arms, how precious were the tears that forced their way down his manly cheek! How delightful the proud feeling of his mother, who knew her son had not, even to save himself perhaps from a prison, swerved from the path of honour—that he had not hesitated an instant as to the course he ought to pursue! How sweet and graceful was the emotion of Lucy, who clung to this loved brother, and felt that in him she could repose every thought! So great had been their joy at again beholding him who had been separated from them for the first time since he had arrived at manhood, that they did not perceive the entrance of another person till Henry, turning round, introduced Sir Charles Mortimer.

I am afraid,' said that gentleman, as Mrs. Melville kindly bade him welcome, ' that at such a time as this I shall be deemed an intruder.'

'Henry's friend—one who has kindly nursed him in illness, and shared the responsibility of his actions, can never be deemed such by his mother and sister,' replied Mrs. Melville; 'Lucy will tell you the same.'—' She will, indeed,' said Lucy, offering her hand in token of friendship, which was gladly accepted.

Fairford, immediately after the trial, returned to Marian, by whom he was received with tears of joy. The following day Henry, accompanied by his sister, called to see Rose and Albert; need it be said he was received by both with kindness? It cost him a severe pang to observe the sad alteration a few weeks had made in Rose; a blight had too evidently fallen on this sweet flower, which gave but slight hope of permanent recovery.

'I have persuaded Albert and Rose to accompany me into the country, whither I return to-morrow, thinking if anything can avail to restore Rose to her wonted health, it will be her native air,' said Mrs. Sommerville to Henry and Lucy, as they left the room to take their departure.

'I think so indeed,' replied Lucy, 'and God grant that it may not only restore her to health, but her spirits likewise!'

Henry said nothing—his heart was too full. The sight of Rose had banished every feeling but anguish from his mind, and as they turned their steps homeward, scarce a word escaped him. Lucy loved and respected his feelings too much to offer any remark. She felt that it was best to allow him to indulge them unheeded. She herself had shed many tears when alone over the alteration that had taken place in Rose, consequently she could not be surprised that Henry should feel it severely.

Marian was sitting alone with Fairford over the breakfast-table when a letter was handed to her by the servant. The address was in a small but elegant hand, and the post-mark showed it to come from Italy. At this discovery she was so overcome, that she was near fainting, but with a strong effort she subdued her emotion, and, tearing it open, read the following words :—

'MY DEAR MADAM,
' I received your letter, and in reply beg to state that I am not the person you are in search of, having been born in Italy, and from which country I have never been absent for a day; neither have I, that I am aware of, any relatives in England. This, I think, will convince you that it is utterly impossible I can be the brother you are desirous of finding.
'I am, my dear madam, respectfully yours,

'CHARLES MORELAND.'

The very sight of this name, the name of a brother so dearly loved, again had the effect of recalling the past to her memory; and, dropping the letter from her hand, she covered her face, and wept.

Fairford kindly entreated of her to communicate to him the cause of her distress, and, placing the letter in his hands, she made him acquainted with everything concerning it.

'I know no reason that this Charles Moreland should so distinctly deny himself, were he, in truth, your brother,' said Fairford, when she had concluded, 'and consequently must believe him when he says he is not.'

'Then, of course,' replied Marian, 'it would be useless to proceed further in the matter.'

'I certainly think so,' returned Fairford.

'Well, then, I will be advised by you, and allow the matter to drop. I have a painful task to perform,' she continued, after a short pause; it is to pay a visit to my brother and his wife. 1 received a note from him yesterday, to the effect that they were going into the country, and desired to see me before they left town, and I do not like to refuse him, though I fear it will be almost too much for me.'

'You must endeavour not to allow it to be so,' replied Fairford.

'I will,' she returned.

Consequently when in the course of the morning she called, and was admitted into her brother's dwelling, though her cambric handkerchief was constantly held to her dark eyes, yet she was certainly far less really affected than either Rose or Albert; feelings, indeed, which are constantly upon the surface make much less impression on the mind than those which are subdued. Thus, those whose sorrow, let it come from whatever source it may, is most violent, is always sure to be evanescent; while others whose deep-seated grief is little marked by a common observer, mourn in secret for a much longer period. We do not mean to say persons are capable of governing their feelings; on the contrary, we are assured that to a great extent such is not the case. Some are differently constituted to what others, are and in consequence have more command over their feelings, be they of joy or sorrow. Marian we have seen, was one whose feelings were not of the most subdued or quiet kind, and therefore nothing affected her for a very long period. Albert, on the contrary, showed but little outward signs of grief, but his heart retained the impression of sorrow for years after its impress on Marian was totally effaced; unless any untoward circumstance recalled it to her memory, then she would apparently feel the pang as deeply as when it first stung her, but at other times she was light-hearted and happy, while Albert was ever melancholy and reserved even to his sister. It was wounding her self-pride, yet Marian considered it her duty to apologise to Rose for the suspicions she had engendered in Albert's mind regarding her, and which she now felt convinced were utterly groundless. With a sweet smile, Rose assured her of her forgiveness.'

' As you are going into the country,' said Marian, 'we shall be separated for some time ; but, upon your return, we shall, I hope, be more than ever united.'

Rose and Albert reiterated the wish. Mrs. Sommerville, more in compliance with what she deemed the wish of Albert, than her own desire, gave Marian a cordial invitation to accompany them, which was politely declined, and with rather a formal leave-taking, they separated. The following day found Rose and Albert once more among these sylvan scenes where they had first met, and, as Rose's strength would permit, they again wandered as they were wont previous to their marriage among her native hills; together they were happy;

a sweet contented smile, and yet melancholy withal, for ever sat upon Rose's features. But, like him, she seemed averse to society, even avoiding that of Agnes and her brothers: to be alone with each other seemed the sole happiness of each, and though little they conversed, there appeared a charm in each other's society that knit their hearts and souls as one. It was touching to see how each depended on the other for every drop of comfort they felt or knew. Mrs. Sommerville often wept, as she watched her altered child.

'And yet, as she is happy, why should I complain?' she remarked one day to Agnes, when conversing with her on the subject.

'Why indeed, my dear mother,' replied Agnes, encouragingly, though tears bedewed her own eyes, 'we should be thankful to know that she is happier than she has been before since her marriage; still it is such a strange, melancholy happiness that it makes me wretched even to witness it.'

'I hardly recognise the altered Rose as my own darling child, whose merry laugh was music to my ears.'

'It is doubtless greatly the effect of illness,' urged Agnes, 'and as she gets stronger, much that now makes you uncomfortable, will most probably disappear.'

'God grant it!' returned Mrs. Somerville.

Of all that mourned the sad change in Rose, not even her mother deplored it more bitterly than the warm-hearted father of Agnes. Tears would frequently trickle down his sun-burnt cheeks, as he gazed upon her pallid face and attenuated form, and it required all Agnes's gentle gaiety to prevent him brooding too much over it.

'Well, girl, it is, as you say, useless to repine, and yet I would rather have died while she was the gay and frolicsome bird that used to sing with heart unknown to care.'

'Say not so, dear father,' she returned, 'it sounds unkind towards myself.'

'I meant it not so, girl; you must not think that,' and he pulled her towards him, and fondly kissed her cheek; 'ye will not think so bad of your poor old father, eh, girl?'

'No, no,' replied Agnes, fondly returning his embrace.

After a month spent in the country, Albert and Rose returned together to town without any apparent amendment, either in her health or spirits. The first who welcomed their return were Lucy and Henry: they were kindly, indeed warmly, received by both, for they felt they were much indebted to them, especially to Lucy, who had, tenderly and unsolicited, save by Henry, nursed Rose through a dangerous illness, when forsaken by those, whose duty it was to have extended to her the helping hand; yet Lucy and her brother had the delicacy to perceive that Rose as well as Albert preferred being alone; this induced them to call but seldom, and Marian (whose grief in the course of a few months wonderfully abated) having, when they took possession once more of their town house, paid them a visit, and found them, as she afterwards declared to Fairford, 'so gloomy and reserved, that it actually affected her with *ennui* for several days afterwards, was not much disposed to renew her visit; and, finding they preserved the same melancholy exterior as months rolled on, at length ceased to call altogether, except as a matter of form, and on very rare occasions. 'It is certainly most unaccountable,' she observed, 'that my brother and his wife should not only live so entirely excluded from society, but should also look, and indeed act, as though some heavy calamity had befallen them: had it been me who was thus affected, it would not be surprising; indeed it is wonderful how I manage to keep up my spirits as well as I do,' and here her cambric handkerchief was in requisition. Fairford, to whom these observations were made, of course did his best to mitigate the sorrow of the fair young widow, and banish the tears from her bright eyes, and in truth we are bound to declare that he succeeded so well, that they shortly gave place to smiles,

Since the occurrences above related, the reader will have the goodness to suppose three years to have elapsed—scarcely three years, and yet how much has happened in the interval. Agnes, the fair and blooming Agnes, has become the mother of two sweet children, one, a lisping, romping boy of two years old, who climbs up his grandfather's knee, and coaxes him to tell him some old story about the fairies, or sing him a song; who loves to talk of his little sister Rose, and feels proud at being able to sustain her tottering footsteps across the floor, while she, only a year younger, just begins to lisp the name of brother, and laughs and claps her dimpled hands the moment she catches sight of Farmer Foster, and not unfrequently risks a fall in her eagerness to reach him. Both these sweet children are equally beloved by Mr. and Mrs. Sommerville, but they are not their only treasures, for their eldest son, who, at the time Henry was about being united to Agnes, so earnestly disclaimed matrimony, is now the happy husband of the daughter of a neighbouring farmer, who has lately made him the delighted father of a fine boy: their second son still remains at home with them, so they are not left entirely alone; nor does Agnes, in her new and increased duties, forget the one she voluntarily took upon herself of supplying to Mr. and Mrs. Sommerville the place of the absent Rose; no, were she in truth their own daughter, she could not possibly show them more duteous love and care. In this sacred task she is aided and assisted by her brother's wife, who feels for them an equal regard : and oh ! it is sweet to their parents to mark the unity of feeling that exists between their children ; the delicate health of Rose, whom they but seldom see, being the only thorn in their path, and of which Mrs. Sommerville remarked to her aged partner, ' We should not complain when all else is so fair and bright : it is a bitter drop in our cup ; but let it not poison our whole happiness. Every one has some trial, and this is ours ; let us therefore bend meekly to it.'

Marian is no longer a widow, but has, a second time, entered the marriage state, and given her fair hand to (the reader, we are sure, has already guessed to whom) Mr. William Fairford : they had been friends long before Edward's death, and the painful circumstances attending

which brought them in such close contact, that, before many months had passed, each felt the company of the other to be so pleasant and agreeable, that they were never happy apart. The fashionable world began soon to talk loudly or the impropriety of such constant and familiar intercourse that took place between the young and pretty widow and the gay and gallant cavalier.   Marian was the slave of appearance, and could not, for the world, bear to be talked of, or her conduct animadverted upon, and therefore told Fairford, with tears in her eyes, that however grieved she felt to be obliged to interdict his visits, he must, for the future, desist from calling when she was alone.

Fairford was quite taken by surprise, and stammered out an apology for having intruded his
No. 18.

company so much upon her, which, he assured her, he would not have done, had he not flattered himself that he was not wholly indifferent to her.

'Neither are you,' replied Marian. 'I regard you as a brother, a dear and tender brother; but the world will not give credit to such feelings existing between us; in short, Fairford, they will not believe you are content with the love I so freely bestow upon you, but accuse you of desiring a warmer affection.'

'Nor are they wrong,' replied Fairford, 'I acknowledge, Marian—you will allow me to call you so—that I have long aspired to create a regard for myself in your bosom, warmer than friendship; if you deem me presumptuous in hoping that I might succeed in my desire, I trust to your generosity, at least, to forgive, since it was the kind trust you reposed in me that alone induced me to hope.'

'Fairford,' returned Marian, after a pause, 'I will not allow any fastidious feeling of delicacy to stand in the way of my own, and I also fully believe your, happiness. The tender care you manifested for Edward, whose deathbed we watched together, and afterwards the kindness you showed to myself, must be my excuse, if any be needed, for thus again so speedily yielding my heart: there is my hand,' she continued, stretching it towards him, 'if you think it worth accepting, take it, and with it my entire affection.'

Fairford received it with eyes sparkling with gratitude, and pressing it in his own, carried it rapturously to his lips.

'There is one thing I desire of you,' said Marian, 'and that is, not to think ill of me for thus so soon forgetting one whom I once loved with the most ardent affection.'

'Were it possible I could think bad of you,' replied Fairford, 'I must also think ill of myself.'

'Men do not usually argue so,' returned Marian.

'To argue otherwise would not only be erroneous, but unjust. I desired your love as the best blessing Heaven could bestow upon me; and yet, but for this conversation, which gave me an opportunity of declaring sentiments, I should not have dared to impart them to you, at least for the present.'

'I hope,' replied Marian, earnestly, 'we may neither of us ever have cause to repent your having done so.'

'It is utterly impossible that I should ever repent it,' returned Fairford, 'and if constant and untiring affection——'

'That is all I desire,' interrupted Marian, 'but oh! if you should ever grow weary of me.'

'Think not so badly of me,' replied Fairford; 'you have won not only my love, but esteem, and that should convince you that you have nothing to fear for the future; it is, I assure you, no passing liking that I entertain for you, but a deep, firm, concentrated passion.'

'Yet think well,' urged Marian, 'before you take the irretrievable step of uniting your fate to mine; remember that I am six years your senior, you being but two-and-twenty, while I number eight-and-twenty years.'

'I do not forget it, dear Marian; but with that full in my memory, I am certain it is in your power to make me happy beyond what ordinarily falls to the lot of mortals.'

'I certainly,' replied Marian, 'do understand your temper and disposition.'

'Better,' interrupted Fairford, 'than any one else on earth; to you, and you alone, can I open my whole heart, and if, as is sometimes the case, I am affected with melancholy and low spirits, your presence is always sufficient of itself to charm it entirely away; and for the trifling difference in our ages, any person unacquainted with us would undoubtedly take me for the eldest.'

'If,' said Marian, after a pause, 'you feel that you could be happy with me, more so, indeed, than with any other, here, as I before said, is my hand, and be assured that nothing shall be wanting on my part that can in any way contribute to your happiness.'

'Dearest Marian,' returned Fairford, clasping her to his bosom, 'you have indeed made me blessed; and in gratitude for this precious gift,' and he pressed her hand with ardour to his lips, 'thy welfare shall be my constant study.'

In a short time they were married, with every prospect of happiness, for it was a marriage founded on mutual love and esteem; nor were they disappointed, for nearly two years had now glided imperceptibly on, and found them as perfectly happy as it is possible to be in this world. Fairford was justly proud of and gloried in Marian, while she, having learned wisdom by experience, and entertaining a high opinion of his moral character, never sought to debar him from the company of his own sex, even though the club frequently withdrew him from her; at the same time, being naturally of a lively disposition, his home was rendered so cheerful and pleasant, that he always returned to it with increased joy after a short absence, and ever felt that though sometimes induced to seek amusement away from it, that there alone his heart dwelt, and Marian, with easy, playful gaiety, would welcome him home, and without one word of chiding for his absence, but with sweet smiles and tender kisses, make him feel how dear his presence was to her.

We must now communicate to the reader another wedding which has taken place, though but a few months since, and which we think bids fair to be also a happy one: it is no other than that of our old favourite, Lucy Melville, who has given her fair hand and gentle, loving heart, to Sir Charles Mortimer, with the full consent of Henry and her mother. They were, as we have before said, a happy family; and the thought of separation could not be borne by any of them; and so they still continue to reside together, Sir Charles making a pleasant addition to their number. So truly amiable and kind, so richly gifted in all that makes a woman lovely, it was no wonder that she captivated the heart of Sir Charles Mortimer, an avowed admirer of the beauties of the mind, in preference to a pretty face or figure. Yet Lucy was averse to marriage. She had loved once, and been bitterly disappointed in the object upon whom she had lavished her young affections; and it required every persuasion Sir Charles was master of to induce her to listen to his suit. Indeed, she at last gave him a positive denial, alleging as her reason for doing so, that she never intended to change her situation, but Sir Charles remembered the old adage, 'Faint heart never won fair lady,' and consequently was not content to abide by her answer, but became more constant than ever in his attentions, which Lucy at first repulsed with almost chilling coldness, but at length her heart melted. It was not in a woman's nature, whose affections are disengaged, to be for ever indifferent to the addresses of one who, in addition to manifesting the strongest affection towards herself, is likewise aided by prepossessing manners, and a handsome face and form. No. Lucy was obliged at last to acknowledge her heart was conquered, and yielded a captive to the gallant knight.

Henry had from the first moment he suspected Mortimer's feelings toward his sister, made his character and disposition his peculiar study, unintentionally as it were drawing him into conversation on various topics, thus learning his sentiments, on what he deemed important subjects; and, having at length perfectly satisfied himself that Mortimer was in truth worthy of possessing his much-loved sister, gave him every encouragement in his suit.

'If you once, my dear fellow, succeed in winning her affections, they are yours for ever,' said Henry, one day when conversing with his friend about Lucy.

'I am convinced of it,' replied Mortimer, 'and consequently do not despair of gaining her yet.'

Neither did he; but persevered till he succeeded to his most sanguine wishes. Between Lucy and Marian there had never existed the cordiality since the unfortunate death of Edward that had before that event so marked their intercourse. Lucy certainly entertained the same warm friendship towards Marian, but Lucy was devoted to her brother, and Marian could not bear the idea of meeting Henry; indeed, she even ventured to express herself warmly on the subject of the duel, even venturing to censure Henry's conduct very freely before his sister. This Lucy, though making every allowance for Marian's feelings, could not endure quietly, and much as she herself regretted Edward's death, yet she never for a moment considered Henry had behaved otherwise than honourable in every sense of the word. 'Had he not, indeed,' she urged, while conversing with Marian on the subject, 'boldly come forward, and stood his trial, and had not his country taken the same view of his conduct that she did herself—had he not been proclaimed innocent—and was not the proclamation received with unbounded applause?' But all Lucy's eloquence failed to convince Marian, and when she was united to Sir Charles Mortimer, a still stronger barrier was placed between them, so they ceased to visit each other altogether, never meeting save in public, and then they only formally bowed. This at first grieved Lucy, but, pleasing herself with the certainty that Marian was happy in her second union, and needed not her friendship, she grew in time content. It was with unbounded delight that Henry gave away his sister at the altar to a man he felt confident was every way worthy of her.

'Now, indeed,' he whispered to his mother, as they returned from the church, 'if it should please God to remove us, we shall have the satisfaction of knowing that we have secured Lucy's happiness.'

Thus much has taken place in the course of three revolving years—a long time to look forward to, but, when past and gone, never to return, it seems as nothing. With Rose and Albert scarcely any change had taken place. Since the sad affair which caused Rose so severe an illness, he had never taken pen in hand as an author; and had entirely relinquished his pursuit after fame. Content with the laurels he had won, he gave himself up to the enjoyment of the society of one who so truly loved him. They were never apart, never absent from each other for a single hour, mixed in no society, kept no company, but lived together in entire seclusion. And it was strange to mark how much Rose had grown to resemble Albert; the expression of their countenances, and also the *contour* of the face was so strikingly alike, that though one was fair as alabaster, and the other very dark, yet they might well have passed for brother and sister. The lovely bloom which betokened at once health and beauty, and which had sat upon her cheek, matching in its unrivalled loveliness the colour of the rose, was gone forever, leaving her face fair and white as unspotted marble. The dimples, too, from her cheek had flown: she had no longer the appearance of the soft, glowing beauty that had characterised her a few years previous. Still there was a sweet and interesting expression in her face, as though sickness and sorrow had grieved to eclipse so much loveliness, and in pity had left the expression, to show what it had once been. Alas! there is nothing on earth so fragile and fading as beauty; and yet how much it is coveted, how richly it is prized, even when we know by sad and bitter experience how easily it is effaced. A little sickness, oftentimes less of trouble, will suffice so to mar it, that we shall scarcely recognise the beauty of a few weeks back. Oh! think of this, ye who pride yourselves wholly on your good looks; spare some time from the cultivation of the graces of the person to devote to the graces of the mind—to beauties that never perish, but in the grave—that never decay or grow old: whereas the sweetest face and form, if they escape even the ravages of sickness and trouble, must naturally, in the course of a few short years, fade. And then, when age creeps on you, if you have neglected to cultivate your mind—if, priding yourselves so much upon your beauty, you have never thought it worth while to be amiable and obliging, but have indulged in a proud capricious temper that has prevented any one loving you for yourselves alone, apart from all admiration of your beauty—where then, we ask, when that is decayed and gone, can you look for happiness and comfort, when age creeps over you, if you have never, by your kind and conciliating manners, endeavoured to render yourselves beloved? You cannot possibly expect, when age, with its concomitant trials, comes upon you, to reap that harvest of kind actions and affectionate attentions you have never sown. No, it cannot be. Then while you are young and happy, and everything around you looks bright, sow the precious seed of affection, and cultivate those inward graces, that make a woman lovely in the sight of all, and depend, should trouble or sickness overtake you, and mar the beauty of your person, you will then reap an abundant harvest, and feel far better pleased and satisfied at being loved and admired for the beautiful graces that adorn your mind, than you ever were for your pretty face and lovely form. Not that for a moment we decry, or desire to undervalue what is styled beauty; on the contrary, we love to look upon it, as on one of God's masterpieces, and should think it equally culpable for a woman to neglect her person as her mind. All we wish to impress on the young is, not to make their person their entire study, but also to cultivate and adorn their minds, since, after all, engaging and amiable manners are everywhere preferred to pretty faces. Poor Rose was certainly more loved and treasured by her husband now that her greatest charms of person were flown, than she had been in the brightest and proudest days of her beauty. Her health was exceedingly delicate; and though she had borne up uncomplainingly for three years, yet she was evidently sinking slowly to the tomb. Albert's whole thought and care was for her; often in heart-broken anguish would he hang over her as he marked her short, quick breathing, and saw with agony the hectic flush upon her cheek—that certain indicator of an insidious disease which ever selects the fair and young for its prey. Oh! if the last three years of tender, unvarying love could make up for the one deep wrong he had done her, and which, alas! was the fatal cause of her illness, he had made her ample amends. The constant anguish of mind he endured both from the fatal secret which ever robbed him of repose, and the slow wasting decay of one who so tenderly loved and clung to his dark destiny, had wrought powerfully upon his frame: his form was attenuated in the extreme, and he was sensible of great weakness consequent on the slightest exertion. These signs of disease he hailed with delight. 'I shall not survive her,' he inwardly exclaimed, with joy pictured on his pallid countenance, as the certainty of Rose's death forced itself upon his mind; yet he sedulously concealed from her the symptoms of indisposition that affected him, and even spoke of the future, as though they were both certain of spending many years on earth, and Rose sometimes seemed so well in health, that he almost doubted whether she would not have to experience the inexpressible anguish of surviving him; and at the thought only of what her sufferings would be, should such prove to be the case, he was obliged to hurry from the room to conceal the tears that rushed in torrents to his eyes, and Albert was an altered man. The sweet simplicity of Rose's faith in a superior Being, who was able and willing to pardon all sinners, no matter what their guilt, or how deep its dye, and which she had expressed so touchingly in their mutual converse, had been productive of great benefit to Albert's mind: the mist gradually cleared from his eyes, and he began to see the erroneous doctrine he had adopted in its true light; and though he did not entirely renounce it, he no longer used it as a shield behind which to screen himself from the sins he had committed and now deeply deplored; and though he felt it was impossible to undo his sins, yet he resolved, in the language of Scripture, ' to go and sin no more;' and whenever he now alluded to his transgressions, he did not ascribe them to the workings of fate, but to his own evil passions, and earnestly and humbly did he implore pardon for them of his Maker; and though still, for many reasons, a melancholy man, he no longer regarded himself as cursed above his fellows: on the contrary, he blessed his lot, in possessing so sweet and dear a treasure, as his loved, and still, even in sickness, lovely, Rose. Oft when he clasped her to his bosom, or she would rest her aching head upon his shoulder, and in that posture fall asleep, would he gaze upon her fair face, or stroke back the soft tresses from her forehead, and while he held her to him, feel that in her he possessed all that his soul ever yearned for; and then the dread, the cold, sad chill, that ran through his veins, that he held her by only a single thread, which each hour was in danger of being snapped asunder,—oh! the thought was fraught with such intensity of anguish that his whole frame shook; and tears, bitter scalding tears, would force their way down his cheeks, yet checked instantly she gave the slightest signs of awakening; and though his heart felt ready to break, a smile greeted the upturned eyes that gazed upon his face with an expression of love deeper than words can convey. How beautiful is love—nothing on earth can compare with it! How fragrant and sweet is its lightest expression; how self-denying, how unwearying, are all its efforts! Oh! beautiful indeed is love; it throws a grace round every action—charms every heart, and imparts a feeling of sacredness in its very devotion. Such was the love that animated the bosom of Rose and Albert; it was breathed in every word; cast a halo of brightness round their path; and made each anxious to bear any sorrow if they could prevent the other from feeling its sting. Thus Rose, though she felt her days on earth were numbered, carefully concealed it from Albert; and when she observed his sunken eyes and hollow cheeks would inwardly exclaim,—

'Oh, that I might be spared to bless and cheer him to the end—to whisper words of hope and comfort, to soothe his dying hour, to receive his latest breath; then, when all is over on earth, join his loved spirit in another and a fairer land, where we may for ever dwell, without one thought of sorrow! Henry and Lucy were almost the only persons admitted to see them, and they often turned away to hide the tear as they witnessed the tender expression of love so evident in all their looks and actions.

'I cannot bear to see you so melancholy, dear Rose,' said Lucy, one day, soon after her marriage, when she had called to see her; 'you ought to endeavour to go out into society a little more; you were once the very essence of gaiety.'

'To be gay,' replied Rose, smiling faintly, 'is not always to be happy.'

'I know it,' returned Lucy, 'and yet I would rather see you gay than see you as you are now.'

'That is really unkind of you,' replied Rose, 'for so far from being melancholy, as you fancy I am, I was never so happy and blessed as I have been the last three years.'

'I am glad to hear you say so, dear Rose, and yet—'

'And yet what?' said Rose.

'I scarcely know myself,' replied Lucy; 'but what I meant to say was, that though I love my husband and enjoy his company exceedingly, it does not prevent me mixing in society, or make me feel a distaste for the company of others; in short, my happiness makes me cheerful and lighthearted, while yours, on the contrary, appears to make you sad.'

'Stop, dear Lucy,' replied Rose; 'you and I are very different, so also are our husbands: you are in the enjoyment of excellent health—I am sinking under the effects of a lingering and wasting disease. Sir Charles is gay, by nature fond of company, and though, I am certain, devotedly attached to you, still you do not constitute his all; whereas Albert is naturally averse to society—of a quiet, studious turn of mind, and has but me only in the wide world, who understands and appreciates his character. This, Lucy, should be sufficient to keep me, as you call it, in seclusion, did not my health unfit me for scenes you can mingle in both to your own and husband's satisfaction.'

Albert's entrance at this moment put a stop to the conversation on that subject, but Lucy felt the truth of Rose's argument, and said, too plainly, that before many years, perhaps, even many months, they would both be laid in the quiet grave, for neither, she was certain, would long survive the other. Lucy's kind and gentle heart caused her to feel this severely on her own account, but still more bitterly did she deplore it on her brother's. Henry, she had not long discovered, loved Rose—yes, loved her with all the warmth of a first and passionate love; this, knowing it to be a perfectly hopeless love, he had endeavoured to conceal from his sister, but in vain: she had discovered all; and though, with that delicacy which characterised her in every action, she had kept it from his knowledge, yet she was well acquainted with the secret he thought known only to his own bosom, and strove by her cheerful conversation, and not unfrequently assumed gaiety, to prevent his thoughts from dwelling too much upon the unfortunate object of his love. Henry was not insensible to his sister's kindness, and endeavoured, as far as he possibly could, to repay her, by casting from his mind the feeling of sadness which was too often an inmate of his heart. As Rose's health visibly and rapidly declined, Albert sought the advice of the most eminent of the medical profession, who strongly advised, as the best remedy, that she should seek a warmer climate, and mentioned Italy as a suitable spot, in which to spend the ensuing winter. At the name of Italy, Rose perceived that Albert shuddered, and even turned paler than usual, but when they were again alone, he said, with a forced calmness,—

'My dearest Rose, you have heard the recommendation of your physicians, and which I intend to profit by; and shall therefore make immediate preparations to leave our native land. You would like, I am sure, to bid your parents and brothers farewell; and as we cannot now be parted, as we once were, we will, my Rose, if agreeable to you, both go to them to-morrow, and remain a few days, previous to our departure from England: does this, dearest, meet your approbation?'

'Perfectly, dear Albert! We will no more be parted, as you say, even for an hour; all places are alike to me, so that you are by my side.'

Accordingly, the next morning found them ready to start on their journey, and before evening closed in, they were once more beneath the roof of Mr. Sommerville. Their arrival was hailed with gladness; but when Mrs. Sommerville learned the object of their visit, she was overcome with sorrow.

'Oh, let me entreat of you,' she said, addressing Albert, 'to alter your determination. Your own health, as well as that of Rose, is very delicate. Consider how wretched you will be in a strange land without one kind friend to soothe or attend to you, should one, or both of you, grow worse instead of better.'

'My dear madam,' replied Albert, 'if it is the will of fate that such should be the case, we must endeavour humbly to bear it; and yet,' he added, glancing affectionately at Rose, 'this dear one would indeed, as you say, be lost in a foreign land, should I be snatched from her, which God in his mercy forbid.'

'Think not of me, dearest Albert,' returned Rose, sweetly, 'I should quickly follow you! My spirit would join yours in the skies, where we shall meet, never again to part.'

Albert pressed her hand tenderly in his own, while, making an effort to overcome the emotion, which visibly shook his whole frame, he spoke as follows:—

'There is a secret, a dreadful secret connected with my early life, that I have never imparted even to you, my Rose, fearing the knowledge of it would turn the love you feel for me, and which I so dearly prize, into hatred and abhorrence.'

'Stop, stop, dear Albert, I know it all. I have long ago, in our early married days, learned that secret from the lips of Marian, and think you, my husband, far more sinned against than sinning.'

'And is it possible that you know all, and yet can love me with that tenderness you so constantly manifest? It is true, as you say, that I was sinned against, still I have sinned in no light degree.'

'Say no more on the subject, dear Albert; being convinced that I know all, never let this conversation be renewed between us. It must, I am sure, be painful to you to revisit Italy: let us, therefore renounce our project and remain in London.'

'On the contrary, dear Rose, I am now more than ever determined to pursue it. Knowing my painful history, you will not be surprised when I tell you that there is one who would gladly receive us both, and be unremitting in kindness and affection—one who, should we be forced to part, would bless and soothe the survivor. This,' he added, turning to Mrs. Sommerville, who, during the conversation between Albert and Rose, had sat perfectly silent, gazing from one to the other, with anxious countenance, 'this, I should think, will remove all fears from your mind, and you will be willing cheerfully to part with Rose, the more especially as her physicians recommend it as the most likely means of restoring her to health.'

'It is sad indeed to part with her,' returned Mrs. Sommerville; 'yet it being for her good, I will endeavour, as you say, cheerfully to resign her for a time, hoping that she may be again restored to me in renewed health and vigour.'

'I shall,' said Albert, 'write immediately to Naples, to apprise my friends of our intended visit; and though I hope to arrive almost immediately after the letter, yet I would rather they had an intimation of our coming, than take them entirely by surprise.'

Accordingly he shortly after withdrew to fulfil his intention, and Rose being left for a short time alone with her mother, Mrs. Sommerville endeavoured to draw her attention to different objects, spoke of Agnes' lovely children, and likewise the son of her elder brother, whom she had never seen; but though Rose, evidently out of respect for her mother, endeavoured to appear interested, yet it was but too plain that her every thought and affection was given entirely to Albert. Although Rose and Albert remained at Mrs. Sommerville's for a week, yet active preparations were going on in town for their immediate departure from England, and in a short time a letter arrived to acquaint them that all was in readiness, and Rose once more bade adieu to the home of her youth. The parting between herself and relatives was affecting in the extreme; Mrs. Sommerville clung to her with the intense agony of a mother, who looks upon her child, she fears, for the last time, and it required all the tender affection of Agnes and her sons to reconcile her to the loss of a daughter she had ever loved so well. Rose herself was much moved by her mother's grief, yet Albert, she felt, was dearer to her than all besides, and for his sake she controlled the emotion that threatened at one time nearly to overpower her. At length the parting kiss was given to all, the lingering pressure of the hand was over, the smothered farewell was whispered in broken accents, and Rose, supported on Albert's bosom, was whirling away towards the metropolis. How dear and pleasant everything seems that we are conscious of soon being forced to leave! In the hour of parting from them, perhaps for ever a new and endearing interest is awakened on behalf of all that has ever come in contact with us: each well-known room, and each object that it contains, reminds us of scenes and days long gone by, hallowed, perhaps, by the recollection of the sweet and mutual exchange of affection, or a thousand nameless feelings, be they of joy or sorrow, which the rooms we are about to leave have witnessed, and in a manner appear connected with the past. We envy not the man who can with cold indifference part from scenes he has long dwelt among, who feels no tender emotion swell his breast. As he looks his last upon even the humblest spot, where perchance he may have endured hardship and privation, and is about to leave it to seek a brighter destiny, then he already sees in imagination days of happiness and plenty arise that he has long sighed after, and with delight proposes to embark on what he deems a joyful enterprise. Yet, oh! in the sad hour of parting, how differently will the past be coloured! All that before appeared wrapped in gloom and sorrow, if he be possessed of right feeling, will now subside into trivial ills, or if that may not be, even the remembrance of the trouble will throw a sacredness around the spot, and the teardrop glistening in the eye will bespeak the feelings of the breast. Thus Rose and Albert felt, as, arm in arm, they wandered through the different suites of rooms that comprised their mansion for the last time. The study, that had witnessed the grief of Albert at Rose's supposed baseness, and Rose's intense agony at the accusation, was yet dear to their hearts, and here they lingered, gazing around on each well-remembered object, with a feeling that they might, perhaps, never again behold them.'

'But oh!' in thought, said Rose, turning her eyes lovingly on Albert, 'we shall often be here.'

'Yes,' replied Albert, resting his hand on the table; 'here I have spent many hours of bitter grief, relieved only by giving it vent in poems, which have breathed in every word, anguish; and which none of the many who have read and applauded them ever for an instant thought was the offspring of an almost broken heart of a wearied and exhausted frame, of one who was glad by any means to seek at least a partial oblivion of the sorrows by which he was encompassed, rendered a thousand times more bitter by the consciousness that they were alone to be attributed to the sin of his youth; and now,' he added, half musingly, 'I am about to seek those climes I had never once thought aught could induce me to look upon again. Yet there I feel I shall find a grave—yes, my dust shall mingle with his, and he, enshrined in bliss, will pardon all the past—will forgive his brother that one act he has for so many years bitterly, truly deplored. Oh! yes, sweet thought, I feel that I shall obtain forgiveness, not only of him, but of my God.'

It was evening, and during their stay in the study, twilight had deepened around them, so that now they could scarcely behold each other's countenance; but as Albert thus spoke, he was conscious of the increased pressure of Rose's hand upon his arm, and folding her to his bosom, they mingled their tears together. Oh! sweet hour of twilight, when day and night seem almost to meet and embrace each other, filling one's mind with pure and holy feelings that mount up to the very threshold of Heaven. The rapt soul at this still hour seems to expand within us, and sacred thoughts take place of all others; the cares and trials of the day melt into nothingness, and though our hearts are too full for converse, yet we inwardly bless the soft hour of twilight and of solitude.

Early the ensuing morning, having previously taken leave of their town friends—few in number, but truly and devotedly attached to them; among the most prominent of which were Henry and his sister Lucy; indeed these two, with Mrs. Melville, Sir Charles Mortimer, and Marian and Fairford, comprised all they knew, or cared for, in London—and having taken an affectionate leave of them, they stepped into the carriage which was in waiting, and drove rapidly off to the sea, where a vessel was in readiness to convey them to their destination. Money can procure every luxury, even at sea; and Albert being at no loss for that truly necessary article, they found excellent accommodation provided for them, and began their expedition with every auspicious omen. The weather was dry and beautiful, the wind favourable and pleasant. Albert and Rose stood upon the deck, and watched the white cliffs of England receding from view, till they became a speck in the distance; and long after they had wholly disappeared, they remained in the same position, gazing towards the spot where they had obtained the last glimpse of their native land. Albert's thoughts had wandered back to the time when, buoyant with youth and health, he had trod the deck in the pride of manhood, and by his side, a dear and younger brother, whom a dying father had bequeathed to his love and care, and whom he then loved with the tenderest fraternal affection. Oh! now, where was the freshness of soul, the fond, warm hopes which then animated his bosom, and tinged all by which he was surrounded in glowing colours? Gone, alas! fled for ever. No more, oh! never more on him could the freshness of the heart descend like dew; and though hastening once more to that land of beauty and romance, no fond hopes were cherished in his bosom—no thought of once more viewing, in the company of one he loved, the bright and beautiful in

Nature.   Other passengers who surrounded them were, with bright and happy hearts, picturing to themselves and each other the delight they should experience on viewing Naples, famed for the most lovely scenery in the world.   To him the name of Naples called up, as it were by magic, such sad and bitter thoughts that for a time he almost repented having resolved to undertake this voyage; but then he looked on the fair and pensive countenance of his young wife, who, bending over the side of the vessel, watched the waves as they dashed past them; and as the thought came over her, with the impress of certainty, that she had bidden an eternal adieu to her native land, the tears, large and bright, dropped from her eyes, and mingled with the salt water of the ocean.   Albert roused himself instantly.

'Come, my love,' he said kindly, 'it is time you retired to your cabin; the air is too cool for you here.'

Rose made no reply, but suffered him to lead her in silence from the deck.   When they had gained their cabin, Albert, seating himself by her side, endeavoured, by kind and gentle conversation, to make her forget her sorrow.   She was not, indeed she never could be, unmindful of his love, and in her turn spoke cheerfully of the future, and of their happy return to England with renewed health.   Their voyage was altogether a pleasant one, neither of them suffering from that terrible bane to travellers, sea sickness.   Much of their time was spent on the deck, Rose, to whom travelling was new, loving to watch the waves rolling over and over, and eventually dashing against the sides of the vessel, and more especially to gaze upon the setting sun, sinking to rest—a beautiful sight on land, but far more splendid when viewed at sea.   Those who have witnessed it will be ready to acknowledge that there is no work of man that can in the least compare to the work of God—nought half so sublime and beautiful as the wonders of his hand.   Rose had a mind, which though little cultivated, was formed by Nature to love and admire the beautiful, and when Albert, in glowing language, expressed the admiration he felt, she timidly though fully responded to him.   Thus the time passed quickly on, and before they had even begun to be weary of their voyage, their vessel anchored in the bay of Naples, and they obtained a beautiful view of that great and opulent city, with its castles, its harbour full of ships from all nations, and its churches, palaces, and convents beyond number.   The sight even of this city appeared to revive a thousand painful thoughts in the mind of Albert, and again he inwardly drew a comparison between the present and the last time he had seen it, when it first burst with all its glory upon his astonished eyes; when his brother, young and enthusiastic, gazed upon it with him, and memory recalled even the exact expressions that had fallen from his brother's lips, in praise of the country that lay thus extended before them.   Rose could only gaze, and gaze again with renewed rapture; yet, as she noted Albert's quivering lip and humid eye, her feelings took the tone of his, and melancholy filled her heart.

'I know well what he must feel,' thought Rose; 'and for me alone has he revisited this place, so fair and beautiful to look upon, but associated in his mind with such painful reminiscences as to eclipse all its beauty.'

Thus, each wrapt in thought, they stood side by side gazing half vacantly on the lovely scenery stretched before them.   The hurry and bustle of the other passengers, who were in haste to land, disturbed not their meditations: no, there they stood, apparently unconscious of what was passing around them, till all had landed but themselves, when the captain, stepping up to Albert, politely inquired if it were not his pleasure also to go on shore that evening.   He started from his reverie, and, with a stern and fixed look, signified his intention to do so; and then, turning to his fair companion, while the sternness that sat upon his brow gave place to a tender concern for her welfare, he gently guided her footsteps to the land.   A carriage was quickly procured, and Albert, having seated Rose, gave his directions to the man, and placed himself by her side; then, veiling his face with his hands, he sank back in the carriage, evidently desiring to avoid the sight of scenes that called up such sad thoughts.   Rose spoke not, but softly her hand glided into his, which she tenderly pressed, signifying, in this mute manner, that she understood the nature of his feelings too well to intrude upon them with words.   After a short drive, the vehicle stopped in front of a picturesque and romantic-looking villa, whose rich and costly exterior bespoke the inmates to belong to the highest class of society—a broad avenue led to the grand entrance, which was adorned by some beautiful statues, and also several elegant fountains of water, and bordered on each side with a variety of flowering shrubs, which perfumed the air with the most delicious odour—a large balcony surrounded the villa, and which, like the avenue, contained orange trees and other beautiful plants.   As Albert assisted Rose to alight from the carriage a servant was in readiness to receive them, and they entered into a superb hall, paved with marble of different colours, richly wrought with lapis lazuli, porphyry, and other valuable stones.   This splendid hall was lighted by a large window at the farther end, which was composed of stained glass of different colours; the walls were covered with some fine basso-relievos of white marble, and round the sides were arranged the family statues, some of them evidently very ancient.   Albert's step was weak, and he trembled violently as he placed his foot inside this truly enchanting villa; yet he endeavoured to assume a calm demeanour, and addressed a few words to the servant in Italian, who, answering in the same language, bowed low; and, beckoning them to follow, led the way through several suites of rooms, each corresponding in richness of design and beauty of architecture with the hall we have described, and at length knocked at the door of an inner apartment; but receiving no answer, after

repeating the knock, he opened it, and discovering it empty, motioned for them to enter; and with a few words addressed to Albert in his native tongue, the servant bowed, and withdrew.

Thus left alone with Albert, who, seating himself, covered his face with his hands, and gave free vent to the emotion he had concealed in the presence of the servant, Rose had time to glance around the room; it was an elegant and spacious apartment, with high-arched roof,

No. 19.

magnificent architecture, and, like the hall, was lighted by a large window of stained glass, through which the sun shed a subdued and mellow light upon a superb crucifix of pure white marble, which stood upon a table of ivory, richly inlaid with mother-o'-pearl: all the furniture in the room was of the same massive and costly description. Rose felt almost awed as she gazed around and above her—to her imagination, indeed, it more resembled some enchanted palace than aught else, so utterly unlike was it to anything she had ever before even dreamed of; and, creeping closer to the side of Albert, while she retained his hand firmly in her own, she continued perfectly silent, scarcely knowing what next to expect. After the lapse of a few minutes, a door in the middle of the apartment, facing the one by which they had themselves entered, was thrown open to its fullest extent, and a tall, majestic-looking woman appeared on the threshold. Albert started from his seat, and, pronouncing the name of Rosalia, advanced with trembling steps to meet her. She stretched towards him a particularly small and delicately-formed hand, while her lips moved, as though she were essaying to speak; but not the slightest sound escaped her. Albert eagerly seized the hand she presented to him, and carried it respectfully to his lips, at the same time addressing her in Italian. Again her lips moved, and still her tongue refused to give utterance to what she wished to say. She was evidently violently affected by some powerful emotion, which she was striving earnestly to overcome, and at length succeeded in speaking a few words: the purport, being in a strange language, was of course utterly unknown to Rose; but the sweet, musical tone of the stranger's voice gave her such exquisite pleasure that she could but desire to hear her speak again. Nor was she disappointed. Having conquered her emotion, the stranger again spoke—and this time with more apparent ease. The tone of her voice was low, but so exceedingly musical, that the notes vibrated on the ear, even after she had ceased speaking. During the few minutes' conversation she maintained with Albert, Rose was at liberty to note her appearance. She was tall, Rose remarked, beyond the generality of her sex, but of the most elegant and exact proportions; her deportment was majestic in the extreme. She was evidently approaching towards middle age, which was more shown from the sedateness of her demeanour, and the quiet repose of her features, than aught else; her complexion was of a clear olive, and perfectly colourless; her hair, of which she had a great profusion, was jet black, and arranged in the Madonna style; her fore-head was high, noble, and commanding; and her features had the appearance of being chiselled out of marble, by the hand of the sculptor, so regular and faultless was their construction; her eyes, large, black, and piercing, though occasionally subdued to the most melting softness, and ever and anon, as the conversation between her and Albert varied, Rose marked a tear glistening on the long-fringed lids. Her dress was composed of a long black robe, which fitted tight to her figure, thus displaying the beautiful proportions of her bust to the greatest advantage; she wore not the slightest ornament, with the exception of a rosary, which was suspended round her neck, and to which was attached a rather large crucifix. Albert and the stranger had continued conversing in Italian sufficiently long to allow Rose time to remark all this, when she suddenly became aware that they were speaking of herself: this was evident from the manner in which they both looked towards her. Rose was confused at the searching glance which the stranger cast upon her: observing which, she approached, and kindly taking her hand in her own, bent down and pressed a fervent kiss upon her brow, and then, to Rose's astonishment, addressing her in English (which language she spoke with the greatest fluency) bade her welcome to Italy.

'Your health, Albert informs me, is exceedingly delicate; he also is sadly changed since I last beheld him. I trust that the beautiful climate of Naples may be the means of restoring you both; if tender care and kind nursing can be of service to you rest assured of finding both in Rosalia Parinelli.'

It was not the words alone, kind and gentle as they were, nor the look of tender love and pity she cast upon Rose's pallid countenance, but the musical tones of her voice, which touched the heart of Rose, who, incapable of answering, could only return her embrace.

' She is doubtless fatigued,' said Donna Rosalia, turning to Albert, ' and would like to retire for a short time, and then touching a bell, a female servant entered, to whom she spoke in Italian, who then motioning for Rose to follow her, led the way from the room, and up a broad staircase of white marble, reaching the top of which she turned to the left, and crossing an ante-chamber, opened the door of a room, which was fitted-up as a sleeping apartment, in a rich and costly style; near the window was an ivory table, similar to the one Rose had seen below, but larger, on which was a splendid crucifix, and also an exquisite statue, in pure marble, of the Virgin Mary, with the infant Christ in her arms: the beauty of the workmanship was so nice and exact that it could bear the closest inspection, and yet be pronounced faultless; the expression of the face of the Virgin was so sweet and heavenly, that Rose could scarcely withdraw her eyes from it. In front of the statue and crucifix, which stood side by side, were laid two richly-embossed books of Paternosters and Catholic Prayers; and on the floor, two cushions of purple velvet, for the accomodation of persons wishing to perform their devotions; corresponding with this bed-chamber were two dressing-rooms, each fitted up with every comfort, even to luxuriousness.

The young Italian who had conducted Rose to this apartment, now offered by signs to assist her in changing her dress, which under her skilful hands was soon completed. Her toilet, being of the simplest style, never occupied her long, and, in a short time she again joined Albert and Rosalia in the room below. They were engaged in earnest conversation, but as it was carried on in Italian, the subject could not be ascertained by Rose, who, seating herself at a little distance from them, listened with delight to the musical tones of Rosalia, which contrasted strangely with the deep, manly tones of Albert. They seemed contesting some point, and Rosalia appeared with reluctance to give way to Albert's wishes, and once more touching the bell, gave some order to the servant in which Rose distinctly caught the name of Charles. ' I shall see him then,' was her inward exclamation; ' the brother of my Albert'—he who has for so long time languished in voluntary exile from his country and friends. I wonder not at Albert's quivering lip and trembling frame; how painful will be the meeting of the brothers, after so long and mournful a separation! the thoughts of both will naturally recur to Florence, once so loved by both, and her untimely end.'

Her meditations were at this moment interrupted by the entrance of a youth, whom Donno Rosalia led by the hand to Albert, who received him with an emotion so powerful, that it shook his whole frame; his face assumed an ashy paleness, his brow contracted, and it was with difficulty he gave utterance to a few words. Rosalia, in order to give Albert an opportunity of recovering his self-possession, turned to Rose, and introduced the youth as her nephew.

' It is fortunate,' she remarked, ' that Charles can speak and understand English equally with Italian, as it will make him a very agreeable companion to you, and I am certain he will do his best to amuse and entertain you. For myself, I rarely go out; but if your strength will permit, Charles, I am sure, will take a delight in pointing out all that is worth seeing in this city; will you not, my love ?'

' Certainly, dear aunt, nothing could afford me greater pleasure,' and he stretched out his hand to Rose, who, the moment he spoke, was prepossessed in his favour, for his voice had the same musical tone that so delighted her in his aunt, and with evident pleasure she received the offered hand, which pressing in her own, she felt his palm to be soft and yielding as that of a woman's; and as Donna Rosalia joined Albert, who had walked to a distant part of the room, Charles seated himself by her side.

' My aunt has not told me by what name I am to address you,' were the first words he uttered, as he gazed upon her fair transparent skin, and auburn tresses which flowed in rich profusion over her neck and shoulders.

' Call me Rose,' she returned, bending her soft liquid blue eyes upon the dark flashing orbs of the youth, which bespoke his temper to be fiery in the extreme, that is, when roused; for at other times, he had all the softness and gentleness of the dove. He seemed scarcely to have numbered fifteen summers, yet was remarkably tall for his years; his form, though slight and boyish; yet showed fair and symmetrical proportions; his face was exceedingly handsome, of olive complexion (though scarcely so darkly tinted as his aunt's), while the blood kindled to a deep glow upon the cheeks; his black hair shone like the plume of the raven's wing, and hung in thick masses of curls over a finely-formed forehead; he certainly bore a strong resemblance to his aunt, and might well indeed have passed for her son, instead of her nephew Rose looked on him with pleasure and delight, and replied to the many questions he put to her concerning England, of which country he seemed desirous of learning all that he could, with evident pleasure.

' I have a great wish to visit England,' he said, after a short pause; ' but my aunt is very much averse to my doing so, and I should be sorry to disobey her, even to gratify my own ardent desire.'

' Have you no parents ?' said Rose kindly. The expression of his face, which was usually gay and volatile, assumed an air of deep melancholy at this question; and a tear trembled on his long, black eye-lashes, as he replied,—

' No, dear Rose; my mother, I have been told, died in giving me birth.'

' And your father !' said Rose, with deep interest. ' None has ever breathed that name to me. I know, I feel there is a mystery connected with it—a dark and terrible mystery.'

' I have, lady,' he continued, and his dark eye flashed with indignation. ' sometimes been led to suspect the purity of my mother; but my aunt has repeatedly assured me' that I was born in wedlock—more she will not say, though I have often urged her to disclose to me everything connected with my parents; this,' he continued, drawing a locket from his bosom, and presenting it to Rose, ' is the portrait of my mother.'

Rose took it in her hand, and gazed upon the resemblance of a most beautiful woman; the face was one that could not fail to attract attention, even from the most commonplace observer. It strongly resembled Charles both in features and expression, and the coral lips, just parting into a smile, disclosed teeth of ivory whiteness. Rose gazed on it some minutes in silence, and then, heaving a sigh, was about to return it to Charles, when, chancing to turn it over, a small braid of hair caught her attention; it was set round with small precious stones of great value, and looking at it more closely, she discovered they spelt the name of Florence.

This, then, was the portrait of that unhappy lady, and she it was who was the mother of Charles; and his father—oh! she could not for a moment doubt who that father was—the name he bore told all. Yes, yes! the wretched brother of Albert, who had planted the dagger in the breast of the mother, stood in the tender relation of father to her child. 'Unhappy wanderer,' thought Rose. 'Alas! his own act has severed him from the delight of owning such a son as the youth now seated by her side—a son he might well have been proud to acknowledge, who united at once the warmth and ardent spirit of his mother with the soft and endearing gentleness Marian had described as peculiarly belonging to Charles. Nobility was stamped upon his young brow; while his dark eyes at one moment flashed with the fire and ardour of his mother, and the next melted into the soft liquid brightness of his father's. As these thoughts passed through her mind, she dropped a tear of mingled pity and sorrow for the fate of one so lovely, on the portrait she still retained in her hand.

'Dear lady,' said the youth, perceiving her tender emotion, and gracefully kissing off the tear which had dimmed the lustre of the glass upon which it fell. 'Dear lady, you have a kind and gentle heart thus to feel for the untimely fate of another. I oft have wept over this precious relic, but even to me she bore the sacred name of mother.'

'Oh! had she lived, she would have been justly proud of such a son,' interrupted Rose, who already began to feel an elder sister's interest and affection for the dear, ingenuous youth, and which she sought not to conceal.

When they retired for the night, Albert inquired of Rose what she thought of the friends to whom he had introduced her.

'I like them much, very much.' replied Rose, eagerly, 'Donna Rosalia is indeed a delightful woman; and her nephew, oh! never did I know so graceful and engaging a youth.'

'You speak in warm terms upon so short an acquaintance,' returned Albert, mournfully.

'The acquaintance is as you say short,' replied Rose, 'but I am sure I have formed a correct opinion of both. I thought, dear Albert,' she added, after a pause. 'to have seen your brother.'

'He started in amazement, while bitter grief was depicted on his countenance.

"My brother,' he repeated, in heart-rending accents, 'alas, Rose! I thought you told me you knew my unhappy story.'

'So I did, dear Albert,' returned Rose, earnestly; 'do not, I entreat of you, distress yourself. I was not rightly informed in every particular, and can now well understand why he should avoid this spot equally with England.'

'Oh God!' said Albert, , every word you utter convinces me you are entirely ignorant of all that occurred in this house, when I was last here. Oh, had I known that you were indeed unacquainted with that awful affair—I should never, never, Rose, have brought you to this spot, under any circumstances; indeed, we should not have been now here, had I not considered it absolutely necessary for the restoration of your health. Oh, Rose, my adored wife—who has alone succeeded in making life endurable to me—when you know all, as you must and shall, you will no longer regard me with the tender affection you now feel; but will cast me from you, as a being to be abhorred—shunned.'

'Oh! talk not thus wildly,' cried Rose, throwing her arms round him with affectionate warmth, 'nothing, nothing can alter my love for you. Let me, I beg of you, remain without the knowledge of aught that could possibly tend to lower you in my estimation.'

Albert clasped her fervently to his bosom. 'My own, my pure and innocent Rose—oh, it would kill you to know the guilt which encompasses your husband.'

'Then never, never let me know it,' replied Rose, kissing his cheeks and forehead. 'You are not guilty to the extent you would make me believe—you, who never, since our acquaintance, even trampled on a worm, but was ever merciful and kind to all. Oh, Albert, dearest, not even your own words would ever induce me to think ill of you.'

'My own Rose,' he returned, fondly embracing her, 'I have done wrong thus to excite you. I fear it has already injured your health—forgive me, my love, and we will no more, at present, dwell on this painful subject; yet, rest assured, at some other time, you shall be made acquainted with the truth. I will not seek to palliate or excuse my guilt.'

'Say no more, dear Albert,' interrupted Rose; 'let us forget this conversation, equally painful to us both.'

Rose was sensible that Albert passed an almost sleepless night, and he arose in the morning with a harrassed and dejected appearance. On descending to the breakfast-room, they were kindly greeted by Donna Rosalia and her nephew, who were already up and waiting their arrival. Albert conversed during the meal but little, and at its conclusion Donna Rosalia expressed a wish to converse with him alone for a short time, while Rose availed herself of Charles's offer to show her over the house.

'Not that there is much worth seeing, dear Rose,' he said, 'but being a stranger, the picture-gallery and our private chapel may perhaps interest you.'

'I do not doubt it,' said Rose, rising to follow him. He led the way through numerous suites of rooms, each vieing with the other in magnificence and beauty till at length they gained the picture-gallery! Here, Rose lingered a long time; each picture charmed and interested her greatly, but one, far more than all—on that she gazed, and gazed again, each time with renewed pleasure; she could scarcely, indeed, tear herself from it. It was the full-length portrait of two young Italian maids glowing fresh and warm in youth and beauty; the one, Charles informed her, was Donna Rosalia; the other, her sister: the unfortunate and unhappy Florence, who had fallen, she could not now doubt, by the hand of Albert—of one who had paid to her his first and early vows of love; but who, jealous of the favour shown his brother, had, in a fit of passion, deprived her of life. But where was Charles? An outcast, from all who were near and dear to him—a wanderer, none knew where. Oh, sad must be his fate, dark indeed his doom! But was he, in truth, the father of the youthful Charles who bore his name, and now stood in silence by her side? At this thought, she cast a full and searching look on his handsome form and face, but could see naught there that bore any resemblance to the description Marian had given her of her brother, save in the soft and gentle manner he sometimes assumed. The brother of Albert was described as fair, and possessing blue eyes, and hair light as her own; while the nephew of Donna Rosalia was perfectly Italian; no one, to look upon him, would for an instant suspect that English blood flowed in his veins. He was indeed finely formed and handsome, but his beauty was entirely of the foreign cast. She had remained absorbed in these thoughts some considerable time, and would doubtless have remained so much longer, had not Charles, gently touching her arm, inquired if she would not now like to visit the chapel. Casting a last look on the portrait of Florence, she turned from the gallery, and followed her youthful guide. The private chapel to which he now introduced her was small, but of elegant construction; the tabernacle was the most splendid of all she had yet seen and was composed entirely of lapis lazuli, and occupied the most prominent position in the chapel; the sacristy was also very rich, facing which were several porphyry and marble monuments of exquisite workmanship. Here, too, Rose lingered a long time, admiring all she saw, the richness and beauty of which absolutely astonished her.

'If this chapel,' said Charles, 'which is comparatively undecorated, please you so much what will you think of the cathedral, which even I (who am accustomed to behold it) acknowledge magnificent in the extreme?"

'I scarcely know, indeed,' said Rose; 'but you have made me desirous of visiting it, and I must needs again enlist your services as guide.

'A pleasant office, dear Rose, and one you will only find me too willing to perform: but come, I have not yet shown you my library, and I am anxious to do so; it is on the same side of the building as we are now, and therefore will not tire you to reach it.'

Rose assured him it would afford her infinite pleasure. Leaving the chapel, the room they now entered was the smallest in the villa, and though the floor, like the others, was composed of coloured marble, yet the room strongly resembled an English library; shelves were ranged round the room, on which were arranged an infinite variety of books, among which Rose was pleased to observe several volumes of Milton, Shakspere, Dryden, Bolingbroke, Bacon, Pope, Byron, and Moore, not in the translative, but in the best editions of the original.

'Here,' said Charles, who manifested an enthusiastic delight for poetry, 'I have spent some of my happiest hours.'

'I am pleased indeed,' replied Rose, 'that you have made English authors your favourite study.'

'Oh! everything connected with England,' he replied, with increased enthusiasm, 'has long been my delight, but it is time we separated to dress for dinner; only let me tell you, Rose, that while you remain with us, I shall be proud, if you will so far oblige me, as to consider this room your own, and unhesitatingly make use of it whenever you feel inclined to peruse any of these authors.'

'It is I, dear Charles, that shall feel proud to be allowed to do so.'

Thus, days and weeks passed on: in the meantime Rose did not forget to write to her parents and friends in England, and with delight they read an account of the improved state of her health, and of the kind and affectionate treatment she experienced from Donna Rosalia and her youthful nephew; and oh! her tender mother was overjoyed to discover in her letter something akin to her former playful gaiety, and this was gladly hailed by all as a sure forerunner of her ultimate recovery, and many tears of joy were shed over the unconscious letter, which conveyed to them the joyful tidings. Indeed, it was wonderful how much Rose had improved during the short time she had been at Naples. The climate, which, indeed, is one of the warmest in Italy, appeared to suit her constitution in every respect. It was now autumn, but the weather clear, fine, and warm; indeed, it would have been almost insupportably hot, had not the air been constantly refreshed by the sea-breeze. Albert, with joy, beheld this change in Rose, and though he felt his own health daily declining, he sedulously kept it from her knowledge, and he delighted to witness the friendly intercourse that existed between her and Donna Rosalia's nephew; and yet, at times, when the boy would manifest a tender affection and concern for her welfare, he viewed it with evident uneasiness; and, when once Albert discovered Rose in the library, reading aloud a volume of Moore, while Charles, seated at her feet, gazed upon her lovely face, to which the bloom was gradually stealing back, while her small, white hand, resting upon his head, was almost hidden beneath the thick clusters of raven curls, he looked upon the two, both so lovely, yet so unlike, for a few minutes in silence, and then, in a harsh, discordant voice, called Rose away. Starting at the sound of his voice, she instantly cast aside the book and joined him.

'You are very fond of the company of that boy,' he said, as soon as they were alone, trying to assume a gentle tone.

'I am, dear Albert,' replied Rose, ingenuously; 'the company of no one but yourself ever afforded me so much pleasure.'

Albert appeared for a minute or two struggling with himself, whether or not to impart some intelligence to Rose. Seeing he paused, she said mildly,—

'I fear, dear Albert, you have imbibed some antipathy to the youth. I am grieved to observe it, for I am confident, if you knew him as well as I do you could not fail to love him.'

'And do you love him?' inquired Albert.

'I do,' replied Rose; 'he is a boy indeed or uncommonly quick perception and talent for his years, and, were you to enter freely into conversation with him, you would, I am certain, regard him as much as myself; and then he is ever so thoughtful and attentive, even to my lightest wish, that were he my brother, I could scarcely feel more attached to him.'

Albert said no more at that time; he loved Rose, and had the greatest confidence in her love for him, which prevented him for a moment feeling the slightest jealousy, on account of the regard she nourished in her gentle bosom for the Italian youth; on the contrary, he would have been pleased to remark the growing friendship that existed between them, had he not observed in the youthful Charles a something bordering on a more tender affection than that of friendship. Yes, young as he was, Albert began to entertain fears that he loved Rose, and how to check this passion, without disclosing the truth, he knew not. Sometimes he determined to mention it to Donna Rosalia, and then again he was confident she would insist upon making Charles acquainted with all that had occurred, and this thought deterred him from taking the step he most wished.

'I am certain of Rose,' he said, inwardly debating with himself; 'but, alas! if this unhappy youth should nourish a fatal passion for her, it may be the means of destroying him —of adding another victim to those who have already fallen through my means; and yet, I cannot bear to have my guilt proclaimed—to be shunned and abhorred by those who are nearest and dearest to me. But a little while, and I shall be unconscious of all that may be said regarding me; till then, I will watch this youth, and endeavour to keep Rose as much apart from him as possible.'

With this resolution, Albert contented himself for awhile, and yet he had so many private conferences with Rosalia as to leave Rose much spare time to devote to Charles, who seemed happy only in her presence. He had been brought up so entirely with his aunt, associating with few of the Italian nobility, that it is not to be wondered at he was somewhat effeminate in his manners and conversation. His education was superintended by a Catholic priest, who for many years had resided in the house, and now fulfilled the double office of tutor and confessor. Rose had not been out much (beyond the grounds of the villa, which were indeed beautiful and extensive) since her residence in Naples, but one fine warm evening Donna Rosalia proposed for them all to take a row, the water being beautifully calm and smooth. This meeting with the approbation of all, they were soon in readiness. Donna Rosalia and Albert were seated at one end of the boat, and Rose and Charles at the other. The sailors pulled vigorously at their oars, and they soon found themselves in the middle of the Bay of Naples, which is so wonderfully diversified by all the riches both of nature and art, as scarcely to leave an object wanting to render its beauty complete. The extensive cost is surrounded by a vast variety of mountains, valleys, promontories and islands, covered with an everlasting verdure, and loaded with the richest fruits; and the rich country stretching towards Porlici, covered with noble houses and gardens, appearing only a continuation of the city, and all around an amazing mixture of the ancient and modern; some rising to fame, others sinking to ruin. Rose, to whom alone of the party this splendid scenery was new, looked upon all around her with awe-struck delight, and when the setting sun sunk entirely to rest, the scene was even yet more lovely, the heavens exhibiting a most beautiful appearance, the eastern part of the hemisphere being of a rich deep purple, and the western of a bright beautiful yellow glow, and then presently up rose the moon, large and full, and looking like a ball of fire, rising from the waters. The scene was one that naturally sunk the mind to pleased and calm meditation, and all of them remained for nearly an hour without speaking a word, when suddenly the sailors began their evening hymn to the Virgin, beating time with their oars. The music was simple, touching, and melancholy, and in perfect harmony with the scene ; the cadence swept low, yet full over the waters, till it died away in the distance, leaving the mind in admiration of the soft pathetic strains. Charles was the first to break silence.

"What think you, dear Rose, of the evening song ?"

'Oh : it is beautiful, more than beautiful,' she replied, bending her eyes, which were swimming with tears, on his face.

'And yet, it has made you melancholy,' he returned, resting his hand on hers.

'Oh! but it is a sweet, soothing melancholy—it brings, dear Charles,' she replied, pressing his hand kindly in her own, 'with it sweet pure thoughts, which raise the soul far above this world—yes, fair and beautiful as is the present lovely landscape, which lies before our enraptured gaze, it must sink into nothingness when compared with heaven: Oh! how bright and beautiful, then, must heaven be !'

The boy listened in profound silence, his eyes fixed on her fair face, upon which the soft moon shed a subdued and gentle light, and as he gazed on the transparent skin and lily whiteness of the English girl, while her auburn tresses were waved gently by the ambient air, he thought that nothing could ever match its beauty and grace. His own dark hand was still clasped in her fair one, and he felt as though he could thus sit and gaze upon her for ever ; yes, young as he was, the heart of Charles was becoming insensibly touched by the soft and tender passion of love—a passion so new to him, that he could not define it even to himself. It has been said, and we think with much truth, that a man's first love is generally placed on a being that is unattainable, and most frequently on a person older than himself. Thus it was with Charles—he loved, although he knew it not. Rose was sensible of feeling a strong and powerful interest in him, and, looking upon him almost as a child, had shewn him the regard and affection of an elder sister, which she, in truth entertained for him ; and the charm of her presence, her sweet beauty, and the consciousness that she fondly regarded him, had made an impression on the heart of Charles, not easily effaced. It may seem strange to some readers that one so juvenile as Charles should thus early become susceptible of the tender passion ; and it would, perhaps, be so in our own cold climate, but in the bright and sunny land of Italy it is far different, and instances are numerous in which many equally as young as Charles have become deeply enamoured, nor has it proved an evanescent feeling ; on the contrary, it has more frequently deepened into a strong and lasting passion. The evening was indeed beautiful—the moon shone bright upon the water—the waves were high, but smooth and equal, and followed one another with a slow and even pace, which tempted the party to remain out longer than they had previously intended. Albert had spoken not since he took his seat in the boat, but gazing almost vacantly around him, while melancholy was stamped upon his pallid brow, remained absorbed in thought.

'There is something in the calm stillness of such an hour as this,' said Donna Rosalia, in her low musical tones, 'that produces a feeling in my breast unknown to it at other times.'

Albert started, and, as though her observation recalled some painful thoughts to his memory, covered his face with his hands, and continued silent. With deep sorrow, Rose observed this, and longed to whisper to him some words of affectionate condolence ; but no opportunity was afforded her of doing so, and, seated apart from him, capable only of witnessing his sorrow, she became restless and uneasy. The beauty of the scenery no longer afforded her delight, and she was thankful when their boat reached the shore, and they again entered the villa.

Although little has been said concerning Donna Rosalia, yet she was kind and affectionate to Rose in the extreme. Nothing on her part was wanting that could in any way tend to promote the happiness or comfort of her fair young guest. Rose felt, and was grateful to her for this kind consideration for her welfare ; and though she tenderly and passionately loved her husband, yet she could not be indifferent to the affectionate attention and regard of Charles, who studied her every look, knew and fulfilled her wishes before she had time to express them, and never seemed so happy as when engaged in some service for her. Rose felt all this, and lavished upon the boy the sincere affection of a sister, at the same time, she was sorry to observe that much of the gay and volatile spirit which had animated him on their first acquaintance, had gradually given way before a deep and settled thoughtfulness ; indeed, there were times when she observed upon his young brow an expression of sadness strongly resemling that which so constantly sat upon Albert.

'I am afraid, dear Charles,' she remarked one morning as he entered the room where she was sitting, 'that my company has produced the effect of making you melancholy, and I must positively insist upon your not being so much with me ; it is sad, indeed, that my sombre spirit should cast a shadow upon your hitherto bright and buoyant one.'

'Oh! do not say that, dear lady,' replied Charles, 'I assure you I am very far from sad, and have now come to solicit you to accompany me to the cathedral. You have already expressed a desire to inspect it, and as Mr. Moreland is engaged with my aunt, will not, I hope, offer any objection.'

'So far from it,' replied Rose, 'it will give me great pleasure to accept your invitation.'

The distance from the villa to the cathedral was short, and Rose would have preferred walking, had not Charles informed her that the custom of the country forbade persons of his aunt's rank, or any of her guests, from doing so; and, consequently, the carriage was ordered for the purpose of conveying them thither. The cathedral was a venerable gothic building, supported within by sixty columns of oriental granite, some of them extremely rich; and the walls and vaulted roof were entirely encrusted over with ancient mosaic—the pavement, in particular, struck Rose as the most splendid and rich of anything she had seen since her residence in Naples. It was composed of sepulchral monuments of the finest marbles, porphyry, lapis lazuli, and a vast quantity of other valuable stones joined together, representing, in a sort of mosaic, the arms and insignia of the persons whom they were intended to commemorate. The altar, too, was magnificent in the extreme, being of massive silver, exquisitely wrought, representing in relief some of the principal stories in the Bible.

'Well,' said Charles, impatient at Rose's silence, 'what do you think of it? Is it not a splendid place?'

'It is,' replied Rose, 'but my admiration is blended with awe—a feeling, dear Charles, that you, who have from infancy been accustomed to this charming country, and the beauty and riches with which it abounds, have never, I dare say, known.'

'Oh yes, dear lady, I have often, while standing beneath this venerable building, been struck with a sensation of awe at its grand and imposing appearance, especially when I gaze upon those marble and porphyry monuments, some of them nearly seven hundred years old.'

'Have they, indeed, been executed so long?' replied Rose, advancing to inspect them closer.

'They have, dear lady,' he returned, 'and yet, you see, they are of very tolerable workmanship.'

'How splendid is that altar!' said Rose, turning towards it.

'It is very rich,' replied Charles, 'but I must call your attention to those ropes, which are embroidered with oriental pearl, and are now four hundred years old.'

'Amazing,' returned Rose, 'they look as fresh as if done but yesterday; this seems indeed a land of wonders.'

'There are yet some things,' replied Charles, 'that you have not seen, which are looked upon as the greatest riches the church contains.'

'Indeed,' said Rose, 'I am lost in surprise at the splendour and magnificence that everywhere meets my eyes; and am, indeed, wholly unprepared for more.'

'Look here, then,' returned Charles, directing her attention to a large silver box, curiously wrought, and enriched with precious stones, of great value, 'this box contains some bones of St. Peter, and also of John the Baptist.'

'Is it possible?' replied Rose, gazing on the box, with a feeling of almost sacredness for what it was supposed to contain.

'Yes,' returned Charles, 'and they have been known to perform very wonderful miracles.'

To this, Rose made no reply; her Protestant education induced her to reject at once the idea of miracles being performed in the present day; but, knowing that Charles had been early taught, as part of his creed, to give it his most implicit belief, she would not on any account breathe a word that might shake his confidence in the faith of his religion; and while standing beneath this ancient structure, surrounded by splendour and magnificence, hitherto beyond even her conception, her thoughts flew back to the simple undecorated village church, where but a few plain marble tablets told of departed worth, where by her mother's side she had bent her knee in prayer, and, in language beautiful in its simplicity, given God hearty thanks for his present goodness and preservation, and invoked his merciful blessing for the time to come. The contrast was more forcibly brought to her memory, as they now began to celebrate their church service, and it seemed to Rose sadly overcharged with parade and ceremony, the number of genuflections before the altar, the kissing of the friar's hand, the holding up of his robes by inferior priests, the ceremony of throwing incense upon the flock, and many other things, after a little while absolutely wearied her, and she felt glad when the service was brought to a close.

Rose and Charles lingered till all who were assembled had taken their departure, when they together walked once more round the cathedral, stopping to admire the numerous statues and monuments, each vieing with the other in the beauty and costliness of its workmanship. Charles, who but very seldom visited the cathedral seemed to feel equal pleasure with Rose, and, over and anon explained to her the meaning of the insignia with which they were decorated, or interpreted the inscriptions on the tombs. And they were alone, yes, alone, surrounded by the dead, and the trophies, which had distinguished them while living; there is ever a solemnity connected with the crumbling remains of mortality, and here it was especially called forth. A most profound stillness prevailed, which alone was broken by the soft tones of their whispering voices, save when their footsteps, light and gentle as they were, echoed and reverberated through the building. Now and then, in their slow walk, they

[See page 155.

stopped before the monument of some one freshly entombed, who had been snatched away in the very bloom of youth; these created a far stronger sympathy in the minds of the young and handsome pair, than when the inscription told of those 'who had borne the heat and

No. 20.

burden of the day,' and at length descended to the tomb, full of years and honours. For them to die appeared natural; there was nothing startling or deeply impressive as regarded themselves in the transition of the aged from this world to another, and who (if the inscription on their monuments spoke truth) had passed a long and well-spent life, and might now be safely concluded to have reached that happy haven which is promised to the righteous; but there was something that spoke loudly to themselves in the contemplation of the monuments that were reared to the young. Like them, perhaps, they had clung to earth, 'beloved and loving many riches,' and the enjoyment of all that makes life pleasant had invited their stay. And it might have been with a fond lingering desire to remain here, that they were compelled to exchange this world, they trusted, for a better, and over these stones they dropped the sympathetic tear. Rose had drawn forth her white pocket-handkerchief to remove the traces of emotion from her fair cheek, as, leaning on Charles's arm, they turned from a monument of even unusual richness and beauty, and which was but recently raised to the memory of a young Italian lady, of high rank and talents, and whom the inscription spoke of as having possessed extreme loveliness of person and mind.

'I thought,' said Rose starting, 'I saw a dark figure this instant gliding before us; did you observe it, Charles?'

'No, dear Rose, I saw nothing; neither, I think, can any one have passed without my having observed it.'

'And yet,' replied Rose, 'I could almost have declared with certainty that a tall, dark figure glided noiselessly before us, a few paces, and then suddenly disappeared behind yonder statues.'

'It is easy to ascertain if such be the case,' said Charles, releasing himself from his fair companion, and hastening in the direction she had indicated; while thus left standing alone for a few minutes, Rose felt an involuntary shudder run through her frame, while at the same time a sense of dread came over her which she could not account for. Charles quickly returned.

'It must have been your imagination, dear Rose,' he said, as soon as he joined her, 'as I have searched all round the spot, without perceiving any one.'

Rose felt relieved by his presence. 'Yes, dear Charles, it must, as you say, have been imagination, and yet I was foolish enough to allow it to alarm me; but come, let us proceed— I may not have another opportunity of visiting this cathedral, and am, therefore, desirous of inspecting it thoroughly.'

'If it be really your desire to do so, dear lady,' replied Charles, 'I will guide you to a part that you have not yet seen, and which, though more retired, still contains many statues of the ancient kings, famed for their antiquity, as well as for the costliness of the marble out of which they are sculptured.'

Rose expressed her wish to be conducted to that spot, and they walked together towards an inner chapel, dedicated to the patroness of the city, and who was held in great veneration— more so, indeed, than even the Virgin Mary herself. The spot directly leading to this chapel was, as Charles had intimated, in the most retired part of the cathedral, celebrated chiefly for its antiquity, and here, as he had also said, Rose found much to admire in the statues. While walking from one to another, and scrutinising each, a small white marble tablet, evidently of recent workmanship, and without even the slightest ornament, caught Rose's attention, as bearing a strong resemblance to what may be found in any church in England; but, looking closer, she saw with surprise the inscription was in English, containing only a name, the age of the individual, and the date of his death, in commemoration of whom it was placed there. On this tablet the eyes of Rose were riveted, and Charles, who had not as yet observed it, was surprised to find she trembled violently, and that she leaned heavily on his arm for support. Looking on her face, he was shocked to see her countenance blanched to a deadly white; in her emotion, she had dropped her handkerchief on the marble pavement, but the raised finger of her left hand pointed in explanation to the tablet. Quick as lightning, Charles' dark eye followed the direction of hers, but no sooner had it rested upon the spot, than he was affected in the same manner as Rose. His olive complexion was instantly divested of the rich bloom that usually sat upon his handsome face, his lip quivered, and his whole frame gave evident signs of his being powerfully moved. Suddenly, with an action as graceful as it was unexpected, he raised his hat, and standing thus with his head uncovered, his dark eyes, that often sent forth such fiery glances, now melted into the most touching softness, and turned towards Heaven, while his lips moved as though breathing a prayer for the soul of the departed. Rose remained in the same attitude with her arm extended, and finger pointed to the tablet, that had caused them both so much emotion, while a large pearly tear stood in either eye. Yes, there they were, side by side, each gazing on the same spot, apparently unconscious of all else, and lost in grief and surprise. On one side of them was a large gothic window of coloured glass, representing our Saviour extended on the cross, and through which the sun shed a refulgent but mellow light upon their upturned countenances, making the contrast between the two more strikingly apparent—the fair, and now as white as the marble upon which they gazed, while her auburn hair, stealing from under her bonnet, floated loosely on her shoulders; there was a freshness of youth and beauty visible even through her fading charms, and a feminine grace in the outline of her slender form as perfect as when it possessed rounder and fuller proportions, while Charles, the very type of youthful beauty, whose symmetrical form and exquisitely proportioned limbs gave promise, when a few more years should have matured them, of changing the now somewhat boyish form into that of the full beauty of manhood : tall and stout now, beyond his years, he supported the slight and fragile Rose upon his arm, who clung to him as though he were at once capable of sustaining and cheering her fainting spirit. They had remained in the position we have described for some minutes, when both were startled by a sob, or rather groan; surprised at the unwonted sound, which seemed to proceed from behind one of the statues, without speaking a word, they moved almost noiselessly to the spot, and beheld the figure of a man, evidently English by his dress, prostrate on the pavement before the very tablet that had so affected themselves. A large statue that intervened between them had hitherto concealed him from their observation. He seemed in the very agony of grief, which found vent in sobs and groans. Surprise kept Rose and Charles for awhile motionless, till the stranger, suddenly raising his face, which had previously been bowed to the ground, discovered the features of Albert; at the same instant, the words seeming to burst from an overcharged heart, he exclaimed, his eyes, which were, swimming with tears, fixed on the tablet,—

'My poor, my murdered brother !'

Horrorstruck, Rose instantly, with gentle force, drew Charles away, who, with flashing eyes, the instant he caught the words, had, half unconsciously, laid his hand upon his stiletto.

'Come, come, dear Charles,' she whispered, when she had withdrawn him a short distance from Albert, 'let us, this moment, leave the cathedral, and hasten home.'

'As you please, dear lady,' he replied, yielding to her desire, and in a few minutes they were once more seated in the carriage, which was moving rapidly towards the villa.

'It is sad,' said Charles, who was the first to speak, 'that the only token I should ever have of a father, is the monument that is erected to his memory; and oh! lady, it is evident he must have closed his existence ere mine began : he never even looked upon his child. This would have been melancholy, had it been the decree of Heaven; but we have heard from the lips of one who called him brother, that this was not the case, but that my parent was cut off in his youth by the hand of another; who that other may prove to be, we have yet to learn, but let me once obtain that knowledge, and I dedicate myself, heart and soul, to revenge his death.'

'Oh, stop, stop, dear Charles, you know not what you say : speak not so rashly, I entreat of you, consider,' added Rose, endeavouring to assume a calmness she was far from feeling, 'you have no proof that the monument we have this day seen was erected to the memory of your father.'

Charles shook his head as he replied,—

'The name, dear lady, tells me all. I have long felt assured that my father was of English birth, and from the circumstance of bearing the same name as myself, together with the intimation I received from my aunt previous to your arrival, that a near relative of mine intended paying me a visit, caused me to regard Mr. Moreland (even on my first introduction to him) as my uncle ; and now, dear lady, I am convinced that his murdered brother stands to me in the character of a parent.'

'Oh, do not,' said Rose, earnestly, 'so hastily form your conclusions: you have yet but slight grounds for supposing the brother of my husband to be your father.' The words, 'my husband,' caused Charles a pang he could scarcely account for ; he was conscious of feeling an affection for Rose stronger than for any other person he had ever known, his aunt, to whom he was much attached, included ; but there was something about Albert—a sort of a cold melancholy reserve, which, so utterly opposed to his own open confiding disposition, had occasioned a feeling of distrust towards him in the breast of Charles, and which latterly the increased sternness of Albert had deepened into a settled dislike. The words, 'my husband,' had for the first time partially opened the eyes of Charles to the real regard he entertained for Rose; yes, reminding him that she was married, they had caused thoughts and feelings to flit across his bosom entirely unknown to it before, and as he gazed upon the fair being seated by his side, who had unconsciously awoke such tumultuous thoughts and feelings within him, the tears gathered in his eyes, and stole gently down his cheeks. Rose, perceiving his emotion, and attributing it to a far different cause, sought by kind and gentle words to cheer and soothe him; but, alas ! it only swelled the tide of grief that lay heavy on his heart. Pressing the small white hand (that in her earnestness Rose had laid upon his) with fervour to his lips, he promised to wait patiently till time should divulge to him his real parent, and not thus wildly seek revenge until, at least, he had communicated with her.

I feel almost sure,' said Rose, 'that your father is still living, and will, perhaps, ere long, discover himself to you, but any attempt, on your part, to seek an explanation, concerning that tablet we have to-day seen, may end in the frustration of your wishes; therefore, dear Charles, let me advise you to mention what you have witnessed to none, not even your aunt.'

'I will be guided entirely by you, dear lady,' replied Charles, 'feeling confident that you are the best judge.' After this they both continued silent the remainder of the drive, each busily engaged in thought, Rose's mind filled with the image of Albert's brother. She had proof now that he was indeed no more—that he must have lost his life about the time Florence was supposed to have been killed by his hand. Coupling this with the words of Albert, ' my murdered brother,' she shuddered, and her thoughts became agonised, which she strove, but in vain, to cast them from her. And then the intense grief of Albert. Oh! how bitter must his suffering be, and she, who would have sacrificed all that was dear to her to have soothed his sorrow, and, if possible, to bid it cease, had felt herself unwillingly compelled to leave him alone prostrate on the cold marble, giving vent to his overcharged feelings in tears and groans; he had perceived her not, and she felt, with innate delicacy, that he would have deemed even her an intruder upon his sorrow; he believed no eye witnessed the agonised grief that rent his very frame. No; thinking himself entirely alone, he had uttered the words which caused such a tumult of sorrow in her breast.

'My murdered brother!' Alas! by what hand could the unhappy Charles have fallen—he whom Marian had described as being so universally beloved? Albert, she had seen, bitterly deplored his death, even though years had elapsed since the fatal occurrence; while these thoughts filled the mind of Rose, Charles was equally absorbed, but not to forgetfulness of his companion. No, she it was on whom his imagination was engaged; yes, her image was in almost entire possession of his breast; revenge, that passion so strong in an Italian, had given way before her gentle pleading. And though she failed to remove the impression from his mind, that the tablet recently raised to the memory of Charles Moreland was in truth his father, yet, all thoughts of avenging his death vanished at her bidding, and gave place to more gentle feelings. 'Sweet Rose,' was his inward exclamation; 'you little know the nature of the regard I feel for you; till this moment I knew it not myself, and, now that I have discovered it, it must remain buried in my bosom for ever: to breathe it to any one would be to deprive myself of the only joy I can ever know. To see her, to speak to her, to be able even, in a remote degree, to tend to her happiness—this will hereafter constitute my all of earthly bliss.' Thus each engaged with their own thoughts, they spoke not, till the carriage stopped in front of the villa, when Charles, instantly rousing himself, assisted Rose to alight, and, drawing her arm through his own, led her into the house. When Rose and Albert again met, she observed traces of agitation in his face, that she well knew how to account for. Her own appearance was also dejected, which Albert perceiving, kindly inquired the cause, and it cost Rose a great effort to conceal from him her visit to the cathedral; she was so unaccustomed to deception, that she was frequently very nearly betraying it.

'I think, dear Albert,' said Rose, throwing her arms round his neck, 'that as my health is so much improved, we may now safely return to England.'

'Why so, my Rose?' he replied, kindly returning her embrace; 'are you already weary of Italy, or do you pine for the friends you left behind?'

'Neither, dear Albert; while you are with me, I could be happy anywhere; and for this country, I think it delightful in the extreme, and, so far from wearying of it, I see beauties to admire in it every day.'

'And the climate,' said Albert, 'undoubtedly suits your constitution?'

'Let my improved appearance vouch for that,' replied Rose.

'Then why, my love, propose to return so soon? I had fully purposed staying through the winter.

'If you were only as much improved in health as myself,' returned Rose, 'oh! how gladly, thankfully, would I stay, not only the winter, but for years; but alas, alas!' she continued, gazing with agony upon his attenuated form, his hollow cheek, and sunken eye, 'my husband, my all on earth! I cannot help seeing that you are daily, nay, almost hourly, growing weaker; let us then, Albert, leave this spot at once, and seek some more congenial clime.'

'This climate, dear Rose,' he returned, kindly, ' is the finest and healthiest in all Italy, and does, I am sure, agree with my constitution as well, or better, than any other, or I would, my love, comply with your wishes.'

'Oh! it is not the climate, dear Albert, but this place recals such sad scenes to your memory, as to embitter every pleasure or drop of comfort that might otherwise be enjoyed by you. It preys constantly on your spirits, and, as a mutual consequence, on your health also.'

'You are right, dear Rose, in your conjecture, so far as this place does indeed recal scenes and days long past, but never to be forgotten; but that my constitution is giving way, I will not, dear love, conceal from you.'

'Oh! then, dear Albert, since you confess so much,' replied Rose, bursting into tears, 'you will consent to flee this place instantly.'

'Oh! why, why,' she continued bitterly, 'did we ever come here? Was it indeed to preserve my life at the expense of yours? Oh! rather, a thousand times rather would I have died.'

'My own dear Rose,' replied Albert, folding her to his bosom, 'you sadly mistake my love, It is not this place, nor any reminiscence it recals, that has weakened my health or enervated my frame. I have been dying for years, slowly but surely, and God only knows how much longer I am destined to remain on earth. I may be years longer before my spirit, free and unshackled, joins my sainted brother's in the skies.'

'Oh! Albert,' replied Rose, sobbing, 'I cannot, cannot bear to hear you talk thus; we must not, will not be separated.'

'Only for a time,' returned Albert, with a calmness Rose had never before observed in his manner—'only for a time, my love, and there we shall again meet, where I shall never more have occasion to wipe away your tears.'

'Do not distress yourself, my Rose,' he added, after a pause, 'we know not yet the decree of fate; it may be ordained that I shall yet remain on earth with you for many years to come, If not, my love, depend you will never want for kind and considerate friends.'

'I shall not need them, dear Albert,' said Rose, giving vent to a fresh burst of tears,' 'we are too linked, too closely united, ever to be parted—we must live or die together.'

'We must, my love,' said Albert, tenderly kissing her cheek, 'bow to the omnipotent will of God!'

Rose could only weep on her husband's shoulder, and cling to him, as though she were in instant danger of having him snatched from her.

From this day Rose more particularly marked that Albert's health declined, yet his spirits seemed to rise in proportion. Much of the melancholy that had characterised him was gone, and in its place there sat a lightness on his brow which gladdened her heart, and made her sometimes fancy that he was approaching towards convalescence. He conversed often, and cheerfully, both with her and Donna Rosalia. Of Charles he took but little notice, and Rose, fearin he should think himself neglected, as his aunt was much engaged with Albert, found many opportunities of amusing him, both with her company and conversation. The boy felt grateful to her for this kindness, and showed by the bright and merry smile which ever illumined his countenance in her presence, how much he valued her company. On venturing to speak to him of Albert, and her own anxiety on his account, Charles seemed surprised that she should entertain any fears regarding his health.

'Oh! do not, dear lady, give way to sorrow. I feel confident there is no danger to be apprehended from Mr. Moreland's illness; indeed, he is surely far better in health than when you first came here.'

'Oh! that I could but think so too,' replied Rose; 'his spirits certainly are much improved, but his bodily health, I fear, declines.'

'I would not deceive you, dear lady, who have ever shown such kindness to me,' said Charles, 'therefore, did I think Mr. Moreland dangerously ill, I would not hesitate to say so; but I assure you such is not my opinion; on the contrary, I firmly believe he is now fast recovering.'

'God in heaven grant that you may be right,' replied Rose.

Thus hoping even against hope, her spirits buoyed up with the cheerful anticipations of Charles, Rose mistook the hectic flush of disease for the bloom of returning health; and then Albert seemed, especially at times, so cheerful, so unlike an invalid, that notwithstanding his evident weakness, she looked forward with a feeling of almost certainty to his ultimate restoration. And poor Rose, much improved in every respect by her residence in Naples, yielded herself to the delight of seeing Albert overcome the melancholy that had for so many years been his companion; and often, indeed, was he obliged to turn away to hide the starting tear, as, seated by his side, she pictured in glowing colours forthcoming years of happiness and joy.

'How delighted all our dear friends in England will be to receive us again, especially with such happy countenances! I am afraid, dear Albert, that of late we have been very selfish, scarcely ever receiving those whom we well knew were deeply interested in our welfare; but for the future we will make them amends for our seeming unkindness.'

Thus spoke Rose, when conversing with Albert, who, though pained to see that she so fully anticipated his recovery, yet could not undeceive her as to his real situation.

'You must promise me, Rosalia, as a further proof of your affection for me and mine,' said Albert, one day when sitting alone with her, 'to extend your utmost care and tenderness to my poor Rose when I am gone; let her and Charles know my unhappy story, nor seek, dear Rosalia, to extenuate my guilt to them. Suffice it, that great as my sin has been, I can now feel that I am forgiven, and, were it not for the sweet innocent I must leave behind me, should be thankful to lay down life's weary load.'

'All that claims love or care from you,' she replied, gently, 'will ever be loved and cherished by Rosalia, but the one you now recommend to my care is loved and treasured for her own sake.'

'I cannot attempt,' returned Albert, 'even to thank you for all the kindness I have experienced at your hands, but God, while he punishes the guilty, never allows virtuous deeds to go unrewarded. He, dear Rosalia, will bless, and amply repay you for all.'

'The little I have done,' replied Rosalia, 'deserves no such commendation as you bestow; I have loved Charles from his birth, as though he were my own son—indeed, is he not the child of an only and tenderly beloved sister? And as for Rose, your young and interesting wife, none, I am sure, could be long in her company and fail to feel a strong and endearing affection for her.'

'I am content,' replied Albert, 'to leave her to your tender care and keeping; you have known what it is yourself to suffer grief and anguish at heart, and consequently are capable of administering to the sorrows of another.'

Although Rose entertained, as we have intimated, but few fears regarding Albert, yet she often felt grieved at his apparently desiring her absence. Had she followed her own inclinations, she would never for an instant have left his side, but this he would not allow her to do; on the contrary, he insisted upon her taking regular exercise. She seldom, indeed, went beyond the grounds attached to the villa, but they were extensive, and laid out to appear even more so than they really were. Naturally possessing a great fondness for flowers, she was delighted with the orange trees, the citrons, bergamots, and pomegranates, which gave forth a most delicious perfume; but what pleased her far more was to see, growing in rich profusion, flowers, similar to what she had cultivated in her own little garden appertaining to her childhood's home, such as larkspur, Flos Adonis, Venus' looking-glass, hawkweed, and very fine lupins. Of these she each evening gathered a nosegay for Albert, who, when strong enough, would accompany her walk through the grounds.

When Charles observed her fondness and preference for these flowers, that bloomed alike in her own native land, and learned from her lips the cause, he was seized with a similar passion for them, and the breakfast-table and library were always adorned with a fresh-gathered bouquet, composed entirely of these flowers. This compliment to her taste and feelings could not, of course, be otherwise than gratifying to Rose, who repaid him with smiles and thanks—not that Rose was indifferent to the beautiful sweet-scented flowers of Italy, but, when absent from our own, our native land, the slightest thing that recals it to our memory is ever loved and prized. This it was that made Rose, in one of the few rambles she took from the villa, delighted to come suddenly upon a field, covered with the richest white clover, intermixed with a variety of aromatic plants, which perfumed the air for some distance; but the walk which most pleased Rose, and which she was more desirous of repeating than any other, was by the sea-shore. Here she loved to wander, especially of an evening, when she could watch the setting sun and the up rising of the moon, and then her thoughts would fly back to England, and she would picture to herself her joyful return to the friends she had left. Charles, as we have before intimated, manifested an ardent desire to learn all he could concerning England.

'I think,' said Rose, when they were conversing together about her native land, 'I must persuade your aunt to allow you to accompany us; when we return thither, she surely will not be afraid to trust you with Albert and myself.'

The boy's eye brightened at the suggestion, and his face gave token of extreme delight, which vanished as the thought arose, that he should not be able to obtain Donna Rosalia's consent.

'I am afraid,' he replied, 'that my aunt will object to part with me, even for a few months; we have never been separated, and much as I am desirous, dear lady, of accepting your kind offer, I would not perfect my own happiness at the expense of hers.'

Rose rejoiced to see this excellent trait in the boy's character, and replied—

'Is it impossible, Charles, think you, to prevail upon her to go with us likewise? I can promise you both a warm welcome from kind and affectionate hearts. Supposing Albert to be your uncle, you will find in his only sister Marian, an aunt who will love you scarcely less than Rosalia.'

'And have I indeed, dear lady, an aunt in England? Tell me, does she resemble you? I mean is she fair, with light air?'

Rose smiled, as she replied—

'No, dear Charles, she is, on the contrary, dark, and much like Albert: she loved her brother, her whose tablet we saw in the cathedral, with the most devoted affection. I have heard her speak of him in the warmest tones, and supposing him to be the father of yourself, she will, I am certain, extend her affection to you.'

Charles paused for a few minutes, and then said thoughtfully—

'I have often wished, but never, dear lady, had the courage (so fearful was I of offending you) till now, of asking you to inform me of the particulars relating to the death of him I feel convinced was my father; as Mr. Moreland's sister spoke to you about him, she doubtless acquainted you with the manner of his death. I ask not now, for the purpose of seeking revenge, for your sake, I will forego all thoughts of such a thing; therefore, dear lady, I trust you will not deny my request.'

'Not for an instant, dear Charles, would I, were it in my power to comply with it, but I assure you that it is not; when I left England, Marian fully believed him still living, and not the slightest intimation had I ever received of his death, till we discovered the tablet, which placed it beyond all doubt.'

'Alas! then,' replied Charles, 'I am convinced there is some terrible secret connected with his fate; the words of Mr. Moreland in the cathedral assure me that he came by his death in an unfair manner.'

'There is, dear Charles,' said Rose, evidently affected, 'without doubt, a sad and, as you say, a terrible secret connected with it; but what that secret is, we cannot at present tell; has your aunt never mentioned him to you?'

'Never, dear lady; of my mother she has spoken, and presented to me the locket containing her portrait, but when I have inquired for my father, she has answered me only with tears, and such bitter sorrow the name apparently awoke in her bosom, that I have foreborne to press her on the subject.'

'I can scarcely think,' said Rose, looking earnestly on the youth, 'that the brother of my Albert is the father of yourself, for Marian, as I this moment told you, frequently spoke of him to me, and described him as being fair, and light haired as myself, while you, dear Charles, are very dark.'

'So was my mother,' he replied, drawing forth the locket, and gazing on it with fearful eyes, and pressing it to his lips, he exclaimed aloud,—

'Sweet image of the sainted being who gave me birth, and, in doing so, gave her own life in exchange for mine,—great indeed must thy sufferings have been, when thou wert doomed ere thy child saw the light to lose thy husband by the base hand of an assassin.'

'Unfortunate being,' said Rose, 'what joy she would have felt had she lived till now, and owned thee for her son!'

'I was assured that my father was English, and that has ever given me an interest in the land of his birth,' replied Charles, 'and if I can but prevail on my aunt to accompany you back to England, how delighted I shall be to visit that country!'

'It is dear to me,' said Rose, 'as being my native land; and with all that is said against its climate, I own I love it well, and though inferior in richness and beauty to the sunny land of Italy, yet there are many sweet and pleasant spots to be found therein, which I would not exchange even for the verdure and fertility of Naples.'

'All you say, dear lady, but inspires me with a more ardent desire to behold it.'

'And yet,' said Rose, smiling, 'when you view it, you will, I make no doubt, think my description partial.'

'You who have been accustomed from infancy to the splendid scenery of Italy, will scarcely think England otherwise than flat and uninteresting.'

'I am at least prejudiced in its favour, and prepared to love and admire it more than any other land on earth; and you, dear lady, will use your influence with my aunt to induce her to comply with our wishes.'

'Marian would indeed be delighted to see you,' said Rose, half musingly. 'But you will allow me to remain under the same roof with you,' said the boy, while a shade of anxiety passed over his expressive countenance. 'Surely,' said Rose, quickly, 'if you desire it; though I know Marian will want you much with her, especially if you are the son of her brother Charles, to whom she was much attached, and even now, I fully believe, anticipates seeing him again.'

'In heaven I hope she will,' returned the youth, 'but on earth—never.'

Rose took the earliest opportunity after this conversation to mention to Albert her wish that Donna Rosalia and her nephew should accompany them, when they returned to England.

'Charles has, dear Albert,' she said, 'a great desire to do so, and, if you persuade his aunt, I have no doubt but you would succeed in gaining her consent.'

Albert turned aside his head, but made no reply; Rose was surprised, but still more so, on looking into his face, to perceive that it was wet with tears.

'My dear, dear Albert,' she exclaimed, throwing her arms round his neck, 'if I have offended or grieved you, pray, pray forgive me!'

'There is nothing to forgive, my Rose,' he replied, folding her in his arms; 'heed me not, I beseech you,' he added, as the tears still bedewed his cheek.

'Tell me, at least, the cause of your sorrow,' she returned, 'that I may share it with you; you will not deny me, love, this gratification?'

'I have none, dear Rose,' he replied, 'and can only excuse myself on the ground of feeling weak and low, this evening; do not allow it, my love, to trouble you.'

'I cannot help it,' replied Rose; 'I thought, dearest, that you had succeeded in entirely banishing melancholy from your mind.'

'So I have, dear Rose, and I bless God for it, who has enabled me to feel that great as my guilt has been, it is all forgiven; and you it was, my love, that first taught me to seek pardon of a God, and a merciful God; you have, my Rose, been of great service to me, more, deed, than you are yourself aware of; and yet once I wronged, deeply wronged, and suspected you, who was all purity and innocence.'

'Mention it not, dear Albert, I entreat of you. Let us speak of something more cheerful than the past; you were not offended, dearest, at my proposition of taking Donna Rosalia and Charles to England with me when we return thither.'

'Certainly not, my love; but I scarcely think Rosalia will consent to do so.'

'Why not, dear Albert? Charles is most desirous of going, and his aunt seldom refuses him anything.'

'She has, I believe, indeed I have heard her say as much, a deep aversion to travelling, and you see yourself in what complete seclusion she lives.'

'She does, dear Albert, and yet I think she might be induced, for the sake of her nephew.'

'Well, my love,' interrupted Albert, 'there is plenty of time to consult her on the subject; we do not propose leaving here for several months, and we know not what may occur in the interim.'

Days and weeks glided smoothly and happily along. Rose and Albert frequently heard from their relations and friends in England, and as frequently forwarded them accounts of their own welfare. Albert's health gradually but certainly declined, of this himself and Donna Rosalia were perfectly aware; but Rose, unfortunately, saw it not. On the contrary, it was perfectly evident that she nourished the brightest hopes for the future.

'Poor child,' said Donna Rosalia, one evening, when Rose, who had regained much of her own light and buoyant spirits, fondly kissed Albert's cheek, and left the room to take her accustomed walk round the grounds with Charles—'poor child! she little dreams how ill you are, or in what danger she stands of having you snatched from her. The blow will descend the more heavily by coming upon her unprepared; it would be a kindness, Albert, to inform her of your danger.'

'Not for the world, dear Rosalia,' he returned. 'I once never thought to have seen her so well, and at the same time so cheerful again; and oh! I feel it indeed a blessing to see her thus restored to her wonted health and spirits. I am now content to die; and though I am convinced that my death will wring her heart with anguish, yet why should she be grieved before the time? Sorrow will come upon her soon enough; then force not the tear from her eye, while there is no cause for her to shed it. Consider, dear Rosalia,' he continued, 'that though we are both aware I never can recover from my present indisposition, yet I may still live for many months, and it cheers my heart, and makes me thankful to see her happy; and though I knew the fond hopes she cherishes can never be realised, yet never by word or action will I consent to dash the cup of joy from her lips till it is inevitable, and then, I trust, she will bear my loss with resignation. To your kind and tender care I leave her, and you must promise me, that, should she desire to return to England, you will yourself accompany her, and restore her safe to the arms of her fond parents.'

Rosalia seemed struggling with an emotion that choked her utterance, and kept her for a few moments silent; but overcoming it, she answered it in her own low, silvery tones—

'Your confidence in me is not misplaced; when you are gone,' and she seemed to utter the words with difficulty, 'Rose shall share my kindness and affection equally with Charles, and I willingly give you my promise never to lose sight of her so long as I live. If, indeed, it is (as it most naturally will be) her desire to return to her parents, I will myself deliver her to them. Nothing shall she require that love and tenderness can procure.'

'I thank you,' replied Albert, 'and I know I can depend on you. This is not the first time I have delegated to you the office of friend and comforter, and well I know you performed the trust.'

'Not only for your sake,' returned Rosalia, 'for I was equally interested in the fate of a sister, and now I look upon Rose as my child; her sweet disposition has so endeared her to my heart, that I feel for her as if she really bore that tender relationship.'

Their conversation was here interrupted by the return of Rose and Charles: the evening having turned out wet had driven them back again to the house.

Although Albert was certainly sinking under the effects of disease, yet sometimes he was so well as to be able to join Rose in her walks, while at others he was confined to his room. It could not of course escape Rose's notice that he was frequently very unwell; but then, seeing him again so much recovered, and at all times more cheerful and talkative than had been usual with him previous to his arrival in Italy, she indulged, as we have said, in high hopes for the future, and spoke of her own and Albert's restoration to health in her letters to her parents and brothers with so much confidence, as to fill all their hearts with joy; and, like her, they fondly pictured the happiness of the return once more to them. Already, in imagination, they viewed her blooming in all the sweet charms of health and joy. These feelings were fully participated in by Lucy, now Lady Mortimer, and her brother Henry. A melancholy had marked his demeanour ever since the departure of Rose; but now that Lucy read to him, with beaming countenance, the

letters she received from her friend, containing so pleasing an account of her renewed health, and which throughout breathed an air of cheerfulness that had of late been foreign to Rose, a happy and delighted surprise filled the breast of Henry. To know that she was well and happy, constituted the greatest joy his heart could feel. It had pained him, more than any but himself ever knew, to witness the sad and melancholy change that had taken place in Rose, and which he had despaired of ever seeing removed. It was, therefore, with a joy, in which no selfish feeling mingled, that he became sensible, through her letters, that she was once more the gay and light-hearted Rose she had been in days gone by.

Charles and Rose were particularly partial to the library, and therein they spent some of the happiest hours the youth had ever known; it was such a delight to have a companion who could understand and appreciate his admiration for the best English authors, who encouraged and confirmed his taste for all that appertained to England, loved as being the native land of a father he had never known; and fondly did he cherish the idea that he should visit it in the company of her who had so unconsciously won his youthful heart, and content he would have been for hours to sit at her feet, and hear her discourse of the land of her birth; and already was the boy familiar with the names and excellent qualities of those who were dear to her, and loved them because she did the same.

'Dear lady,' said Charles, as seated in the library facing a large gothic window of stained glass, which commanded an extensive view of the shrubbery, which was thickly planted with orange trees, citrons, and a variety of other aromatic plants, and bordered on each side by a row of exceedingly large American aloes, numbers of them being in full blossom—'dear lady, how pleased I should be to see the friends that had been so kind to you, especially her you call Lucy; I love her now from your description alone.'

'And you would, dear Charles, much more if you come to know her; she is all that is kind, gentle, and generous. Oh! none, indeed, that ever knew Lucy, could help loving her; and I, more than others, have reason to love and remember her, for she nursed me through a long and dangerous illness, and clung but closer to me in sorrow and distress.'

'Dear, noble lady,' replied Charles, with an air of almost reverential affection, 'I hope one day to see, to know her, and love her as you do.'

Their conversation was here interrupted by Donna Rosalia, who called Rose from the room, saying she wished to speak to her for a few minutes. Rose immediately complied, and Charles, thus left alone, sunk into a deep reverie, from which he was aroused by the entrance of some person; and not doubting it to be Rose, who had promised to return, he hastened in the direction of the door: it was evening, and the farther end of the room was dim and obscure, and Charles was unable to perceive Rose; but as he extended his hand to lead her to the chair she had left but a short time before, he said—

"I am glad you have come back, dear Rose, I had almost begun to despair of your doing so, and I am never happy but in your presence, and now you will stay and talk to me, I hope, a long while; I could listen to you, dear lady, for ever.'

The warmth of his feelings had betrayed Charles into expressing himself more strongly than usual, and now, receiving no answer, he dreaded that his speech had offended her, and began to think of offering an excuse for his warmth of manner; but before he had time to frame his thoughts into words, the person he had made certain was Rose walked towards the window; and standing in the full light of which, Charles was thunderstruck to perceive Albert; surprise kept him silent for a moment, and in the next, covered with confusion, he could only stammer out,—

'Mr. Moreland!'

'Ay,' replied Albert, 'it is I whom you have been addressing, and not my wife; and I wonder not at your confusion; nay, I rather wonder at the familiarity of your address to Rose; how could you have supposed it would be received?'

Charles was naturally very proud and high-spirited, and consequently could not break the tone of sarcastic contempt in which Albert addressed him—his blood was fired immediately, and rushed tumultuously to his very temples, as he replied to Albert—

'How could I suppose it would be received?—why, as Mrs. Moreland ever receives what I say to her, with kindness and affection.'

'It is false,' returned Albert, 'you know it to be false.'

'I know that you lie,' replied Charles, anger taking place of every other feeling in his bosom.

'Boy,' rejoined Albert, 'how dare you speak thus to me?'

'How dare you to insult me?' replied Charles; 'boy as I am, I will not bear it patiently,' and he laid his hand upon his stiletto.

'It is your duty,' returned Albert, 'to submit to me; you owe me duty and obedience.'

'I owe it to you!' said Charles, 'I understand not your words.'

'I nevertheless speak plainly, and again repeat what I before said,—that you owe implicit obedience to me.'

'Who are you, then, that have a right to exact such from me?' replied Charles.

There was a pause of a few seconds, during which the two remained facing each other, Charles's face burning with anger, and his eyes flashing with painful excitement, his right hand still resting on his stiletto; while Albert, deadly pale, and his lips quivering, seemed debating some point in his own mind; then suddenly raising his eyes to those of Charles, said in a low but emphatic voice, in answer to his question, 'who are you?'—

'Your father!'

Oh! had the stillness of that hour been broken by a loud and appalling burst of thunder, it would not have wrought upon Charles the effect caused by these two words.

'Your father!' his cheek instantly vied with Albert's in whiteness, his eyes beamed with a soft and tender feeling, and releasing instantaneously his hold of the stiletto, he sunk upon one knee, and gracefully raising the hand of Albert to his lips, bedewed it at the same time with a tear, as he repeated, 'My father, alas! I knew not I had a parent living, I deemed that the same hand had indirectly destroyed them both.'

'Some day,' replied Albert, melting into softness, 'you shall know the unhappy history of myself and your mother: when that day comes, judge not too harshly of your father, for great as his guilt may be, a son should pity, and if possible, forgive him.'

'He should, and doubt not that he will,' returned Charles, affected even to tears.

'But why did not Donna Rosalia acquaint me that you were my parent? Ah! she knows how often I have inquired for a father, and with what joy I should have welcomed one.'

'Blame her not,' replied Albert, 'she was anxious on my arrival to introduce me to you in my true relationship, and it was with difficulty I prevailed upon her to abandon her own wish, in deference to mine.'

'And you, dear Charles, I wished to conceal from you your parentage, till the grave should have closed over my guilty head. I deemed, perhaps rightly, that you would hate and despise me on account of the sins I have committed, but you will wait till I am gone, and then from your aunt you will learn all. I have desired her to conceal nothing from you; my time here is short, a few more weary months at most, and my spirit will have taken its flight.'

'Impossible!' replied Charles, ' ah! surely, surely. I shall be spared the misery of losing a father, at the moment I have found him, ere I have had an opportunity of showing him my love and duty.'

'The decree has gone forth,' returned Albert, ' my time here, as I have before said, is limited, else I would not, even now, have discovered myself.'

'And why?' replied Charles, as a blush mantled to his cheek, 'were you ashamed to acknowledge your son?'

'No, no,' said Albert, 'I have found you all my proudest wishes could have desired.' He hesitated a moment, and then added, ' Charles, answer me truly, you love Rose?'

A still deeper glow mantled to his cheek at this abrupt question, but he strove to answer calmly and with the least show of agitation possible—

'It is impossible to be so much in her company as I have been, and fail to do so.'

'It was the certainty that I interpreted your feelings towards her rightly, that impelled me in a manner to declare the relationship that exists between us, and you now see, I hope, the imperative necessity of stifling the ill-fated passion in its birth.'

'I have ever seen and felt it,' replied Charles, modestly, 'it was quite sufficient for me to know that she was your wife, that alone convinced me when I discovered the sentiments she had created in my bosom of the utter hopelessness of my love, and I needed not,' he added, rather proudly, ' the additional knowledge of your being my father to induce me to hide the passion deep in the recess of my own heart.'

'And yet the words you supposed you were addressing to Rose when I entered the room'—

'Were those of friendship only,' interrupted Charles, ' though perhaps warmer than my usual manner of speaking to her, yet, I am proud to say,' and he raised his head and drew up to his full height,' that I am certain Rose regards me with the fond affection of a sister.'

'Our family,' said Albert, ' have proved, beyond many others, into what sad consequences the indulgence of such an ill-fated passion as yours may lead. It is on this account, and for your own sake alone, that I warn you to be careful; better, oh, far better, had you resolved never to see her more, than trust to the self-control you may fancy you possess over your own feelings. When I have breathed my last, which cannot, will not be long, Rosalia will repeat to you a tale, heartrending in the extreme, from which you will learn a lesson, that never, I think, will be effaced from your memory. One young and amiable as yourself lost his life, the cause of which was solely attributed, in the first place, to his indulging in a passion for the wife of another; therefore, Charles, let me entreat of you instantly to banish it from your bosom. You know not where it may lead you; you mean, you feel honourable now, I am certain; so did he whose name you hear, and though you will never, I am equally certain, receive the temptation to swerve from the path of honour that he did, yet at least to encourage a hopeless affection is unwise and foolish, as it can only result in misery and sorrow to yourself; will you, therefore, promise me to banish the passion from your bosom?'

'I will promise,' replied Charles, 'submissively to strive my utmost to do so; and it is with bitterness I give the promise, for it is the only source of consolation I hoped to find was in secret to nourish the love you now bid me stifle.'

'You are very young,' replied Albert, 'and at your age it is easy to overcome a boyish liking, which arises chiefly from Rose having been the first interesting female into whose society you have been thrown; when you come to see and know others, you will yourself be surprised at your present infatuation.'

'Never,' replied Charles, firmly; 'neither call it infatuation, as it is no such thing, nor indeed,' he continued, bitterly, 'is it so easily overcome as you imagine.'

'Not for my own sake, nor any feeling connected with self, do I desire it.' rejoined Albert; 'my days are numbered, and were I capable of any jealous feeling (which under our relative positions is impossible), all earthly ideas must soon vanish from my bosom: death is the inevitable lot of us all; and but for my poor Rose, I should be willing, nay, eager to obey its summons.'

The conversation was at this instant interrupted by a piercing shriek, and Rose, who had, unknown to them, entered the room, and caught the last words of Albert, rushed forward; and, throwing herself into his open arms, fainted on his bosom: with tender care he tottered (such was his own weakness) with his lovely but insensible burden to a sofa, and laying her gently down, bathed her hands and face with water. 'Sweet innocent,' he said, as he bent over her, 'what misery and anguish have I not caused thy tender bosom; thou, so free from guilt thyself, hast drunk from the poisoned cup of another; and it was I that held it to thy lips, that tempted thee to the draught by kind, persuasive words. Alas! alas! how much have I to answer for.'

Charles could only gaze on the pair, while the tear that stood in his eye spoke the sad feelings of his breast; he longed to offer Rose assistance, in endeavouring to restore her to consciousness; but the conversation he had held with Albert kept him back, and though he ran eagerly to obtain water, he only placed it near Albert, and then withdrew a few paces. Rose quickly recovered her senses, but it was to an agony heartrending to witness.

'Dear, dear Albert, my own loved Albert,' she exclaimed, as she clasped her arms round his neck, and sobbed out her sorrow upon his bosom, 'you talked of dying, of leaving me alone in the world.'

'Not alone, my love,' he said, nearly as much overcome as herself; 'you are loved, and will be cherished, fondly cherished by many.'

'But you, Albert, my husband, constitute my world: here are none on earth that I care for, in comparison with you. Oh! would to God that I had died, for to live to be separated from you is too dreadful even to think of for an instant; the bare thought rends my heart with anguish, and distracts my very brain. Oh! do not, pray do not leave me.'

'My own love,' said Albert, 'calm yourself, I entreat of you; the will of God we know to be omnipotent, and must bow to His decree.'

When Charles saw that Rose gave signs of returning consciousness, he crept from the room, and informed Rosalia of what had occurred. She hastened to the library, and, seeing the distress of Rose greatly affected Albert, and dreading the consequences of emotion on his weakened frame, besought Rose to control her feelings.

'You are really destroying the life you are so anxious to preserve, by thus giving way to your distress,' said Rosalia, kindly, but firmly; 'and if you cannot avoid doing so, I must insist upon your leaving him.'

'Oh, no, no,' said Rose, 'do not part us while we both live; let me remain by his side, and I will never again allow my distress to overcome me; I will master every feeling: see, I am now calm, my tears shall cease to flow, and I will not so much as breathe one word of anguish.'

'I meant not unkindly, my child,' replied Rosalia; 'none can enter more deeply into your feelings than I, but we must consider Albert. I see he already stands in need of refreshment, and had better retire at once. You know, Albert,' she continued, turning to him, 'how precious your life is to all here, and will, therefore, consent to follow my advice.'

Albert bowed his head in token of submission; indeed, he felt greatly exhausted in body and mind; the events of the evening had wrought powerfully upon his frame, and he passed a restless and feverish night. Rosalia's care had, almost immediately on his arrival in Naples, provided the most eminent medical skill, in the hope that they might be able to administer to his disease, and perchance restore him to health; but in this hope she was quickly undeceived. The physicians had, on their first visit to the patient, declared the utter imposibility of aught they could do availing to eradicate the disease, which they pronounced of too long standing to be removed by any earthly power; at the same time, they considered that tender nursing and restoratives, carefully administered, might tend greatly to prolong life, but they particularly desired that his mind should be kept perfectly composed, and nothing allowed to excite or depress him, as it would undoubtedly facilitate the progress of the disease.

With this knowledge Donna Rosalia was not surprised to find Albert the ensuing morning considerably worse, and though in the course of a day or two he again rallied a little, yet from that evening he perceptibly declined. Rose, true to her promise, never after allowed him to witness her sorrow and anguish of heart; frequently, indeed, would she leave the room to shed the bitter tears she could not restrain, yet would she carefully remove all traces of them before she again returned to his side. To wait upon him, to watch his every look, to whisper words of hope and love, to join with him in ardent prayer to the Almighty, that they might be re-united in another and a purer world,—this was her only joy and comfort.

'We shall meet again, we part but for a season. I shall wait for thee at Heaven's gate, and be the first to welcome thy beloved spirit to the skies. The thought of the sweet joy that then will be ours should reconcile us, my Rose, to the sadness of parting. Think, think, how mournful it would be, were we to be separated for ever; but such will not be the case. God has, I feel certain, pardoned my sins, and we shall spend a blessed eternity together,—no more sorrow, no more tears, all, all, peace and joy.'

Thus spoke Albert, for, though weak and exhausted in body, his mind was firm and strong in faith, and he looked forward to his end with perfect resignation, that never but once wavered. It was a beautiful calm autumnal evening, and so warm, that the window, which commanded a view of the ground attached to the villa, was thrown open, and the sweet perfume of the orange and citron trees rushed in, filling the room with a delicious odour. Seated on one side of the bed, and sunk in calm reflection was Donna Rosalia; on the other, the pale and spiritless Rose, whom constant anxiety and watching had robbed of the bloom that had bidden fair to return to her lovely face.

'Raise me,' said Albert, in a faint voice, 'and let me once more gaze upon the setting sun.'

Instantly complying with his request, they supported him in the bed with pillows; he turned his face (which was wan and colourless, though his eye sparkled with a bright and un-earthly lustre) towards the sun, now sinking in grand sublimity to rest; he gazed on it for some minutes without speaking, but the tears gathered in his eyes, and rolled, unheeded, down his cheek.

'Why do you weep, dear Albert?' said Rose. Is it at the thought of parting? See, I weep not, though I must be left behind.'

'The sun,' said Albert, still gazing intently on it, 'will rise as bright to-morrow, but I shall see it not—never again shall I behold our dear own native land.'

'Oh! think not of that, dearest Albert,' returned Rose; 'you are going to a land more fair and bright. When your eyes have closed for ever upon the sweet scene that now lies spread before them, they will be blessed by a vision far more lovely, such as mortal eye hath never seen.'

'I know it, dear Rose, I know it, and feel it now; it was but a moment of weakness. A mist for a short time obscured my sight, but it has cleared away, and I am ready and willing to go, to change this earthly for an heavenly scene; and oh! my Rose, let us part with hope in our bosoms and smiles upon our lips, in the certain expectation of a speedy reunion.'

'It is that, and that alone, dear Albert, that has so far supported my fainting spirit, and it will, I doubt not, sustain me through the sad hour of parting; for it is sad to part, even though we were sure to meet to-morrow.'

'If you return to England, my Rose,' said Albert, after a short pause, 'tell Marian, indeed all our friends, that they were in my thoughts at this solemn hour, and that, though we were doomed to meet no more on earth, I fully hope to meet them all in heaven. Oh! let me not miss one : this, tell them, was my last prayer.'

'They shall know it all, dear Albert,' returned Rose, in a low, subdued voice. Rosalia's face was buried in her handkerchief, and she spoke not.

'Where is Charles?' resumed Albert. The youth, who had been seated behind his aunt, now rose and approached the bed.

'Give me your hand,' said Albert, 'and accept at the same time my farewell blessing. You are a good youth, and though I have never publicly acknowledged you as my son, it has been that you should never blush to your own father. My guilt is great; but your aunt will impart to you the sad truths connected with it. You will promise me this, Rosalia, and it will, I hope, prove a warning to him.'

With difficulty Rosalia pronounced the words—

'I will.'

'For yourself,' continued Albert, 'I can only say, you have proved for years the best and kindest friend I ever knew: your reward I leave to God, as I am myself incapable of offering any. To your tender love and care I leave these two—I need not say love and cherish them, for I know, I am sure, you will, though we worship the same God under a different form; yet, dearest Rosalia, I am assured we shall meet in heaven. Oh, Charles,' he continued, turning to him, 'let the unhappy history of thy father act as a warning to thyself; and oh! fail not, I charge thee, to meet me at the footstool of God. If spirits are allowed to look down from heaven, and watch over those they loved on earth; rest assured that I shall often be near thee, and before thou givest way to temptation, reflect that, probably, thy father's eye is on thee; and now farewell, my son, for a few short years, and then join me in that land of bliss to which I am fast hastening.'

The youth was too deeply affected to speak; he could only press his father's hand, and give vent to his sorrow in subdued yet audible sobs.

'Rose,' said Albert, 'let me rest my head on thy tender bosom, and die where I have so loved to live; and oh, dearest, believe that thee, above, far far, above all others, do I most regret to leave.'

'Think not of me, dear Albert,' she said, pressing her lips to his cold and bloodless cheek, 'I feel willing to resign you. There was a time when my heart rebelled against the will of God, and I murmured at his decree; but it is passed—I feel that, had you been spared a few years longer, death would have parted us at last.'

'For a time—only for a time, love. I but go before, and you—'

'Will shortly follow,' said Rose. 'Oh! yes, my Albert, I shall quickly join you.'

'I know it,' replied Albert.

After this, silence prevailed for some time, while the shadows of evening gradually deepened around them. Albert, who had been sleeping on the breast of Rose, suddenly roused, and looking around him with a smile of ineffable sweetness, gently whispered—

'I am going—kiss me, love,' he added, fixing his eyes, which were already glazed with the dull cold film of death, upon Rose; and, as he stooped to do so, he faintly uttered the word, 'Farewell!' and all was over with him on earth.

Thus lived, thus died he. 'Never more on him shall sorrow light or shame.'

'He is gone,' whispered Rose, tenderly laying him on the pillow, and then, casting herself on her knees by his side, with clasped hands and upturned eyes, seemed breathing a prayer for the departed spirit. Rosalia and Charles followed her example, and though tears plentifully bedewed their cheeks, no wail or loud lamentation disturbed the stillness of that chamber; on the contrary, not even a sob was heard. Thus they remained profoundly silent for more than an hour, and though the darkness had gathered round them, no voice or even motion gave token that the living shared that chamber with the dead; and when it became necessary to perform the last sad offices, no stranger was allowed to intrude—Rose, assisted by Rosalia, did all that was necessary. They would both have deemed it almost a profanity to have allowed other hands than their own to perform the last mournful task for the departed; they had loved and waited on him whilst living, and they did not, as is too often the case, rush from his presence, as though they were affrighted of him, when dead.

'He is at rest,' said Rose, when they had laid him in his coffin and dressed the room, not in the sorrowful insignia of mourning with closed blinds, and walls hung in black, but the windows thrown open, admitting the fresh pure breath of early morning, and throwing an air of cheerfulness around the room, while a nosegay newly gathered, and consisting of flowers that he most loved, stood in a large vase at the foot of the coffin, and gave forth a sweet and soft perfume. Rose and Rosalia were seated on either side, gazing on the quiet, tranquil face of him they loved.

'He is at rest,' repeated Rose again, 'and I thank God for it.'

Charles, who was sitting at her feet, raised his eyes to her countenance, and beheld an almost unearthly lightness on her pallid face, which made him shudder with a forewarning that not much longer would she linger here.

Together they chose his grave—a quiet, green, shady spot, refreshed with the early dews of morn, and bathed at night in the soft light of the moon. Never did Rose leave his side till the coffin lid was closed, and shut from her sight that face upon which she had so long loved to gaze. It rent her heart to feel that she had looked her last upon him.—'But, oh!' she exclaimed, striving to check the tears that forced themselves in torrents from her eyes, 'I forget not almost his last words, 'we shall meet again.'—And no violent agitation marked her demeanour, when she saw him laid in his quiet grave, and heard the hollow sound of the earth, as it fell upon his coffin; on the contrary, a slight observer might have thought her wanting in that bitter sorrow which mostly marks the nervous; but oh! she knew that his spirit, that dearest part, was enthroned in bliss, that he had only gone before her to a better and purer state of existence, where she would shortly join him; and this calmed the violence of her grief, and bade her sorrow cease. On their return home after the mournful ceremony, they sat together conversing calmly on the departed, and tenderly dwelling on the best traits of his character.

'I,' said Donna Rosalia, 'knew him many years longer than even you, dear Rose, and never shall I forget his kind and noble disposition: when we first became acquainted, I was myself ardent affection, but he early placed his affections on my sister Florence, the mother of you, Charles,' she added, turning to her nephew, ' who gave him every encouragement, and, ere he had been six months in Naples, they were married in the private chapel belonging to our villa, none being present at the ceremony except the priest, who united them according to the forms of the Catholic Church, Charles the brother of Albert, and myself. I need not, my children,' she continued, ' tell you that Florence was exceedingly handsome, for you have both seen her portrait, and that speaks in warmer terms of her personal beauty than I can do; but Charles, Albert's youngest brother, I may say, without flattery, was one of the handsomest young men I ever beheld, delicately fair, while his pale auburn hair hung in loose curls round a face remarkable for the sweetness of its expression. On this young man, of so opposite a style of beauty to herself, Florence on his first introduction cast a very favourable eye, nor did he seem backward in returning her advances. Myself and Florence first became acquainted with Albert and Charles by meeting them at an evening party, held at the house of a mutual acquaintance. That evening I danced with Albert, and my sister with Charles. On our return home, we conversed about our partners, and I found that Florence was as much pleased with the manner and attentions of Charles, as I had been with Albert. After this we frequently met, and for a few short weeks I indulged in the brightest hopes, both for Florence and myself; but alas! the charm was never doomed to be realised. No sooner had the brothers obtained a more intimate footing in our family than Albert showed a marked and most decided prefrence for my sister, which Charles observing, he with a melancholy reserve endeavoured to avoid his company as much as possible. Piqued by this conduct in the one she best loved, Florence made a show of seeming pleased with Albert's attentions, thinking by this conduct to induce Charles to declare his affection, but alas! it had a contrary effect. He no sooner perceived that she received Albert with apparent kindness and pleasure, than he withdrew from her society altogether. Interpreting this into a want of affection for her, Florence in an ill-fated hour accepted the proposals of Albert, and though I have reason to believe she afterwards repented doing so, yet her proud spirit would not allow her to retract, and she consented with an outward show of pleasure to be privately united to Albert. The day was fixed, and Charles, to oblige his mother, to whom he was much attached, consented to be present at the ceremony. When Florence was made acquainted with this, she manifested a much greater degree of interest in her toilet than usual; and as, on the morning of her bridal day, she took a parting glance at the mirror, her dark eye flashed with joy at the beauty it presented to her gaze, more, I am convinced, from what she told me, because Charles would be there to view and admire it, than for the man whom she was about to call by the endearing name of husband. When she entered the chapel, leaning on my arm, Charles and Albert were already there : the latter flew to meet us, and with rapture led his lovely bride to the altar. Charles moved not from his position, and but slightly bowed to myself and Florence. Yet, as his eye rested for a moment on her warm and glowing beauty, and caught the expression, half of reproach and half affection that she cast upon him, he trembled and turned pale. The day, though fine and bright at the commencement, towards noon became overcast, and the evening set in very wet, yet it was with difficulty Florence and Albert could persuade Charles to accept a bed under our roof. For myself, I urged him not; I knew his feelings too well to enable me to do so. Albert most affectionately loved Florence, indeed I have heard him say she was the first woman that ever made an impression on his heart; and he believed that he was fondly loved in return, and having the most implicit confidence in her honour, and not even suspecting the nature of her feelings towards Charles, he never for a moment deemed there was the slightest impropriety in the constant and habitual intercourse that took place between them; indeed it was some months before an explanation ensued between Charles and Florence, and then it was unsought for on his part. He would have avoided her company, had she allowed him to do so; but immediately after her marriage with his brother, she insisted on his attending every party she went to with Albert, and in a short time prevailed on him likewise to become an inmate of our villa. In vain did I beg of her, with tears in my eyes, not to expose herself to the temptation of his company, reminding her that, now she was the wife of another, it would be wise, especially as Charles himself desired it, to be as much apart from him as possible; but, alas! Florence seemed bent on destruction, and heeded nothing I said.

'But what, alas! could be expected from such familiar intercourse between two persons, evidently attached to each other? Charles would frequently remain alone with Florence when Albert was absent, and when she had been married scarcely six months, Charles and herself (as I gathered from what she afterwards told me) mutually confessed the affection they entertained for each other.'

'Alas!' exclaimed Charles, ' he heard from her own lips that her love had ever been his, why did I but know this sooner? What misery it would have spared us both! now, now, it is too late. How I have loved, madly loved thee, Florence; but I deemed that thy love was given to my brother, and now it is guilt to love thee—to encourage thy love in return. That which would once have been so precious to me is now a curse; but, oh, we must part at once, and for ever; with the knowledge that you love me, I dare no longer trust myself in your presence.'

'Oh! say not that,' returned Florence; 'deny me not the small gratification of seeing you. Oh! never, never had I married Albert, but I thought you scorned my love—that you despised the wretched Florence.'

'We must part,' said Charles, in a melancholy voice. 'Albert is my brother, dear to me as my own life. I feel that I am injuring him even by this conversation.'

'Oh! no, no,' returned Florence; 'it were cowardice to fly. Surely we have sufficient command over our feelings to forbid for a moment a thought arising in our minds unworthy of ourselves or dishonourable towards him. We can in secret love each other as a fond brother and sister. Say you consent to this? You will not leave me?'

With such words as these Florence, on her death-bed, confessed to have prevailed upon the unhappy Charles to abandon his intention of quitting Naples: still she declared that her only desire was to keep him near her, and that no thought of sin entered either of their bosoms till the ill-fated hour when Albert accidentally discovered Charles in her dressing-room. I had been myself absent from home one morning, but as I believed Charles to be at a distance, I felt no uneasiness regarding Florence, whom I left entirely alone, Albert himself being engaged from home that morning, nor did we expect his return till evening. It unfortunately occurred, that, shortly after my departure, Charles returned, and this being made known to Florence, who was engaged in her dressing-room, she desired the servant to request him to come to her. What conversation took place between them I know not, or how they came to lose the self-command they had hitherto preserved over their feelings; suffice it, that Albert, who had been absent, arranging for the departure of himself and Florence to England, suddenly returned, and hastening to the dressing-room of Florence, to impart to her the pleasing intelligence that he had secured accommodation for her in a vessel that was shortly to sail for his native land, became an eye-witness of his own dishonour. Enraged to madness at the sight, and scarcely knowing what he was about, he seized the stiletto, which, according to the costume of the country —and since his marriage with Florence, he had, in compliance with her wish, adopted—he wore by his side, and raised it with the intention of plunging it into her breast; Charles, seeing the action, quick as lightning, flung himself before her and received the point of the fatal weapon in his heart. His passion calmed; instantly he became aware of the dreadful deed he had committed. Words cannot do adequate justice to the dreadful and heartrending grief of Albert: throwing himself on the body of his murdered brother, he bathed his face with his tears, conjuring him by every endearing and tender epithet, to pronounce his forgiveness—but, alas, Charles heard him not!

Florence's grief and anguish was scarcely less than Albert's, yet she implored his pardon for the sake of her unborn child, which she assured him was his own; but he spurned her from him as the guilty cause of all.

You may judge of the horror I experienced on my return home to hear the tragic scene that had been enacted in my absence; yet my first impulse was to fly to Albert to conjure, to pray him, on my knees, that instant to quit Naples; it was with difficulty that I prevailed on him to do so, but at length I gained his consent to comply with my request, on condition that I would myself superintend the funeral obsequies of Charles, and watch over the health and welfare of Florence, whom he felt he could never look upon again. Need I say that I gladly complied with his request? And we parted, I fully believed, for ever; but such was my love for him, that I inwardly resolved to dedicate myself to a life of celibacy. After Albert's arrival in England, I received a letter from him, in which he informed me that it was his earnest desire to have the half of his estate, which, by a deed of gift, he had made over to his unfortunate brother, distributed in charitable gifts among the deserving poor of Naples, and asked as a favour that I would see his wish obeyed. Nothing could I have refused him, but this was in

ROSE SOMMERVILLE.

itself a blessed and holy task, and I willingly undertook to perform it, and have done, and still continue to do so.'

'Your mother, Charles,' she continued, turning to her nephew, 'survived your birth but a few days; and, placing you in my arms, bade me love you as the offspring of the unhappy an deeply-injured Albert. Previously to her death, she acquainted me with all I have now informed you, and died invoking blessings on my head, so that I loved and cherished you as a son. Albert and myself constantly corresponded up to the time he again visited Naples. And now, my children, I have told you the entire truth, keeping nothing back, and I think you will agree with me, that however deeply Albert felt his own guilt, he was certainly more sinned against than sinning. I had forgotten to mention, Charles, that you received the name of your uncle, in compliance with the wish of your father.'

Donna Rosalia ceased, and there was a silence of some few minutes, each being engaged with their own thoughts.

'I knew,' said Rose, who was the first to speak, 'that my Albert was less guilty than he wished me to believe; but all the actors in that scene have now passed away from earth peace to their manes! and let us not deem too harshly of any.'

Charles pressed Rose's hand in his own, thus mutely thanking her for sparing his mother's memory.

Rose, in the course of a day or two, wrote to England, informing them of the sad tidings of Albert's death, and of his peaceful and happy end, and the kind message, he desired on his dying-bed, should be delivered to them.

'My dearest mother,' she wrote in conclusion, 'I feel that we shall never more meet on earth, and I can only reiterate the dying prayer of him I shall shortly join——may we all meet together in heaven! Shed no tear, I beseech you, for me, for I am assured that for " me to die will be gain." want not for even your tender love and affection, for it is all supplied to me in the Person Donna Rosalia, of whom I cannot speak in terms sufficiently commendable; therefore, dear mother, have no care or anxiety for me; assure all my dear friends in England that they are not, and never will be, forgotten by me while life and breath remain.'

Thus wrote poor Rose, in the full consciousness that her departure was at hand. The shew of returning health that had manifested itself on her first arrival at Naples, had long been banished by the anxiety and exhausting attention on the sick bed of Albert, and all the former symptoms of consumption had come back with redoubled force. She suffered at times much distress from a harassing cough, which completely destroyed her rest; but she bore it with exemplary patience, a murmur never escaping her lips. The kind attention of Donna Rosalia and Charles she ever received with fervent gratitude, and frequently, when assailed with such extreme weakness as to cause long and repeated fainting fits, she would between the attacks strive to smile; and, though unable to speak, thank them for their care and tender love, with an expressive glance of her soft blue eyes. Once, when Charles shed tears, as he witnessed her rapid progress to the tomb, she stretched out her thin, warm hand, and when he pressed it to his lips, bathing it at the same time with his tears, she gently chid him for thus giving way to sorrow on her account.

'Oh! rather,' she said, while a heavenly smile played over her pallid and wasted features, should you rejoice to think that I am soon to join him I loved so well on earth; it would be cruel to desire to keep me here when my soul so longeth to be gone.'

'Pardon these tears, dear lady,' replied Charles; 'they are shed not for you, but myself; selfish I know they are, but you will forgive them.'

She thus lingered in a state of extreme weakness and great suffering for two months, and then her gentle spirit took its flight. Not even Charles could regret it, or wish her back again to earth; no, both himself and Donna Rosalia were thankful to lay her by the side of Albert, in the quiet spot she had herself chosen. She looked beautiful even in death, and a sweet smile rested on her countenance, once so transcendently lovely; and though the lids had closed for ever on those soft blue orbs that had so oftentimes been lighted up with tender love and kindness, yet she only appeared in a calm and refreshing sleep. Death had cast no shadow on her fair young brow, and, to gaze on her slumber, it seemed that of an infant's balmy rest. Charles strewed around her the flowers of her native land, which she had so loved and cherished while living; and it was with difficulty they could induce him to look his last upon her tranquil face. Oh! he could not bear the thought of closing the coffin lid, while she thus looked so beautiful, and returned again and again to gaze upon her; and when at length convinced that he should see her no more on earth, but that she had passed away for ever, he repeated to himself from one of her favourite authors—

> ' She was not made,
> Through years or moons, the inner weight to bear,
> Which colder hearts endure till they are laid
> By age in earth.'

They slept together; yes, Albert and Rose, so fondly united living, were not long divided even by death. Donna Rosalia and Charles felt the loss of them both deeply; indeed, it affected the whole after-life of Charles, not that he became a moody, melancholy man, but it chastened not destroyed his once volatile spirit. On Rose's death, he lost all desire to visit England with her; in Naples, he had passed many happy hours, and in Naples she slept her last long sleep of death, and from that spot he never wished to stray: he caused a small piece of ground surrounding the grave of her and his father to be enclosed with railings, and the cultivation of this spot became the sweet resource of his leisure hours; and on it the fairest flowers bloomed, and cast their perfume on the ambient air. The memory of Rose was ever present to his bosom, and whatever had been loved or admired by her, was rendered sacred in his eyes. In the course of years he was united to a beautiful and amiable Italian lady, of his own age and rank which union afforded him every earthly bliss, and was blessed with a numerous family of sons and daughters. The eldest of each were named respectively Albert and Rose; and on the green shady spot where their grandfather and his fair young wife reposed, the children would of an evening assemble with baskets of sweet-scented flowers to strew upon the grave. A beautiful, health-beaming, happy group they were, and among them was a Charles, a Florence, and a Rosalia. Charles and his amiable wife had the pleasure of rearing all their lovely offspring, and seeing their sons grow into honourable, noble-hearted men; and their daughters into gentle, amiable, and lovely women. Of Donna Rosalia, we need say no more than that she lived to see the children of her beloved Charles playing around her knee; herself ever looked up to with mingled respect and affection by the entire circle. Mr. and Mrs. Sommerville were, of course, deeply affected by the intelligence of their daughter's death, although in a measure prepared to receive it; yet they sorrowed not without hope—the certainty that she had reached that blissful shore, where they hoped in a few short years to join her, mitigated the violence of their grief, and they could without murmuring resign her; and, though untimely deprived of their daughter, they found a constant source of comfort in their sons and their partners; and not only lived to see their children's children, but likewise those of their grandchildren.

Agnes was ever a particular favourite with the old people; but this caused no jealousy or unkind feeling in the others. They felt that she had earned their favour, by many years of kind consideration and attention to their feelings; and her father, old Farmer Forster, lived for many years, beloved and respected by all. Sir Charles Mortimer, and his truly deserving and amiable lady, enjoyed many years of sweet domestic intercourse, made more blessed to Lucy by its being constantly shared by her tender parent and much-loved brother. Henry never married, but found much joy and pleasure in the company of his little nephews and nieces, and among these, as well as in Italy, there was an Albert and a Rose. The little girl who bore this name being fair and delicately made, was more especially favoured by Henry than the others, although he dearly loved them all. Marian and her husband were happy in each other's society, and having no children, they were more enabled to indulge their taste for company and places of amusement than they otherwise would have been. Marian, soon after Rose's death, received a letter from Donna Rosalia explaining to her all that had occured in Italy connected with her brother Charles's death, and confessing the letter Marian received from Italy, in answer to her own, was from the pen of Charles the son of Albert, and dictated by herself, she, not then being at liberty to enter into particulars, took that mode of convincing her that the Charles Moreland she imagined her brother, could not, by any possibility, bear that relationship to her. Marian was at first much shocked on hearing that Charles's death was the result of a wound he received from Albert; but it made plain many things that seemed strange, and fully accounted for the deep-seated melancholy of Albert. She was not, we have previously seen, of a nature to grieve long, and being fondly attached to her husband, and spending the greater part of her time amid gay and animating scenes, she soon appeared totally to forget the unhappy fate of her brother.

————————

And, now we have taken a review of, and dismissed the whole of the dramatic personages that have figured in this our history, nothing remains but to do the same by the readers; therefore, hoping he will not consider the time spent in the perusal of these pages entirely thrown away, we desire to shake him by the hand, and for the present bid him farewell! though not without the hope of one day meeting him again.

ELLEN T.

THE END.